DARK MOON

Also by Alton Gansky

The Prodigy

J. D. Stanton Mysteries
Vanished
A Ship Possessed

DARK MOON

ALTON GANSKY

GRAND RAPIDS, MICHIGAN 49530 USA

We want to hear from you. Please send your comments about this book to us in care of the address below. Thank you.

GRAND RAPIDS, MICHIGAN 49530 USA

ZONDERVAN™

Dark Moon
Copyright © 2002 by Alton L. Gansky

Requests for information should be addressed to:
Zondervan, *Grand Rapids, Michigan 49530*

ISBN 0-7394-2794-6

Interior design by Beth Shagene

Printed in the United States of America

To Naomi Gansky ("New Daughter"), who this year joined our family through marriage. Thanks for bringing even more love and joy to our family.

CHAPTER
ONE

THE CALIFORNIA NIGHT WAS PERFECT. NOT A SECOND OF IT passed without the complete appreciation of Marcus Stiller. The cold gnawed at his ebony cheeks and ears, but it was a small price to pay for the joy of doing what he loved. Not even the dull ache that hovered just over his kidneys, the result of several hours of stooping, could take the luster off the evening, nor could the brisk breeze that shook the needles of the nearby pine trees. Above him the black dome of the evening sky hung inverted like an obsidian-colored bowl. Stars shimmered like sequins on a black evening gown. Even without the benefit of his telescope, the distant specks of light seemed close enough to touch. To Marcus, they begged to be caressed by someone who knew them, someone who understood them, someone who loved them.

Pressing one of the four direction buttons on the electronic controller he held in his gloved hand, he waited for the Orion 200mm telescope to change the direction of its unblinking gaze.

"I'm freezing," Terri Lynn said, slapping the sleeves of her heavy coat.

"Don't be such a wimp," Jason Coogan shot back. "Where is your sense of scientific adventure?"

"Tucked away safe and warm in my head," Terri retorted. "Not that you'd know anything about having stuff in your head."

Jason sighed melodramatically. "Just like a woman."

"All right, you two," Marcus said, looking up from the eyepiece of the telescope. He chuckled as he looked at his two students. Jason Coogan was a brash twenty-year-old with a genius-level IQ. His friends called him "Whiz," as did Marcus when they were outside the college classroom where Marcus taught physics and astronomy. Whiz stood just two inches shorter than Marcus, which made him five-foot-eleven. He wore his hair greased back and a two-day growth of stubble on his Mediterranean chin. Rounding out his carefully orchestrated rebel image was his ever-present white T-shirt and leather vest. Since the temperature was in the low forties, Jason's getup was hidden beneath a thick down coat borrowed from Marcus. Whiz was bright, but common sense was a stranger to him. It hadn't occurred to him that the mountains were colder this time of year. "Scientists don't criticize one another's gender, Whiz. They make fun of their research. Try to get it right."

"You're not taking his side, are you?" Terri asked, her face forming a pout. Marcus knew it was an act. Of all his students, only she could keep up with Whiz's academics and wit. Despite appearances the two were fast friends. Like Whiz, Terri was a student enrolled in one of Marcus's classes. Her chestnut hair hung on each side of her face.

"Of course not," Marcus replied. "I'm just trying to fill out the conversation a little. Oh, and Whiz, you're lucky my wife didn't hear that 'just like a woman' crack. She'd throw you off the balcony without a second thought."

"Who needs to be tossed off the balcony?" Lucy Stiller asked as she stepped through the sliding glass door that separated the expansive redwood deck from the warm rooms of the Stiller's mountain home.

"Whiz," Terri said. "And it's not too late. I can give you several reasons. I might even pay to have the deed done."

"No need," Lucy said with a broad smile. She was carrying a tray with four mugs. Diaphanous steam floated skyward. "I would be happy to do it for a friend."

"You gonna let them threaten me like that?" Jason asked Marcus.

Marcus turned to his wife and winked. She was a tall woman, an inch shorter than he. Her chocolate-colored skin was a shade lighter than his own. A striking woman, she had modeled while in college to earn money for tuition. She had been told many times that she could have made a career in front of the photographer's lens, but she had declined. Medicine was her calling from childhood, one to which she had listened faithfully. Now as a senior resident of Fontana Municipal Hospital, she was living the life she had always known she would. "Don't ask me for help. I've been thrown off the balcony enough times to qualify for frequent-flyer miles."

"Poor mistreated baby," Lucy teased. "I brought hot cocoa."

"Great," Terri said. "I could use it."

"Have anything to put in it?" Whiz asked with a smirk.

Lucy set the tray down on a plastic outdoor table and threw an icy glance at the young man. "I didn't know you had passed your twenty-first birthday."

"I haven't, but who cares? We're at a private residence high in the mountain community of Pinewood. It's a beautiful night and we're among friends. Who's going to know?"

Marcus cleared his throat and pantomimed someone throwing another over the rail. Whiz screwed his face into a frown and shrugged.

"Okay," Marcus announced. "We're ready." He moved from the telescope to a white plastic patio table two feet away upon which sat a laptop computer. Electric and video cables connected the device to the telescope. The ash-colored image of the Moon was centered in the screen. Whiz and Terri joined him at the makeshift desk. Lucy sat in a plastic chair next to the table where she had set the tray of mugs. "Terri, you take the keyboard. I'll turn off the deck light. We'll need a few minutes for our eyes to adapt to the dark."

Terri took a seat on the bench before the table. Whiz stood behind her, peering over her shoulder.

"Here, take this," Marcus said to Whiz. He handed him the telescope's electronic controller. The device was slightly larger than Whiz's gloved hand and had a back-lit keypad that glowed a pale orange. "You can slew the telescope with the arrow keys or punch in celestial coordinates."

"Great," Whiz said. "What shall we find? A binary star system, or maybe a—"

"We've found what we're looking for," Marcus said.

Whiz looked at the monitor in disbelief. "The Moon? You're not serious."

"He's serious," Lucy said. "He loves the Moon."

"Isn't that like going to a fancy restaurant and ordering macaroni and cheese?" Terri asked, clearly disappointed. "We can see the Moon any night."

"That's the point," Marcus said. "The Moon is our closest companion in space, and we still know very little about it."

"What's left to know?" Whiz asked. "It's been studied for decades."

"More than you imagine," Marcus answered. "Less than twenty-five percent of its surface has been adequately mapped. We still don't know how it was formed, what it is made of, or why it's there."

Marcus leaned over Terri's shoulder and pointed at a button on the computer keypad. "Push this. It will tighten the shot." Terri did so. "Any idea what you're looking at?"

Terri shrugged. "A crater."

"That's right," Marcus said. "The Crater Plato. It's high in the northern hemisphere of the Moon. Just south of it is Mare Imbrium, the Sea of Rains."

"Except there are no seas on the Moon," Terri said. "It's a desolate, barren, waterless world."

"Not completely waterless," Marcus corrected. "It's true that there are no seas on the Moon. The large, flat, dark areas are called seas, *maria* in Latin, but they are large expanses of flat land. The rest of the Moon is made of ridges, mountains, and craters. There is, however, water."

"Lunar Prospector, 1998," Whiz said flatly.

Marcus saw Terri roll her eyes. "That's right. Some think that there may be as much as 330 million tons of water in the regolith."

"Lunar soil," Whiz explained.

"I know what regolith is," Terri snapped.

"Really?" Whiz replied.

"Yes, really. Sometimes it's called mantle rock. It's loose material that rests on the surface."

"I'm impressed," Whiz said.

"Most of the water is believed to be at the Moon's northern pole," Marcus continued, "with some at the southern pole and perhaps more in the permanent shadows. That opens up the possibility . . ."

"Colonization," Terri said, anticipating Marcus.

"Exactly. Hydrogen and oxygen can be made from the water, providing fuel and air." Marcus could tell that the

interest of his students had been whetted. He continued drop-
ping little tidbits of lunar information. "Did you know that
the crust on the dark side of the Moon is thicker than on the
side that always faces us?"

"I read that somewhere," Whiz said.

"The crust is thirty-three miles thick on the near side and
sixty-three miles thick on the far side. What would that be in
the metric system, Whiz?"

Whiz paused for only a moment, then replied,
"Approximately sixty kilometers and one hundred kilometers
respectively."

"Right," Marcus said. "Now let me show you something." Marcus took a seat next to Terri and turned the computer toward himself. "I'm going to give you the one-minute
lecture on astrophotography. The telescope is equipped with a
CCD video camera . . ."

"CCD?" Terri asked.

"Charge-coupled device," Marcus explained. "They're
electronic devices used in everything from fax machines to pho-
tocopiers. It's part of the video system on the telescope. The pictures can be directly recorded into the computer for analysis at
a more convenient time."

"Or a warmer time," Terri said with a shiver.

"You volunteered for this extra-credit assignment,"
Whiz said.

"Okay, here's what I want you two to do. Each of you is
going to practice capturing photos from the video feed. Do
about ten each. That's about all my hard drive is going to hold.
Practice slewing the camera with the controller."

"What are you going to do?" Whiz asked.

"I'm going to go sit by my wife, drink hot cocoa, and
watch young minds at work."

"Don't you mean, get out of the cold wind?" Terri said.

"Well, that too," Marcus admitted with a broad smile.

THE CLOCK ON THE DESK in Marcus's home office read 12:30. *Half past midnight*, he thought. *I should be in bed*. But bed would not come for at least another hour. He was a night owl, a habit developed during countless hours stargazing as a teenager. While other young people his age attended parties, went to movies, or hung out at the pool parlor, Marcus spent his evenings alone building telescopes and using them to bring the universe closer to home. Now, at the age of thirty-two, he still stayed up late and stared at the stars. Things had changed, of course. While he still spent time outside peering through the eyepiece of one of his telescopes, he now did most of his work inside his warm, well-appointed home office. Whiz and Terri would be surprised, maybe even angry, to learn that he had another telescope mounted in its own domed observatory. The observatory, which stood on a foundation at the side of the house, was just large enough for his sixteen-inch Starfinder Dobsonian telescope. Motor-driven, computer-controlled, and camera-equipped, the whole system could be operated from the comfort of his office. Images would appear directly on his computer monitor.

As good as it was, it still was no match for the adventure of standing in the cold night air peering at the sky. Terri and Whiz needed that experience, and Marcus had wanted to give it to them.

Now, with only the light of the computer monitor to illuminate the room, he studied the video captures made by his two favorite students. Once presented with the task, they had set aside their quibbling to focus on the assignment. They had done well, working together like meshing gears. The end result was a series of exceptional digital photos of the northern hemisphere of the Moon. The resolution was sharp, the detail easily discernible. It was all familiar territory to him. He had logged hundreds of hours studying the one side of the Moon that perpetually faced Earth. His knowledge of the gray orb was encyclopedic. Others studied distant stars, some searched for answers to questions of cosmology, while yet others pursued the sexier planets of the solar system, but Marcus was enthralled with the object closest to his home—the Moon.

He allowed his eyes to trace the familiar form, to analyze the geological structures and to—

"What . . . ," Marcus muttered aloud. He leaned closer to the image on the monitor. Something wasn't right. Something was there that didn't belong. He pursed his lips in frustration. A *smudge*. On his pictures, a *smudge!* That meant that something was on the mirror of his telescope. But how could that be? He was compulsive enough to the point of neurosis about his equipment. It was inconceivable that dirt or grease or something had marred his expensive eye to the heavens. Unless Whiz or Terri . . . He dismissed the idea. They had worked at the computer, not with the telescope itself.

Still, there it was.

With a click of the mouse, he enlarged the picture to better study the smear. Perhaps he could tell where the smudge was. Marcus's mind ground to a halt. The image was wrong in almost every way. It didn't match the Moon's terrain, the color was wrong, and he had never seen the likes of it before, despite his thousands of hours staring at its surface.

Red. A light crimson blotch was tucked just beneath the Crater of Plato and at the extreme north end of the Mare Imbrium. There appeared to be no depth to it as he would expect with a ridge or a cliff. It would be easy to miss without a trained eye. No wonder Whiz and Terri hadn't noticed it.

"A light anomaly," he told himself. Perhaps lens flare, the reflection of a light from an unknown but otherwise earthly source. Marcus shook his head; the answer did not satisfy. Everything he was seeing argued against the conclusion. The aberration seemed a natural formation or discoloration. But that seemed wrong, too. The Moon was a static place. There were the occasional moonquakes and even minor meteorite impacts, but the surface never changed color. It never had and couldn't now. In the 350 years people had been turning telescopes toward the Moon, no one had seen a new crater, not to mention something like this.

Swiftly switching between the other pictures, Marcus discovered that the blotch appeared on two other images that showed the narrow band of high ground just south of Plato. More disturbing than the number of appearances was the consistency of the discoloration. It was an uneven shape, roughly that of a malformed butterfly, and its orientation and size was consistent in each of the three photos. That implied that it was truly on the Moon's surface and that something, a shadow or lens flare, had not caused the image. And if the aberration had been caused by something on the telescope's mirror, or by an electronic gremlin in the CCD, then it would have appeared in different locations on different photos. At the very least, it should be seen on every picture.

Marcus wanted verification.

It took only moments for Marcus to activate the Starfinder, enter the computer commands that would direct its unblinking eye to the Moon, and locate the crater named Plato. The telescope, which Marcus had bought, made improvements to, and used on a daily basis, had cut into his income deeply. With the addition of a high-end CCD camera, the tiny custom-made observatory enclosure, photo-enhancing software, precision-drive, and a host of other enhancements, Marcus was out the cost of a luxury car. Without Lucy's income from the hospital, he would never have been able to afford it.

The image from the telescope played across his monitor. It took less than three minutes for Marcus to find the Moon and focus on the mystery spot. He found what he was looking for, and it made his stomach turn.

)))) ● ● ((

SHE SAT UPON THE BED. She had a bed and because she was sedate and obedient, she had walls without padding. She even had a window. It didn't open and it had flat iron bars on the outside, but the glass was clear, letting in the outside world. Except for the daily exercise periods on the grass-carpeted grounds behind the institution, the window provided the only view of the world in which she used to live.

That was long ago—a lifetime ago, a different era, when she was a person with a future, a home, and a career. A time before the dreams, the unrelenting, hellish visions that hunted her. That was before the doctors, before the sedatives—before this place.

The Moon was shining high in the night sky, but it seemed to grow dimmer as it continued its slow descent toward the horizon. Since her window faced west, she could not watch the ancient orb rise, but she would wait for it patiently until it had passed its zenith and started its gentle fall down the nighttime dome. She would then stand by the window staring at it as if by the very act of scrutiny she could transport herself from the confines of the mental hospital to the lunar surface.

She was a smart woman and knew that no human could live without protection on the frigid surface of the Moon. Death would come in seconds. For her—Julie Waal, former real-estate agent, former wife, former person—that death was a comforting desire.

Rising from the bed, she walked barefoot to the window and pulled her terry-cloth robe closed and held it to her breasts. Slowly she reached forward with one hand and touched the glass of the window as if touching the Moon itself. The smooth surface felt cool on her fingertips. She allowed her eyes to trace the thin reflection of her image. Blonde hair, once lush, now stringy, hung limp to her shoulders. Lips which had not borne lipstick in eighteen months reflected back a pale rose color. Ice-blue eyes stared without blinking. What had she become? When did it happen? How did it happen? More importantly, *why* had it happened?

Julie Waal began to cry for the third time that day. Her reflected image and the sight of the Moon blurred in the wash of tears.

A tingling began at the back of her head. She sucked in a lungful of air. The tingling moved forward, like a thousand ants marching inside her head.

"No," she said, raising her hands to her ears and pushing at the side of her head. "No, no, no." She had not had an "experience" for days. Why now? Why had they returned?

She turned toward the bed and staggered forward, striking her shin on the metal bed frame. A cry of pain escaped her lips as she crumpled to the floor and rolled onto her back.

The ants marched forward.

"Not again," she cried and pulled at her hair until it felt like her scalp would detach from her skull. "Leave me alone. Go away!"

Images. Colors. Sensations.

Evil. Pain.

Terror.

The sound of pounding filled the room. It grew larger and with each thump pain raced down her neck. Bright lights exploded in her brain. It took several moments for her to realize that the pounding sound was coming from her head striking the floor. Thump, bump, pounding. Pain. But no matter how hard she slammed her head on the floor, the tingling continued. The images flashed neon bright.

"Noooo!" she screamed.

More noises. Footsteps. Voices.

"Get her arms." They were harsh words, angry tones.

"Stop squirming!" Another voice demanded.

Them.

"No. Leave me alone," Julie protested as she tried to pull herself from their grip. "Don't touch me!"

"We're going to help you."

"You're one of them, aren't you?" Julie shouted. Without waiting for a reply, she brought a knee up in a fierce kick and felt it contact something.

There was a cry of pain followed by a stream of hot curses. "Can't you hold her legs?"

"Not and give her the injection."

"Then sit on her."

A pressure dropped on Julie's chest, crushing the air from her lungs. Opening her eyes she saw the fat man in the white suit that brought her dinner each night. "Get off me," Julie demanded, but there was insufficient air to broadcast the words louder than a whisper.

"Hold still," the man on top of her commanded.

A sharp stabbing pain erupted from her right arm followed by a scorching sensation, as if someone had injected acid under her skin. Julie tried to scream. Still no air.

"Hey, go easy," the other man said. "You're going to hurt her."

"What do you care?" the fat man said. "You were complaining that she kicked you."

"That's no excuse to rough her up. You're not supposed to be giving injections anyway."

"I've seen it done a hundred times."

"So what? That doesn't make you a doctor . . ."

The burning spread up Julie's arm. A moment later she fell into the black sea of unconsciousness.

CHAPTER
TWO

A DISTANT SOUND PERCOLATED THROUGH THE SHROUD OF sleep that covered Marcus. It seemed familiar and he was sure he could identify it if he tried, but he had no intention of making the effort. It was Saturday morning, his day to sleep in. He rolled over and reached for his wife. Lucy was gone. She was an early riser no matter the day of the week. She had often said that sleeping in was a waste of time. It was not unusual for her to arise at 5:00 in the morning, spend forty-five minutes on the treadmill, make coffee, shower, and be ready to face the day by 6:30. Marcus had to be chiseled out of bed like a fossil. He arose early only by force or the fear of losing his job.

Marcus noticed something else: the smell of bacon. Every other day of the week was started with a dry bagel or high-fiber cereal, but Saturday was different. There were no rules for Saturday. Leisure and pleasure were the only requirements. He and Lucy would read, watch movies, shop at the mall down the hill from their Pinewood home, or simply do nothing. It was an agreement they had made during Marcus's graduate school days. Lucy was finishing medical school and their schedules robbed them of any free time. Once they had survived their grueling education, they determined to set aside a day for mindless activity. It was a commitment they had stuck to for years.

The door to the bedroom opened slowly. "Marc?" Lucy's voice was soft, gentle.

Marcus groaned into his pillow.

"There's a phone call for you, Marc."

"I was up late last night," Marcus said in a gravelly voice. Now he knew that the ringing of the telephone had awakened him. "I'll call them back later."

"It's Dr. Lansing," Lucy said. "He says you e-mailed him something last night."

"I don't care—" Marcus sat up in bed, fully awake. The pictures. "Of course." He reached for the remote phone that Lucy held in her hand.

"I guess I won't be needing the bucket of ice water after all," Lucy said with a mischievous smile as she walked from the bedroom. "Breakfast will be ready in about ten minutes."

"Dr. Lansing," Marcus said into the phone. "Sorry to keep you waiting."

"I didn't wake you, did I?"

"Of course you did. I was up late."

Lansing laughed. "I see that. The time stamp on your e-mail says 2:10. Getting your fill of infomercials?"

Marcus felt his heart rate pick up. Dr. Philip Lansing was his mentor and a well-known astrophysicist at the California Institute of Technology—the same school where Marcus had studied. Since Marcus's graduation, Lansing had taken a teaching fellowship at MIT in Cambridge, Massachusetts. The two had kept in contact over the years. "Did the pictures come through okay?"

"Clear as a bell," Lansing answered. "You took these with that fancy setup you keep bragging about?"

"Yes." Marcus swung his legs over the side of the bed, pushed his feet into his slippers, and, dressed only in a pair of flannel pajamas, walked to his office on the other side of the house.

"Interesting." Lansing's voice was slipping into the professorial tone Marcus always associated with the man. As Marcus made his way through the living room, passed the kitchen, and entered the office, an image of his former instructor came to mind. Dr. Philip Lansing was a large man who was fond of rich food and all things scientific. His girth was matched by an insightful, logical mind that had enshrined him as a giant in the field of astrophysics and cosmology. Marcus could see him stroking his gray-tinted goatee or scrunching up his nose to reposition his thick glasses. "Odd choice on the artificial coloring, I must say."

Most pictures of astronomical objects were artificially colored for better analysis and sometimes for pure aesthetics. Colored pictures of nebulae and galaxies that appeared in magazines were far more interesting than their paler reality.

"I didn't add color," Marcus said. "What you have is the raw photo." Sitting at his desk, Marcus pinched the phone between his ear and his shoulder, freeing his hands to open the file that held the printout of the images he had taken early that morning.

"No color?" Lansing said with surprise.

"Correct. You're seeing it just as it was captured." The comment was greeted with silence. "Dr. Lansing?"

"I'm looking at a picture of the northern part of the Moon and there is a red discoloration in the Mare Imbrium. You're saying that you did nothing to highlight that area?"

"That's correct. What do you think?"

There was a pause before Lansing answered. "There's nothing wrong with your imaging system or telescope?"

"All in perfect order. I also have several other shots taken with the telescope slewed to a slightly different position. The anomaly remains consistent in size and shape. Not only that, I have pictures from both my telescopes."

"Odd," Lansing said softly.

"To put it mildly. That's why I sent one of the photos to you. I was hoping you would have some answers."

"I don't," Lansing said bluntly. "If this came from anyone other than you, I would have tossed it in the trash. You're not playing a game with your old professor, are you?"

"Have you ever known me to play games with science?"

Lansing grunted. "No."

"I take it that you're just as lost as I am about this." Marcus leaned back in his leather chair.

"More so," Lansing admitted. "I'm an astrophysicist, not a planetary geologist. You know more about those things than I do."

"You're being modest."

"I don't waste time with modesty," Lansing said. "Not when it comes to the science to which I've devoted my life."

Marcus smiled. Lansing was, above all, intellectually honest. He was just as likely to brag on himself as he was the work of others. He had often said that the only emotion allowed in science was passion. Everything else was counterproductive and fogged the reasoning mind.

"You may have made a real discovery here, Marcus. I'm glad I sent this on."

Marcus froze. "Sent it on?"

"Of course. Your e-mail had only the picture and one sentence, 'What is this?' I'm trying to find out. So I sent it to another astronomer for verification and comment. Don't worry, you'll get credit for the discovery, if there is one."

"I wasn't worried about credit," Marcus said.

"What are you worried about, then?"

"I don't know," Marcus replied. "I thought we could talk about it first."

Lansing sighed loudly. "You must get over this college student insecurity," he said flatly. "It has plagued your career. You've earned your academic chevrons. You have a PhD after your name, just like I do, and from Caltech at that. You could be teaching in a major university instead of a small liberal arts college, but you keep yourself reined in so tightly."

"I like my students, I like what I do, and I like where I live." Marcus had had this conversation with Dr. Lansing before. He didn't want to repeat it now. Teaching had always been his goal, not professional research, and he didn't want to deal with the "publish or perish" politics of university life.

"All right, Marcus," Lansing said. "I won't beat that horse again."

"Who did you send the picture to?"

"This has to be verified, Marcus, or someone else will lay claim to it."

"Who got the picture?"

"A friend I went to grad school with. He's a wizard at lunar science."

"Does this wizard have a name?"

"Father Benjamin Sicarello."

"Father?"

"He's with the Jesuits and the Vatican Observatory. He's a likable enough fellow and does good science."

"I would like to have done more work before passing it on to anyone else."

"I know you would. That's why I sent it before I called. Listen, Marcus. I have taught for a great many years. During that time, I've seen only a handful of students with your intellect and natural grasp for astronomy. I did what I did because I'm proud of you and I think you deserve some credit. If this turns out to be something significant, you'll be able to write your own ticket to a teaching post anywhere in the world."

"I like my part of the world just fine, thank you." Marcus was sure he heard his old friend quietly moan.

"Anyway," Lansing said, "Father Ben will get back to us soon. He's not one to let grass grow under his feet."

"Are you sure that was wise?"

"Yes, Marc, it was wise. My guess is that we'll hear something by tomorrow, assuming he can get some telescope time."

"Is he in Gandolfo?" Marcus asked, referring to the papal summer residence in Castel Gandolfo, outside of Rome, where the Vatican maintained one of the oldest astronomical research institutions in the world.

"Oh, my, no," Lansing said with a chuckle. "He's in Tucson at the Vatican Observatory Research Group with the University of Arizona."

"It's a good facility." Marcus's hopes began to rise. His mentor had seen some value in his find and passed the word on to a trusted friend. What could be bad about that?

"He can be trusted, Marc," Lansing said. "If it's nothing, he'll tell us outright, then we can forget about it. He has no tolerance for the political games that some of our brethren play. You can expect a straight, professional answer with no strings attached."

"You'll let me know when you hear from him?"

"Of course. I'll give you a call tomorrow one way or the other."

"I'll be out for much of the day. Do you have my cell phone number?"

"Yes, I do. Don't forget, tomorrow is the day."

Marcus nodded to the empty room. "Tomorrow is the day."

)) ● ● ● ((

JULIE WAAL LAY ON HER BED as still as a corpse. Her eyes were closed as if in sleep, but her mind was frenetic with thought. Her left shoulder ached from the brutally delivered injection, both wrists were bruised, and her bladder felt close to splitting. Her ribs were tender and the back of her head felt like a baseball was growing out of it. But she lay motionless and listened to the conversation being held over her.

"We saw her go nuts. One minute she's staring out the window, the next she's screaming and banging her head on the floor. She's going to have a world-class headache when she wakes up."

"It's a good thing we had her under video surveillance."

Julie knew the voices. A year and a half of confinement in the Pacific Institute for Family Care had allowed her time to know everyone who worked in her ward. She liked only two or three; the rest she distrusted with every fiber of her being.

"We had to act quickly," the fat man said. It was the same attendant that had sat on her last night. If he was still around, then it must be before 8:00 in the morning. That's when the shift change took place.

"You exceeded your authority," the other man said. It was Dr. Peter Bernard. "You had no right injecting her."

"It was an emergency situation."

"Medication can only be dispensed by medical personnel. I should fire you, Gordon."

"But you won't. I'm good at what I do, and I don't mind getting my hands dirty."

"Why didn't you call me sooner?"

"She seemed all right to me," Gordon replied without emotion.

"Be clear on one thing, Gordon. I may be your uncle, and I may owe your father a huge debt for putting me through medical school, but there is a limit to my patience. There's only so much I'll overlook, and you are very close to that limit."

"Whatever you say, Dr. Bernard."

"Send in one of the nurses. I need to examine her for injuries."

"I can stay if you want," Gordon said. Julie could hear the leer in his voice.

"No thanks," Bernard snapped. "You've done enough. And just to make sure we're clear on this: If this gets out, or if you ever medicate one of my patients again, you can kiss your job good-bye. Now go get the nurse."

As soon as Julie heard the door close, she allowed herself to relax slightly. Maybe Dr. Bernard would release the restraints on her arms and legs so that she could go to the bathroom.

〇〇〇●●●〇〇

GORDON HAD SENT THE NURSE IN, just as his uncle had demanded of him. He would play the obedient employee for now, at least in front of the old man. Like a soldier on a mission, he quickly made his way to his desk. The desk was a counter with six video monitors showing views of various patient rooms. Every twenty seconds, the images would change to a new room, moving systematically through the ninety-bed private hospital. With a touch of a button, one monitor froze on the scene before its camera's eye. Leaning back in his chair, Gordon watched his uncle and the middle-aged nurse begin the physical exam of Julie Waal. *This was better than television*, Gordon decided. He had thirty minutes before the shift change at 8:00, and he planned to enjoy every moment of it.

〇〇〇●●●〇〇

"I KNOW IT'S NOT MY COOKING," Lucy said as she took another sip of coffee. "You married me for my cooking."

Marcus looked up from the plate of eggs and bacon at which he had only poked. "I thought I married you for your money."

"Surprised, weren't you?" Lucy let slip a little smile. "By calling upon my years of medical training and experience, I have determined that you are distracted. Did talking to Lansing depress you?"

"Depress me?"

"Lansing always depresses you," Lucy said. She leaned forward with both elbows on the table, giving Marcus her full attention.

"No, he doesn't. Dr. Lansing is my friend, my mentor."

"And every time he calls you slip into a mild funk."

"I wasn't aware of that."

"Really?" It was a one-word response, but Marcus understood every nuance carried in the tone. Lucy was nothing if not insightful.

"I suppose you're right," Marcus admitted. "He still intimidates me, even over the phone."

"You feel you don't measure up," Lucy offered. "We've been over this before, Marc. You stand in no man's shadow. You're every bit as intelligent as he."

"But he has stature in the scientific community. I'm an outsider."

"You've published," Lucy countered. "Doesn't that count for something?"

"I've published, but not in the best journals, not the ones that make a difference." Marcus pushed away from the table. He had had this conversation too many times. "Besides, that's not what's on my mind."

"The pictures?"

Marcus looked at his wife, puzzled. He hadn't mentioned the photos to her. He wasn't attempting secrecy; he had just been too absorbed in thought to bring it up.

"Dr. Lansing mentioned that you e-mailed him a picture last night," Lucy explained.

"Ah," Marcus said. He rose from his chair and started clearing the dishes. "Want to see them? They have me puzzled."

"I'm no astronomer, but I'd like to see what it is that has taken you away from our Saturday breakfast."

Marcus felt a wave of love wash through him. How had he been so lucky as to have not only a pretty and sensitive wife but also a smart one? "If I take you to dinner, will it make up for my wandering attention?"

"It's a start. You may have to take me to a movie, too."

"Wait a minute, I think I'm getting worked here." Marcus set the dishes down, stepped to Lucy, and took her in his arms. "You know you're still the brightest star in my universe, don't you?"

"It's the only universe I want to be in." She kissed him deeply. "Now show me the mystery of the cosmos that you've discovered."

"It's just an anomaly, but an interesting one. Do we do the dishes first?"

"Nope. I feel irresponsible this morning." Lucy took Marcus by the hand and walked to his office.

The morning sun poured through the office window, bathing the darkly paneled room with warmth and light. Lucy stood by the window, letting the sun illuminate the printout of lunar pictures she held in her hand. "These were taken last night?"

"Yes. Those are the shots Whiz and Terri made. They did a good job." Marcus stepped behind her and pointed to the blotch. "At first I thought it was an equipment problem, but I've ruled that out."

"And you have no idea what it is?"

"Not a one. Dr. Lansing had no ideas either."

"So what's next?"

Marcus related his conversation with Lansing and Lansing's decision to share it with Benjamin Sicarello.

"A priest?" Lucy said with surprise. "What's a priest going to do?"

"He's a Jesuit," Marcus explained. "They're an order that finds some fulfillment in academic pursuit. There have been many clerics who have advanced the cause of science. Our early understanding of genetics came from experiments performed by a monk, Gregor Mendel. Isaac Newton wasn't a man of the cloth, but he wrote more about spiritual matters than scientific ones. I suppose there's room in the world for stargazing priests."

"You sound like your father," Lucy said.

"Yeah, I suppose I do."

Lucy turned and faced Marcus. "I'm not going to be able to go with you tomorrow," she said. "I'm covering for Dr. Turner. His wife gave birth yesterday."

Marcus frowned. "You know I hate going down there alone. It's a two-hour trip each way."

"I know, but I can't help it. Dr. Turner covered for me when you wanted to go to that convention earlier this year. It's only fair that I help him out now."

Marcus sighed. It was only twenty past eight and he was already having a bad day. "I understand."

"You could postpone going. Maybe we could sneak down to San Diego later this week. I can try to arrange it—"

"No, that's okay. I missed last week. I should go tomorrow."

"You need to make peace with this, Marc." Lucy's tone turned serious. "It's not good letting this go on month after month. I can talk to one of the hospital counselors for you if you want. I'm sure they would be glad to meet with you."

"No. I'll resolve this my own way. I don't know how, but I will."

"We can get a book on tape for you to listen to." The playfulness had returned to her voice. "That'll make the time go faster."

"If I take you to the mall, you mean," Marcus said with mock suspicion.

"See, you are a smart man. And remember, a movie is included in the deal."

"Okay, just stay out of my popcorn," Marcus said.

"Maybe I will, maybe I won't." They kissed again.

◖◗◕◕◖◗◐◖

BENJAMIN SICARELLO PLUNKED HIMSELF DOWN in the antique oak chair that held its position behind his metal desk. The chair had been a gift to him by his parish priest before Ben, an eager, inquisitive nineteen-year-old, went off to seminary. That was thirty-five years ago, and the chair had traveled with him everywhere he had been assigned. It gave him a sense of ownership and provided a tangible connection to his past. The chair, despite its age and constant use, was in excellent shape. Ben kept up repairs like a car fanatic did with a classic vehicle.

His desk was another matter. More than one colleague had observed that Dr. Benjamin Sicarello, S.J., had the world's most organized mind and most disorganized desk. While he held in his brain vast catalogues of information, both scientific and theological, he seemed quite incapable of filing papers. For that, he had Judy Lawrence, a wizard of systematization and punctiliousness. Ben was sure she chanted her mantra, "A place for everything and everything in its place," at least a hundred times before rising from bed. So efficient were her efforts that one wag had quipped, "Ben, if you ever win the Nobel Prize for astronomy, Judy will have the prize money organized by serial number before you leave the building." Not a week went by that he didn't sing her praises to some envious colleague. He did his work and Judy cleaned up after him. It was a beautiful relationship.

It was because of Judy's efforts that his desk was clean and orderly, unlike the way he had left it the night before. On its surface rested three blue file folders, each with a typed label on

the tab: Messages, Schedule, and Letters to Be Signed. He
hadn't told her that he would be in this Saturday, but Judy
somehow knew. *Organized and precognitive*, Ben mused. Ben
ran a hand across his bald head and opened the first folder.
Inside were a dozen pink slips with phone messages and an
equal number of printed e-mail messages. One had an attached
page: a photo of the Moon.

Such things were not unusual. Amateur astronomy was a
major hobby, and curious sky watchers from around the world
would e-mail him or some other staff astronomer asking,
"What is this?" In every case it was a well-known heavenly
object, so Ben started to set it aside until his eye caught the
sender's name: Dr. Philip Lansing.

"What are you up to, old man?" Ben muttered to himself
with a knowing smile. The two men had studied together at
Caltech and, even though Ben was two years his senior, Philip
had been dubbed the "old man," all due to the premature gray
that highlighted his temples and streaked his ever-present
goatee. Ben stroked his own, now gray, beard.

The message was short: "What do you think? Philip."

Ben removed the paper clip that held the color-printed
image from the e-mail and glanced at it. Northern hemisphere
of the Moon . . . a pretty good picture, although something was
lost in the printing . . . a good but amateur telescope was used,
and—

Ben blinked several times in disbelief. "What is that?" A
second later he was on the phone to Cambridge. As the phone
across the nation began to ring, Ben opened the file marked
"Schedule." Before him was a white sheet of paper with information divided into four columns: PERIOD, TO, INSTRU-
MENT, and FOR. Walvoord was scheduled to use the VATT2
for observation of Kuiper Belt objects. Ben was not scheduled
for any of the telescopes for at least two weeks. That would be
too long. He would have to pirate away an hour from
Walvoord. He would hear about that, but what good was being

director of the Vatican Observatory in Arizona if you couldn't throw your weight around a little.

"Hello," said a familiar voice on the other end of the line.

"Philip, it's Ben."

"I've been expecting your call."

"I'll bet you have," Ben said with a laugh. "I'll just bet you have."

CHAPTER

THREE

RIVULETS STREAKED ALONG THE WINDSHIELD OF MARCUS'S five-year-old Ford F–150 pickup truck. What had been a rainstorm a few minutes before was now an annoying mist. Spray from the tires of other cars misted the glass with water and oil from the road. The freeway shimmered like a river of black water. Gusts of wind swept across the road, rocking the vehicle.

The small of Marcus's back hurt. The drive to San Diego from his Pinewood home had taken an additional forty minutes. An overturned eighteen-wheeler had backed up Interstate 15 for miles, closing the freeway to just one passable lane. That was behind him now. What lay ahead was more nerve-wracking. As he drove through the San Diego community of Kearny Mesa, he glanced down at the passenger seat and caught sight of the audio version of the latest Dean Koontz novel. Lucy had bought it for him to help pass the time, but Marcus had yet to open the package. His mind was elsewhere.

When he had been stuck in the oozing traffic of the freeway, he retraced yesterday's events. The trip down the mountain to the flat land of Ontario and the mall had been enjoyable. After five years of marriage, he could still honestly say that Lucy was his best friend. Any time he spent with her was a treat. The movie, however, failed to capture Marcus's attention. Instead, prompted by the dark of the theater, he let his thoughts sail moonward. The day could not pass fast enough. Marcus had planned a night of moon watching. He wanted to repeat the shots of the previous evening and make a comparison. But a heavy cloud cover had obliterated the night sky. There was to be no observation. The same cloud cover that thwarted last night's plans began dropping sheets of rain by 9:00 p.m.

San Diego, like all major cities, was a composite of smaller communities, hunks of humanity that made up the greater metropolis. It was in one such enclave that Marcus had grown into adulthood. Born in Santa Barbara, he had moved to the south bay city of Chula Vista with his parents. A city in its own right, but still part of San Diego County, it was situated on the border between Mexico and California. His father, a chief in the Navy, had been assigned to the Naval Training Center.

Today Marcus would not travel to the south bay. Instead, he pulled from the freeway and motored down Genesee Avenue. His stomach tightened as he did.

A side street led him to a single-story set of pink buildings with white trim. It was the ugliest color of pink he had ever seen. He had felt that way the first time he saw the place and every time since. An empty parking space awaited his arrival, and Marcus steered the pickup truck into place. Switching the vehicle off, he sat motionless, looking at the front door. Someone had hung a smiling jack-o-lantern from the door handle. Paper ghosts hung in the windows, kept company by a crooked-nose witch riding a cardboard broom.

No sense in putting it off, he thought, and then felt an immediate flood of guilt. It wasn't that he minded the trip, or the obligation; it was the sense of helplessness, the clear understanding that no matter how smart or clever he was, he could never make a difference. Not now.

Taking his cellular phone from the seat next to him where it had rested alongside the unopened audio book, Marcus stepped from the truck and locked the door behind him. He pressed his lips together and steeled himself for what awaited him.

Buildings possess their own particular smells. Growing up, his house always smelled of fried chicken, okra, or other delicacies. His mother had been reared in the South and knew of no other cuisine. Nearly every meal had something fried, and Marcus missed that greatly. As he opened the entrance door and stepped in he was greeted with the unmistakable odor of a medical facility. The air was redolent with body scent, alcohol, fresh washed linen, warmed food, and hospital disinfectant. The concoction assaulted his nose as it had every time he had stepped through the entrance doors, and over the last six months he had crossed that threshold many times.

Marcus lowered his head, fixing his eyes on the floor to avoid the sight of the wretched souls who lay on their white-sheeted beds, oblivious to the world around them. His footsteps echoed off the highly polished, beige linoleum floor and rebounded from the pale green walls. A beeping sound came from his right, but he didn't need to look to know that it was a heart monitor.

Why does he have to be so far from the entrance? Marcus asked himself. The journey through the wide corridors had always been a trek of discipline and discomfort—a hike through a desert of hopelessness. It was a march he made with driven purpose, like a man hustling across a bed of hot coals. He did it for only one reason—his father. *How Lucy deals with this stuff every day is beyond me.* Marcus corrected himself. *She doesn't deal with this every day.* Sure, she worked in a hospital, but that was different—very different. In the hospital there was hope. This was a hopeless place, devoid of any optimism, stripped of any glimmer of confidence. There was nothing here but death, sure and certain. Not just any death. A lingering, postponed demise that didn't have the decency to be prompt. Here, in this building, lay all those whom Death could not be bothered with, neatly tucked away in their rooms like a man might tuck away his socks in a drawer. Here were the spent shells of men and women who had been robbed of meaningful life. They were biological machines with no off switch. Food came through a shunt surgically implanted in their stomachs or a tube threaded through their noses. Oxygen came in through a thin, clear plastic tube. Waste exited through similar tubing. Tube upon tube, and every conduit pirated away a little more of their humanity, and diminished their dignity.

What kind of universe allows such things? Marcus wondered as he trudged forward.

The door to room 21 was slightly ajar. Marcus hesitated, taking several deep breaths of the sour air. A faint, sweet voice seeped through the one-inch opening between the door and its jamb. It was a voice he recognized, a voice that filled him with the warmth of love and the chill of anxiety.

Marcus pushed the door open and entered. Everything was the same as the last time he had been here: pale green walls, clean but scuffed floors, a single window overlooking a tiny courtyard, and a fluorescent light that hummed relentlessly.

Also the same was the frail black man on the hospital bed, his rich, ebony skin hanging loosely on his face. His only motion was the slow rising and falling of his narrow chest. On the nightstand next to the bed rested several items that had been important to him in life: wire-rim eyeglasses; a blue baseball hat with gold lettering that read *USS Michigan*, the last submarine on which his father had served; and a family picture. The glasses had not been moved or the hat worn in six months. One item was missing from the stand—a Bible.

A woman sat next to the bed. Her face was drawn but glowed with an inner peace. Her friends called her Abigail, but Marcus called her Mother. She held the King James Bible in her hand. It was her voice he had been hearing as she read the Scriptures to his father.

"Hello, Mother," Marcus said softly. "Have you been here long?" He already knew the answer.

"Awhile," she said. Her voice was trimmed with a Mississippi accent that had persisted despite the fact that she had not been back to the state since she was a teenager, a time far removed from her present age of sixty-three. "I came over after church. I went to the early service like I always do. The reverend gave a good talk."

Marcus walked forward and kissed his mother on the forehead. "You need to take care of yourself, Mom. Spending hour after hour here can't be good for you."

"Don't you fret about me. This is where I belong. This is where I'll be. The Navy kept your father and me separated for months on end. I'm not going to waste a minute of the time we have left together."

All Marcus could think of to do was nod. He let his eyes trace the form on the bed. His rational mind told him that he was gazing at his father, but the man hardly resembled the one he had called Dad. He was too thin and his skin the wrong shade of ebony. A new sadness filled Marcus. This was why he hated coming here. He loathed this place, not because he was unconcerned for his father and mother, but because there was nothing he could do. The coma had deprived his father of a meaningful existence, stolen his mother's husband, and left him without a father. He had been encouraged to speak to his father. The doctors and nurses had all urged him to assume that every word was heard, every emotion felt, even if there was no visible response. There was plenty of evidence to show that coma victims heard all that went on around them.

That fact notwithstanding, Marcus had trouble following the advice. He found it almost impossible to believe that the motionless man had ever been the father he remembered as robust, active, and quick to laugh. Marcus remembered a game of one-on-one basketball played at his parents' home when his father was fifty-five and he was just twenty-four. His father had cleaned his clock. True that Marcus possessed no natural athletic ability, but he was far from sedate, especially in those days. The bottom line was that his father seemed full of endless energy and perpetual youth.

That was before the stroke six months ago. It came without warning and with a suddenness that belied belief. A blood vessel in his brain had exploded like a bomb, laying waste to the man's power to reason, to feel, even to move.

"You look tired, son," Abigail said.

"Do I?" Marcus smiled at his mother. She was being forced to hike through hell and she was concerned about his weariness. "The drive down was a little more difficult than usual," he said. "The rain and an accident slowed things down."

"I pray no one was hurt."

That was just like his mother, praying for strangers. "I don't think anyone was."

"How's that wife of yours?"

"She's fine," Marcus replied. It was all small talk. Since the accident, that was all they had.

"He missed you last week," Abigail said with a nod toward his father.

"How can you know that?" Marcus asked softly. He felt guilty for not coming down last Sunday. He had awakened slightly ill, something he attributed to the Italian food he and

Lucy had eaten the night before. By 9:30 he had felt much better, but chose not to make the trip to San Diego.

"We've been married a very long time," Abigail responded. "Forty-two years. A husband and a wife learn to communicate with more than words after that many years."

Marcus nodded. "I didn't feel well. I called you to let you know."

"I remember. I'm just saying that he missed you."

"I missed him, too."

His mother gave him a strange glance. Marcus understood the unspoken message. Stepping over to the supine figure of his father, he leaned over and kissed him on the forehead. "Hi, Dad," he said a few decibels above normal speech. Before the accident, his father had complained that his hearing was failing. "I'm sorry I missed last Sunday. I thought about you all week." He paused, wondering what to say next. One-sided conversations were so difficult. "Lucy sends her love. She's working at the hospital today and couldn't come. She's sorry that work got in the way."

A long, painful pause followed.

"She's a smart that one, that Lucy," Abigail said, breaking the silence.

"I think so," Marcus said. He pulled the second chair in the room closer to the bed and sat down. "What were you reading to Dad?"

"Psalm 139," she said.

"His favorite," Marcus said with a smile. "I don't know how many sermons he preached on that passage." After retiring from the Navy with twenty-five years of service, his father had returned to school to study for the ministry. Four years later he had a college degree from a small Bible college in San Diego and his first church. The advantage of enlisting in the service at eighteen was that his father was barely middle age when he retired, allowing plenty of time for a new career. Since he had his retirement pay and benefits, he was able to take a small church that could not afford to pay a full-time salary. Chief James Stiller became Reverend James Stiller. The Central Missionary Baptist Church grew under his leadership, and Marcus learned all there was to know about church life and life in the public eye. To the very private sixteen-year-old Marcus, the attention was a burden, and he spent much of the rest of his teen years trying to live up to the image that the congregation had of the "preacher's boy." It was unfair. It was his lot in life.

"He likes it when I read from the Bible. It brings him peace."

"I'm sure he does," Marcus said, not feeling sure in the least.

"Will you stay for dinner?"

Marcus shook his head slowly. "I can't today, Mom. I have classes tomorrow and I'm not ready. I'll be up half the night getting my lesson plan pulled together."

"Or looking through that telescope of yours."

If the weather clears, Marcus thought. He wanted to explain the odd discovery he had made, but decided against it. His mother had no aptitude and less interest in things of science. His dad was different. He was a man of deep faith, but also one with an abiding and unabashed curiosity. Unlike Marcus who struggled to reconcile what he heard on Sunday with what his teachers and professors were teaching him, James Stiller moved easily between the two worlds of faith and empiricism. Somehow, Marcus had never had the conversation that would shed light on the epistemological bridge his father had built between the distant shores of belief and science. It was an oversight Marcus deeply regretted.

"They ask about you at the church," Abigail said.

"That's nice," Marcus said. "They're good people."

"They're worried that you left the faith, that you've gone after strange gods."

It was a church euphemism. The "strange gods" were the sciences that many saw as an affront to God. "I haven't left anything, Mother. They needn't worry."

Abigail nodded, which Marcus understood was not a gesture of agreement but a simple courtesy, an acknowledgment
that she was listening.

"Well, I guess I can't blame them." Abigail closed the Bible
and folded her aged hands over the black leather cover. "They
thought you would follow your father in the pulpit."

It was a sore subject. "Not everyone can do what Dad did.
I don't have the gift for it."

"God would have given you what you needed."

"I don't want to argue, Mom. I love you and Dad. No son
has more respect for his parents or their beliefs, but maybe God
gave me a different set of gifts."

"He's going to use you, boy. You know that. You know
that right here." She leaned forward and touched his chest. Her
hand seemed smaller, more arthritic than the last time he saw
her. He worried for her health.

"Sure, Mom, I know that."

"You may know it, Marcus, but you don't *believe* it."

As if letting his assent be known a moan erupted from
James. Marcus glanced casually toward his father. It was one of
a host of sounds he made since slipping into the coma. Abigail
leaned back in her seat.

"I tell you what, Mom. Lucy and I'll come down early
some Sunday and go to church with you. That way the church
can see that I haven't turned into a devil and we can spend the
day together."

Abigail nodded.

"Do you need anything, Mom? Are you eating? Do you
have enough food? How's the car running? What about the
house?"

Abigail quieted him with the wave of a hand. "Everything
is fine with me. The church has been wonderful. They still pay
your father his full salary and I have his pension. It's more than
I need. I pay people to do the things I can't. It gives me more
time to spend with your father."

"If you need anything, anything at all—"

"I'll call. I promise."

"Okay."

"There is one thing you can do for me and your father. You can lead us in prayer."

Marcus tensed and hoped it didn't show. He prayed so little these days. Standing, Marcus helped his mother to her feet and they stepped to the bed. Taking his mother's frail hand in his own, Marcus reached forward and touched his father's arm. The skin was soft and warm. There was no response. Marcus expected none. Then, bowing his head, Marcus prayed aloud, uncertain of what to say. One halting word followed another.

Outside, the sky darkened another shade.

◗ ◗ ◖ ● ◖ ◖ ◖

THE FOGGINESS OF HER MIND was clearing like a mist under a determined sun. She had no sense of time, of day or night, or the passage of evenings. How long she had been restrained in the hospital bed was beyond her. A day? Two days? A week?

It hurt to think. It hurt to move. The fat man was responsible for the latter; the drugs accounted for the former. Still she had to think, and she knew that she would have to move. The sedative was wearing off, and her behavior would dictate if she were to receive more. Julie didn't want more. Nor did she want anything for the pain. She needed her mind clear. Better to be in agony and thinking, than painless and confused.

She was being watched and Julie knew it. When the attacks came—and that was what she considered them, attacks—her reasoning faculties were overpowered in a tsunami of emotion. What she knew no longer mattered, only surviving the assault.

The back of her head pounded. She could feel the knot of swelling under the scalp. That meant something, but what? Reason dawned. If there was still a bump on her head, then the attack must have happened recently, maybe just a few hours ago—certainly not more than a day.

But what did it matter? A day, a week, nothing was different. She was still institutionalized, restrained, and drugged. Most of all she was still alone.

It hadn't always been so. At first she had visitors. Friends and coworkers would come by on a regular basis. If she weren't in the middle of an "episode" they would stay and visit. Her husband visited daily—initially. The friends were the first to go. Her husband continued to visit, when he had time. His visits decreased. She hadn't seen him in a month.

Any moment now, she thought, *he'll stroll in here. He'll be wearing a gray suit. He always wears a gray suit.* "I'm sorry," he'll say sadly, "something came up. I've been real busy. It's been a zoo in Sacramento." He would sit with her for a few moments, then say, "Boy, I've got to run. I've got a meeting at the district office in half an hour." He would leave. Just like he left the time before and all the times before that. No amount of pleading, no quantity of reason, no flood of tears could convince him to stay, let alone have her dismissed from the corner of hell in which she was confined.

Julie tried to focus, to get her brain running again. She wondered how long it would be before Daniel stopped showing up at all. *Having a crazy wife was a hindrance to an up-and-coming state assemblyman*, she concluded. Voters might think that insanity was contagious. Still, she was his wife of eight years. The state capital was close to five hundred miles away, so daily visits were impossible while the assembly was in session. At first she pleaded to be taken with him even if it meant being institutionalized in Sacramento.

He refused. Julie knew that he would always refuse. It was just a matter of time before he found a way to quietly divorce her, leaving her stranded and alone. Without income or family she would be transferred to a state hospital. Once there, she would fall through the administrative cracks never to be found.

Death would be better.

"Please, God," she whispered. "There must be a way out. Even death would be better than this. Hell can't be worse. Please, God, help me or kill me, just don't leave me here."

A hot, desperate tear escaped the corner of one eye, rolled down her cheek, and fell to the coarse white sheet.

"Please, God. Please." The silent prayer of desperation wafted heavenward. "Just take me."

CHAPTER

FOUR

FATHER BEN SICARELLO FELT ODD. NOT NORMALLY A demonstrative man, Ben nonetheless felt like jumping and shouting. He also felt the cold of confusion. On the computer monitor before him was a tight, crystal-clear image of the Moon. He had magnified the computer image until just the southern rim of Crater Pluto filled the screen. To get the image, Ben had to pirate time away from a researcher from the University of Arizona. The scientist whom Ben had usurped said nothing, made no complaints, but his displeasure iced the room. Ben made a mental note to send a bottle of wine to the man.

By agreement, the U. of A. had scheduling rights to the VATT for twenty-five percent of its use. The Vatican Advanced Technology Telescope was a 1.8 meter at the Mount Graham International Observatory near Safford, Arizona. It was one of three telescopes operated at the site by the Vatican Observatory. In addition to the VATT were the newly finished Large Binocular Telescope and the Submillimeter Telescope Observatory—a telescope that viewed the universe at the microwave frequency. The VATT was the best choice for observing the Moon.

Ben typed a number into the keyboard and watched as the color of the Moon changed. He was using a computer program that allowed him to colorize the image, making certain details easier to observe. He shook his head in disbelief and puzzlement. He could not be seeing what he was seeing, but the image was undeniable. He had no answers, only questions.

Glancing at the clock on his desk he saw that it was close to 2:00 in the afternoon. His stomach growled. He had not eaten since last night. Once the images of the Moon had been electronically captured, he had spent the next few hours studying the images, tinkering with it using imaging software. Everything he tried left him more mystified. He had kept at it until 1:00 that morning. Once home and in bed he had mulled over his findings, slim as they were, until he fell asleep.

Sunday morning had begun early as it always did. During Mass, he found his mind wandering back to the images, to the lunar mystery. Whatever it was, it had captured his every thought.

As soon as Mass had ended, Ben had made his way back to his office and began work again. Not that there was much he could do. Toying with the images confirmed that the Enigma, as he had named it, was as real as anything he had ever seen. And he had no idea what to make of it.

He sighed heavily and leaned back in his chair. It was time to make the call he was dreading. Ben was a systematic man who liked to have everything in its place, whether it was the books in his library, or the theology in his mind. His desk was often a mess, but his mind was always orderly. When things were in order, he was content; when things were out of place, he quickly became irritable. He was irritable now.

Closing the imaging program, Ben called up his personal address book on the computer, selected the name Philip Lansing, and clicked the dial icon. A second later the sound of a dial tone followed by a ringing came over the speakers of the computer.

"Yes," Lansing said sharply.

"Did I wake you from your Sunday afternoon nap, Professor?"

"As a matter of fact you did, Ben. I was having a wonderful dream."

Ben laughed. "God save us from the dreams of middle-aged men."

"Are priests allowed to dream?" Lansing asked.

"Sure. Ever since Vatican II." There was a pause, then, "We have to talk, Philip."

"It's real then? You've confirmed it?"

"It's real. Who did you say found this?"

"A former student of mine, Marcus Stiller. He's in California."

"I assume he's at your old stomping grounds, Caltech," Ben said.

"No," Philip answered, "he teaches at a small liberal arts college."

"A small college?" Ben said, and then wondered if he sounded superior. He quickly added, "Not that there's anything wrong with a small college."

"No need to soft-pedal around me, Ben. I chew him out about it all the time. The man is brilliant; he could be tenured in any major university with an astronomy program."

"Marcus Stiller." Ben mulled the name over in his mind. "The Stiller Enigma it is then."

"Stiller Enigma?"

"Yes," Ben said. "He found it, it gets his name."

"Any ideas as to what it is?"

"Not a clue," Ben admitted. "I'm going to send you the images I took last night in an e-mail. It's going to be a big one. Do you have PGP?" PGP stood for Pretty Good Protection. It was a cryptology program used to protect e-mail.

"Yes."

"Good. We can't keep this under wraps very long. The Moon isn't all that far away. Someone else is going to see this and make an announcement. I suggest you get this Stiller on the phone and start talking about how to go public."

"I can do that," Philip said. "Send a copy to him, too. I'll give you his e-mail."

"Does he have encryption software?"

"I wouldn't be surprised, but if he doesn't, he can download it off the Net."

"Okay. You both will have everything within the hour. After you have had time to look at my report, we should have a conference call."

"Got it," Philip said. "Thanks, Ben. You're the best."

"Don't sing my praises yet. All I've done is verify another man's discovery. Beyond that I'm in the dark."

◖◗◖◗●◗◖◖

JULIE HAD BEEN WATCHING THE SPOT for some time. With no clock in sight, she could not know how long. It terrified her. Her stomach was knotted in fear, chills ran down her spine, and, worst of all, the ants inside her skull were back.

The process had been slow, but the sedative had worn off. That was the good news. She could think again, she could reason. With the sedative gone she could once again create and hold a thought. The bad news was that the visions could return at any time. She determined to remain calm. There would be no thrashing about, no cries of fear, no banging her head on the floor. That's what put her in the five-point restraints that now held her to the bed. She could move her toes and her fingers; she could even turn her head from side to side, but the leather straps around her wrists and ankles and the one around her waist kept her pinned to the bed.

It was as she lay on her bed staring at the ceiling that she first saw it. Initially it was just a dot, no larger than might be made by the head of a ballpoint pen, too small for anyone but her to notice. But this room was her world. Confined for countless days, she had come to know every inch of the cubicle. Strapped to the bed as she was now, there was little she could do but sleep or stare at the ceiling.

The dot was directly overhead. A coincidence? What were the odds that a single dot would be directly over her head? Why not one foot to the left or right? And why hadn't she seen the dot before?

Those concerns were being eclipsed. The speck was growing. At first it had been too small to determine its color, but now she could see that it was red—crimson red. As it grew, the depth of its color intensified.

Minutes began to stretch. Seconds ticked by so slowly that it seemed as if time had ground to a near halt. She watched the spot grow; there was nothing else she could do. From a pinpoint to a dot to something the size of a pea, it grew, expanding outward, pushing its border out millimeter by millimeter.

As it grew, it developed a thickness, a third dimension.

Calm, she told herself. *Remain calm. No outbursts. They'll bring more drugs. They'll hurt you again.*

The spot on the ceiling grew. It was now the size of a quarter. Its color had remained the same bloodred.

"It's not real," she uttered so softly that if anyone had been in the room they would not have heard it. "It . . . is . . . not . . . real."

She closed her eyes and willed the sight to be gone. She could make it go away, she told herself. If it was all in her mind, then she could make it go away. All it would take was concentration and a belief in herself.

She opened her eyes.

The scream caught in her throat.

A portion of the spot was hanging down, like a thick mucous drop. It hung from the ceiling by an ever-increasing gluey strand. It was no longer just a spot, it was a drip, and Julie knew that it would lose its grip and fall—fall on her face.

Remain calm, she ordered herself, but her body had its own ideas. Acid flooded her stomach as she looked at the repulsive drop. Her muscles cramped into tight knots of flesh. Perspiration coated her goosefleshed skin. She pressed her eyes shut and waited. Waited. Waited. Waited.

Nothing.

Slowly she opened her right eye—just her right eye.

The drop fell.

Julie felt it hit her forehead. It was warm and thick and putrid. She tried not to move. They were watching her. She knew that. The camera was behind a black plastic bubble in the ceiling. They watched her all the time and they were watching her now. If they saw her thrashing about, they would come back and if they came back . . . "Stop it!" she commanded herself. "Stop it. Stop it. It's not real."

The fluid slid down her temple.

Opening her eyes, she looked at the bloody spot and saw another drop form. As it gave way, so did Julie's resolve.

The scream that she had stuffed down so deeply in her gut burst forth like a siren.

Another drop fell.

Another.

THE SLAB OF SLATE-GRAY CLOUDS that had been overhead when
Marcus left for San Diego had broken into clusters of dark cotton. They were moving south over the mountains like a fleet of
ancient sailing ships. He was glad to see them go. This time next
month, clouds like that would be dropping snow, not just rain.
The radio had said, however, that another storm was on its way.
Marcus hoped the break would be long enough for him to
make more observations.

The drive home from San Diego had been just as grueling
as the trip down. Seeing his father always made Marcus feel as
if he had been run over by a truck. He loved his father, there
was no doubt in his mind about that. It was the helplessness
that bothered him. Nothing in his life had prepared him for
what he had just faced. Seeing his father less than alive but not
dead tore at the fabric of his soul. What does one do? Pray for
death? Hope for healing? Turn and walk away?

Then there was his mother. To Marcus she was a saint. No
one could have had a better mother than she. But she was not
well; the stress of caring for her father had deprived her body
of vitality. He worried about her. She was a fiercely independ-
ent woman who insisted on driving and caring for herself. Six
months from now would he have both parents in the hospital,
one in a coma, the other exhausted?

He shook his head as he turned up the street that led to his
house. That was a problem for the future. All he could do now,
he decided, was to take each challenge one at a time.

Once the car was parked in the garage, he went into the
house and fixed a pot of coffee. The house was cold. Lucy loved
living in the mountains even if it meant an hour's drive to work
each day. Her only complaint was the cold. For most of the
year, Pinewood offered a mild climate, but winter could sweep
in quickly. The late October change had arrived on time. Soon
the nights would be routinely below freezing and the days not
much warmer. Marcus turned on the forced air heater so that

the house would be warm when she arrived home. Maybe they would go out to dinner tonight.

As he waited for the drip coffeemaker to do its job, he walked into his office to check his e-mail. A few moments later, he was reading a note from Philip Lansing:

Interesting news. Go to the Web site listed below and download the PGP program. You'll need it to open a message from Father Ben in Arizona. He wants a conference call this evening. Amazing stuff, Marc. Take a look at his report and see if you can wrap your mind around it.

The clock on the computer read 4:32. Lucy wouldn't be home for at least another hour, maybe two. That should give him more than enough time to review the file. He wondered why the insistence on PGP? Marcus knew of the encryption program but had never seen any personal use for it. He clicked on the site address provided in the e-mail and began the downloading process.

Something was up, and it was time to find out what.

)◗◖●◗◖◗◖

DR. PETER BERNARD HAD A PROBLEM, a crisis big enough to bring him into the office on a Sunday afternoon. It was a predicament similar to those he had faced before, but this time things had been moved into the red zone. And he owed it all to his stupid, self-centered nephew, Gordon.

Punching the rewind button on the remote he held in his delicately thin hand, he watched the scene he had been viewing play backwards. When he reached the desired point in the tape, he stopped the rewind and pressed "Play." He felt sick as he watched it.

The tape showed Julie Waal standing at the window looking out into the night. One minute later she was screaming, pulling at her hair, and thumping her head on the linoleum floor. He continued to watch as Gordon and another attendant rushed

in. Julie thrashed about and managed to land a kick to the
young intern's thigh. Watching Gordon climb on top of the
woman to control her mildly bothered him, but what made
the pit of his stomach drop like an elevator whose cable had
snapped was the sudden appearance of a hypodermic needle
in Gordon's hand. He watched as Gordon popped off the plastic
safety cover and then plunged the needle into the upper arm of
Ms. Waal. He did it in one fluid motion and much harder than
was necessary. It was amazing that the needle didn't break off
in the woman's arm. Bernard was certain he had seen Gordon
smile throughout the process.

Bernard turned off the television and tossed the remote on
his desk. A routine problem teetered on the edge of becoming
a catastrophe.

Restraining patients was a normal practice in a mental
hospital. Patients could be violent and in their frenzy could display enough strength to intimidate a professional football
player. But there were limits. Only qualified personnel were to
dispense meds. Gordon was an orderly; he had no right giving
that injection. He put Ms. Waal and the hospital at risk. And
it would be Bernard who would bear the blame.

Gordon had to go, but that was no easy task. Gordon's
father was Bernard's only brother and Bernard owed him
money, a great deal of money. There were medical school
expenses, private practice costs, and two bad business ventures.
Gordon's brother had been there each step of the way, pouring
out tens of thousands of dollars like it was pocket change. He
could do it; he had made millions in the early days of tech
stocks, before dot-coms became dot-bombs. He had bought
Microsoft and Intel stock when they were still affordable. But
he was a man of principle. He required that his children work
until their thirtieth birthday before receiving a cut of the riches.
Bernard knew Gordon hated his father for it, but there was
nothing he could do.

When Gordon failed to find employment, his father turned to Bernard. How could he say no to the man he owed more than he could ever repay?

Perhaps he should show the tape to his brother. Bernard dismissed the idea. The tape had to go. It was evidence, evidence that could fall into the hands of the authorities. That image sent a shiver down Bernard's spine.

He rose from his chair and walked from the office, making his way to the surveillance room, the room where Gordon spent most of his time. Sunday was Gordon's day off. A tall, thin man sat in the swivel chair at the desk.

"Hello, Dr. Bernard," the man said with surprise. "What are you doing here today?"

"Paperwork," Bernard answered. "Always paperwork. I need to check on a patient. You can take your break now."

"I just came off my break."

"Then this is your lucky day," Bernard said with a forced smile. "Take another one. I'll keep an eye on things."

"Whatever you say, Doc." The man rose and left the small office.

Bernard sat down in the still-warm chair and swiveled it so that he could face a rectangular box on the counter. He slipped the tape he had been watching into a slot, closed the top, and depressed the button marked "Erase." A powerful magnetic pulse hummed to life. In two seconds the tape had been wiped cleaned. He removed the cassette and set it in a file box marked "Blank."

As he swung his chair back around, he took in the images on the monitors. Patients rested in their beds. One stood in the middle of his room rocking back and forth, something he did for at least twelve hours a day. Other monitors showed padded rooms.

Things seemed normal. Then he stopped. The bank of monitors flashed from one room to the next every twenty seconds, limiting the number of monitors needed to cover the ninety beds in the private hospital. With a quick gesture, Bernard punched a button that prevented the monitor from moving on to the next room. Bernard leaned forward and studied the image.

It was Julie Waal's room; she was still confined to the bed, but instead of lying still, she was jerking her head from side to side as if in the grips of a seizure.

"Now what?" Bernard moaned. He stood. Before exiting the surveillance room, he picked up the phone and called for a nurse. He started down the hall to the room of Julie Waal.

FIVE

CHAPTER

M s. WAAL?"

The voice seemed distant and thin. Julie refused to open her eyes, knowing what awaited—another vile drop suspended over her head. It would hang from the ceiling seconds longer than seemed natural, then fall, splattering on her face. No matter how much she tried to move, the dripping found her. If she lay still, the drops landed on her forehead, just an inch above her eyes. If she turned her head to the right or left, then the drops would splat close to her ear.

It was more than the fetid blood drops that terrified her. The crimson fluid seemed . . . intelligent, willful. Once it was on her skin, it did more than pool on her forehead or stream down her face. It moved. It crept. It crawled.

She was crying. Though she knew crying would do no good, it was beyond her strength to stop. So she wept in heaving sobs. At first she had screamed, shouting for help, but no help had come. Now, shivering in her own terror-induced sweat, she let the inevitable happen. She could not think, she could only feel, and what she felt was the frigid, probing fingers of fear.

"Ms. Waal?"

It was the voice again. This time it was a little stronger, a little nearer. "Can you hear me, Ms. Waal?"

A familiar voice.

"If you can hear me, please open your eyes."

"No, no, no." She forced the words through her teeth.

"Shall I get a sedative, Doctor?"

Doctor? A familiar voice. A male voice. Doctor.

"No," he said.

"But, Doctor—"

"I said, no, Nurse. Just stand by."

Doctor. Nurse. Sedative. Familiar terms. Familiar voices.

"Please, Ms. Waal. Open your eyes for me."

A soft hand touched her forearm. It was warm, as a human hand should be. It was a hand she had felt before. It was a voice she had heard before.

"Open your eyes now, Ms. Waal. You can do it, open your eyes."

It was waiting for her. She knew that as sure as she knew she was strapped to a bed in a mental hospital. If she opened her eyes, if she parted her lids just a little, another drop of obscene liquid would find its mark. It would enter her, seep into her mind, infecting her soul. Her soul was all that she had left. She couldn't allow it to be contaminated.

"It's all right, Ms. Waal," the doctor said. "I'm here with you. Nurse Richardson is here, too. You like Nurse Richardson, don't you?"

Nurse Richardson. An image of a large woman with gray and black hair, a round face, and a sweet smile played in her mind. Julie nodded.

"Of course you do."

A spark of recognition lit up her dark thoughts. "Dr. Bernard?"

"Yes, Ms. Waal, it's Dr. Bernard. Now open your eyes for me."

Julie bit her lip and searched within herself for that reservoir of courage that would allow her to face the hideous thing above her and found it. Through tightly clinched teeth, she sucked in a deep, noisy breath and snapped open her eyes.

The ceiling was above her, but it was a blank canvas of painted drywall. No bloodstain, no spot, just the flat expanse of gloss white with only a fluorescent light fixture interrupting the smooth inverted plain. Everything was as it was before.

"My face," Julie said.

"What about your face, Ms. Waal?"

"What's on my face?"

Dr. Bernard shook his head. "I don't see anything. Do you feel something on your skin?"

"I thought . . . I thought . . ."

"What did you think, Ms. Waal?"

Julie sighed. She was confused. Nothing made sense. "I thought something was on my face."

"What did you think was on your face?" Bernard's words were firm but caring. He had the tone of a healer. Not like the fat man. Not like Gordon.

"I thought something was dripping on me. Something from the ceiling." She paused, uncertain how much to tell him. More than anything, she wanted to be free of this place. To walk the streets like normal people, to watch television, to eat junk food, to know that she could go wherever she wanted, whenever she wanted. But she would never leave as long as they thought her insane. "I was . . . having a bad dream."

"Did it seem like a dream to you, Ms. Waal?"

"Yes. Yes, of course. Why?"

"You were very upset," Bernard said. "Nurse, bring me a cool washcloth, please."

Nurse Richardson responded immediately. Julie watched as she disappeared into the bathroom and returned with a white facecloth and a towel. Bernard took the cloth and touched it to Julie's head. The dampness felt good.

"You've been perspiring. That must have been some dream, Ms. Waal. Why don't you tell me about it."

Julie didn't want to. "It was just a dream. Everyone has bad dreams. Even normal people have bad dreams."

Bernard nodded as he gently dabbed at Julie's face. "I have them from time to time. I find them very unsettling."

Julie chuckled mildly at the understatement. "Unsettling is a good term."

"I think it terrified you, Ms. Waal," Bernard said. "I also think that you would feel much better if you would tell me all about it. I can't help unless I know everything that is going on."

"I want to go home, Doctor. I don't belong here."

Bernard frowned. "I wish you could go home. Maybe someday soon you can. But first we have to find out what it is that troubles you."

"I'm not crazy, Doctor." Julie turned her head away and looked out the barred window. Out there was the real world. Somehow she knew she was part of something larger than herself; part of the fabric of existence of which the rest of the world was ignorant. They could not understand.

"Crazy is a term we don't use here, Ms. Waal," Bernard said firmly. "You know that. You're here because we can help you. This is what we do. A dentist fixes teeth, a surgeon heals bodies, and we deal with emotions and the mind."

"It's more than emotions, Doctor," Julie said softly. "It goes beyond emotion."

"How so?"

Turning her face back to Bernard, Julie abruptly said, "I don't want to be tied down any longer."

"We had to restrain you because you tried to hurt yourself yesterday."

"I won't hurt myself." As she spoke the words, the lump on the back of her head began to throb as did the bruises she had received at the hands of the orderlies.

"We have to be sure of that," the doctor said.

Julie fell silent for a moment then said, "I will have to talk to my husband about yesterday when he comes to visit." Julie saw Bernard tense.

"Yes, of course you do. I want to talk to you about that." Bernard turned to Nurse Richardson. "I need a few minutes alone with Ms. Waal."

"Doctor, you have a policy about not being alone with any female patient."

Bernard's tone hardened. "I know my own policies, Nurse. Now please leave us for a few moments."

"Very well," Richardson said. "If you insist."

After the nurse had left, Julie said, "You're worried that my husband will bring legal action against the hospital."

"We . . . My staff was just doing their job, Ms. Waal. You were out of control."

"I was given an injection."

"Not unusual in a hospital."

"By an orderly?"

"How do you know that it was an orderly who gave you the injection?"

"I was there." Julie was surprised by the firmness of her voice, but she had to play this card. It was the only card she had. Inside she quivered like a frightened rabbit, but she had to appear strong or she could remain strapped to the bed for weeks, being let up only long enough for a little exercise and to use the bathroom. And if she remained strapped to the bed, the blood on the ceiling would return, slowly driving her mad.

"Well, of course you were, Ms. Waal. What I meant was—"

"You were testing my memory, my perception, Doctor. I know what you were doing. I see things. I see horrible, terrifying things, but I am not stupid. I am as rational as any of your staff. Maybe more so than some."

"You refer to Gordon."

"Imagine this, Doctor," Julie offered. "My husband comes to visit. I tell him about yesterday, about how an orderly injects me with a sedative. I show him the bruises on my arms and ribs where that pig sat on me. He becomes concerned and begins to ask questions. He smells a lawsuit, or better yet, decides that the State of California should investigate facilities like this to see what kind of abuses are going on. Since his wife is institutionalized at this hospital, he begins here. Soon, investigators from departments you haven't even heard of start showing up on your doorstep, rummaging through your files, talking to your staff, looking at your bank account."

"I get the picture, Ms. Waal," Bernard said. Then, still holding the washcloth, he put his hands behind his back. "When was the last time your husband came to visit?"

A punch to the stomach would have hurt less. *Bernard must know the answer to that question,* she reasoned. He must know it had been nearly a month and that no one else had visited in that time. Despite the turmoil she felt, her countenance remained unchanged.

"I don't mean to be rude, Ms. Waal," Bernard continued, "but it has been quite some time."

"Of course it has, Doctor. You don't know much about politics, do you? This is the busiest time of the year. Everyone at the capitol has some bill they want to push through before the holiday break. My husband told me that it would be a few weeks before he could get back to visit. However, I expect him in the next day or two. Maybe even today."

Julie watched the doctor's Adam's apple shoot up and down. He had swallowed hard, and what he had swallowed was a lie.

"What is it you want?" The kindness of his voice had evaporated in the heat of fear.

"Remove the restraints."

"And if you have another episode—"

"I promise not to hurt myself." Julie nodded at the camera mounted to the ceiling. "You watch me twenty-four hours a day anyway. I can't even go to the bathroom without one of your staff leering at me."

"They don't leer, Ms. Waal. You have full privacy in the rest room. You know that."

"Release the restraints, Doctor. I promise to behave and to keep our little secret."

"I can up your meds—"

"No. They fog my mind. No more medication."

"You must have some. We are supposed to be treating you."

"Okay. No *new* meds. Just leave the current dosages where they are. I can live with that." Julie had to concede something. Ten years in real estate had taught her the finer points of negotiating. One such point was to always have something to surrender so the other party could feel a sense of victory.

"If you try to hurt yourself, the deal is off. Can we agree to that?"

Julie nodded. "Yes."

Bernard lowered his head and sighed. Julie knew that this went against everything he had been trained to do, and that she was pushing him into a corner. She also knew that Gordon would hear about this. There was satisfaction in that.

"Very well," Bernard said.

"One more thing."

"You're pushing it, Ms. Waal."

"I don't want to see that orderly again."

"Gordon?"

"If he comes into my room again, then I tell my husband what you allowed him to do. Agreed?"

"He has a job to do, and I didn't allow—"

"Let him do it elsewhere," Julie interjected.

Dr. Bernard nodded reluctantly and then began to release the leather straps. To Julie, he looked like a defeated general facing his soldiers.

That's step one, Julie thought. *Now comes step two.*

○ ◐ ◑ ● ● ◑ ◐ ○

The download had gone smoothly, although it had taken close to half an hour. As much as he loved living in the mountains, Marcus often wished he had access to faster Internet providers. Phone lines worked fine for general net surfing, but downloading large files was a chore. The image files from Benjamin Sicarello in Arizona had bogged his system down. Once in the computer, he was in business. He spent the next thirty minutes drinking coffee and marveling at what he was seeing.

The pictures that Whiz and Terri had made with his telescope were wonderful, but paled compared to those now displayed on his computer monitor. The images had come as an attachment to an e-mail. The note had been short:

Here are some photos for your consideration. These were taken with the VATT, 1.83 m., f/1, at the Mount Graham International Observatory in Arizona. Operator =Benjamin Sicarello. Other info in the report sheet. Allow me to say, 'Wow.' I propose we call it the Stiller Enigma. Talk to you soon.—Ben.

"Stiller Enigma." Marcus chuckled. He felt good about seeing his name associated with an astronomical find even if it was just in an e-mail. Ben had included color-enhanced shots as well as a short report. Marcus consumed it all like a hungry man, but when he had digested everything, he was left with little more than he started with. The VATT pictures were clear and crisp, showing much more detail than his telescope could deliver. Still, the blemish appeared to be just that, a smudge on the Moon, as if someone had spilled cherry Kool-Aid on the lunar surface.

The phone rang, startling Marcus. His heart tripped quickly for a moment. He picked up the phone on the third ring. "Hello."

"Is this the famous astronomer, Marcus Stiller?"

"Hello, Philip," Marcus said with a chortle.

"You received the e-mail from Ben?" Philip always cut to the chase.

"I'm fine thank you. And you?"

"We're scientists, Marc, we don't need all the pleasantries. Did you or did you not receive Ben's e-mail?"

"I got it. I've been studying the shots for the last half hour."

"I've been studying it a lot longer than that. This is quite a find. What do you think it is?"

"A blotch."

"That's your considered opinion?" Philip asked with friendly sarcasm. "A blotch?"

"That's about it," Marc admitted. "I've run it through my imaging software a dozen different ways, as did your friend in Arizona. Even the best resolution shows nothing more than a discoloration."

"Wait," Philip said suddenly. "I have another call coming in. This may be him."

Marc found himself on hold.

"Marc," Lansing said a minute later. "I've got Ben on the other line. I'm going to make this a conference call." Marcus listened with amusement as Philip tried to figure out how to combine three phone calls into one.

"Two degrees in physics and two in astrophysics and you can't work your own phone?" Marcus prodded.

"Physics is easy, stuff with buttons is hard. Wait, here we go." There was a slight clicking sound, then, "Marc, you still with me?"

"I'm here."

"Ben?"

"Present."

"Okay, it looks like we're all connected," Philip said with authority. "Marc, I would like you to meet Father Benjamin Sicarello, director of the Vatican Observatory in Arizona."

"It's a pleasure Dr. Sic . . . Father Sicarello," Marc said, uncertain which title to use.

"Call me Ben. I must admit, you've knocked my socks off with those photos." His voice betrayed no accent. Marcus had expected him to sound Italian, but instead, he sounded as if he had grown up in the West.

"Serendipity, I'm afraid," Marcus said modestly. "I wasn't looking for it. Two of my students took the photos, and I noticed the anomaly later that night."

"I don't believe in luck, Dr. Stiller—"

"Just Marcus or Marc, whichever you prefer."

"Okay, now that we're all buddies," Philip said, "let's get down to business. What are we looking at and what are we going to do about it?"

There was silence.

"I take it that no one has a clue," Philip said.

"I admit to being in the dark," Marcus said.

"I wish I could offer more, but I can't," Ben admitted. "More study is needed. Without it, we're just fishing."

"Okay, let's talk about what Marcus should do next," Philip said.

"Me?"

"Yes, you," Philip replied. "It's your discovery and it needs to go in the books that way. I like Ben's idea of calling it the Stiller Enigma, at least for now."

"You're not serious. That's fine between us, but—"

"No buts about it, Marc," Philip interrupted. "If you don't announce this, someone else will. You deserve the credit."

"I think a press conference is in order," Ben said. "The sooner the better. A few press releases to the right scientific periodicals are needed, too."

"Wait a minute," Marcus said. "What do we announce? 'Hey, guys, there's a really neat spot on the Moon. Have you seen it?'"

"I'd doll it up a little more," Philip said. "And it's not 'we' but you. You will be the one making the announcement. We're just the guys who documented your find. Trust me, you'll come out smelling like a rose."

"How about Caltech," Ben said. "Could you fly back to your old alma mater, Phil?"

"You bet. It will tick off people here at MIT, but Caltech is still home and Marcus is a graduate. It's perfect."

"All that's left is the time," Ben stated.

"Do I get a say in this?" Marcus asked.

"Certainly," Philip said. "Pour out your heart."

Marcus took a deep breath and tried to formulate his thoughts. Things were moving too quickly, and becoming public too soon. More work needed to be done. Still, they were right, anyone—a backyard astronomer with a mediocre telescope—could see the Enigma, but a press conference? That seemed a bit much. "This seems a little fast, guys."

"It is, but the world moves fast these days," Philip said. "You have made an interesting, maybe even great, discovery. You deserve the credit. Besides, once the announcement has been made, then the real science can begin. Trust us on this, Marc."

Marcus reluctantly agreed.

"Okay, here's what we do," Philip said. His words came in a torrent of syllables. "I'll prepare the press releases. My secretary is great at that kind of thing. Ben, can you make more observations?"

"I'll see what I can do. The schedule is full, but I'll pull a few strings."

"Great," Philip enthused. "Marc, you should think about the wording of your announcement. I'll have my secretary send you a copy of the print release. I'll also pick the publications. Any special ones you think we should contact?"

Marcus felt like a raft in the rapids. "Um, not off the top of my head."

"Okay, I'll call Caltech and set up a place and time. I'll let you know when I can fly out there. Does that sound good to everyone?"

"It sounds great to me," Ben said. "Marc, don't worry. We'll stand with you, but this will be your baby. You'll love it."

Marcus wondered if that was true.

CHAPTER

SIX

MARCUS STOOD ON HIS BALCONY GAZING UPWARD,
seeing nothing but a fresh, thick bank of clouds drap-
ing the night sky and obscuring his vision. He had
hoped to take more pictures of the Moon, to glean
more detail of the Stiller Enigma. The phrase still
seemed silly to him, but Lucy had thought it an honor.
She wanted to celebrate, so in a few minutes they would
be leaving for dinner at Bennie's Chateau, Pinewood's
only upscale restaurant.

Yet Marcus didn't feel like celebrating. The day had been an emotional grinder. The excitement he felt in the wee hours of Saturday morning, the difficult drive to San Diego Sunday, the sight of his ailing father, the confusion over the lunar spot, his inability to make observations, the pending press announcement—all worked to turn his thoughts into a boiling stew.

A sudden breeze rustled through the pine trees and sprinkled a cold mist of water across his face. He shivered.

"You're going to catch pneumonia standing out there," Lucy scolded. "Where's your coat?"

"I'm just taking in a little fresh air," Marcus said.

Lucy joined him on the balcony. The clouds thinned enough for the Moon—still more full than gibbous—to push through a hazy ivory light. "Clouds are not your friend," Lucy said. Like Marcus, she wore no coat.

"No, they're not," he agreed, his eyes still fixed above. "Nature has conspired against me."

Lucy shuddered as another breeze rolled over the deck. Marcus turned and looked at her and said, "What are you doing out here without a coat? It can't be more than forty degrees." Lucy said nothing but cast a questioning look at her husband. "Oh," Marcus said, chagrined at his foolish question.

"I thought I'd freeze to death with my husband," Lucy said with a smile. "That way, the neighbors could find two frozen people."

"Okay, you win. Let's go inside and grab our coats. Dinner awaits."

Bennie's Chateau was in full swing. Sunday night brought out not only the local mountain residents, but those from the communities below—the "down the hill" crowd—who desired a nice dinner in the mountains. The restaurant was situated in a large Tudor structure with a steeply peaked roof. The interior decor was a confusion of styles that mysteriously worked well together. Dark wood paneling covered the walls from floor to ceiling, simulated gas lamps hung on the walls over the booths, and imitation Persian carpets covered the floor. The atmosphere was cozy and warm, albeit eclectic.

Marcus and Lucy sat in the corner of the dining room next to two large windows. It had begun to rain again, splattering the tinted glass. Marcus stared out one of the windows.

"Do you think it will turn to snow?" Lucy asked.

"It's possible." Marcus continued his vigil of the icy rain.

"Every year is different," Lucy said philosophically. "Some years it snows early, other years late. It snowed on Mother's Day once. Remember that?"

Marcus didn't respond.

"Marc?"

Nothing.

"I was abducted by an alien," Lucy said evenly.

Marcus grunted.

"I'm having an affair with him," Lucy said. "He's not tall, dark, or handsome. In fact, he's short, gray, and terribly ugly, but he did offer to show me the world."

Marcus blinked several times and turned his attention from the window to his wife. "What are you talking about?"

"Oh, you *are* listening."

An embarrassed smile crossed Marcus's face. "I seem to be a little distracted."

"A little? Your body is present and accounted for, but I can't say the same for your mind. What's bothering you?"

"Bothered isn't the right word for it. I'm just ... distracted by all this."

Lucy nodded. "By all this, you mean the Stiller Enigma?"

"It's a silly name."

"No, it's not," Lucy said. "You discovered it. Why shouldn't it get your name? That's tradition, isn't it?"

"Generally, but not always. But that's not the point. I just have a bad feeling about all this."

"A bad feeling?" said Lucy. "Are you sure you're not just a little nervous?"

"You know that I'm a meticulous man," Marcus said. "I like things orderly, everything in the right place."

"That's true enough," Lucy agreed. "You're the only man I know who organizes the glove compartment of his car."

"I'm not that bad, am I?"

Lucy nodded. "Worse."

"Anyway," Marcus said, "this Stiller Enigma has had all the order of an avalanche. I know that Philip and Ben are looking out for my place in history, but I can't help but feel that I'm missing something."

"Like what?"

Marcus laughed. "If I knew that, then I wouldn't be missing it."

Lucy reached across the table and took Marcus's hand. "Part of the adventure of life is found in its uncertainty. Good things often lie just around the corner. People find them. Life is not a script, dear; it's an adventure. We choose how we want to live our lives and then we do the best we can. Along the way both good and bad come. This is a good thing. Let it happen."

"I'm sure you're right," Marcus replied. He felt no such certainty, and he knew no reason why.

○ ◐ ● ● ● ◑ ○

BEN SICARELLO FELT UNEASY as he set his Bible down on the small dining room table. He rubbed his weary eyes and leaned back in the wood chair. Soon he would leave his small bungalow home in the tiny community of Safford, Arizona, and make his way up the serpentine road to the Mount Graham observatory. He had been fortunate enough to secure another hour of observation on the VATT from a colleague. It was going to cost him time out of his own research schedule next month, but he could live with that. At least he would have an opportunity to take a few more shots of the lunar surface.

The Moon traveled around the earth at 2,300 miles per hour taking twenty-seven days, seven hours, and a handful of minutes to complete a single orbit. Since the earth rotates on its axis, the time between new moons was always a little longer, twenty-nine and a half days. That meant that the Moon appeared in a slightly different spot of the sky each night, about thirteen degrees to the east. It also meant the Sun would strike the lunar surface at a slightly different angle. Perhaps something new could be seen.

Ben leaned over the Bible again and studied the words on the page. Unlike the Bibles in the homes of most people, this one was written in Greek. The New Testament had been written in Koine Greek nearly two thousand years before. To Ben, for whom languages were a hobby, the Greek used in the twenty-seven books of the New Testament was a miracle in itself. No other language could match it for detail or could carry so many levels of meaning in a single word. It was truly a scientist's language. Such a realization was confirmation for his blending a life of faith with the rigors of scientific investigation.

He knew that most people saw faith and science as polar opposites. To him, however, they were inseparable. How one could look at the universe and not see a Creator was beyond him. How one could look for a Creator without looking at the creation was equally mystifying. Science and faith were not oil and water, but more like the oxygen and hydrogen atoms that combined to make the water—volatile individually, stable when combined.

It had been a Jesuit teacher in his high school that had shown Ben the perfect blending of belief with evidence, of science with faith, and of past wisdom with contemporary knowledge. For him it had been a natural progression to enter the priesthood as well as choose the Jesuits for his work. The training had been rigorous and demanding, and he loved every moment of it.

Pushing the remembrances aside, Ben picked up his pencil and continued his translation. He could have read the passage from an English Bible, but there was no challenge in that, and every translation carried with it the assumptions of the translators. No one could convert from one language to another without a bit of his thinking being embedded in the text.

Ben had been uncomfortable most of the day. His phone conference with Philip and Marcus had done nothing to alleviate the nagging discomfort. Generally not an emotional man, Ben was nonetheless perplexed by the feeling. What need was there to be uncomfortable? None. If anything, he should be thrilled to have been part of the discovery.

Jealousy? Was he envious of Marcus Stiller? After all, he was the director of a prestigious observatory, while Marcus was only a teacher in a small college. Ben shook his head, dismissing the idea. None of that mattered. Learning mattered. Knowing mattered. Discovery mattered. Marcus deserved the scientific claim that was about to come his way.

Ben focused on the job at hand. He knew the passage well, but translating it now seemed important. The words before him were in the Apocalypse of John the apostle, the sixth chapter. At last he put his pencil down and read the words.

"And I gazed when he broke the sixth seal, and there was a great earthquake; and black as sackcloth made of hair became the sun, and the whole moon became as blood." Revelation 6:12.

○ ◗ ◖ ● ◐ ◖ ○

"HOW DO YOU THINK Dr. Whitaker will respond?" Lucy asked as she cut a small bite from the herb chicken breast and raised it to her mouth.

Marcus swallowed a bite of blackened meatloaf, then washed the spicy food down with a sip of tea. "I hadn't thought about that," he admitted. Jacob Whitaker was the president of the college where Marcus taught.

"Do you think he'll be upset that you're not making the announcement from his campus?"

"He could be," Marcus said. "I'm not a research professor so he has no right to be, but I'm sure he'll see it as a missed public relations opportunity. Caltech is really the better idea."

"So you don't expect any repercussions?"

Marcus shook his head. "Nothing serious. I imagine I'll have to explain myself."

"You could mention his name and the name of the school. That way they would get some mileage out of the PR," Lucy suggested.

"That's a good idea. Maybe I should invite him to attend."

"Couldn't hurt."

A soft ringing erupted from the cell phone that lay on the table next to his plate. He answered, listened, and then hung up. "That was Philip. The press conference is on for tomorrow afternoon at 3:00. He's arriving in the morning. Father Ben will do the same. They arranged their flights to arrive close together. Ben will arrive about half an hour before Philip."

"What time?"

"Ben's flight from Arizona is scheduled for a 10:30 arrival; Philip at 11:00."

"Ontario or LAX?"

"Ontario thankfully. I imagine we'll just stay down the hill until the press conference. Ben has more pictures to show me. Philip has arranged for a conference room where we can meet. The press conference will be held in Beckman Auditorium."

"At 3:00."

Marcus could see the wheels of his wife's brain spinning. She bit her lips and narrowed her eyes when deep in thought. "I'm on duty until 6:00, but I might be able to get someone to cover the last few hours for me. I'd like to be there."

"I'd love to have you."

"Hand me the phone," she said, pulling a small leather folder from her purse. She opened the personal directory and began scanning the names. "This may take a few minutes," she said as she took the phone, "but I shall prevail."

○ ◑ ● ● ◐ ◐ ○

JULIE WAS BACK AT the window again, looking through her reflection into the dark night. The Stygian sky was costumed in broken clouds, pieces of which moved through the atmosphere like ice floes in a nearly frozen river. But the Moon was up and visible through the occasional break in the clouds. Water drops speckled the windowpane, blurring the ivory orb, but Julie maintained her watch. The minutes passed fluidly, marked only by the moving of the Moon through the sky.

Julie reached forward and touched the glass as if she could push her hand through it and caress the wet night air.

The Moon was different. Not just in its shape. It was no longer full like it had been two nights ago when she had been watching it, two nights ago when the attack came. Still, it was mostly full, and it cast a pale, lonely light through the fractures in the clouds.

Julie began staring at the moon four weeks before. She had no idea why. Gazing at Earth's eternal partner at first seemed right, then mandatory. Early on she believed that she was amusing herself. Confined to her lonely room, Julie had little to keep her active mind occupied. Before, watching the Moon was entertainment. Now it was an irresistible compulsion.

Over the month she had watched the full moon slowly erode in the sky, diminishing with each passing day until its white light was gone. She remembered from school that this was called the new moon, the time when the Moon was between the earth and the Sun, lost in its own shadow.

That had been a lonely time. She knew it was out there, hung in airless, frigid space, but she couldn't see it. She longed to see it. Then it began to return, first as a thin crescent that reminded her of a white fingernail. Each day it grew in size until once again it shone with its full face.

A child's poem floated up through the murky sea of her mind. It was something her mother had taught her when Julie was in preschool. She spoke the words softly, too soft to be called a whisper. "I see the Moon, and the Moon sees me. God bless the Moon, and God bless me."

Was God on the Moon? she wondered. Was that why she stared at it so? "God bless the Moon, and God bless me."

Julie did not feel blessed.

○ ◗ ◗ ● ● ◗ ◖ ○

PETER BERNARD SAT IN THE VIDEO monitoring room watching Julie over the closed-circuit surveillance system. Thanks to his moronic nephew Gordon, she had won. She had manipulated him with the skill of a top negotiator. She was a lovely woman, with piercing eyes and beautiful blonde hair. The hair was stringy and unkempt now, but that was not her fault. There were no mirrors in the room, nothing in which she could see herself. He had thought that best, but at the moment he was unsure.

He was angry with her. She was using the bad judgment of another to get what she wanted from him. His was a difficult job. Few physicians chose the field of abnormal psychology as a life's work. There were more lucrative, less stressful areas of medicine to practice. Nonetheless, it was a field that had seized his interest early in medical school and was showing no signs of letting go. That was fine with him.

In most cases, the patients he treated had no hope for a normal life. Disease, drug abuse, trauma, and scores of other causes could scramble the delicate mind. Occasionally, he could provide medical treatment through drugs and counseling that would lessen the symptoms of a mental patient. Some, however, were hopeless. Medical science had nothing to offer those whose minds were somehow wired incorrectly. There was so much that science didn't know, so much that medicine could not do.

In those cases, the patients would be institutionalized for life, many on a regimen of medication that suppressed their illusions, diluted their emotions, or just sedated them into passivity.

Julie was marching to join the ranks of the hopeless, and Bernard felt bad about that. Especially since much of it was his fault.

CHAPTER
SEVEN

THE CLOUDS THAT HAD COVERED MUCH OF SOUTHERN
California were gone. The fall storm had come, dropped
an inch and a half of rain, and then continued south to
the Baja Peninsula. Marcus, who preferred that rain be
limited to daylight hours leaving the night sky free of
overcast, was glad to see the storm move on.

The effects of the storm, however, lingered. Wet
streets glistened in the morning sun. Cars that shared
Interstate 10 with him kicked up an unrelenting spray of
water tinged with the detritus of rubber and oil left by

the countless autos that traveled the freeway every day. The mist streaked his windshield as the wipers struggled to squeegee away the tainted liquid.

"You still remember the way?" Lansing asked from the passenger seat.

"To Caltech?" Marcus responded with a small laugh. "I spent nearly seven years there. I think I can find it."

"Just checking," Lansing said. "As I recall you weren't very good with directions. Didn't you once get lost going to the cafeteria?"

"Not lost. I was just numb after sitting through one of your lectures."

Ben Sicarello laughed from his seat in the back of the Toyota sedan. Marcus and Lucy had exchanged cars for the day. She had been unable to get free of her obligations at the hospital, but not for lack of trying. "You have numbed countless minds over the decades, Philip."

"It's a dirty job, but someone has to do it. Nonetheless, several of my students have shown themselves to be promising scientists—Marc included."

Marcus had picked the men up at the airport in Ontario, California, and was now piloting them to the California Institute of Technology in Pasadena.

"I've made arrangements for a conference room where we can pull our thoughts together. The press conference will be held at the Beckman Auditorium. That should be more than enough room for the media."

"I can't believe you've set all this up so quickly," Marcus said.

"This is unlike most scientific discoveries where the investigator labors away in seclusion on some obscure aspect of physics or a deep space object. The Stiller Enigma is in our own backyard."

"It's in the backyard of six billion people," Ben added. "Speak now or forever listen to someone else talk about your discovery."

They were right. Marcus had mulled over the decision about holding a press conference. Lansing and Ben had plowed forward like great ships pushing through the ocean. By the time Marcus had seen the wisdom in the decision, they had already had a media conference scheduled, a place chosen, and the details worked out. No grass was growing under their feet.

"Marcus," Ben said. "I have new photos for you to look at. I've also set them up in PowerPoint so that you can use a laptop computer to display them on a monitor. It looks pretty good, if I do say so myself."

"A priest with no humility," Lansing said. "That's what I like about you, Ben."

"I have plenty of modesty," Ben retorted. "I just don't remember where I put it."

Marcus smiled. It was like being in college again. There was something in most academicians that forced them to role-play. With competing scientists, they could be cold, aloof, and even rude. But among friendly peers, they were like any other men: jovial, quick with a friendly jab, and filled with reminiscences of the "old days."

"I didn't bring my laptop with me," Marcus admitted.

"I did," Lansing and Ben said in unison.

"It looks like you guys have it all covered," Marcus commented.

"That we do, Marc," Lansing said. "That we do."

○) ● ● ● ○ ○

THE CONFERENCE ROOM WAS a small affair near the Dean of Students office. Ben Sicarello had set up his laptop computer and started the presentation program. The college had provided a small television to which Ben had connected the computer, allowing the three men to view the slides without hovering like vultures over the laptop's screen.

"These are images I took from last night's observation," Ben said. "Conditions were good."

"They're marvelous," Marcus exclaimed. He was looking at the face of the Moon. The orb was ashen gray, unlike the bright ivory that appeared to the naked eye.

"First I did a general survey of the visible surface, one quarter at a time. There was nothing out of the ordinary. I then concentrated on the north rim of Mare Imbrium where it shares a ridge with the Crater Plato." The image changed to a tight shot of a large crater with a dark floor the same shade of gray as the Mare Imbrium. "The Montes Alpes are to the east."

"Which telescope did you use for these?" Lansing asked.

"The 1.8 meter Alice P. Lennon Telescope, just like before. It's a good one, and Mount Graham is one of the best places on earth to make observations. Light and air pollution is at a minimum."

"This is a great presentation," Marcus said. "Can we print out the images and create a media packet?"

"Absolutely," Ben replied. "We can add it to the material you gathered."

"If we're going to do this," Marcus began, "we should put our best foot forward. By the way, I've invited a few people."

"Oh, really?" Lansing said with a surprised expression. "More media?"

"No. Jason Coogan and Terri Lynn. They were the two students who took the original pictures. I'm just going to introduce them. It's as much their discovery as it is mine."

"Not really," Lansing countered. "It was your equipment they used, and it was your keen eye that spotted the abnormality."

"You have a problem with them being here?" Marcus asked, not unkindly.

"Not at all. You just have a nasty habit of shortchanging yourself. This is your discovery. You can have anyone here you want."

Ben added, "They have as much right, if not more, to be here as we do. All Philip and I did was corroborate your find."

"I invited someone else," Marcus said. "Dr. Whitaker." From the puzzled looks on their faces, Marcus could tell that the name rang no bells. "Dr. Jacob Whitaker is the president of my college."

"Ah," Lansing said knowingly. "Trying to head off any political problems, eh? Good thinking. Of course, you'll have plenty of offers from universities after this news breaks. Doors are about to open for you."

"Unless this turns out to be a big bunch of nothing," Marcus said.

"It won't," Ben said. He nodded at the monitor. "There's something there that wasn't there before. It's unique. It's interesting, and best of all, it's a mystery, and the world loves a mystery."

Marcus studied the image again. The red smear was less consistent in tone than when he had first seen it a few days before. It was mottled with some areas darker and more crimson than others. The new pictures brought no revelations. The enigma was still enigmatic.

Something else had changed. Marcus couldn't identify it at first, but he sensed it. He squinted as he studied the image more closely. Lansing was saying something, but it sounded like little more than a dull drone in the distance.

"Marc?"

It was starting to register on his mind. Something was definitely different.

"Marc? You still with us?"

"It's growing," Marcus said flatly, struggling to believe his own words.

"What?" Ben said.

"It's growing," Marcus answered.

)) ● ● ● ((

THE PHONE IN DR. BARRY WENHAM'S George Washington University office rang to life, startling him from the research paper he was editing for the *American Journal of Physics*. He snapped up the hand piece. "Yes, Beverly, what is it?" He listened for a moment, then said, "Who? Okay, I'll take it."

He punched the white flashing button on his phone. "This is Dr. Wenham."

"Thank you for taking my call," a male voice said. "My name is Don Holm of the *Los Angeles Register*. I'm the science editor. I wonder if you would care to comment on a press release I received this morning."

"That depends on the subject matter, Mr. Holm."

"It has to do with the Moon, Dr. Wenham. Did you receive the release?"

Wenham glanced over his desk. It was tediously neat and orderly. Not a paper clip was out of place. "No, I didn't. I've read all my mail and memos for the day. Apparently I was overlooked."

"I'll have someone fax you a copy immediately," Holm said professionally. Wenham gave the reporter the fax number. "I'm surprised that you didn't receive a copy."

"Why is that?" Wenham asked.

"Well, you are the science advisor to the president."

"True as that is, Mr. Holm, I don't receive a report of every discovery made or paper published. If I did, I would spend my days doing little more than reading about what others have said or done."

"I understand, but this one seems . . . different."

"Different? How so?"

"The press release carries three names: Dr. Philip Lansing of MIT, Dr. Benjamin Sicarello of the Vatican Observatory in Arizona, and Dr. Marcus Stiller."

"I recognize Lansing's name. I've read a paper or two that he's published. I don't the know the others."

"So they're not big names then?"

Wenham sighed. A science writer for the *Los Angeles Register* should know that the scientific community was no community at all. "The world of science is a big one, Mr. Holm.

It has many fields and subspecialties. Tens of thousands of trained people labor in their respective fields known only to those who share the same interest. I'm a physicist by training. I know a great deal about physics, but there are fields in which I know nothing. My research has been in the field of theoretical condensed-matter physics. I'm very good at that. I can even work around in M-theory, string theory, and a couple of other areas, although they're not my forte. Lansing is an astrophysicist. I assume that the gentleman from the Vatican Observatory is also involved in space science of some sort. I know very little about those areas. They could be 'big names' in that field and I wouldn't necessarily know it."

"I see," Holm said. There was a pause, then he blurted, "They say there's a spot on the Moon."

"What kind of spot?" There was a knock on the door. Wenham covered the mouthpiece and said, "Enter." Beverly walked in with a two-page fax. She handed it to Wenham.

"They don't say specifically," Holm replied. "They call it an 'unidentified anomaly on the lunar surface.' Whatever that means."

"I have the fax. Give me a second." Wenham scanned the message quickly. "Intriguing."

"Can I quote you on that, Dr. Wenham?"

"Sure, but it will be a one-word quote. I'm afraid I can't help you on this."

"How do you think the president will respond?" the reporter pushed.

"To what?" Wenham countered. "To a two-page fax that says a previously uncategorized spot has been discovered on the nearside of the Moon? There's not really much to respond to, is there?"

"I was hoping for a quote."

"Okay," Wenham said. Since becoming science advisor to President Larry Rendel two years ago, Wenham had answered hundreds of questions from reporters and quoted the president on many occasions. The fact that the quotes never came from the Oval Office was of little concern to him or to the media. The White House rules were to stay within stated guidelines and not embarrass the president. "President Rendel follows the world of science as much as his time allows. He is always pleased to hear of new discoveries and congratulates these men on their hard work."

"That works," Holm said. "Thanks for your time."

"You're welcome," Wenham said. "By the way, is the *Register* going to have someone there at the press conference?"

"I plan on being there myself."

Wenham said. "I wonder if I could impose upon you for a favor."

"You want to see my article as soon as I finish it," Holm said. Wenham could hear the smile in the man's voice.

"If it's not too much trouble."

"Sure. I don't mind doing a favor for someone who has the president's ear. Who knows, I might need a favor someday."

"I get the point, Mr. Holm. Just remember, I can make a call to a dozen different news sources and get the same material."

"I'll fax it to you just as soon as I have it."

"Thank you." Wenham hung up and then buzzed for his secretary. Beverly stepped into the room less than a minute later. "Beverly, there's a press conference at 3:00 Pacific time." He looked at his watch. "That's about half an hour from now. I need you to make a few calls and see if anyone is covering it live. Maybe we can catch a broadcast over the Internet. Call NPR, CNN, and whomever else you can think of that might have someone there." He handed the fax back to her. "I doubt you'll have any luck, but it looks like the kind of thing that the media will take to."

"Yes, sir. Will there be anything else?"

"Yes. There are three names on the fax. See what you can find out about them."

"Okay." Beverly left the office.

Wenham leaned back in his chair. For some reason, he felt disquieted.

○ ◐ ◑ ● ◐ ◑ ○

JULIE STOOD STARING OUT THE WINDOW of her room. The dark clouds had given way to a cobalt blue sky. Wind rustled the leaves of the oak tree outside her windowpane. She heard nothing. The safety glass of the window was too thick to allow the pleasure of sound in. She focused on the green leaves, then on just one leaf, then on just one of the jewel-like drops resting near the leaf's jagged edge. Would the drop, pushed by the wind, shaken by the vibrating leaf, fall from the edge?

She felt like that drop: teetering on the edge of oblivion. The leaf was her sanity. Too much shaking, too much wind, and she would lose her touch with this world and fall into the hell that hovered just at the edge of her sight, just behind her eyelids.

The drop, she reminded herself, had no will. It did what it did because it had no choice. Without volition, it fell from the sky and clung to the tree because the law of physics demanded it. She, however, had choice—at least some choice. The madness that plagued her had failed to win her over. She had fought, resisted with every ounce of strength and determination she could muster. Determination welled up in her like a geyser. She would not surrender her sanity. Disease might steal it, might pirate it away, but it would have to fight for that conquest.

It was the drugs that concerned her. When they gave her the injections, or the pills, she was forced to abdicate her control to a chain of molecules designed by people she would never meet. The pills helped her sleep, but they fogged the world, distorting it so much that she could no longer see it in its true form. Her brain felt hazy. They gave her the drugs when she panicked. When the visions came, she would naturally respond with the terror they elicited. Then they would come with their syringes and leather straps to tie her to the bed. The only solution was to refuse to respond emotionally, to turn off that part of her brain that harbored the impulses to flee.

Could it be done? She was no machine. Like everyone else, emotions were biologically wired into her. Of course, that wasn't the real issue. It wasn't what she felt that mattered, but how she expressed those feelings. If she could remain calm, she could avoid the mind-numbing sedatives. She could feel whatever came her way, terror, abject fear, as long as she didn't let it show.

Easy words. Noble concept. But was it possible? *It had to be,* she decided. *It simply had to be.*

As if testing her resolve, a prickly chill crawled up her spine and spread through her chest. Her scalp seemed to contract, pulling tight on her skull. The ants began marching in her brain again.

Julie stared at the drop on the leaf on the tree in the yard under the sky. *Ignore it,* she said to herself. *Ignore it. It's just a daydream. It's not real. It's just a movie in my head, a very real movie, but nothing more.*

An urge to look down percolated in her mind. How did she always know where to look? She refused. *The drop. Just watch the drop.*

She stared at the small glistening bead and wished she could project herself into it. Being a microscopic organism suspended in a drop of water was immensely preferable to her present existence.

The urge to look down became more intense. The impulse grew rapidly, like a fire doused with gasoline. Look down. *Look down.* LOOK DOWN.

She stared at the drop outside her window, her eyes fixed in an unblinking gaze. It couldn't make her look down. Not if she didn't want to. It was her decision, she told herself, her decision and hers alone.

The chill in her spine grew colder.

The ants in her head marched faster.

Perspiration peppered her brow.

The drop was so lovely. It was round and smooth and so very, very clear—a tear shed by the distant sky. It was as pure as she was polluted, contaminated by a madness she could not understand.

A ray of sunshine pushed through the leaves of the tree and fell on the droplet. Julie could see the colors of the rainbow on its surface. Red, orange, yellow, green, blue, indigo, violet. All so beautiful. She raised a shaky hand and wiped the sweat from her brow.

LOOK DOWN.

Julie did.

She bit her lip until it bled.

EIGHT

BECKMAN AUDITORIUM WAS A MODERATE-SIZED BUILDING near the center of the Caltech campus. The building was circular with toothpick-shaped columns supporting a roof that looked like a flattened cone. Inside, the nearly thirty members of the media seemed swallowed by the cavernous lecture theater. A crew from a local television station set up a camera on a tripod and ran a cable to one of the several microphones on the dais. Some in the group took seats while others joked with their peers.

Marcus's stomach was churning madly and his heart fluttered. He was accustomed to speaking to groups, but only in the classroom. This was different. These were seasoned and professional reporters.

"Kind of gets the blood moving, doesn't it?" Lansing asked Marcus.

"Not to mention the stomach," Marcus replied.

"You're not nervous," Lansing declared.

"I'm not?"

"Of course not. You're excited. People confuse the two emotions all the time."

"Ah, I see." Marcus didn't see.

"You ready for all this?" Whiz asked.

Marcus turned to face the young man. He was seated next to Marcus and next to him was Terri. Whiz had foregone his usual leather vest and white T-shirt. In honor of the press conference, he was wearing a long-sleeved white shirt and a pair of cords. He had even shaved. Marcus had to hide his surprise. "It doesn't matter, Whiz. It's here. It's going to happen."

"I feel like I should say thanks," Whiz said in an uncharacteristically soft voice.

Marcus raised an eyebrow.

"I mean for including us," Whiz explained. "You didn't have to do that. It was your telescope and all. We just snapped a few shots."

"You and Terri deserve to be here. Credit should be given where credit is due."

"I don't suppose this will get me out of the final exam," Whiz said with a smile.

"Not a chance," Marcus shot back. "In fact, you may have to write a paper on it."

"Gee," Whiz replied sarcastically. "Could I? You're too good to me."

"I aim to please," Marcus said. A movement at the back of the auditorium caught his eye. A man in a three-piece blue suit stepped through the doors, took a quick look around, spied Marcus, and raised his hand. Marcus returned the greeting.

"Is that the good Dr. Whitaker?" Lansing asked.

"That's him," Marcus answered with a nod. "That's my boss."

"He looks like he's dressed for a job interview," Lansing quipped. In all the years that Marcus had known him, Lansing had never voluntarily worn a tie. His appearance was as casual as his mind was disciplined. "What's his PhD in?"

"EdD," Marcus corrected. "He has a doctor of education degree."

"I see," Lansing said. Lansing was a good friend and able scientist. He was also an intellectual snob. Any degrees other than those taken in a hard science were pseudo degrees to him. Marcus had once overhead him tell a life science professor that biology was the science a man turned to if he couldn't do real math. The man had simply replied, "Be sure to say that to the surgeon who does your bypass surgery."

"He's a good man," Marcus said.

"Just not punctual," Lansing snipped. "We're five minutes late. It's show time." Lansing turned to the lectern and pulled a single piece of paper from the pocket of the beige sports coat he wore and cleared his throat loudly. The dry guttural sound echoed from the public address system. Immediately the members of the press took their seats. The lone cameraman switched on the tiny flood lamp of his camera and a harsh white light shone on the podium. Lansing waited for another moment to allow Whitaker time to make his way down front and take a seat in the front row.

"Thank you," Lansing said. "I'm Dr. Philip Lansing of the Massachusetts Institute of Technology and a former astrophysics professor here at Caltech. First, I would like to thank you for taking time to attend this very important news conference and Caltech for allowing us the use of this facility. I know your time is valuable, so without further ado I introduce Dr. Marcus Stiller, professor of astronomy at Inland Empire College." He turned to Marcus and said, "Marc," then stepped away.

Marcus's tripping heart went into overdrive, pounding like a hammer in his chest. He slowly rose and took his place behind the stand. Lansing gave his shoulder a reassuring squeeze before returning to his seat. Before they had stepped into the auditorium to finish setting up the presentation, Lansing had stopped Marcus, looked hard into his eyes, and said, "This is important, Marc. It's a huge time for you. Don't let your nerves blow it. Enjoy every moment."

It was good advice, Marcus had decided. Why not enjoy it? He took a deep breath and said, "My name is Marcus Stiller. You have my vita in the press kit you were given when you arrived today, so I'll cut to the chase." The sound of his own words encouraged him. Trepidation was ebbing; exhilaration was flowing. "Last Friday, while making lunar observations from my home, two of my students took several interesting photographs. Those students are here today."

Marcus turned to Whiz and Terri and motioned them to stand. "Jason Coogan and Terri Lynn, both second-year students, made the photographs using a reflecting telescope and a CCD capture instrument." To his students he said, "Thank you." They took their seats. "Later that night, while analyzing the photos on my computer, I noticed an anomaly. A large discoloration appeared in the Mare Imbrium just south of the Crater Plato. After a thorough check of my instruments, I communicated the find to Dr. Lansing, whom you met a moment ago. Upon his review, he contacted Father Ben Sicarello, PhD, at Mount Graham International Observatory in Arizona. Dr. Sicarello has made two observations of the lunar surface using the 1.8 meter Alice P. Lennon Telescope. He was able to verify my observation and made additional images. I have some of those images here for you today."

Lansing was seated behind a laptop computer. He punched a button and the bland face of the Moon appeared on the

screen of a large projection television the university had provided for the occasion.

A voice came from the crowd. "Will we be able to get a
copy of these pictures?"

"Yes, we'll have an additional packet for you when you
leave." Marcus looked at the image on the screen. "This is a
picture of the Moon as it might be seen in any telescope. North
is up in this picture."

"What's that mean?" a woman in a green jumpsuit asked.

"Most telescopes invert the object in their view. That is,
the picture is seen upside down. This has to do with the telescope's optics. I just wanted you to know that up was really up
on these images."

"Thank you." She jotted a note in her notebook.

"Next picture, please." The slide changed. "Here is a rea-
sonably close image of the crater named Plato. It is situated high
in the northern hemisphere and is approximately 109 kilometers across. As you can see . . ."

"Can you convert that to miles for us?" someone called out.

"Well," Marcus began, "a kilometer is just over six-tenths
of a mile, so—"

"Sixty-seven point five-eight miles," Whiz said loudly.

Marcus smiled. There was a reason why the young man
was called Whiz. "Sixty-seven point five-eight miles," Marcus
repeated. "To continue, you can see the discoloration just below
the crater in the north end of the mare."

"Mare?" came another question.

"Yes," Marcus said. "The Moon has many features. The
two most obvious are craters and maria. Maria is the plural for
the Latin word *mare*. *Mare* means 'sea.' In the seventeenth century observers saw the dark areas of the Moon and assumed them
to be oceans. Hence, *mare*. You'll recall that Neil Armstrong and
Buzz Aldrin landed the Apollo 11 lunar module on the Sea of
Tranquility. That's the Mare Tranquillitatis. There are fourteen
such mares on the near side of the Moon, none on the far side.

The traditional naming has stuck. Craters are usually named after famous or mythical people: Plato, Atlas, Tycho, and so on. Mountain ranges are named after mountain ranges on Earth."

Marcus paused and was awash in silence. "Anyway," he said, resuming the topic, "just below the Crater Plato is a discoloration. This anomaly is previously unrecorded and has been confirmed by Dr. Sicarello and Dr. Lansing."

"What is it?" a man asked.

"We don't know," Marcus admitted. "More observations need to be made. I imagine other scientists will be examining the area in the days ahead. Hopefully some reasonable answers will be forthcoming."

"You introduced Dr. Sicarello as Father Sicarello. Is he a priest?"

Marcus was taken aback. What did this have to do with anything?

Ben stepped forward to answer the question. "Yes, I'm a Jesuit. I work with the Vatican Observatory."

"In Rome?" the woman in the green suit asked.

"No," Ben said with a kind smile. "As Professor Stiller said, I'm in Arizona. The Vatican Observatory and the University of Arizona share the facility on Mount Graham."

"Why did they call you?" the woman asked. "Is there a religious significance to the spot?"

"Dr. Sicarello was asked for his help because he's a qualified astronomer and had access to quality equipment. He is also a former classmate of Dr. Lansing." Marcus felt that control of the situation was slipping from his fingers. "Ladies and gentlemen, if I could have your attention—"

"Does the Pope have an opinion of the spot?" a new voice asked.

"I doubt he knows of it," Ben answered. "You folks are the first to hear of the Stiller Enigma."

"The Pope doesn't know about this?" the woman asked. "Will you be telling him personally?"

This is getting out of hand, Marcus thought. *They're missing the point.* To his surprise, Ben didn't answer. He remained statue still behind the lectern.

"Father," the woman began again, "will you be informing the Pope personally?"

Ben said nothing. The crowd of reporters shifted in their seats as if on cue. More moments of silence passed until each reporter sat transfixed on the speechless Ben. Marcus started to say something, but Ben held up a hand. Marcus joined the silence.

Seconds dripped by, then Ben said softly, "The Stiller Enigma is a significant discovery. Soon articles on it will be appearing all over the globe. Newscasters will discuss its importance before television cameras. If I were a reporter, I would want to be on the leading edge of this monumental find. If I were seated where you are, I would want to get as much information about the anomaly as possible, and not waste my time hunting for a story that is not there. The fact that I am a priest as well as an astronomer has nothing at all to do with this. It is an easy truth to see, don't you think?"

No one answered.

Ben turned to Marcus. "I believe you have the floor again."

Marcus felt awkward. Ben had just regained control of the reporters as easily as a man might reel in an unruly dog with a sharp snap of a leash. He cleared his throat, then said, "What makes this anomaly so interesting is that it is unprecedented. The Moon is a static, sterile place. No appreciable change to its surface has ever been noted. It looks the same today as it did thousands of years ago. Until last Friday night, that is."

The words were coming easier now, and the reporters were paying close attention. "As to what the cause may be, I couldn't say. I can say that it did not look like this a few weeks ago."

A hand in the crowd went up. A slovenly dressed man in a wrinkled coat was asking to be recognized. Marcus called upon him.

"How big is this thing?" the man asked.

"Currently it is about 210 kilometers east to west; about one hundred kilometers north to south."

"One hundred thirty miles by sixty-two miles," Whiz chimed in before being asked.

Another hand went up. "So the Moon's dirt is changing color?"

"Regolith," Marcus said. He spelled the word. "The loose rock and dust of the Moon is called regolith. It's too early to say that the regolith is actually changing color. We have, however, ruled out several things, including instrument error."

The green-suited woman raised her hand and Marcus recognized her. "I mean no disrespect by this question, Professor, but so what? Why should my readers care about a spot on the Moon? The Moon's old hat and has been since the early seventies."

Lansing harrumphed and Marcus gave him a quick glance, doing his best not to smile.

"The Moon is the closest object to Earth," Marcus said. "As such, everyone has seen it. The old saying 'Familiarity breeds contempt' applies here. Many assume we know all there is to know about the Moon. The truth is that there is a great deal we don't know. For example, we don't know how the Moon was formed. There are several good ideas, but they remain unproven. We don't know why there are maria on the near side of the Moon, but not on the far side. Of the inner planets, Mercury, Venus, Earth, and Mars, only Earth and Mars have moons. Our Moon is quite large in relation to our planet, much larger compared to the size ratio of other moons to their planets. In a nutshell, the more we know about the Moon, the more we know about Earth."

"But it is just a discoloration," another reporter stated.

"True, but I think you're missing the point," Marcus said. "As I said earlier, the Moon is a static place. It changes only minutely. There is no atmosphere or running water to cause erosion. Geologically, the Moon is barely active. There are occasional moonquakes, but they are minor, not releasing any

more energy than a firecracker. In fact, the Moon is so static
that the footprints left by Neil Armstrong and all the other
astronauts who followed him will remain unchanged for thousands of years."

Marcus studied the crowd of reporters. They were listening intently but seemed unimpressed. He had expected nothing
more. While a few of the nation's major newspapers covered
science-related stories, most did not. Science was a waning
interest in the United States.

One man stood suddenly. He was a rail-thin man with a
hawkish nose and hair the color of coal. "Professor Stiller," the
man began, "I'm Donald Holm of the *Los Angeles Register*."

The *Register* was one of the largest and most prestigious
newspapers in the country. Holm was the paper's science editor.
Marcus had read many of his articles and found them accurate
and insightful. "Yes, Mr. Holm. I'm familiar with your work."

"Thank you. Did I miss something earlier or, when you
were describing the size of the enigma, did you say, 'Currently
it is about 210 kilometers east to west, about one hundred kilometers north to south'?"

"I believe that is what I said," Marcus answered.

"So you did use the word *currently*?" Holm pressed.
"Does that mean that there has been a change in the size of the
enigma since your first observation?"

Marcus stiffened. He had discussed with the others
whether or not to reveal the spot's increasing size. They had
decided to withhold the information until another observation
could be made. Marcus knew he had let it slip. "We're still
investigating that, Mr. Holm."

"But you do have reason to believe that it may have grown
in size?" Holm was pressing the issue.

"It's too early to tell," Marcus said.

"I see," Holm said. His manner was erudite and gentle-
manly. "As I understand it thus far, there have been three

observations made: the first from your home observatory and then two by Dr. Sicarello from Mount Graham. Is that correct?"

"It is."

"And those observations began just last Friday night?"

"Yes." Marcus knew he was being led.

"So from Friday night until the last observation on . . ." He paused and looked at the briefing packet that had been handed out to the reporters. ". . . Sunday, the object in question grew sufficiently to be seen through a ground-based telescope?"

"That's what we hope to find out in the near future," Marcus said.

"I see," Holm said. "But it is safe to say that you have reason to believe that it has changed size."

Marcus paused, then said, "Yes."

"Then, in light of your statements about the lunar surface being a static place, this new discovery is even more astounding. You have not only seen something that wasn't there before, you're seeing something that is changing before your very eyes. Is that right, Professor?"

"It is."

There was a moment of silence as the reporters took in what they were hearing. Then the questions began, questions that Marcus could not answer.

◗ ◗ ◖ ● ◖ ◗ ◖

LOOK DOWN!

The inner voice within Julie shouted at her, but she would not look down again. She had looked down once and what she saw had terrified her. Panic welled up in her like molten rock in a volcano. It had taken every strand of strength she had to contain her screams. Instead, she bit her lip and squeezed her eyes shut so hard they hurt.

But even with her eyes closed, she could see it: the crimson puddle of blood at her feet. She was standing in it, a spreading, pooling, pond of blood. Julie had no idea where the blood was coming from. Was it seeping up through the floor? Or was it coming from her? If it was streaming from her body, then she knew she was moments from death. No one could lose that much blood and live.

But she didn't die. She didn't even feel weak.

LOOK DOWN!

No! she screamed in her mind. She struggled to remain unmoving. Surely the hospital staff was watching her through the closed-circuit system. If she panicked, they would come and sedate her again. She had to remain calm.

LOOK DOWN!

The voice in her head was powerful, threatening, like a ranting, raving dictator.

LOOK DOWN!

Despite her overwhelming fear, Julie slowly lowered her head. *I will not look*, she said to herself. *I will not look.*

Julie opened her eyes.

The blood was still there, a wide patch of viscous red. It covered her feet. Trickles of blood moved up her legs as if they had a will of their own. But the most shocking of all, the most soul-tearing sight was not the blood, but what was just below its surface. Things were moving. Small things. Wormlike things, just below the surface of the blood pool. They wiggled. They writhed. They moved toward her feet.

Julie felt her knees weaken, her legs shudder involuntarily. Her heart skipped and fluttered. She gasped noisily and closed her eyes as tightly as she could. But the image remained there, flashing in her consciousness. Julie raised her hands to her face. They were fluttering like the leaf of a tree. Her skin began to burn.

The ants were crawling in her head again.

"Oh, no," she groaned aloud.

She felt something new, something different—something repulsive. Whatever was crawling just below the surface of the blood was now on her legs. Wriggling. Slinking. Slithering. They were working their way up her calves and thighs.

Julie felt her legs give way and she collapsed to the floor.

CHAPTER

NINE

THE SUN WAS SETTING, DARKENING THE WASHINGTON, D.C., sky to a dull black. Dr. Barry Wenham leaned back in his leather chair and rubbed his eyes. He was tired and wanted to go home, but the loose ends of his job kept him at the desk. He tried comforting himself with reminders that Pennsylvania Avenue would be grinding to a halt as thousands of government workers made their way home. At least he wasn't fighting traffic.

The phone rang sharply. Instinctively Wenham looked at his watch. It was nearly 8:00, two hours past his normal office hours. His secretary was gone for the day. He would either have to tolerate the ringing or answer the phone himself. He snatched up the receiver.

"Dr. Wenham?" the caller said. "Still hard at it I see."

"I was headed out the door," Wenham lied.

"I won't keep you, Dr. Wenham. This is Don Holm of the *LA Register*. We spoke earlier today."

"Yes, I remember, Mr. Holm. Was the press conference everything you hoped it would be?"

"As a matter of fact, it was. Very interesting, this spot on the Moon. They're calling it the Stiller Enigma."

"After Marcus Stiller?" Wenham said. He picked up a brown folder and opened it. Inside were three pages. At the top of each page was a name, the names given him by Holm during their first conversation. His secretary, Beverly, had researched the men and prepared a short vita on each. There was nothing remarkable in the report.

"That's right. He discovered the spot with two of his students. He teaches at a small liberal arts college."

"Hmm," Wenham said. Thanks to Beverly, this was information he already had.

"I know what you're thinking: Not much real science goes on in a small college."

Holm had nailed Wenham's thoughts. That would explain why there was so little information on the man. Still, the other two scientists were men with solid credentials and were backed by reputable institutions.

"They gave a good presentation. Photos, computer graphics, the works. I wish all press conferences were so interesting. Sure beats covering the problems faced by spawning salmon."

"Was there a press kit?"

"Yes."

"How would I get a copy of that?" Wenham asked.

"I thought you might ask that. I've already taken care of it. Got a pencil and paper?"

Wenham pulled a fountain pen from his pocket and removed a single sticky note from his desk. "I'm ready."

"I'm going to give you the URL to my personal web page. I've scanned everything from the kit and uploaded it to my site. You can download it from there."

"Thank you," Wenham said, "but I don't think you did all that just for me."

"I would have," Holm said. Wenham felt he was sincere. "But I did it this way so that some of my expert sources can review the material. This has all the markings of a great story."

"So it seems," Wenham replied. "Now what do I owe you for your courteous efforts?"

"I'm thinking of doing a piece on you. You know, the man who advises the president. That sort of thing."

All things have a price, Wenham thought. "I'll be happy to help, but not tonight."

"I was thinking of next month. My plate is full at the moment," Holm said. "Oh, and one more thing—"

"I'll let you know what the president thinks," Wenham said, anticipating the next request.

◗ ◗ ◖ ● ◗ ◖ ◖

THERE WERE VOICES—distant, hollow, indistinct. They floated about in her mind like a freed cobweb on a warm breeze. Julie fought to rise from the depths of unconsciousness and break the surface of awareness. She struggled to order her thoughts, to make some sense of the sounds around her.

"How long . . . been like . . ." There was something about that voice, something that ignited the synapses in her brain.

"Thirty minutes . . . arrived." Another familiar voice. Male, like the first one.

"Injuries?" The first voice.

"No, sir. None. We thought that . . . head."

The words were starting to make sense. The voices were becoming more distinct.

"That's good," the first voice said.

"You should know, Senator, that this is her second attack in as many days."

Senator! Her husband. Her husband had finally arrived. Regaining consciousness was now imperative. She had to speak to him, to beg him to take her from this place.

The blackness in her mind lightened to a milky gray.

"It is to be expected," State Senator Daniel Waal said.

"I suppose," the second voice answered. Julie recognized it as Dr. Bernard's. "We sedate her to keep her calm, but a course of constant sedation is . . . can be dangerous. Not the results we had hoped for."

"I see," Daniel said. "What now?"

"I suggest you leave her here and allow us to continue to monitor her behavior. I see no need to change our approach. Some good may come out of these tests."

"She can't go out in public like this," Daniel said.

Help me, Daniel, Julie screamed in her mind.

"I'm afraid that's true," Bernard replied.

"We should stay the course," Daniel offered. There was a strain in his voice, an uncertainty. His words sounded distant again, as if he had moved away from her bed.

Daniel, wait. I'm coming. I need just a minute. Wait. Stay.

"You will keep me posted," Daniel said firmly. That was his way. Direct, always to the point.

"I shall," Bernard said. "I'll walk you to the car."

Daniel. Daniel! Julie continued to scream. The words were loud in her mind, but her lips remained locked in silence. *No. Stay. Stay, please. Don't leave me here. I'll die if you leave me!*

The milky gray of her mind turned white.

"No need, Doctor. I can find my way." Daniel paused. "I have some urgent business in Sacramento for the next few weeks."

Daniel, please.

"If I'm out of line here, Senator, then please say so," Bernard began. "Is it true that you may make a run for the governor's office?"

"It's too early to talk about such things now, but there are those who are pushing for it."

"You have my vote."

DANIEL!

"Thank you, Doctor."

Don't leave, Julie pleaded silently. *Daniel. Daniel! Oh, God, please*—". . . don't leave!"

The sounds of the last words were different. It took a moment for Julie to realize that she had spoken aloud.

There was silence.

"Daniel?" Julie said softly.

Footsteps. A hand touched her arm, a hand she knew well. It was Daniel's.

"Julie? Can you hear me, Julie?"

"Stay, Daniel. Please stay."

"I'm right here."

Julie opened her eyes. Hovering above her was the face of the man she had married so many years ago. A man she had loved; a man who loved her. Was that still true?

She raised his hand and slowly brought it to her lips, thankful that she was not restrained. She kissed his fingers. "Please stay, even if it's just for a few minutes. I want to talk to you."

Julie looked past Daniel and into the face of Dr. Bernard. She saw him blanch.

"I'll stay . . . for a little while."

Julie smiled. For the first time in a month, Julie smiled.

○ ◗ ◖ ● ● ◖ ○

THE HOSPITAL'S RECREATION ROOM was expansive and filled with round wood-topped tables, leather sofas, and two large televisions. Several patients, each dressed in pale green pajamalike garb, sat around one table where a young man played solitaire while carrying on a conversation with himself. The others watched and occasionally kibitzed. The player seemed oblivious to their suggestions.

Another patient stood in one of the corners rocking side to side. A few watched an old *Match Game* show on one of the televisions. The other television was blank. Two women watched it anyway.

Julie took in the sight. She had not been outside her room for several weeks. Not since she had an episode in front of the other patients. Her terror-laced scream had frightened some of the other residents, requiring every orderly, nurse, and doctor to race to the room in an effort to reestablish order.

"You look good," Julie said to Daniel. They were seated on one of the plush sofas. The furniture was expensive but the room wore an unpleasant smell. Daniel seemed uncomfortable.

"Thank you," he said softly.

His eyes darted about the room, never settling on hers. She loved his eyes, deep blue and reflecting a keen intellect. She had always been able to tell what he was feeling by his eyes. When agitated, they fluttered nervously; when angry they narrowed and darkened; when laughing they sparkled like stars in the night sky.

"Thank you for staying," Julie said. "I've … I've missed you."

"I've had trouble getting away," Daniel said. "This is a tough time of the year. I'm working a lot of hours."

Julie wondered if he was working alone, or if he had already replaced her. "I understand. It's just that it has been so long since I've seen you. I don't know how long. It's hard to keep track of the days here. They won't let me have a clock or a calendar."

"I'm sure they know what they're doing," Daniel said, turning his gaze toward his wife. "They must have some reason. Anyway, I've called and talked to the doctor several times. He's keeping me posted on your treatment."

"That's not the same as seeing you, Daniel. I'm so alone here. You know how sociable I am. I would have loved to talk to you on the phone. Even that would help."

Daniel frowned deeply. "This is hard on both of us, Julie. When you have your episodes, I feel helpless. Besides, the doctor doesn't want you to get too excited. He thinks that brings on the attacks."

"It doesn't," Julie retorted. "Being ignored doesn't help."

Daniel's frown darkened and his eyes narrowed.

"I'm sorry. I really am glad you're here." She reached out and touched his hand. His skin felt warm and soft. How long had it been since she had been held? How long since she had felt a caress?

"I'm afraid I can't stay long," Daniel said.

"I know," Julie replied with a sigh. He never stayed long. She couldn't blame him. She hated this place. How could she expect him to be comfortable here when she longed for nothing more than to be as far away as possible?

"The doctor says that you've had several more . . . episodes."

She nodded. "A few, but I think I'm getting better at handling them."

"He says you were screaming at the top of your lungs." His words were thin, uninvolved, distant.

They had been in love once. She had idolized him; he had worshiped her. Then the erosion of familiarity undermined the foundation of their relationship. He began to spend more time at the office, and she did the same. When he was elected to the State Senate, she remained behind to keep her business afloat, flying to Sacramento every other weekend. A marriage could not thrive just on occasional meetings.

"Daniel," Julie began, "this place is not good for me. They sedate me too much. Some of the orderlies are rough and hurt me. Couldn't I go home with you? I think I can control these attacks if I could just get out of this place."

"You know that wouldn't be wise," Daniel answered. "I wish it were otherwise, but it just wouldn't be prudent."

"I'm a prisoner here," Julie said, raising her voice. She caught herself. She spoke softly, "They keep me locked away."

"It's for your own good."

"It's not for my own good. They lock me away so they don't have to deal with me. Then they take your money and call it treatment."

"Julie, I can't take you home."

"How about just for a visit? Just a day or two."

Daniel shook his head. "The doctor advises against it."

"I won't embarrass you. I promise."

"I'm not worried about that."

"I think you are. That's all you've ever been concerned about. Ever since you were elected you've worried that I might cost you votes. I'm your wife, Daniel. I have rights. I deserve better treatment."

"You know better than that, Julie. I've loved you and love you still. Your illness makes that hard for you to see."

She nodded her head. "I'm sorry. It's the medications. They make me loopy. It's like being on an amusement park ride, without the amusement. I think they're making me worse."

"I understand," Daniel said. His words were cool. Julie doubted that he did.

An icy shroud of silence fell on them. Daniel began to look around the room again. A few moments later, he glanced at his watch. Julie knew he wanted to leave.

"I'm sorry about pressing you to take me home. I know that would be difficult, but I am feeling a little claustrophobic. Could we take a walk outside? Just for a few moments. I know you can't stay long."

"I don't know if we should."

"You'll be with me. Ask for an orderly. They'll do it for you."

"I don't know, Julie."

"Five minutes. That's all I ask. Just five minutes. A few moments in the sun."

Daniel glanced at his watch again. "Okay. Let's see what we can do."

Julie smiled. "Thank you."

○) ◗ ● ◖ (○

"I THINK IT WENT WELL," Whiz said, taking another swallow of soda.

Marcus shot him a wicked glance. "You think so, eh?"

They were sitting with Lansing, Ben, and Terri at a Denny's near the Caltech campus. Before Marcus was a half-eaten hamburger and a small pile of french fries. Terri and Whiz's plates were clean. Lansing drank coffee and picked at a salad, clearly unsatisfied. Ben had consumed a turkey sandwich and tea.

"Sure," Whiz replied. "You did great."

"I expected it to go differently," Marcus grumbled.

"Really?" Terri said. "How so?"

"You saw what happened," Marcus said. "For most of the press conference they looked bored and put-upon."

"They looked interested after you mentioned that the spot was growing."

"I didn't mention it; that reporter from the *Los Angeles Register* brought it up."

"You were planning on keeping it secret?" Whiz asked.

Lansing stepped in. "We learned of it shortly before the press conference. It was too early to mention the spot's expansion. We needed verification."

"The pictures aren't enough?" Whiz asked.

"Science is based on observation, young man. Repeated observation." Lansing pushed his plate away. "A single observation is never enough. We need to take more pictures, make precise measurements."

"Then what?" Whiz asked.

"Then your professor here publishes the results," Lansing replied.

"Along with Dr. Sicarello and Dr. Lansing," Marcus added. "They've done the bulk of the work so far."

"Nonsense," Lansing said. "This is your baby and you're going to have to run with it."

"Now there's the problem," Marcus said. "I have a great home observatory, but I'm not equipped to do the kind of research that needs to be done."

"I've been thinking about that," Ben said. "How about conducting some of your research at Mount Graham?"

"Mount Graham?" Terri asked.

"The Vatican and the University of Arizona work together at the International Observatory at Mount Graham," Ben explained. Turning to Marcus, he said, "We could work together on the project."

All eyes turned to Marcus. "That's a wonderful offer," he said. "I would have to get someone to cover my classes, but I should be able to pull that off. Whitaker seemed pleased at the publicity the college will receive with this whole thing."

"It's settled then," Lansing said in his typical bulldog style. "I'll pull some strings at MIT and see what additional help we can get."

"So what's it mean?" Terri asked.

"What does what mean?" Marcus said.

"The spot," she said. "I know you need to verify the fact that it's expanding, but we all know that it is. Don't we?"

"Yes," Marcus admitted.

"So what does it mean?" Terri pressed. "What is it? Why is it growing?"

The question was not new to Marcus. Ever since seeing Ben's latest pictures, he had asked himself the same thing many times.

Terri continued, "What I can't figure out is why, if the Moon is such a stagnate place as you say, this thing suddenly appears and grows. Why now?"

"Those are all good questions, Terri," Marcus said. "And right now, I can't answer any of them."

"But we will answer them," Lansing boasted. "We will get to the bottom of it. It's the way of science."

◖◗◗●●◖◗

THE LATE AFTERNOON SUN washed over Julie as she and Daniel walked through the walled courtyard of the hospital. It was as good a feeling as she had felt in weeks. The sun's rays were warm and offset the slight, cool breeze that caressed her hair and face. She wore her robe over the hospital-issue green jumpsuit. The old worn robe was the only thing she owned of her previous life. It had become a source of security and a material token that her entire life had not been spent in an institution.

"It's a glorious day," Julie enthused.

"It's a little damp," Daniel replied, referring to the moist remains of the previous night's rain. "It wasn't much of a storm, just enough to wet the ground."

"It didn't rain this morning?" Julie asked.

"No," Daniel said. "Just a little last night. There's still some unstable air." He looked up at the few remaining clouds.

"You were in town last night?" she asked.

Daniel seemed to tense. "Well, I got in late."

It was late afternoon now. Julie wondered why he had not come to see her sooner. She started to ask, but he changed the subject.

"What do you see?"

Julie was confused. "What do you mean?"

"Your visions," he explained. "What do you see?"

When the visions first began nearly two years ago they had been short and indistinct. They lacked the graphic sensory explosive images that haunted her now. She used to call them "daymares" because they only happened when she was awake. As the weeks passed the images became more severe, crescendoing until they overshadowed every aspect of her life, took captive every emotion.

"Things," she said with a dismissive shrug. "Awful things." She didn't want to talk about this. Not now. She wanted to breathe air that hadn't been cycled through an air-conditioning system and didn't carry with it the acrid smells of a hospital.

"What kind of things?"

"Do we have to talk about this? It's such a pretty day. Can't we just enjoy it?"

"I want to know," Daniel said.

She had to appease him. If she refused to answer, he would become angry and cut short their stroll. She didn't want that. She desired more than anything to feel grass beneath her feet, to hear leaves rustling on the tree, to smell fresh air. But the darkness of her thoughts frightened her. Julie feared that by simply thinking of the visions, by dragging them up from the dungeon depths of her subconscious, a new one would swarm upon her.

"They're horrible," she admitted. Tempted as she was to play down the sights, she knew that Daniel would catch her in the lie. He might be selfish, but he was nothing if not insightful.

"Are they like the ones you had before coming here?" asked Daniel. Julie had shared her visions openly with Daniel, hoping for his support. At first, he had been compassionate. He arranged for the finest doctors to see her, but when none could help, he became distant. A crazy wife was a detriment to a politician.

"They're never the same," she said. "Each vision is different. Only the blood is the same. There's always blood. Sometimes other things."

"What other things?" Daniel pressed.

"The Moon. Sometimes I see the Moon in my visions. Sometimes just the blood. There's no rhyme or reason to it, Daniel, they just come. I feel like something is crawling in my head, then I start seeing things."

"But they're just your imagination," Daniel said. "They're not real."

"They seem real to me," Julie shot back. "When they happen, I can't tell what's real from what's in my head. I not only see these things, but I sense them in every way."

"How?"

"It's not like watching a movie or television. I not only see the images, I can smell them, feel them. To me they are as real as anything I ever experienced—as real as your presence here."

Julie stopped, crouched down, and picked up a fallen oak leaf. She saw another one and picked it up also.

"What are you doing?" Daniel asked.

"Leaves. I think they're pretty."

"They're wet," Daniel objected.

"I don't care. They won't let me go outside; maybe I can bring some of the outside into my room."

"You're still a sentimentalist," Daniel commented. Julie knew this was hard on him. He was not a callused man, but he had never been demonstrative, not even before her illness. He had once explained to her that most men were emotional cripples, unable to organize and access their deeper feelings. It was part of being a man in the western world. There was nothing he could do about it, nor did he care to try. Unable to manage her situation, he became academic in his approach. Not knowing what to do, he did nothing.

"That's the whole point, Daniel," Julie said, looking down at the leaves in her hand. "I'm the same person I've always been. My illness has not changed me. I'm still the woman you married. I know we had a few problems before the attacks came, but we would have worked those out."

"I wish that were true, Julie. I really do."

"It is true."

Daniel turned and faced her, placing his hands on her shoulders. "Listen to me, Julie. I can't see what you see when you have one of these episodes, but you can't see what you're like when you have one. You scream and run. I'm afraid you're going to hurt yourself."

"There must be a way, Daniel," Julie said. Tears were brimming in her eyes. "I can't stay here forever. Each day gets longer. Each moment I feel more alone. You put me here to have my mind healed. If I stay much longer, I may not have a mind worth healing."

Daniel removed his hands and started walking again. "I have no other solutions and neither do the doctors. That's the hard reality of it."

The air seemed to chill. Why wouldn't Daniel meet her halfway? Once again, he looked at his watch. Julie knew her short walk was just about over. Stooping down she picked up a few more leaves and held them in her hand.

"Perhaps we should go back in now," Daniel said. "The wind is picking up."

The wind felt no different to Julie. The chill wasn't coming from the wind. "Will you visit again?"

"I leave for Sacramento this evening," he answered. "I don't know when I'll be back. Things have been—"

"Busy," she said, finishing the sentence for him. It was a line she had heard a thousand times. She sensed it would be a long time before Daniel came back. Maybe months. The time between visits grew steadily longer.

"That's right," Daniel said.

"I guess we better go back then," Julie said. The tears in her eyes had dried. She no longer felt like crying.

"Very well," Daniel said and started toward the metal-framed glass door they had used to exit the hospital and enter the courtyard. It was an auxiliary exit and therefore smaller than the double doors at the front of the institution. Julie followed close behind. He held the door for her and Julie entered the hall. The contrast between the artificial light, the drab colors of the hall, and the beauty of the outside world depressed her. She crumbled the leaves in her hand.

"Your doctor is keeping me informed," Daniel said as he walked her to her room. "I talk to him every week."

"That's good," Julie said without emotion.

At the door to her room, the two paused and gazed at each other for a moment. Words should be spoken, but Julie knew that they would not be uttered.

"Take care of yourself," Julie said.

Daniel reached over and opened the door. Julie looked in at the room that had become her cell. The sight of it sickened her. She turned back to face Daniel. As she did, she placed her hands behind her back and leaned against the doorjamb. The leaves were in her left hand.

"I don't suppose I could have a kiss before you go," Julie said.

Daniel leaned over and gave her a quick kiss on the forehead. As he did, Julie pressed the leaves into the cavity of the jamb where the lock's strike plate was. She hoped that she had pushed them in far enough not to be noticed, but not so far that the tongue of the lock could still latch.

"I wish I could visit more," Daniel said. The words did not ring true with Julie.

"Thanks for stopping by," Julie said. "I wish we could have had a meal together or something."

"Maybe next time."

"Maybe next time," Julie echoed and then stepped into her room. She listened as Daniel closed the door. Julie had heard the door close countless times and knew its every creak. She hoped that one sound might be missing: the sound of the lock engaging.

She heard nothing as the door closed. The tongue of the lock did not have sufficient depth in the jamb to engage.

Success.

Step one was a success.

CHAPTER
TEN

Snippets of the press conference were shown that evening on a Los Angeles television station. Marcus watched with disgust. His careful preparations and detailed presentation had been reduced to a forty-second media bite. The video showed Marcus standing behind the lectern speaking to the reporters. Only three or four lines of his speech were retained. The news anchors summarized the rest into a tight digest that did little more than say, "Scientists have found something unusual on the

Moon—a red spot that wasn't there before. Further study is under way. And now, the weather with Sunny Bob Hall."

Marcus switched off the television with the remote. "Unbelievable. Commercial news. They could announce the beginning of World War III and smile while doing it. I can hear it now: 'China has invaded Japan. Nuclear bombs are falling killing millions . . . now the weather with Sunny Bob Hall.'"

Lucy chuckled. "You never have liked television news very much."

"Every time I watch it, I feel like my IQ drops a point or two. Nothing has happened to the Moon in the last ten thousand years, and when it does, it gets all of one minute of play on the evening news. If a football player broke an ankle they would interview every one of his teammates, his family, and his pet dog."

Lucy rose from her seat and walked into the kitchen. The house had an open floor plan that was common to many California homes. Marcus could sit in the living room and watch his wife work. "What are you doing?"

"Making coffee," Lucy said. "I imagine you're going to be moon gazing tonight."

"The Moon is waning," Marcus said, rising from his easy chair. "I have only a week left before the enigma is obscured in shadow. Then I'll have to wait several weeks before I can make any decent observations."

"Are you going to accept Dr. Sicarello's offer to work with him in Arizona?"

"I've thought about it and don't see how I can pass it up." Marcus strolled into the kitchen and wrapped his arms around his wife. "I just wish I could take you with me."

"I can't leave the hospital," Lucy said, returning the hug. "We're shorthanded already. Besides, you said you'd be gone only a few days at a time."

"True," Marcus said. "We only get a few hours each day, a few days each month. Ben has a lot of authority, but he can't wipe the schedule clean for me. As it is, he's having to call in favors with the other astronomers."

The phone rang, and Marcus broke the embrace to answer it. Lucy returned to her coffee making.

"Hello," Marcus said. The caller identified himself as a reporter for National Public Radio. He had seen the television broadcast and wanted to do a story for the *Morning Edition* program.

"The story will run between four to six minutes on air," the caller explained. "Now that's just the initial story. We would, of course, like to provide updates when new information becomes available."

Marcus was elated. NPR was known for in-depth, quality reporting. This was an opportunity to get the whole story out— at least much of it. Marcus readily agreed and spent the next twenty minutes talking to the reporter.

Before he hung up, Marcus heard a beep in the phone, the signal that another call was coming in. Quickly thanking the NPR reporter, he switched over to the incoming call. It was Don Holm of the *Los Angeles Register*.

"I was at the press conference," Holm said. "Do you remember me?"

"Quite well," Marcus said. The image of Holm standing at the back of the reporters and pressing Marcus with questions was vivid in his mind. It had been Holm that had rightly assumed that the enigma was growing.

"A story will appear in tomorrow morning's paper," Holm said. "But I think we at the *Register* can do better. I'd like to do a follow-up piece, maybe even a series."

"What would you need from me?"

"More information," Holm said. "Updates, too. I'd like to be on your 'first call' list."

"First call?"

"Yeah, you know. I'm one of the first people you call when something significant is found. I think you really have something here, Professor."

"It is significant," Marcus said. "I didn't think your fellow reporters were going to see that. They seemed bored until you figured out it was growing."

"You have to understand the way journalists think. Simply because something has happened may make it news, but a journalist wants more—immediacy. The problem with news is that it is history as soon as it happens. What makes a story interesting is the impact the event has.

"Suppose there's been a murder," Holm continued. "Today few people will stop reading the *TV Guide* to listen to the report on television or bother to read more than the first two paragraphs of a newspaper article. Unless, of course, they know the person, or the murder was weird in some fashion. What really holds their interest is not the fact that someone has been killed but that a murderer is still on the loose."

"So when they heard that the enigma was growing, it made the story more interesting?" Marcus asked.

"Exactly," Holm answered. "They're not reporting something that *has* happened but something that *is* happening. That's why local television stations will interrupt programming to broadcast a high-speed police chase. After it's over, no one much cares."

"I'll be happy to provide you with whatever information I can," Marcus said. "You must understand that this is a scientific investigation and it takes time for things to develop."

"I'm a science editor, Professor. I have a master's degree in geology. I turned to journalism to help popularize science. I know how these things work. However, I think you're wrong."

"Wrong? How?"

"Whatever is going to happen is going to happen quickly. It's not just the scientific community that is going to be shaken up. Have you thought about the global implications of all this?"

"Global implications? No, not really."

"Give it some thought, Professor. Things are about to change in more ways than you can imagine."

JOHN JACOB DEMPSEY SAT on the edge of his worn sofa and rocked back and forth, his arms folded over his abdomen like a man with severe indigestion. Instead of heartburn, he was filled with a churning mix of excitement and apprehension. So he rocked back and forth like a frightened child, alternating between euphoria and utter terror. He often rocked or paced or bounced his legs up and down when he sat. He was a man in perpetual motion, a constant flow of undirected energy.

In front of him the small color television played a reality show with loud, obnoxious contestants, but Dempsey noticed little, unable to focus on it. What occupied his attention was an unfading image in his mind. He could still hear the news reporter talk about the red Stiller Enigma on the Moon. It was now all he could hear.

He muttered to himself: " 'The sun shall be turned into darkness, and the moon into blood, before the great and the terrible day of the Lord come.' Joel 2:31."

He repeated the phrase over and over, his voice filling the small, unkempt apartment. Newspapers were scattered about the room. The walls bore no paintings. Dishes crusted with old and dried food sat on the kitchen counter.

He continued his chant: " 'The sun shall be turned into darkness, and the moon into blood, before the great and the terrible day of the Lord come.' Joel 2:31 ... 'The sun shall be turned into darkness, and the moon into blood, before the great and the terrible day of the Lord come.' Joel 2:31 ..."

It was happening. He had always known it would come in his lifetime. Now here it was. Humankind had reached the threshold. Humanity had come to the brink, and it had happened just as he knew it must. Dempsey stopped rocking, giggled, and then resumed his back and forth motion. Rocking, rocking, with metronome precision.

Emotions bubbled within him in an odd, contradictory solution—a witch's brew of passions. One second he was terrified, the next, overjoyed. Like a thrill seeker who parachutes off a tall building, Dempsey simultaneously felt the joy and terror of the knowledge he had just gained.

It was happening and he was ready. Leaping to his feet he held out his arms, threw his head back, and shouted to the heavens, "The great and terrible day of the Lord!"

A muted voice descended from the apartment above, "Hey, shut up!"

"Infidels," Dempsey said to himself softly. "Unbelievers. Pagans. Heathens." He returned to his sofa and picked up a Bible, its black leather cover worn and frayed, and turned to the back. There he found the concordance, an alphabetical index of key words in the Bible. He turned the pages quickly until he found the word *Moon*. He found the list to be short, too short. Setting the Bible aside, he searched his apartment for another book, a larger concordance. He found it near his bed, under a pile of dirty clothing. Studying the worn, brown cover, he read, *Strong's Exhaustive Concordance of the Bible*. He had bought the large volume at a garage sale for two dollars. In it was every word of the Bible, neatly organized and indexed. Only a fool would sell such a valuable tool for only two dollars. Here was the Word of God organized by word into neat columns. He hugged the book to his chest. His hands trembled.

Returning to the sagging sofa, he opened the concordance and again looked for the word *Moon*. He was pleased to see scores of entries. It would take him some time to read all the verses, maybe hours since reading was not his strong suit, but he would not quit until he had taken in every word. He was bulldog tenacious.

"Terrible day of the Lord," he whispered. "Terrible day."

THINGS HAD TO BE DONE RIGHT, Julie reminded herself for the tenth time that hour. Waiting was the key, waiting and not looking anxious. One misstep and her plan would be discovered. Patience was essential, so Julie did as she always did—stared out the window at the Moon. But for once, she didn't focus on the Moon. Instead she ran the steps of her plan over and over in her head.

The little ball of leaves she had managed to wedge into the doorjamb at the strike plate had kept the door from locking, but there was still the matter of the video camera in the room. At this moment, someone could be watching her, analyzing her body language, looking for any sign that she was about to go over the edge. They would see nothing. No matter how terrifying a vision she might have, she was determined to remain calm. Fortunately, everything around her seemed normal. No apparitions, no puddles of squirming blood—just her room.

There was only one place of privacy—the bathroom. The hospital had allowed her that much dignity since there was very little she could do there to harm herself. Unlike most rest rooms, hers was spartan, devoid of a mirror or a cabinet of any kind. Mirrors could be broken and the shards of glass used as razors. Cabinets could be used to conceal things. Her bathroom was home to a toilet and a shallow basin.

Her time in the bathroom was clocked. Spend too much time out of the camera's eye and someone would soon come through the door to check on her. The bathroom had no lock.

The video camera was situated opposite her bed. While it could see every square foot of the room, it could not see into the lavatory. If she disappeared from the surveillance monitor it would be assumed that she was in the bathroom. Ten minutes was all she was allowed. How far could she get in ten minutes? Julie didn't know, but she would find out tonight.

Another thing Julie didn't know was if the door to her room was monitored. Did a warning light shine someplace if her door was opened? Probably not, she decided. The door was always locked. She could only leave when someone let her out. That meant that she could exit the room and have about ten minutes of free time, assuming no one saw her in the hall.

That was a problem. Once outside her cell, she would be easy to spot by any nurse, orderly, or janitor. Dressed in hospital-issued green jumpsuit and white T-shirt, she would be immediately recognized as a patient. That would quickly end her excursion.

Being discovered carried another horrifying element. They would certainly sedate her more in the future. Escape would be impossible then.

Whatever she did had to be done right the first time. There would be no future opportunities.

Julie turned from the window and crawled under the covers of her bed. A switch by the bed allowed her to turn off the overhead light. A small security light near the surveillance camera continued to burn, casting the room in a pallid glow. She lay facing the window for a few moments, then rolled over to face the door.

Patience, she said to herself. *Patience.*

The minutes oozed by in caterpillar time.

○ ◐ ◑ ● ◐ ◐ ○

"THAT'S A GOOD SHOT," Marcus said. Terri Lynn sat at the computer console in Marcus's office typing commands into the keyboard of the computer that operated the remote Starfinder telescope. "Concentrate on the south edge of the Crater Plato."

Marcus watched as the telescope made the minor adjustments necessary to center the crater in the image.

"I can't believe you let us stand outside and freeze last time we were here," Whiz said. "We could have been warm and comfy in here."

"Comfy?" Terri laughed. "Now that's not a word I expected out of your mouth."

"You know what I mean," Whiz retorted.

"I wanted you to have the experience of gazing at the Moon the old-fashioned way." Marcus stretched. Whiz and Terri had been hovering over the computer and Marcus had been hovering over them. "There's nothing better than stargazing in the brisk mountain air. Besides, you said you weren't cold."

"I wasn't," Whiz said defensively. "This is just . . . better."

"*Comfy,*" Terri said, needling her friend. "Whiz thinks *comfy* is better. Doesn't fit your image."

Marcus saw Whiz roll his eyes. The three fell silent as they gazed at the image on the monitor. Much of the Moon had fallen into shadow, but the area they were interested in was still awash in light. Deep shadows of black painted the edge of the highlands. The image was gray and the surface of the Moon looked as if it was buried in powder. One portion of the Moon, however, looked different: south of the large crater at the Mare Imbrium, the Sea of Rains, was a large spread of red covering the regolith like an angry, swelling bruise.

"How large is the enigma?" Marcus asked. Ever the teacher, he wanted Terri and Whiz to analyze the situation for themselves.

Terri shrugged. "I don't know. We need a scale, something we can use to measure it."

"You have one," Marcus said.

"We do?" Terri replied.

"Yes."

"Plato," Whiz said. "You said at the press conference that Plato was 109 kilometers in diameter."

"That's right."

"You also said," Whiz continued, "that the spot was 210 kilometers wide and about one hundred kilometers north to south."

"Right again," Marcus said.

"So," Terri began, "we can use Plato as our scale and measure the spot to see if it has grown."

"Your job is to tell me how much it has grown," Marcus said.

Terri looked around the desk upon which the computer monitor and keyboard sat and found a piece of paper and a pencil. She held the paper up to the screen, laying it across the large crater. She then drew two tiny lines marking the extreme edges of the rim. Setting the paper back on the desk, she wrote 109 between the lines. Placing the paper back to the screen, she began to measure the width of the red spot, holding her place on the screen with the tip of the pencil. "This is just a rough estimate," she said, "but I'd say that the enigma is two-and-a-quarter units wide—a unit being 109 kilometers."

"That's 245.25 kilometers," Whiz offered. "Give or take."

"I'll show you how to take a more accurate measurement in a minute," Marcus said.

"Wait," Whiz said. "At the press conference, you said the stain was 210 kilometers east to west."

Marcus said nothing. He let his students mull over the implication.

"That would mean that it has expanded by sixteen or seventeen percent," Whiz said with amazement.

"All in one day," Terri added.

"All in one day," Marcus agreed. "So what's the next question?"

"How long before it covers the whole surface of the Moon?" Terri answered.

"Yes, but before we calculate that we need to see if the north-south spread is the same as the east-west."

"Checking for uniformity?" Whiz asked.

"Exactly," Marcus replied. "Not only is it important to know how fast this thing is spreading, but also if it is doing so evenly. There may be some clues in that. Let's do another rough estimate on the north-south direction, then we can move to more accurate measurements."

"Others are doing this too, aren't they?" Terri asked. "Other astronomers, I mean."

"Yes," Marcus answered. "Hopefully several groups are taking a close look at this. We know Dr. Sicarello is doing so in Arizona. Others are sure to be looking."

"Does it bother you that they are looking at your discovery?" Whiz asked.

"Not at all," Marcus said. "That's how contemporary science works. It's not my Moon. If I hadn't noticed when I did, someone else would have in the next day or two. Something like this can't stay hidden. Nor do we want it to."

"What could do this to the Moon?" Terri asked.

"I don't know," Marcus admitted. "But with enough people working on it, we may know soon."

The phone rang and instinctively Marcus looked at the clock on his desk. It was a quarter to ten. He heard his wife cry, "I'll get it."

A moment later, Lucy Stiller appeared in the office. Her face was lined with concern, her mouth pulled tight. "It's your mom," she said softly. "She wants to talk to you about your father."

Marcus snapped up the phone on his desk. He looked at his wife, who continued to listen on the cordless phone she had brought with her from the living room. "Mom?" He listened to the voice of his mother and as he did, his stomach twisted into a tight, hot ball of fear. "I'm on my way." Slowly he replaced the handset back in the cradle.

"I'm going with you," Lucy said.

"Is something wrong?" Terri asked.

Marcus walked from the room without a word. As he did, he heard Lucy say, "It's his father. He's ... not well."

TIME WAS RELATIVE AND IT NEVER SEEMED MORE SO THAN now. The minutes had passed with painful sluggishness as Julie lay in her bed waiting for the wee hours to come. Now outside her room and hiding in a small storage closet off the hall, Julie felt the minutes race past in a torrent of time. If she didn't act quickly, someone would notice that she had not returned from the bathroom and come looking for her. Once they discovered that she was gone, every worker in the building would be notified and her chance of escape would be ended. She had ducked into the four-foot-by-four-foot compartment one minute after she had slipped out the door of her room. She was hiding. Not because she had spied someone from whom she needed to hide, but because the sheer terror of walking out had nearly overpowered her.

Surrounded by mops, brooms, and shelves loaded with cleansers and toilet paper, Julie took several deep breaths and willed her stumbling heart to calm. *Stay with the plan*, she told herself. *Stay with the plan.*

What Julie wanted to do was stroll out the front doors, but those would be locked. She had another concern. Every exit door had an alarm. If she pushed through one of the emergency exits a loud electronic bell would sound and she would be caught before she could make ten yards. She had seen this happen when another patient, an elderly woman, decided to walk home. The alarm had been piercing and the rush of orderlies, nurses, and doctors had been frightening. Doors were out of the question.

But Julie had an idea. It was something she had thought about before, a fantasy she had played over and over in her mind. It would be hard and it was far from foolproof, but it was the only possibility.

Turning the round doorknob with exacting slowness, Julie cracked the door just enough to look down the hall. She saw nothing, but she could look only one direction. The door prohibited her from looking the other way. There was nothing she could do about that. Stepping back into the hall, she silently closed the door behind her and made her way down the corridor. The thin slippers she wore made almost no noise, but it sounded thunderous to her. Pausing and leaning against the green wall of the corridor, Julie removed the slippers and held them in one hand. Barefoot, she continued on.

Julie had been down the hall many times and she knew where each door led. Ahead a door to her left was open and light poured from it into the dim hall. It was the door she feared most. Step after step she crept closer to the room's open maw. Three feet from the opening she stopped and listened. At first she heard nothing. She held her breath and strained her ears.

There was a sound, soft, barely perceptible. It was a sound she had heard before, but had not heard for months. She recognized it in a sudden flash of understanding. Snoring. This was more than she could have hoped, more than she could have wished.

Biting her lower lip, Julie slowly peered around the door-jamb. Inside the room was a counter situated before a bank of video monitors. Leaning back in a tall leather chair was a thin man wearing a white smock. He was sound asleep. A clock on the wall read 2:10.

Julie seized the moment and stepped past the open door, continuing down the hall. Her heart pounded like a piston in a race car. One careful step followed another, but despite her determination to move slowly and carefully, she broke into a jog. The room she wanted was at the end of the hall and she couldn't get to it fast enough. The door was there, waiting for her. A plaque was fixed to the face of the door that read "Cafeteria."

Julie pushed open the swinging door and stepped into the dim light of the room. The cafeteria was a large open expanse of tables and chairs. A single row of fluorescent lights fought back the night. The other banks of lights rested in their dark recesses.

Glancing around the room, Julie was relieved to see the place empty. The chairs were pushed neatly under the tables. Clearly the janitor had already done his work. Julie found relief in that. No need to worry about his walking in.

With her slippers still in hand, Julie walked across the open expanse toward the industrial kitchen she knew to be at the south end of the canteen. As she made her way across the linoleum floor, she glanced at the exit doors along the exterior wall. For a moment she was tempted to push one of the doors open and run as fast as she could. But the temptation had to be resisted. If she were to escape her medical captors, then she would need as much time outside as possible. Seconds could make the difference.

Julie reset her sights on the kitchen. A pair of stainless steel doors separated the room from the dining area. The doors were double-hinged, allowing them to swing in either direction. She was within a few steps of victory. Her plan was simple. A window was situated over the industrial sinks. She had seen it while sitting in the dining room. As workers exited the kitchen, she had been able to see some of the kitchen's layout. Patients were not allowed past the double doors—too many sharp objects for their own good. The window had meant nothing to her until she had committed herself to escaping—then everything took on new meaning. She had no way of knowing if an alarm device had been attached to that window, but she had to take the chance. If she saw that the window was secured by an alarm or fixed so as not to open, then she would make a run for it by plowing through the nearest pair of exit doors—alarms or no alarms. There would be no backing out now.

She reached her hand forward to push one of the swinging doors when it burst toward her.

A startled scream erupted from her lips and she backpedaled furiously. Her heart seized in her chest; her lungs sucked in one distressed breath then ceased. She raised a hand to her mouth. Her eyes flooded with tears.

Standing before her was the corpulent Gordon holding a large, messy sandwich. "Well," he said. "Look who's out of her cage."

Julie took another step back. "Stay away from me." Memories of how he had subdued her, sat on her, and injected her with sedative replayed vividly in her mind.

"You're supposed to be all snug in your bed."

"What are you doing here?" It was a stupid question, she thought, but it was the only thing she could think of.

"Raiding the fridge. It's my break time. The real question is, what are *you* doing here?"

"I ... I ..." Julie realized that there was no answer that Gordon would find believable. "You stay away from me."

"You're breaking the rules. I can't allow that."

Julie backed up another step. She bumped into something. A chair.

"Careful," Gordon said with an evil smile. "We don't want you to be damaged goods." He started toward her. Julie shot around the table, interposing it between them.

"Stay away."

"I can't do that, Ms. Waal. You know that. It's my job to protect you, to help you."

"You want to hurt me. Just like before." He took another step closer. "I'll scream."

"You don't want to do that," Gordon threatened. "We can handle this all by ourselves."

"I won't let you touch me—"

Gordon started for her. Julie threw her slippers at him. She knew they would do no harm, but they were in her hand and they might give her one more second to escape. Gordon flinched. As he did, Julie took several more steps back until she hit another chair. The chair hit the table and she heard a *thunk* behind her. She turned and saw that a set of salt and pepper shakers had fallen over. She reached for one, grabbed it, spun on her heels, and threw it as hard as she could at Gordon. It caught him in the forehead but bounced harmlessly to the floor. Julie knew it was a futile effort. The shakers were made of plastic. Had they been glass—

"You stupid little—" Gordon charged. Julie caught a glimpse of his red face. He was furious.

Turning to the table again, Julie reached for the pepper shaker. As she grabbed it, Gordon's beefy hand snatched hold of her hair. She felt her head snap back. "No one attacks me. Do you hear! No one!"

Julie felt herself being forced to her knees. She wanted to reach for his hand, to pull it away. Instead, she tried to focus on the pepper shaker. She fumbled with the top. It should just pop off. Why didn't it? She pushed and pulled until it gave way. Black pepper poured into her hand and onto the floor. But Gordon was pressing her down, pushing her head closer and closer to the linoleum. Fiery pain raced down her neck and back. Julie knew she could never overpower him. He weighed 150 pounds more than she and was twice as strong. When her head touched the floor, Gordon placed a foot on her blonde hair, making it impossible for her to rise.

"What are you going to do now, Missy?" His words were hot and bitter and they frightened her more than anything she had experienced before, even more than the visions. "What?" Gordon continued. "No response? No words for your pal Gordy?"

Pinned to the floor by Gordon's foot, Julie could not rise, but she could reach his leg with her right hand—the hand with the pepper shaker in it. Julie turned the shaker over and pressed its flat base into the skin just above Gordon's ankle and then pulled as hard as she could. She could feel the edge dig into his flesh. Gordon screamed in pain and took a step back. Julie sprung to her feet, took a step toward the startled man, and blew the small mound of pepper into his face. He screamed and raised his hands.

"My eyes," he shouted.

Julie knew that Gordon was disabled for only a moment. She needed to do more. Grabbing the back of one of the fiberglass chairs, she held it high and brought it down on Gordon's head. He staggered, but didn't fall. Julie swung the chair again, this time catching him on the side. Gordon dropped in a heap, his head hitting the floor, bouncing once.

He lay facedown, moaning. He wouldn't be out long. Julie raced into the kitchen. *It was now or never,* she told herself.

The window was four foot wide. One half of the window could be slid sideways over the other half, letting in air. Julie looked for anything that looked like it might be an alarm and saw nothing. Frantically she clawed at the release that would allow the window to slide. It wouldn't move. She pressed it, pulled it, and slammed her fists on the metal release, but it would not give.

She took a step back, inhaled deeply, and forced the panic from her mind. Stepping forward again, she forced herself to study the window. At the base, she saw the problem. A small aluminum lock held the window in place. It was a cheap window security device that people bought at hardware stores to keep intruders from breaking in. All that was needed was to twist a tiny screw and the lock would come off. Julie did, and the window slid open effortlessly.

She stopped again. There was a screen over the opening, but just a screen. No bars, just a pale plastic fabric. Crawling onto the counter, Julie pushed at the screen. It popped out easily and fell to the ground outside. Julie looked out into the moonlit night, struggling to believe that freedom was inches away.

From the dining room came a loud moan. Julie crawled through the window and dropped to the ground.

The grass outside was still damp from the rain the night before. The cold water clung to her bare feet, but she didn't care.

Julie Waal began to run.

◗ ◗ ● ● ◗ ◖ ◖

MARCUS IMPATIENTLY DRUMMED HIS FINGERS on the steering wheel of their white Toyota sedan. When they first left the house, Lucy had suggested taking it instead of his pickup. Marcus didn't care which car they took, as long as they left immediately. Now, moving down Interstate 15 toward San Diego, he pressed the speed limit as much as he felt he could without being pulled over by the Highway Patrol.

Time crawled by. The miles seemed to be longer, as if his impatience made them elastic. Fortunately, the late hour meant that the roads were free of congestion. Marcus barely noticed the cars he passed as he steered his way south. His mind was filled with a single image: his father lying upon a hospital bed, covered in a white sheet as he breathed his last. The thought ate at Marcus. Another sixty miles separated him from his father, sixty miles that seemed to pass with excruciating slowness.

"Do you think he'll last until we get there?" Marcus asked softly. He had not spoken for the last half hour. Lucy had not interrupted his reflection.

"I don't know," she answered, placing a hand on his shoulder. "No one knows these things. Not even we doctors."

"I know," Marcus admitted. Tears brimmed his eyes. "I'm . . . grasping."

"If any man can hold on, your dad can. He'll wait for you with all his strength."

"He hasn't been aware of anything for months," Marcus said. "He doesn't know if I'm there or not."

"Maybe," Lucy said. "I've come to believe that comatose patients know more than we give them credit for. It's not scientific, but I believe it nonetheless."

"I hope you're right," Marcus said. He wiped at his eyes. "I don't want Mom to have to go through this alone."

"I know, dear. Your mother is strong."

Marcus turned to his wife. In the dim yellow glow of passing streetlights he could see the tears on her cheeks glisten. She understood. She could empathize, having lost both of her parents a few years before. Lucy not only understood his pain, she was living it with him. Marcus was glad she was there.

The next hour passed like a week, but it passed. Marcus pulled the car into a parking stall next to the front door of the convalescent hospital where his father had spent the last six months. He and Lucy exited the car as if it were on fire. Every other time he had come to the place, he had dreaded it. Now he couldn't make his way through the glass doors fast enough.

A woman at the reception desk startled at their explosive entrance, jumped, and asked, "May I help you?"

"No," Marcus said, shaking his head. He shot past her in long strides. "I know where I'm going." He walked with the determination of a freight train on a downhill grade. Glancing to the side, he saw Lucy jogging to keep up.

Twenty steps later, he was there. Without hesitation, he stepped into his father's room, and then came to an abrupt stop. The room was dark except for a single fluorescent light mounted to the wall at the head of the bed. Seated in a vinyl chair was his mother. She held her worn Bible close to her chest. She was leaning over, her head resting on the aluminum bed rail. With her free hand, she held her husband's hand, stroking the parchment-thin skin with her thumb. It was the only indication that his mother was alive.

"Mom?" Marcus said softly as he eased his way to her side. She remained motionless. "Mom? Are you all right?"

The elderly woman looked up into Marcus's face. Her eyes were dull and red from crying. "Marcus. I didn't hear you come in."

"I got here as soon as I could. I'm sorry to wake you."

"I wasn't sleeping, son. I was praying."

Marcus could only nod. "How is he? Any change?"

As Marcus spoke, his father groaned. It was a groan he had heard many times. When he had first heard the sounds, he had assumed that his father was climbing out of the dark world of the coma. He soon learned that coma patients often made such noises.

"He's weaker," Abigail said. "His breathing is not so good. It sounds wet."

Lucy stepped over to the bed, taking the old man's wrist in her hand. She placed two fingers to his pulse. She looked at

Marcus. "Slow and thready." Lucy's expression confirmed what they already knew.

"He loves you, Marcus. He loves you more than anything. Even after you moved off to college, he couldn't stop talking about you. I think he would have burst if he tried to keep all that pride in." Abigail reached for a tissue from a box on the side table. She dabbed at her eyes.

Marcus turned to Lucy. Tears coursed down her face like tiny rivers. "I know, Mom. I love him too."

"Then you need to tell him, son. You go on now and tell him."

Marcus felt awkward. Half of his brain was saying that his father could never hear him, no matter what the others said. He was unresponsive and had been so for over half a year. But another part of his mind pushed him forward. Logic didn't matter. This was his father and whatever words were to be spoken had to be spoken now. No other occasion would exist.

Walking to the other side of the bed, Marcus took his father's hand in his own. He heard a sound behind him and turned to see Lucy pushing an empty chair toward him. Marcus sat and stared at the shell of his father's existence.

Softly he began. The words were disjointed, the thoughts random. He spoke of fishing trips, baseball games, and jokes about his father's preaching. He recounted discipline he had received at his father's hand which he had considered too harsh and unfair at the time, but which he now knew to be the act of a loving father guiding his son to responsibility and respect.

As he spoke Marcus felt his eyes flood with tears, his face turn hot, and his nose begin to run. His heart beat arrhythmically, skipping beats as if it were distracted, no longer paying attention to its job.

The words changed as Marcus continued. Stories of events were replaced by terms of love. Finally, all Marcus could say was, "I miss you, Dad. I miss you."

Marcus's shoulders began to heave as he clamped his eyes shut. Sobs came convulsively, erratically. Marcus moaned then wept as the hot understanding of his loss burned his tender soul. He was awash in emotions he could not control.

A hand touched him on the shoulder. It was Lucy, but he did not look up—could not look up. Instead, he folded over in anguish and rested his head on the side of the bed.

He could no longer think. Thoughts had become too numerous and slippery to be captured. So Marcus wept bitterly. There was nothing more he could do. Each sob said more than words could express.

Six minutes later, the Reverend James Stiller died.

CHAPTER

TWELVE

A COLD BREEZE ROLLED OFF THE OCEAN, UP THE WIDE
stretch of sand, through the mollusk-encrusted wood
columns of the Santa Barbara pier, and over Julie's moist
skin. She shuddered, half from cold, half from fright. The
darkness of the early morning hours hung over her like
a damp blanket. Her feet hurt from the two hours of
walking and running, her thighs and calves burned from
the exertion, and her throat was hot and raw from
ragged breathing. She had made the trip from the mental hospital on the east side of the 101 Freeway to the

beach six miles away in a frantic run. How long she had been running she did not know, but fear propelled each step. Minutes blurred in her mind. In the darkness of the early morning, the Moon was being swallowed by an inrush of thick marine clouds. She fought to suppress her terror.

At first she ran with no direction in mind other than to put as much distance as possible between her and the hospital that had been her prison for so many long months. Then she slowly developed a plan. There was only so far she could go at night. Moving through town or along empty streets at an hour when nearly every law-abiding person was asleep would make her stand out. Surely by now, Gordon would have reported her escape and her attack on him. The police must be looking for her. She had to hide off the streets. That was when she thought of the beach.

The beach had always been a place of solace for her. When she was a child her family made frequent trips to the shore, where she would play in the surf and sand. Those were the best days of her life, the days when her parents were alive, the days when family love flourished—days before the visions.

The sound of the small waves rumbled up the beach to her as if the ocean itself were lonely for her company. The sound of the crashing surf comforted her like a lullaby. She took slow breaths, deeply inhaling the salt air.

Directing her gaze toward the distant horizon, Julie realized that sunup was a short time away. She didn't want to be found, and that meant it was time to move again, but where? She had no money, no credit cards, and no way to pay for a cab or bus ride. She was destitute and alone, but at least she was free.

Rising to her feet, she brushed the sand from her clothes and began a solitary stroll down the shore.

"HOW DID THIS HAPPEN?" Dr. Peter Bernard demanded loudly. He was pacing in his office, his fury barely curbed. The clock on his desk read 4:10.

"It was an oversight," Gordon said. He was sitting in one of the contemporary chrome and leather chairs in front of Bernard's wide teak desk. "The orderly who was supposed to be watching the monitors was ill. He was in the bathroom when she made her escape."

"I've already talked to him. He was asleep!" Bernard shouted. "And where were you?"

"I was on a break. I went to the kitchen to fix a snack," he replied defensively.

"A snack?" Bernard replied, shaking his head at his rotund nephew. "You would do well to skip a few snacks." If Gordon was wounded by the comment, he didn't show it.

"I called the police as soon as I knew what happened," Gordon said. He shifted in his seat, the chair squeaking in protest.

"As soon as you came to, you mean," Bernard shot back. "How could you let that woman get the better of you? You're three times her size."

"I didn't expect her to fight back. At least, not like that." He rubbed the knot on his head.

"I can't believe this has happened," Bernard complained. "Never has anything like this happened to me. I hold you responsible."

"It's not the end of the world," Gordon said. "We'll find her and bring her back. She's bound to show up somewhere. It's just a matter of time."

"Just a matter of time," Bernard repeated. "Well then, I'll let you tell Senator Waal that. Just tell him that you let his wife slip away while you were getting a snack, but not to worry. After all, she's bound to show up sometime soon, maybe on the street, or a homeless shelter, or lying dead in the gutter. I'm sure he'll understand."

"You don't need to get sarcastic. I understand the problem."

Bernard clinched his fists as if he were about to pummel his nephew. "Don't tell me how to speak or act. It's four in the morning and I've been pulled from bed to deal with a catastrophe that you've created."

"It's not my fault."

"You're useless," Bernard snapped. He walked to his desk chair and dropped limply into it. "Where are the police?" he asked after a moment's silence.

"There's only one officer here now. The others are back on the street looking for Julie."

"Ms. Waal," Bernard corrected. "I've warned you about using familiar names when referring to our patients. They're our charges, not our friends."

"Whatever," Gordon said. "Anyway, the other cops are gone, but one is using the phone in the next office. He wants to talk to you."

"Then go tell him I'm here."

Gordon did as he was told, reappearing a minute later with a thin, wiry man in a police uniform. Bernard judged him to be in his early thirties. The leather of his Sam Browne belt, weighted with police paraphernalia, squeaked as he walked into the office.

"I'm Officer Bob Mitchell, Santa Barbara Police," he said with a slight smile. "You made it here in short order."

"I live nearby," Bernard said. "Do you have any word on Ms. Waal?"

"No," the officer answered, "but it's early yet. All our units have been notified. We have her description and your assistant has provided us with a file photo. That will be a big help."

Bernard made eye contact with Gordon. At least he had done one thing right.

"Officer Mitchell," Bernard began, "I can't tell you how delicate this situation is. Ms. Waal is married to a prominent California politician—"

"State Senator Daniel Waal," the officer interrupted. "I understand. We'll do our best to keep things under wraps, but it won't be easy. If I were you, I'd prepare for the worst. The media is sure to find out sooner or later."

"I would like to avoid that," Bernard said sternly.

"So would I, but I've been a policeman for ten years, and one thing I've learned: if there's a story, the media will find it." He paused then asked, "Have you contacted Senator Waal?"

Bernard hesitated before answering. "Not yet," he admitted. "I was hoping that she would be found before sunup. She is on foot, after all."

"It's a big city and there are only a few officers," the policeman said. "Do you have any reason to believe that she had help in getting away?"

"What do you mean?" Bernard asked, taking his seat again. He didn't offer a chair to the policeman.

"I'm trying to understand how a woman could escape a locked room, make her way past your security measures, find a way outside, and then slip into the darkness. That's quite a jailbreak."

"This isn't a jail, Officer Mitchell, it's a hospital. One of the most prestigious in the country, I might add." Bernard felt his ire rising again.

"I understand that, Doctor, but you must agree, it's hard to imagine an insane woman doing so well at escape."

"She's not insane," Bernard corrected. "She has a psychosis that inhibits her function in society. Most of the time she is rational, pleasant, and quite intelligent. She just has periods where she breaks from reality."

"I'll grant you that she's smart or at least clever," Mitchell said. "Stuffing leaves into the lock so that the tongue wouldn't catch is ingenious."

"Yes, I suppose it is," Bernard sighed.

"Is she a danger to others?" Mitchell asked bluntly.

"What do you mean?"

"Could she harm someone?"

"She's never been violent before," Bernard said.

"Yeah, right," Gordon said. "I didn't get this lump on my head over the Internet. She gouged my ankle, threw pepper in my eyes, and then she hit me with a chair."

Not hard enough, Bernard thought. He caught a small smile on the policeman's face. There was something in Gordon's account he found funny. "So she can be dangerous?"

"This is new behavior," Bernard said, trying to sound academic. "I'm sure she was frightened."

"Yes, I'm sure she was," Officer Mitchell said. "I have all I need for my report. We'll let you know just as soon as we find her. In the meantime, I would call Senator Waal. Once we have her, we'll be calling him."

"Is that necessary?" Bernard asked.

"Absolutely."

The officer excused himself, leaving Bernard and Gordon alone.

"You gonna call him?" Gordon asked.

"I have no choice," Bernard said, fearing the senator's reaction to being awakened in the early hours of the morning to learn that his wife had gone missing. This was not going to be a pleasant phone call.

⠊⠊⠊⠊⠊⠊⠊

WHEN THE SUN ROSE, Marcus was there to greet it. He stared at the pink ribbons of light as they pushed through slate-colored clouds. The house, his mother's house, was quiet. Awake all night, he had not even bothered to start a pot of coffee. Instead he paced around the small living room, his head down, his hands clasped behind his back. He took little notice of the furniture he had grown up with. His father had been more inclined to save money than spend it. Much of that saved money had been used to put Marcus through Caltech. The monetary support was a

sacrifice on his parents' part. Marcus felt a sense of guilt perco-
late up in him.

He had tried to sleep after leaving the care facility. He, his
mother, and Lucy had taken care of what paperwork was
demanded, then left. It had seemed so wrong to walk out of the
building leaving his father's lifeless corpse to be cared for by
strangers. How many times had Marcus stepped from that
building after visiting his comatose father? Those times were
different, though. He knew that he could come back and visit.
This departure was final. Most likely he would never step foot
in that facility again. Unless of course, his mother ... Marcus
drove the thought from his mind.

The drive to Abigail's house had been made in silence.
Abigail sat in the front passenger seat of her car while Marcus
drove. Lucy followed in their Toyota. It had taken some gentle
persuasion, but he had convinced his mother that she should
not drive home alone. The hour was late and she was too upset.
"Upset" had been Marcus's term. In truth, Abigail had been as
firm as a rock. There had been no torrent of tears, no heaving
sobs. At the moment her husband died, she closed her eyes and
took one deep breath. "To be absent in the body is to be present with the Lord," she murmured. Marcus recognized the
words as a verse in the Bible. Something from the book of
Second Corinthians, he thought.

Abigail sat statue still holding a small plastic bag on her
lap. This bag held only one book, a worn and tattered King
James Version Bible. The bag also contained the few, meager
possessions of James Stiller: a silver-framed photo of the family,
a blue baseball cap with gold letters that spelled out *USS
Michigan* on it, his glasses unworn for six months, and a gold
wedding ring he had worn on his left hand for forty-two years.
Marcus had watched as his mother had gently removed the ring
from his father's finger. Witnessing the act was horrible, terrible.
He felt as if someone had reached into his gut and scooped out
a large measure of his life.

Once home, Abigail had offered to fix sandwiches for everyone, but Marcus and Lucy declined. Marcus couldn't face food and he knew that his mother was attempting to stay busy to bolster the dam of emotion that would surely have to burst sometime.

"Is there anyone you want me to call, Mom?" Marcus had asked.

"Not tonight, dear." Her voice was strong and even. Marcus wondered why she was so steady when he felt on the verge of a breakdown. "I'll call my sister in Georgia in the morning."

"What about the church? Is there someone there I should call?"

"No one needs to know tonight. It's late. The morning will be soon enough."

Marcus could only nod.

"Your old room is ready," Abigail said. "I put new sheets on the bed just last week."

"I'm sure it will be fine," Lucy said.

Abigail nodded. "I think I'll go on to bed now." Her voice seemed weak.

"Mom, are you going to be all right?"

"The Lord is my strength," the new widow said with a wan smile. "My trust is in him."

"Mom—"

Abigail waved him off. "I'll be fine, son, you'll see. I've been coming home to an empty house for a long time now. I don't like it, but what is, is." She gave a little shrug. "We can talk about the funeral in the morning. There will be calls that need to be made. Can you stay and help?"

"Of course, Mom," Marcus said. "We'll go through this together."

"I called my hospital while you and Marc were taking care of the paperwork," Lucy said. "I'm taking a day of emergency leave."

A smile creased Abigail's ebony face. "My son did a good thing when he married you. No one could have a better daughter-in-law."

"Thanks, Mom," Lucy said, giving Abigail a hug. "You go on to bed. If you need anything, just let me know."

Abigail nodded and walked into the dark and empty master bedroom. The sight of his frail mother walking alone into the room tore at Marcus. He dragged a hand across his face, pushing aside new tears.

Lucy stepped to Marcus's side, took him by the hand, and led him to the worn sofa. She seated herself and Marcus joined her. Wrapping her arms around him, she pulled him close. He offered no resistance.

"I feel so helpless," Marcus admitted.

"I felt the same way when I lost my parents. The accident was such a shock and there was nothing I could do. I was helpless. That's the way death is. It's the price the living pay."

"I keep thinking I could have done more. Visited more. Called more. Something . . . anything."

"There's nothing for you to feel guilty about. You have been and remain a good son. Your father was very proud of you."

"It hurts," Marcus confessed. "It hurts more than I imagined."

"It will pass," Lucy said. "In time, the hurt will be replaced by good memories."

"I hope so."

A soft sound, as thin as a fragrance, floated into the room. Marcus strained his ears to make it out. He recognized it. It was his mother. She was sobbing. Marcus had never seen his mother cry. Hearing it now was devastating.

"I think I had better go to bed," he said, his voice shaky.

He and Lucy rose from the sofa and made the short journey to the guest bedroom.

Marcus wished for sleep, but finally gave up the battle. He dressed in the clothes he had worn the day before, and silently moved into the living room.

He gazed out the front window. The street that ran in front of the house looked like a river of macadam. Pale yellow light fell from lampposts, pooling at the base of their stands. All was silent. All was dark. No lights burned in the neighbors' windows, no cars traveled the residential avenue. The night was as still as it was dark. When he wasn't looking out the window, he was pacing the room that was lit by a single lamp on a stand next to his father's recliner. Minutes ticked into hours and Marcus felt the passing of each one. In the silence of the room, in the still of the night, Marcus came to grips with the loss of his father.

With the emotion subdued, Marcus's logical mind took over. It was a sensation he was familiar with and one he much preferred. There was a great deal to be done today. Funeral plans, death certificates to be requested, insurance companies to be informed, friends to be notified. Unpleasant and painful work, but at least he would be doing something, achieving something for his father. Something he couldn't do before.

The sun began to rise as it had the day before and as it would tomorrow. *My own father's death changed the world so little,* Marcus thought.

○ ○ ● ● ● ● ○

GORDON HAD REMAINED CALM in his uncle's office, choosing to bite his tongue rather than make matters worse. Uncle Peter had a right to be hot, but not to speak to him like he was a wayward child. He deserved better than that. After all, he was a victim. The woman had attacked him, even injured him. Wasn't he owed some measure of sympathy? True, he wasn't the ideal employee, and he was known to show up late or even not at all. But he was family, not some Joe off the street. Bernard owed Gordon's father a great deal of money, and, as far as Gordon was concerned, if he owed Dad, then the good doctor owed him something as well.

"How do you want those?"

"What?" Gordon looked up from his place in the restaurant booth. He shifted his weight, releasing a subtle squeak as his bulk rubbed against the vinyl fabric.

"Your eggs. How do you want your eggs?" The waitress was tall, thin, and stood with stooped shoulders.

"The same way I always want them," Gordon snapped. He had been coming to this Denny's every morning for over a year. The server must have waited on him thirty or forty times. "Over hard. If you can't bounce them, then they ain't right."

"People change their orders, you know," the waitress rebutted.

"Not me," was all Gordon said. His mind was elsewhere.

"No, I guess not," the waitress said. "You're in kinda late, aren't you?"

"Yeah, I'm late. What of it?"

"Nothing. Just making conversation." She turned and was gone.

He had left the hospital that morning and returned to the neighborhood of his tiny apartment in Ventura. Three blocks from the place he called home was the restaurant he frequented almost every day. Bernard didn't pay him enough to afford a decent place in Santa Barbara. He couldn't afford this place if his father didn't send a bimonthly stipend to supplement his salary. Gordon was no fool. He knew the twice-monthly "support" was an effort to make sure he didn't return home. That was fine with Gordon. The only person more demanding than dear old Uncle Peter was Gordon's father.

Thinking of his father only fueled the heat of anger that was percolating in him. Normally he left the hospital at eight, stopped by the local Denny's for a quick bite, returned to his apartment, and slept until three or four in the afternoon. Today was different. He had to wait for his uncle to show, had to speak to the police, had to listen to his uncle describe the depths of Gordon's stupidity and ineptitude. Gordon didn't leave until nearly 11:00. He should be asleep instead of ordering eggs that would be tasteless, toast that had only been touched by butter, and coffee that was bitter as unripe plums. Working graveyard was taxing, especially if one liked to hit a nightclub or two before showing up at work.

This morning, Gordon wasn't sleepy. He should be. He loved sleeping. Always had. From the time he was a teenager he could spend twelve hours in bed without guilt. His father had called him lazy. Gordon never argued. So what if he was. But he was only lazy about what others wanted. When he desired something, he could be tenacious as a pit bull. He could feel that tenacity well up in him. Gordon could endure many insults, ignore scores of disdaining glances, tolerate the low opinion others held of him, but he could not bear being embarrassed by someone he considered his lesser. Julie Waal fell into that category.

Had the woman simply escaped while he was on duty, then he would have shrugged and said, "It happens." But she outsmarted him, gouged his leg, struck his head with a chair, and embarrassed him in front of his uncle and the whole hospital staff. That could not be allowed to stand.

When he left the hospital, he had told himself that the police would find her and that would be the end of that. Now he had doubts. The woman was far more clever than he had thought. She might be able to elude the police, to skirt their search. Assuming they really did conduct a search. The police force was small and had many other things on their plate. They would keep an eye out for her, but he was certain they would not extend themselves to looking under bridges and searching backstreets. It was possible that Julie Waal could make a successful escape. That wouldn't go over well with the senator. Not that what had already happened would be any better.

Somewhere out there was The Woman. That's how he thought of her now. Using her name gave her too much dignity, made her too much of a person. She lost that privilege when she stood up to him in the cafeteria. He should have been more careful, more circumspect, but such caution was not his way.

Besides, she was just a woman who spent her days drugged and confined to her room. How was he to know that she was violent? Gordon thought for a moment, then decided that he should have hit her and hit her hard. He could have later claimed that she had fallen or attributed whatever bruises there were to self-infliction. Other patients did it. Everyone would have believed him if that was the lie he told.

"Here ya go," the waitress said, plunking down a well-used plate in front of him. The eggs looked just right—for a change. "You want more coffee?"

"Have you started serving coffee here? I'm not sure what's in that pot, but it ain't real coffee."

"You don't have to order it, you know," she answered. "Some people get tea, others orange juice."

"I'm a creature of habit," Gordon snapped back as he reached for the salt and pepper. He hadn't answered her question, but she filled his cup anyway.

"Aren't we all?" she said without emotion. "Aren't we all?"

Gordon dismissed her with a wave of a hand and began mixing his food, stirring in pieces of egg with the hash browns. It was an odd practice and Gordon didn't know anyone else who did it, but he did. Every breakfast, he mixed and cut until his plate was covered in a mass of commingled foods; then and only then could he eat.

"Creature of habit," he mumbled to himself. Bits of food dropped from his mouth to the plate. Something was tickling the back of his mind, like a feather from a pillow tickling a sleeper's ear. "Creature of habit," he said aloud.

It struck him like a hand to the back of the head. Maybe, just maybe The Woman was a creature of habit, too. If so, then he might get a lead on her. And if he got to her first, he would prove just how useful he was and Uncle Bernard would have to eat some of his own words.

But where? What habit? *She wanted out of the hospital, wanted out real bad,* he reasoned. Who could blame her?

Gordon hated it and he only worked there. She had to live there—if you could call that living. Living? Those confined in the institute sane enough to know where they were always talked about home . . . going home. Could that be where she was headed?

Slipping a cell phone from his pocket he made a call back to the hospital. The receptionist answered.

"Yeah, this is Gordon. Let me talk to Benny."

"Just a moment," the receptionist said. Gordon thought he detected a smirk in her voice. A moment later, Benny came on the line. Benny did during the day what Gordon did at night, except Benny found some kind of satisfaction in the work. *To each their own,* Gordon thought.

"Yo, Gordy," Benny said loudly.

"Hey, Benny, I need a favor."

"A favor, eh?" The employee sounded suspicious.

"Yeah. Dr. Bernard has me working on this Julie Waal thing. I guess you heard about it." Gordon tried to sound casual.

"I heard. Gotcha with a chair, I hear."

"Yeah," Gordon admitted. "I let my guard drop."

Benny laughed. "I guess so. Must've left a mark."

"I got a lump out of the deal, that's for sure. Anyway, I've got to get to work on this thing. I need Julie Waal's home address." Gordon sensed hesitancy. "I meant to get it before I left, but I forgot. Must be the head wound. I'm already in Ventura and I don't want to have to drive all the way back. Come on, pal. Do me the favor."

"Hang on, I gotta call up the database."

The clicking of a computer keyboard came over the line. "Got a pencil and paper?"

Gordon didn't need one. He would not forget these numbers. "I'm ready." He closed his eyes and listened as Benny gave number and street. "Thanks, bud. I owe you one."

"You owe me a hundred." The line went dead.

"Carpenteria," Gordon said softly. He knew the town. It was a residential area south of Santa Barbara and north of Ventura. It was between his house and the hospital. It would not be hard to find. Not hard at all.

Gordon inhaled the rest of his breakfast.

CHAPTER

THIRTEEN

The din of the previous hours had, at least for the moment, lulled into a quiltlike quiet. Marcus welcomed it. At 8:15 that morning, Marcus had called Bob Brink, the chairman of deacons at the Central Missionary Baptist Church where his father had been pastor. The conversation had been short and to the point. Marcus spoke with a softness and gentleness that belied the emotional Armageddon that went on in his heart. "Brother Brink, this is Marcus Stiller. I wanted . . . I need to let you know that my father passed away late last night."

The news was greeted, not with tears, not with a display of abject sorrow, but with respectful silence. A moment later the deacon utter a single word: "Homegoing." It was a church term Marcus had heard often in his youth. It was a word that his father had uttered many times. No one died at the Central Missionary Baptist Church; they went home.

"Yes," Marcus had managed to say.

"And your mother?" Brink asked. Marcus knew the man well. He had been in the church when the Stiller family first arrived. He was known for impeccable honesty and an unflappable demeanor. He was also a man of few words, as if God had given him only so many to use and he, now close to his own homegoing, was fearful of running out.

"She's doing well. You know Mom."

"I do. Yes, I surely do. She's a strong one. Just like your daddy was. I'll miss him."

"We all will, Brother Brink."

"What can we do?"

The "we" referred to the church. Marcus was aware of what would happen next. Growing up in a minister's home had prepared him. He would hang up the phone, and Brother Brink would make a call or two. Within the hour, most of the church would know that their pastor had died. That's when the calls would come. That's when the doorbell would begin to ring. That's when the hustle and bustle that had carried so many other people who had lost loved ones through the storm of sadness would rush through his mother's house. Marcus would have preferred to be alone, but that was impossible.

"There's nothing to be done right now," Marcus said. "We have some calls to make and the funeral to plan."

"I understand. You call me. You need anything, anything at all, then you call me."

"I will, Brother Brink."

Marcus had been right. The phone began to ring ten minutes later. It rang unceasingly after that. The only time the device wasn't chiming was when Marcus was on the phone to the mortuary. The funeral home's representative asked that they come down to make final arrangements. He also gave them a list of things to discuss. Who would perform the service? Would it be a memorial service, or graveside, or both? Will the casket be opened or closed? Had he made previous arrangements? What clothing should his father be buried in? The list seemed intolerably long, and while the representative was polite and sympathetic, Marcus could not help but think he was going through the motions he had gone through daily for years.

Now Marcus sat on the sofa, Lucy by his side. Six other people, all from the church, were seated on the love seat and dining room chairs that had been brought into the living room. One chair, the one Marcus's father always sat in, remained empty. Three of the visitors were women of Abigail's age. They had arrived within an hour of Marcus's call to Brother Brink and entered the house with tears streaming and handkerchiefs at the ready. Abigail greeted each one with a kiss on the cheek and an offer of refreshment. All declined. All wept. All chatted endlessly. Also there were Brother Brink and two deacons.

The conversation centered on their sorrow over the loss and the great memories they had of Pastor Stiller. "Do you remember that time the fire alarm went off in the sanctuary?" one of the ladies asked. "It was a horrible sound. It even woke up some of the deacons." There was gentle laughter. "Pastor Stiller never missed an opportunity to make a point about the Gospel. Right there, right on the spot with that piercing wail from the fire alarm, he says, 'If that sound were the sound of the last trumpet, would you be ready?'" This brought a heartier laugh.

The minutes oozed by in a thick trickle. Marcus was feeling weary, the strain becoming heavier with each passing moment. A solitary man, Marcus hated gatherings and groups. The only exceptions were the classes he taught. But that was different. That was a neutral setting, composed of people he barely knew, and one in which he controlled the conversation. There was no control here, just a steady stream of visitors and the unending ringing of the phone.

Abigail took it all in stride. Her voice was strong, her attention sharp, and her hospitality in high gear. Tears ran down her face from time to time, but she wiped them away as quickly as they came. Watching his mother, Marcus realized that she was by far the stronger of the two. He wondered where her strength came from.

The sun continued to rise in the sky, pouring its effulgence on Marcus's dark world. The higher the sun rose, the dimmer his emotions became. When his father had died, he immediately became concerned for his mother. That concern shielded him from the truth before him. Like an astronaut's space suit, it provided a cocoon of protection from the deadly cold and vacuum of personal loss. Now that he could see his mother persevering through the strain, unbending before the sorrow, he was left to deal with his own emotions. For the most part, Marcus hated emotion.

Unlike the character Spock in the old television show *Star Trek*, Marcus did not deny he had emotions, nor did he try to suppress them. He simply did his best to avoid them. The only feelings he truly enjoyed without reservation were those he felt for his wife, Lucy. He adored her more now than when they had married. In this bottomless abyss of sadness, she sat by his side doing everything perfectly. She wept when he did, she sat quietly when he did, and she held him when he needed it. Even now, she held his hand and sat close, as if to protect him from the crowd she knew made him uncomfortable.

Marcus wished they would go home. He did not dislike the people. They were wonderful on many levels. They came because they cared. They stayed to lend their strength to those who had been weakened by death's visit. These were noble people. Still, Marcus would have preferred solitude.

"You know, Marcus," one of the ladies was saying. She was a big woman and had taken her place on the love seat, next to Deacon Brink. Marcus had been lost in thought and would have missed the fact that he was being addressed if Lucy had not given his hand a good squeeze. "It's a shame you didn't go into the ministry like your father. You could have followed him into the pulpit. I know the church would have welcomed you with arms open wide." She illustrated this comment by throwing wide her substantial arms, startling Deacon Brink.

"I'm afraid I'm not the preacher type," Marcus said politely.

"Don't write it off just yet, sweetheart," the woman said. "Your daddy came to the work after the Navy was done with him. You might get started yet."

Marcus smiled, then said, "Thank you, but I have a job."

"This is no job, sweetie," the woman went on. "This is a calling."

Marcus didn't want to have this conversation. Some in the church, mostly the elderly women, had assumed that Marcus would slip into the ministry just as his father had, and since they assumed it, they believed it could be no other way. Several in the church had shown shock when it became known that he was going off to Caltech to study astronomy. It had been no surprise to his parents, but it was earthshaking news to some of the members—as if Moses had said no to the Burning Bush. One Sunday, Marcus overheard a conversation between his father, and the very woman who sat in his mother's living room.

"Astronomy, Pastor?" she had said. "He's going into godless science?"

"There's nothing godless about science, sister," his father had replied.

"But it's wrong for a man to avoid the call of God on his life and not go into the ministry."

His father had nodded. "It's just as wrong to go into it if God has called a man to do something else." Then with the laugh that was famous around the church he added, "Let's let God do the calling and we do the listening." That ended the conversation for his father. It didn't end it for Marcus.

"Yes," the woman said, "I do believe you'd make a great preacher. Maybe even as good as your father."

Marcus nodded, then said, "Thank you, but maybe we should let God do the calling and we do the listening."

The woman tilted her head at the comment, then Marcus saw the light of understanding come on. She remembered what his father had said to her many years before.

"God's hand is on Marcus," Abigail said. "He works in each of us differently. That's his way. God has not lost sight of Marcus or any of us."

"Amen," Brink said. "Amen."

The room fell into an awkward and uncomfortable silence. Marcus tapped his foot on the floor and mindlessly drummed his fingers on his thigh. He tried to avoid eye contact. He knew the question on their minds, but as yet had not given it voice. He saw it in their eyes when they entered the house, but they had not asked. As the minutes turned into an hour, Marcus sensed that their resolve was crumbling like an old and strained earthen dam. Each moment that passed meant the dam was closer to giving way.

These were smart people. They watched the news; they read the papers. They knew that the son of their beloved pastor was famous even if it had only been for less than a day. Something was happening to the Moon, something never before seen. Like every man, woman, and child on the planet, they wanted to know what was going on. Marcus couldn't blame them. He wanted to know, too.

The questions that certainly perched in their minds like crows lined up on a telephone wire remained unasked. For not only were these smart people, self-aware and socially aware, but they were kind souls, too. They had not come to ask questions about the mysterious Moon. They had come to mourn with a woman who had just lost her husband of forty-two years, to grieve with a son who had lost a father, and to lament the departing of their longtime pastor. Their Christian nobility would not allow the questions that burned within them to be asked. Marcus admired them for that.

Still, the question would be asked sooner or later. One of them, being human, would break the unspoken prohibition and let slip, "So, Marcus, what is that on the Moon? Is it some kinda alien fungus or something?"

Marcus didn't want to be asked questions, especially ones to which he had no answers. His mind was in turmoil, as if all his thoughts and emotions had been dropped in a blender full of marbles. On the outside, he maintained the air of reason and logic, of control and rock-steady courage. Inside, he was Jell-O that had been left in the summer sun. He decided it was time to make his escape.

Rising from the sofa, Marcus stretched his back, then said, "I need to make some calls. I'm going to use Dad's study. Is that okay, Mom?" His mother nodded but did so only after a moment's pause. Marcus had lied, and his mother knew it. There was no condemnation in her glance, just a knowing. Marcus excused himself and disappeared into his father's familiar study.

○ ◐ ● ● ● ◑ ○

JULIE CONTINUED TO WANDER THE BEACH. In October, only die-hard swimmers, surfers, and tourists were out. The morning had been cool, but the sun warmed the area to the low seventies. At least the fall weather was nice. That was all that was good about the day. She had walked a few miles south along the shore, strolling casually like any meditative beachgoer. Her goal was to be inconspicuous. Walking along the sand in bare feet was a common sight. Once she left the beach, however, it would be a different matter.

"What now?" she asked herself for what must have been the one-hundredth time. As yet, no good answers came. Her mind was still filled with the fog that had been her companion since first setting foot in the mental hospital. She could think, could reason, could put two and two together, but it took effort and wearisome focus. Interfering was the witch's brew of emotion that roiled inside her. She was angry at her husband, fearful of Gordon and the hospital staff, untrusting of the police, and confused about her own state of mind.

As her emotions boiled, she became more perplexed. She had been able to plan her escape and execute it despite Gordon's efforts to interfere. In that, she was lucky, but now she was alone on a nearly deserted beach. Her plans had not reached this far, nor could they. Long-range thoughts had been difficult of late. For months her bloodstream had coursed with sedatives and medications. Her mind had become a yo-yo between misty thoughts and rational, coherent thinking. The good news was that the clouds that shadowed her mind seemed to be thinning.

Of one thing she was certain—she couldn't wander the beach forever. Her last meal had been dinner the night before. She felt no hunger now, but she knew she would. There was no food to be found on the beach, and digging through trash cans was not only demeaning but also sure to cause suspicion. The shore was her haven, but not for long. She had to determine a destination, make a plan no matter how hopeless its success.

Sitting on the sun-warmed sand, Julie stared out across the ocean. *Maybe I should give up the plan,* she thought. *Maybe this life isn't worth it.* The ocean beckoned her. The water would be cold, but that didn't matter. She could strip herself of her clothing, slip into the water, and begin swimming. She was a good swimmer, strong and graceful in the water. At home, they had a pool and she had used it daily, making laps back and forth for thirty minutes without a break. Daniel had often said she should try out for a triathlon, and she would have, if she liked jogging. She didn't. She had no doubt she could handle the swimming leg of things, but would never be able to jog a marathon and ride a bike for 100 miles. No, she'd stick to swimming, thank you very much.

Where was Daniel now? she wondered. Walking the corridors of the state capitol building in Sacramento? Sequestered in his darkly paneled office, weighing matters of state? Why wasn't he here with her when she most needed him? Why had he cut his visits down to just the occasional ten-minute "how-do-you-do"? Despair rose in Julie like bile. So what if she had made good her escape. To what had she escaped? She had nothing but unwanted solitude, fear, anxiety, paranoia, and visions that crippled her mind.

She had escaped the hospital, but she had not escaped her bondage. The chains were still pulled tight around her soul. She was not free. She had no liberty. She carried her prison with her. It followed her wherever she went.

The call of the ocean increased. The waves were small, gentle rollers that tumbled to the sand in a rhythmic, hypnotic dance. Music emanated from each collapsing wave: eerie, soothing, beckoning music. It summoned her to its embrace. How easy it would be to slip beneath the surface and start swimming. One stroke would follow another, each propelling her body through the briny water, taking her farther and farther from shore. She would weary quickly, but that would be all right. That was the plan, the goal, and the purpose of it all. A half a mile out, maybe more, her arms would be too tired to push against the water, her feet too weary to kick. That's when it would happen. There, somewhere in the cold and wet, she would give up. She might be able to tread water for a while, but her body would not be able to sustain it. There was a limited amount of energy in her tissue. When that ran dry, she would slip beneath the blue-green surface. She would struggle at first. That was normal, but it would last only seconds. Then her lungs would demand to breathe, but find only salt water. Water would rush into her lungs; darkness would flood her mind.

It would be over.

The thought of her pool at home came to the forefront of her mind. Pool. Home. Something began to make sense. Home. The fog lifted another inch in her mind. Home was in Carpenteria. Carpenteria was close to Santa Barbara, ten, maybe twelve miles. It was a long way to walk, but not impossible. What was it she had read somewhere? The average man walks about three miles an hour. Of course that was an average man with average shoes on his feet and an average straight path. Still . . .

At two miles an hour, she could walk twelve miles before the sun went down, and she could make most of the distance along the shoreline. There were areas of private beach she would have to skirt somehow, but so what? She was no worse off a few miles closer to home than where she was right now.

Something else bothered her, but it was lodged in the back of her mind. Closing her eyes, she drove out all other thoughts and waited, hoping that the reluctant thought would relent and show itself. It did. Home was a dangerous place. The police would search for her there. It was only logical. Isn't that what people did when they escaped a place they hated? Didn't they go to a familiar place?

"So what?" she said to the ocean. "So what?" The police could find her here as well, or on some street. If she made her way home, maybe, just maybe she could enjoy a day, an hour, or five minutes in the only place she had ever felt secure, the place where love once flourished, the place called home.

The ocean called out to her again, and once more she considered the one-way swim. Then she rose and turned a deaf ear to the water's siren call. "Not today," she said. "I'm going home."

◗ ◗ ◗ ● ● ◗ ◖ ◖

THE HOME OFFICE OF JAMES STILLER always reminded Marcus of old family sitcoms he would watch on television. The father would come home after work, kiss the kids, hug his wife, slip out of his suit coat, don a light sweater, and then, while Mom cooked supper, head into his office to do whatever television dads did. There he would dispense wisdom like an ancient oracle.

"Am I in trouble, Dad?"

"Well, Beav, you know what you did was wrong and you hurt Mrs. Benson's feelings. I really should punish you."

"Gee, I know, Dad, but I'm real sorry."

Then Hugh Beaumont would smile the smile of fatherly love, pat the Beav on the head, and say, "Well, I guess we can let it go this time, but I want you to apologize to Mrs. Benson first thing tomorrow."

"Okay, Dad, I will. I promise."

Life would then resume its happy and peaceful course.

James Stiller was no Hugh Beaumont. He had spent most of Marcus's childhood in the Navy and was gone for long stretches of time, leaving Abigail to provide parental direction. Not that that was bad. No man could have asked for a better mother. Still, his father was absent much of the time. When he was home, he radiated love, gave praise freely, and expected proper and disciplined behavior from his son. Marcus tried to remember a time when his father had lost his temper—not just become irritated, but had truly gone over the edge. He could not think of a single instance.

Marcus knew other Navy families; some were good like his, and others were wretched. He appreciated his father, who seemed always to have time for him. Often, while his father worked at the large, scarred oak desk in the middle of the bedroom-converted-to-office, Marcus would play with his toy cars or building blocks on the shag carpeted floor. The shag carpet was gone, replaced by a beige, low-pile rug. The desk remained. The books were there too. James was an avid reader, and the shelves that ran along two of the walls were filled with books of history and theology.

Behind the desk was an old oak desk chair with curved slats for the back. It had belonged to Marcus's grandfather, who had died much too young. Marcus sat in his father's chair. It squeaked loud enough that he was sure the others heard it even through the closed door.

Marcus spread his hands on the desk. Its oak surface was smooth and dust free. His father had not been in this room for many months, but it looked fresh, clean, and ready for his return. There would be no return. Looking at the bookshelves, Marcus saw they too were tidy, without a speck of dust. Abigail had been cleaning in here, something he imagined she did daily.

On the walls were pictures of family events, several of James in his uniform, and diplomas from high school and Bible college. One photo caught his eye. It showed his father at full weight and height, not the diminished shell Marcus had seen over the last months. He was holding up a tiny fish, no longer than four inches. Beside him stood ten-year-old Marcus holding a trout that was a foot if it was an inch. Marcus laughed to himself. He remembered the trip very well. It was taken at Lake Poway, a small reservoir that was periodically stocked with trout.

They often fished when James wasn't out to sea. Sometimes they would gather together family and friends and spend most of a Saturday floating in a rented boat, their lines dipped deep in the water. On that particular trip, Marcus out-fished his father by catching the most and the largest fish. Dad could only manage to reel in the tiny fish shown in the picture.

"Well, I was just fishing for bait," James had said. "Had I known we were in a contest, then I would have given you a run for your money." From that day on, his father always referred to Marcus as "Ahab" when they went fishing. Marcus wished he could hear that name one more time.

Marcus was uncomfortable. There was a burning just above his stomach and he felt light-headed. For a moment, he thought he might be getting ill, but the sensation soon identified itself. His nose filled with mucus and his eyes began to water. So far he had avoided the harshest emotions of sadness and remorse, but they would not be denied. Sitting alone in the office that defined his father, Marcus felt overwhelmed. Everything he saw, everything he touched, even the smell of the room, reminded him of his father.

Leaning back in the chair, Marcus let his eyes take in the room. It was a warm feeling, which brought his emotions to the surface. It was here that his father studied for the ministry after leaving the Navy. It was here that he prepared sermons every Saturday (those in which they didn't go fishing), and it was here that he and his father had heart-to-heart talks. When Marcus had decided that he wanted to pursue a career in the sciences, he came to this room to inform his dad and found words of encouragement and support.

His eye fell on several books that sat on the right corner of the desk. One was a commentary on the New Testament book of Galatians; another was a hardbound study Bible. "Always, the student, eh, Dad?" There was another book. This one had no title on the spine or front cover. Marcus reached for it and gently, as if he were opening state secrets, pulled back the cover. It was one those bound volumes that held lined, blank pages. At first he thought it was a diary and started to put it down. Inside was the familiar scrawling of his father. He read the first few lines of the first page and quickly discovered that what he held was not a diary but a set of study notes from his father's personal Bible study. Looking up from the thin volume, he saw a dozen other such tomes in one of the bookshelves. Returning his attention to the book, he leafed through its pages, impressed by the detail and logic he saw. There were very few complete sentences, but scores of short notations. Marcus realized that he held the handwritten thoughts of his father.

"I want you to have that," a voice said from the door.

So mesmerized by the simple book that he barely heard the door to the office open, Marcus jumped. "You scared me, Mom."

"I'm sorry. I should have knocked."

"No, that's all right, I was just looking at Dad's notes." Marcus's startled heart settled. "What was it you said?"

"I want you to have that, Marcus," Abigail replied. She entered the room and closed the door behind her. "That one and the others, too. He would have wanted you to take them."

Marcus wasn't sure what to say. "I don't know, Mom. These must be precious to you."

"I have other precious things to remember him by." She approached the desk.

"Here, sit down." Marcus got up from the chair.

"No, sir, you sit down. I've been sitting all morning. My feet have forgot that I have blood. I need to stretch."

Marcus smiled at his mother's humor. "The others still here?"

She nodded. "Lucy is keeping them entertained."

"I'm sorry to bail on you. I'm uncomfortable in groups. Especially right now."

"I know. You've always preferred your own company. Nothing wrong with that." She took a deep breath and looked around the room. "All these books. He loved them. Every night, he'd sit in the living room with some book on his lap. One time, I got mad at him and said, 'You give those books more attention than you do me. I think if you had to choose between your books and your wife, you'd choose the books.'" She laughed. "He said, 'Not hardly. You cook better than they do.'" She laughed a little more, softly, then her mood turned somber. "He reached over and took my hand. 'Baby,' he said. 'You're stuck with me forever. And that's just the way I like it.'"

Marcus saw tears well up in his mother's eyes. He felt the same happen to his own. "He loved you more than life itself, Mom. You know that, don't you?"

"I know it. The same can be said about you. He was always talking about you. Always. He thought you had a great mind. He was right, you know. Take the books home with you,

Marcus. That's what he wanted. That's what I want. A son should have something of his father."

"I have everything of my father in my heart," Marcus said, and for a moment he thought the sturdy dam he had built against his emotions was going to give way, flooding the room. It held. "Are you going to be okay tonight?"

"I'll be fine. Lucy has to get back to her work. You have business to take care of—this whole Moon thing." She paused, and then continued. "It's a shame your father dying when he did. He'd be curious about the Moon and whatever it is that's making it red. He'd ask you so many questions you wouldn't be able to think straight."

"He'd find a way to work it into his sermons, too." His father was well known for sneaking current events into his messages.

"We could bet on that."

Marcus rose and walked around the large desk, taking his mother in his arms. She seemed as frail as a December leaf. "It'll be all right, Mom. We'll make it through this. If you want, you can come and live with Lucy and—"

She pushed away from his embrace. "Oh, no, I won't. I've lived on my own too long. That's all your house needs, two women knocking around in the kitchen."

Marcus started to remind her that he spent more time in the kitchen than Lucy, but he let it go. "Okay, I'm just letting you know the door is always open."

She returned to his embrace and silence covered them. Marcus couldn't remember how long it had been since he had given his mother a good hug. He was determined it wouldn't be that long again.

CHAPTER
FOURTEEN

Gordon rounded the corner in his white Ford Taurus and slowly drove past Julie Waal's house. The home had been easy to find once he had the address. Leaving the Denny's, Gordon had taken a leisurely drive up Highway 101 to Carpenteria. Ironically, he had passed the bedroom community when he left work that morning. There was no need to rush. The Woman was on foot, and it was doubtful that she could have made the distance from the hospital in Santa Barbara south to Carpenteria. The distance was less than twelve miles. He supposed it

could be made by someone in good shape and unhindered by
fear, but although enough hours had passed for her to walk
home, she would have had to do so without hiding. And she was
hiding. He knew that. He could feel it. The woman was paranoid but she wasn't stupid. She would know that the police had
been called. Hiding and moving slowly was her only option.

He wondered if someone could have given her a ride. It was
possible. Some Good Samaritan might see her as a damsel in dis-
tress and give her a lift to the house, but that too was unlikely.
Julie trusted no one. Besides, it didn't really matter. So what if she
got there before him? It would save him some time. As it was, he
was ready to stake out the home. He had even picked up a
couple bags of chips and some soda from a convenience store in
town. While there, he also picked up a map. The street was easy
to find. He was ready to spend the day waiting.

The house was situated in an upscale part of town. It was
a two-story structure and looked brand new. Gordon decided
that Senator Waal spent a fortune keeping up the place, especially since his nutty wife was not there to keep house for him.
The lawn was an immaculate carpet of green. Long flowerbeds
accented the yard with yellow, red, and orange. It was the kind
of house that appeared on expensive design magazines.

Gordon did a slow drive-by and immediately noticed the
familiar markings of a police car parked at the curb. He swore.
He wanted to be the one to find her. He had a point to prove.
She escaped on his watch, something that embarrassed him in
front of his uncle and the other employees. No one had said anything, but he knew the other workers—maybe even some of the
patients—were talking about him. He had to prove that he
couldn't be pushed around, especially not by some crazy woman.

He wasn't afraid of the police. In some ways, he had a
right to be there. The Woman had been a charge of his, so it
was natural for him, as a health-care professional, to come to
the house to check on her well-being. The brutal truth of the
matter was that Gordon hated cops. They were just one more

unwanted source of authority in his life. He hated the way they walked around with godlike superiority, their leather belts weighed down with pepper spray, handcuffs, and a gun, each saying, "Don't mess with me, boy, or I'll haul you in and throw you in the darkest part of the jail." No, if he could avoid speaking to the police, then he would.

Their presence, however, revealed important information: Julie was still on the loose. The opportunity to prove himself was still open, unless, of course, they walked out of the house with her.

Gordon slipped by the house and took in as much as he could see. Two police officers were walking across the front lawn. Apparently they had knocked on the door and had received no answer; now they were searching the side yards. Unless Gordon missed his guess, they would also go around back and look for signs of Julie. Finding none, and he doubted they would, they would probably go house to house. Gordon pulled to the end of the street, made a U-turn, and then parked at the far corner. He was now five houses down from the home and across the street. He would wait. He hated waiting, but he had no choice; he wasn't dealing this hand of cards.

From his parked car, Gordon could see the front of the house. Trees that lined the walkway obscured a small portion of the structure, but he could see enough. The officers, as expected, emerged from the back, walked to the sidewalk, then split up, each making his way to a neighbor's house. *Predictable,* Gordon thought. He doubted they would get much information. It was a workday and most of the houses would be empty. Still, he knew the police would try, which was fine with him. *Let them do the work,* he reasoned. *I'll just sit and take it easy.*

He watched the two officers work their way up and down the street. For a moment, he thought they would come as far as his car, something he didn't want. He had no desire to speak to the police. Just as he was about to start his car and pull away to avoid contact, the officer nearest him turned and hustled back to the cruiser. Moments later the light bar on the roof of the police car came to life. A second after that they were gone, speeding down the street to some urgent call. Gordon heard the sirens go on. Some more pressing need had pulled them away. Gordon had not been seen, and he was happy about that.

JULIE'S FEET ACHED and her ankles were sore enough to bring tears. Before—that's how she divided time, before the hospital and after—she had enjoyed long walks through her residential neighborhood and strolls along the beach. But this was different; she was walking in coarse sand, mile after mile, her bare feet exposed to the sun and grinding action of the ground below her soles. Each step was more difficult than the previous. The tender skin of her feet was battered by her flight from the hospital, through the streets of Santa Barbara, and onto the shore. The sand was softer than the concrete and asphalt that had brutalized her soles, but the tiny pieces of rock ate at her feet, each one taking tiny bites. More than once, Julie had stopped to see if she were leaving a trail of blood behind her. So far, she wasn't, but she felt such a trail could begin at any moment.

To fight off the nagging reminders of pain, Julie imagined her house, the place she had spent so many happy years. The gingerbread exterior was clear as a postcard in her mind. She could see the dark bands of wood trim that so elegantly accented the white stucco. The front yard was small, but covered in a thick grass the color of jade. In back the yard was larger and accented with a flower garden that she had put in with her own hands, weeded weekly, watered lovingly, pruned kindly. That had been eighteen months ago, eighteen full moons. She wondered if Daniel had kept the garden up. She doubted it. How could he water plants in Carpenteria, when he spent most of the year in the state capitol? A dark sadness flooded her as she imagined her exquisitely landscaped backyard given over to weeds.

Surely, Daniel wouldn't let that happen. He loved the house as much as she and had said so on many occasions. He must have hired someone to maintain the garden, if for no other reason than to keep the property value up.

Julie pushed herself forward along the beach. So far she had been able to stay along the shoreline, but she knew that there were several areas ahead where the water came to low, sheer cliffs. She had no idea if she would be able to continue at that point. If the tide were out, there might be enough sand to walk on without having to get wet. The idea of salt water on her raw feet made her ill. She pushed the thought aside and forced her mind to focus on other things. There were too many thoughts in her mind. She felt confused, overwhelmed. Too many desires, too many fears. The ocean still called to her. At times she even thought she could hear a voice in each wave that rolled to shore. She ignored the voices. She ignored the desire to sit and rest; she expelled any thoughts of stopping. Instead, she raised one foot and put it in front of the other. She did it again, and again, and again. The pain no longer mattered. It was, after all, just pain, and she had endured so much more.

So she thought of her garden, she dreamed of her home, she focused on the place where she had last sensed joy and felt happiness. Her place—Daniel's place.

A new feeling percolated to the top of her choppy sea of emotion: guilt—guilt over Daniel. What was Daniel thinking now? Surely Dr. Bernard had informed him of her escape. Was he worried? Was he frantic? Was he angry? The last year before her admission to the hospital he had been angry so often. Something had changed, something beyond her understanding. Daniel was a different man. His language had become coarse, his temper short, his patience even shorter. At some point, for some inscrutable reason, Senator Daniel Waal had stopped loving her. A warm tear, as salty as the ocean to Julie's right, ran down her cheek.

Monotony had been one of the hardest parts of the hospital stay. Between episodes, when her mind was clearer and less doped by injected drugs, she would lie upon her bed and daydream. The dream was always the same. Daniel would arrive at the hospital dressed in the white polo shirt and tan slacks she had bought him for his birthday, gently tap on the door of her room, turn the handle, and peek in.

"Hi, baby," he would say, broadcasting that smile of white and perfectly aligned teeth that had made him so popular with women voters. "What say you and me blow this joint?" Then he would move into the room. It was then that she would see that he was carrying a garment bag. Inside would be her favorite persimmon-colored pantsuit.

In the daydream she would rise from bed and be engulfed in his strong arms. "Daniel?" she would ask with uncertainty.

"I have plans for today," he would say softly. "First we leave here, then we go for a seafood lunch at Fisherman Jack's. We'll order shrimp and scallops. Then I'm taking you home."

"Not back to the hospital?"

"No, never back to the hospital," he would answer. "Never again. The nightmare is over."

He would help her dress. He would kiss her. He would hold her. Together they would walk out of the hospital and into a better future than she could have imagined.

Fairy-tale, a voice said in her head. *Childish wishful thinking.*

"I know," she said aloud. "I know."

Julie plodded on, her head down, tears falling to the dry sand. For a moment, she wished the sand would swallow her like it did her tears.

Julie took yet another step and wondered why Daniel had stopped loving her, why no one loved her.

DR. BARRY WENHAM HAD only been in the Oval Office twice
before and each of those for less than ten minutes, just long
enough to chat with the president and have a few pictures
taken. Beyond that, the only contact Wenham had with the
Executive Office was through e-mail and the occasional report.
Being science advisor was not a full-time job. Being summoned
to the president's primary place of business was more than a
little disconcerting, even though Wenham had expected it. It
was only a matter of time.

President Larry Rendel was seated in a leather wing chair
near the center of the oval-shaped room. Behind him was a
large desk. To his right sat two men in suits, one gray, and the
other dark blue. Rendel wore an ivory shirt with a blue silk tie
and charcoal-colored suit. The tie had been loosened at the
neck. They were involved in a discussion when Wenham
entered the room.

"Come in," the president said. He stood and shook hands.

"Good afternoon, Mr. President," Wenham said after
clearing his throat. He was more nervous than he had been on
his wedding day.

"Thanks for coming," Rendel said. "Please have a seat."
He motioned to another sofa that sat opposite the one occu-
pied by the two men. "You know Bob Sherman from the State
Department and Teddy Thomson, my chief of staff."

"Yes, we've met," Wenham said, then thought, *Never in
a meeting, though. What was the assistant secretary of state
doing in this meeting?* He could understand Teddy's presence;
he was in most meetings. That was one of the things the chief
of staff did. But the State Department was a different matter.

Rendel took his seat again and picked up a file folder.
"We've read your report and have a few questions."

"I hope I can be of some help."

"Good. Let's get down to brass tacks," the president said.
He looked at Teddy and nodded. Teddy was to be the inquisi-
tor. Wenham had heard stories of the president's manner of

operation. He was an observer with a keen mind who wasted little time. Rendel had been a military man, educated at Annapolis; he served his country abroad as a pilot in the Navy. He retired at the age of forty-five and immediately ran for congress in his district of Arizona. Three terms later, he ran and won a seat in the U.S. Senate. After two terms in the upper house he made a surprising run for the White House. At the age of sixty, he narrowly beat out his Democratic opponent in a hotly contested race. That was two years ago. Rendel had grown in the office, indeed, thrived. Unlike most presidents, he looked neither older, nor worse for wear. Instead, he had shed a few extra pounds, gained a tan, and taken up racquetball.

Teddy Thomson was five years the president's junior. A lawyer who preferred politics, he had once been the head of the Republican party. When he wasn't politicking, he was making millions in industrial real estate. Rumors floated around D.C. about Teddy. It was said he could sweet-talk butter out of milk or curdle it with a word. No one wanted to see him standing on his threshold. He could be demanding, even frightening. The prevailing joke was the Marine Corps wanted to clone him to create a master race of drill sergeants. The only man not intimidated by Teddy was the president.

"Why?" Teddy began.

Wenham was nonplussed. "Excuse me?"

"Why the spot on the Moon?" Teddy's words were blunt.

Wenham shook his head. "No one knows. It's too early. I have the Naval Observatory looking into the matter. They don't have the best equipment, but they're in contact with those who do. With better instrumentation available, we might be able to come up with some answers."

"Is the observatory giving you all the help you need?" the president interjected. "Do I need to call them?"

"They've been very responsive," Wenham replied. He then watched the president motion to Teddy again. Wenham's stomach tightened. The chief of staff looked in a sour mood.

"When does it become visible?" Teddy inquired.

"Oh, well, it's visible now even with fairly small tele-scopes—"

"I mean to the naked eye, Doctor."

"Oh," Wenham said softly. How did he mistake such an obvious question? "I can't be sure."

"Guess."

Wenham took a deep breath, closed his eyes, and guessed. "At the current rate of spread, assuming no changes, a week."

"How much of the Moon will be covered then?"

"Percentage wise, I'd say five percent."

"Five percent. The naked eye can see that small a part of the lunar surface?"

"Well, it's more than you might think. The Moon has a diameter of 3,475 kilometers . . . about 2,159 miles through the equator. That means that it presents an area of sixty-eight hundred square miles . . . if it were a disk. It's a sphere, of course, so actually the surface area that we see is larger, but you get the idea."

"Yes, we get the idea." Teddy paused, then asked, "Can it be stopped?"

"Stopped?" Wenham almost laughed, but caught himself. How could anyone stop something happening on an object 240,000 miles away? His desire to laugh melted away when he realized that such a desperate question could only come from a deep need. What were they worried about? "No, it can't be stopped. Of course, it may just go away."

"Just go away?" Teddy parroted.

"Let me explain." Wenham took a deep breath. He was no astronomer and certainly no planetary geologist, but he did know how to gather information, assimilate facts, and find the right people to ask questions. He had prepared for this meeting. "Through the centuries, strange things have been seen on the Moon. Some have seen lights, moving dark spots, starlight flashes, red or orange discolorations, things like that. Most of the time, these are dismissed as faulty equipment, careless observations, interference from our own atmosphere, and such things. A few observations can't be explained away so easily. That being said, none of these observations are taken seriously. They come up; they disappear. That's pretty much it. The Stiller Enigma may do the same thing."

"Stiller Enigma?" the president asked.

Wenham shifted in his chair. "Yes, sir. Marcus Stiller. He's the astronomer who first discovered the aberration."

"What observatory is he with?" Teddy asked.

"He's not with an observatory," Wenham explained. "He teaches at a small liberal arts college in southern California.

"A small college!" Teddy said. "You mean it has no graduate program in science."

Wenham nodded. "Exactly. He was making observations from his home telescope."

"Why didn't one of the big universities see it first?" the president wanted to know.

"Not to put too fine a point on it, Mr. President, almost no one cares about the Moon anymore. There are more interesting things in the universe than a dry and dead Moon."

"Not anymore," Bob Sherman said, speaking for the first time since Wenham entered the Oval Office.

"I don't understand," Wenham admitted.

"Hang on, Bob," Teddy said. "I have a few more questions." He redirected his attention to Wenham. "When will we know the cause of the Stiller Enigma, as you call it?"

"I call it that because that has become the media's term for it. And Stiller did discover it, after all. I suppose he deserves the credit. As to when we will know the cause, I couldn't say. Since the news is out, many scientists are working on identification. They will run spectral analysis and other such observations, most of which are beyond my training. We might have some answers in a week or two, but they won't be conclusive."

"Why not?" Teddy asked.

"Astronomy is science done at a distance. None of it is hands-on, unlike disciplines such as biology, geology, and the like. Observations will be made, then published. The published findings will be reviewed by other astronomers and subject to verification, then—"

"That won't do, Doctor," Rendel said shaking his head. "That won't do at all. There's more here than a scientific curiosity. We can't wait for PBS to do a special *Nova* program on it. I need information now. I need facts and I need them in a steady stream."

"I'll do what I can," Wenham said slowly. There was something he wasn't seeing, but what?

"You're going to be busy for a while, I'm afraid," Rendel said. He leaned back in his chair and crossed his legs. "You know this is more than a spot on the Moon, don't you?"

"I'm afraid I don't."

"Tell him," Rendel directed Sherman.

The assistant secretary of state leaned forward and spoke in a soft monotone. "This spot . . . this Stiller Enigma . . . has been seen by others. We have messages from the French, the Brits, India, and scores of other countries. That's to be expected. The Moon does shine down on everyone, American and non-American alike. One message concerns us, though. It's the Russians. They think we've done something to the Moon."

Wenham laughed despite the tight control he tried to maintain. "That's ludicrous. Do they think we're putting carpet down on the lunar surface?"

No one else joined the laughter.

Sherman continued. "The world is a complex system, Dr. Wenham. It's all tied up in history, power, money, and more. The thing that holds it together isn't trust but fear. Anytime one country gets an edge, everyone else gets nervous. India, North Korea, and other places get the bomb, and we start losing sleep. We're the big kid on the block, Doctor, and we have been since World War I. Anytime something untoward happens in the world, people look at us. This isn't true for every country, but it's spot on for the Russians. They've not directly accused our country of anything, but the subtext is there."

"They must be crazy. How can they think we had anything to do with the Enigma?"

"Actually, Doctor, it's not that strange an assumption."

Wenham was confused. This didn't make sense. He was no politician, but he followed world events. The Russians were always edgy, but to blame the United States for messing up the Moon . . . well, it was moronic.

"Let me ask you something, Dr. Wenham," the president said. "How many non-Americans have walked the face of the Moon?"

"None."

"Exactly. There's millions of dollars of hardware on the Moon, Doctor, most of it made in this country."

"But the Russians have sent craft to the Moon."

The president nodded. "Yes, they did. When they were the Soviet Union, we were in the great space race, and we won. But by comparison, they have left a couple of ham radios up there, while we've dumped the equivalent of a used car lot." Wenham was confused by the analogy and Rendel must have picked up on it, because he continued. "What I'm saying is, our country put more hardware on the Moon than the rest of the world combined. We and we alone have left footprints there. Trip over a piece of hardware and you'll find a sign that says, 'Made in the USA.'"

"But they can't—"

"Yes, they can," Rendel said. "And they will. Not today. Not tomorrow, but if the smear continues to spread, then the world is going to need a whipping boy, and it's going to be us."

"Can't we just explain things in a rational manner? Surely the world can see the foolishness of such statements."

"The world," Teddy said, "will see what it wants to see."

"And explaining such things may not be much help," Rendel added. "All we can say is that we didn't do it, but how do we prove that? We don't even know what the thing is. For all we know, we *are* responsible. Maybe something we left behind started all this. Can you prove it didn't?"

"We have to prove our innocence?" Wenham asked.

"This is international politics, Doctor, not an American court of law." Teddy frowned as if showing disfavor upon a slow child. "No one can lay a defensible charge against us, but we could come off looking bad. Worse yet, our relations with the Russians have been on thin ice the last year. There have been some incidents that you're not aware of, that very few are aware of, that have strained our . . . friendship. Their leadership is paranoid. Do you remember that Russian submarine that went down back in 2000?"

"Yes," Wenham said. "The *Kursk*. The entire crew died."

"They didn't die immediately," Teddy said. "We offered help. We had the equipment that could have saved at least some of the crew, but the Russians wouldn't let us near it. They were afraid we would steal their secrets, and they were willing to let their sailors die to keep us from doing so."

"That's not all of it," Rendel added. "The Russians, and I'm sure the Chinese, will have a few things to say, but they may be the least of our problems. I'm more worried about public reaction."

"How so?" Wenham asked, but he had an idea where the president was headed.

"Do your remember the comet Hale-Bopp? Thirty-nine members of the cult group Heaven's Gate took their own lives back in late March of 1997. They did it in shifts over a period of a few days, with one group helping others take a lethal cocktail of phenobarbital and vodka. They felt the comet was a sign for them to shed their bodies, 'containers' as they called them, so they could join a spaceship that was hiding in the tail of the comet. Sounds impossible to believe when you say it right out loud, but it happened. People killed themselves because of a comet. Others heralded it as the beginning of the end. Late-night radio was filled with so-called experts who were certain that the appearance of the comet was an omen of the apocalypse. And that was for just a comet. What do you think will happen when the red spot on the Moon gets big enough for six billion people to see? Some will say, 'Now isn't that interesting?' Others will say, 'This is an historic event for science.' And a whole bunch of people are going to say, 'This is the end of the world.'"

The president had a point, and Wenham knew it, but what could be done about it? The spot was there. It was real. It was growing, and the news was out. There was no putting the genie back in the bottle now. "Education," Wenham offered.

"What's that you say?" Rendel asked. "Education?"

"Yes. We must be proactive. Talk about the Stiller Enigma in public. Educate the people about the Moon and how this is just a benign change. If we talk about it now, then there should be less irrational behavior later."

The president sighed. Teddy shook his head, and Sherman sat stone still. Wenham felt like a child who unknowingly used a bad word in the presence of adult company. "What?"

"That might work in a perfect world," Teddy said. "This is anything but a perfect world. Did you know that most people believe their government keeps secrets from them, that the White House, Congress, the Supreme Court, and everyone else in D.C. has a closet full of secrets? It's been almost sixty years since the 1947 incident at Roswell, New Mexico, and people still think that we have little gray men in a hangar somewhere in Texas or Colorado. There are more conspiracy theories today than ever before. It's trendy now. Contrails left in the sky by high-flying aircraft are now 'chemtrails' used by the government to forcibly inoculate its citizens, or to control the weather, or to do something else. The Internet is the tool of the Antichrist. Scientists have found Atlantis off the coast of Cuba but are keeping it to themselves. The list goes on. We can—"

"In other words," Rendel interrupted, "we can say what we want, but there will be those who will say we're keeping secrets from them. Just talking about it isn't going to be enough."

"What else can we do?" Wenham asked.

"That's the problem, Doctor. At the moment, there is nothing else we can do, but we must do something. That's where you come in. You're going to be a busy man. Before this is over, you're going to wish I had never appointed you as my science advisor."

Wenham was already wishing that. "What do you want me to do?"

"Get information. I am preparing a memo to go out to any and all government agencies that might know something about this. They will be instructed to cooperate with you fully. NASA, every university that gets money from the federal government, and any others I can think of will be at your disposal. I know you're not an astronomer, so pull some folks on board with you. Get this Stiller guy if you want. He discovered it; maybe he knows more than he's saying."

"I understand—," Wenham began.

"No, not yet you don't," Rendel insisted. "Your life just became busy. There will be reporters, press conferences, and interviews. You are to appear professional and informed at all times. If asked—and you will be asked—say that I am being apprised of the situation daily. There is no danger, of course, but I have a keen interest in such things. Got that?"

"Yes."

"If you're asked about the claims of the Russians, Chinese, Iranians, or any other group, you are to refer them to the State Department."

"Yes, sir."

Rendel fidgeted. He looked tired. "I have a bad feeling about this, Dr. Wenham. A real bad feeling."

Suddenly, so did Wenham.

CHAPTER

FIFTEEN

Marcus came in and closed the front door to his house like a man trying to lock out an attacker. He leaned against the door with his back and took a deep breath. There was no attacker, no pursuer; it was the world he wanted to lock out. In his hands were his father's notebooks, the ones his mother insisted that he take.

"Can I fix you anything?" Lucy asked. "A snack maybe?"

"No, thanks," Marcus said, pushing away from the entrance. "I'm still full from dinner." They had eaten dinner at his mother's—a dinner provided by ladies in the church—and then made the two-hour drive from San Diego to Pinewood. Although he had been gone less than a day, it felt especially good to be home. That relief was punctuated by sharp pangs of guilt. Part of him, a very large part, felt he should have stayed another night. The thought of his mother all alone in the house ate at him, but she had insisted.

"Your Lucy has to be at the hospital tomorrow and you have classes to teach," she had said in a tone Marcus knew allowed for no arguing. "I'll be fine. I love you, but you can't stay here forever. Get on with your life. The funeral is not till Wednesday."

Marcus was prepared to stay through the funeral, but his mother wouldn't hear of it. "You're only two hours away, not clear across the country," she had said. Marcus agreed that he and Lucy would go home after supper. His mother always called the evening meal supper, a Southern trait she had carried with her.

"Those church women know how to bake a casserole," Lucy said. "I'll be full of chicken and pasta for the next two days."

"It comes from years of competing in church potlucks." Marcus walked over to the sofa, set his stack of books on the coffee table, and then plopped down heavily. "My dad used to say that the sin of pride was why we always had such good food at church fellowships, one cook trying to outdo another. I asked him why he didn't say anything about it. He told me the eating was too good." Marcus laughed. "He didn't want to ruin a good thing."

"He was a wise man, your father."

"He was that, all right. Wisdom was his forte." He paused as thoughts of his father danced through his brain. "You know, I will have a glass of milk. Maybe it will make me sleepy. I'm wound tighter than a watch . . . if people still wind watches."

"Big glass or small?"

"Big."

"Okay, after that you're on your own." She moved to the kitchen and opened the refrigerator. "I'm going to bed. I have to go into the hospital early tomorrow, real early. I want to squeeze in six or seven hours of sleep."

Marcus looked across the room at a clock that hung on the wall above the television. It was 9:15, much too early for a night owl like him to call it an evening. "Okay. I think I'll go in the study and check my e-mail and phone messages."

Lucy brought a large tumbler of milk and handed it to her husband. "If there's anything from the hospital, be sure to let me know. I'll be in the shower, then I'm off to bed."

"Will do." He rose from the sofa and gave her a kiss on the lips. She paused for a moment, and then ran a gentle finger along his hairline. It was a simple gesture that said what words could not. She was in this with him all the way. Tragedy and unpleasantness had no effect on love.

Marcus watched Lucy walk to their bedroom, then he crossed the house and entered his office. He left the lights off, choosing to activate only his desk lamp. The fixture was an old style banker's lamp that cast white light to the desk and green light into the room. Marcus liked it dark. He set his father's books and the glass of milk on his desk.

Pushing the button that would start his computer, he sat at his desk. While the computer booted, he picked up the phone. There was a stutter tone meaning that the message service had calls for him. Dialing the number and the code, Marcus waited for the calls. There were thirty-two of them. *Thirty-two.* This was going to take awhile. He began listening to the messages and taking notes. Twelve calls were from friends and colleagues expressing their regrets at his father's passing. One was from the funeral home saying that the funeral director had a couple "tiny" questions. Eighteen calls were from the media. Newspapers from across the country including the *New York Times* and the *Chicago Tribune* as well as several local papers all wanted to ask a few questions. Several calls were from television stations and network programs including *Good Morning America*. The major news magazines had made contact too, *Newsweek*, *Time*, and *U.S. News & World Report*. There were even a few from strangers who had found his number through directory assistance and had been bold enough to call him at home to suggest ideas and offer opinions. Marcus hung up the phone and shook his head. As a rule, he hated the phone. Anybody could call at anytime and disrupt your life.

Turning his attention to the computer, he checked his e-mail. "Unbelievable!" he said aloud as if someone were in the room to hear him. A long list numbering 126 played before his eyes. Most of the e-mails were from the media, too, many duplicating what had been left on his message service. E-mail addresses could be discovered through reverse look-up services. The reporters had made good use of it. Quickly moving through the list he deleted them with the verve of a man mowing a field with a scythe. Marcus was now a famous man and he hated it.

"I'm not dealing with this stuff now," he said to himself. Instead, he shut down his e-mail program and activated the software that would allow him control of the sixteen-inch Starfinder from the comfort of his office. He had not been able to complete his observation of the Moon last night. It was time to have another look.

As they drove up the mountain, Marcus had shifted his gaze from the road to the sky. The Moon was rising high and would be in a good spot for observation and camera work. The terminator line, the line that distinguished the lit surface from that in shadow, had marched further along the face of the Moon. This was good. Contrary to public thinking, the full moon was the worse time to observe. While it was true that more features could be seen, detail was lost in the wash of bright light. And when the Moon was full, light was striking the surface at nearly a ninety-degree angle, meaning there was very little shadow. Shadows enhanced details and helped an observer determine the height of an object. Marcus was eager to take more pictures. If nothing else, it would occupy his mind with thoughts other than death and pesky media people.

Marcus's fingers flew across the keyboard as he entered the search parameters into the software. It was a simple process. The software was designed to find objects in the sky by day and time. All Marcus had to do was choose "Moon" and press enter. Since the software knew the date on the computer and his latitude, it did the rest. Marcus waited while the telescope swung into position. Moments later, Marcus was staring at the blemish on the Moon's face. It had grown, and this excited him.

Following the same procedure as before, Marcus took photos through the CCD on the telescope, saved them on the hard drive of his computer, and took measurements. By his calculations, the stain had enlarged by another eleven percent. That was phenomenal growth. At the time of the news conference the discoloration measured roughly sixty-two miles across; now it was closer to seventy miles. It also seemed to be growing geometrically, meaning that as it got larger, it grew faster.

The phone on the desk rang and Marcus came out of his seat, his heart tripping. A quick glance at the desk clock told him it was a little after eleven. Lucy would be in bed. Quickly, against his desire, he snatched up the phone before it could ring again. Maybe Lucy had slept through the first ring.

"What?" Marcus said harshly.

"Professor Stiller," a familiar voice said. "It's Ben in Arizona."

Father Ben. "Ben, I'm sorry to be so brusque."

"No need to apologize," his voice was smooth and reassuring. "I hope I'm not calling too late."

"Astronomy has taught me to be a night owl."

"Yeah," Ben said with a chuckle. "It's pretty much ruined me, too." He paused, then added, "I heard about your father. Dr. Lansing called me. I'm sorry. It must be tough."

Marcus had made several calls from his mother's house. One had been to his old mentor. "Yeah, it is. I didn't know how much I'd miss him."

"We never do. I lost my father when I was in seminary. Took the wind out of my sails for a long time."

"Was your father a priest, too?" Marcus stopped abruptly, then said, "You know, that may be the dumbest thing I've ever said."

Ben laughed. "No, he wasn't a priest. He was a civil engineer. Specialized in bridges and the like. We weren't that close."

Marcus sensed Ben was uncomfortable. "My dad was a minister," Marcus said to lighten the mood. "I guess you two were in a similar line of work."

"Not really. I'm sure he dealt with people. I deal with distant stars and planets. Speaking of which, I want to send you some information. I've been working on your little discovery."

"It's not so little anymore," Marcus said. "I was just making some observations."

"It's expanding, all right, but amazing as that is, it's peanuts to our spectral analysis."

Marcus felt his heart pick up pace again. Ben had analyzed the light from the enigma. That should tell them something about the composition. "Don't leave me hanging, what did you find?"

There was a protracted pause. "Nothing."

Now it was Marcus who paused. "Nothing? What do you mean, nothing?"

"Precisely that. Nothing. We threw everything we have at it and more. Lansing got the same kind of results. There's nothing there."

"But we can see it. I just took a dozen more pictures of it. It's right there, Ben, right before our eyes."

"I know, I know. I'll send you the numbers, but you're going to draw the same conclusion. Whatever the spot is, we can't measure anything about it, except its size."

Marcus felt as if he had been punched. What Ben was say-ing was impossible. Stars were measured spectroscopically, and they were light-years away. How could something so clearly seen on the Moon not register at all?

"You there, Marcus?"

"Yeah, I'm here."

"Good, I didn't want something else I've observed not to be there."

Marcus didn't laugh at the joke. "Send me what you have. Send it tonight if you can. I'm not going to be able to sleep now."

"I sent it five minutes ago. You should have it by now."

Marcus checked his e-mail again. There it was, a message with several attached files. "I found it."

"I sent the bare-bones numbers and some new photos. The photos aren't much different than the ones we took before aside from the obvious expansion. Of course the lighting is different, but not much else. There's something else."

A twinge of anxiety twisted in Marcus's stomach. "I'm afraid to ask."

"I'm going to tell you anyway," Ben replied. "Are you sit-ting down?"

Marcus said he was. He closed his eyes.

"Okay," Ben began. "We've checked the albedo and com-pared it to the previously known ratio. I wanted to know the light absorption quantities."

Marcus nodded as if Ben could see him over the phone. Albedo was a measurement of reflectivity. When light fell on an object, a portion of that light was absorbed and the remain-der reflected. The ratio of light reflected to the light falling on the object was called albedo. A perfect mirror would reflect all the light that fell on it and therefore would have an albedo of 1.0. Since no surface reflected all light that came its way, albedo numbers were always less than 1.0. The Moon's average albedo was 0.7. Darker material, like the enigma, should absorb more light, and therefore the albedo should be less.

"Don't leave me hanging, Ben. Spill it."

"There's no change. The current albedo is the same as pre-stain observations."

The conversation ceased as Marcus tried to understand, tried to believe, what he had just heard. "Impossible. You made a mistake."

"No mistake, Marcus."

"Yes, there is. There must be. I can see it, Ben. I took photos not ten minutes ago, and a dark red spot appears on every one of them. You've seen it. It must be there, and it must absorb more light than before. You're having fun with me, aren't you, Ben? You're pulling the college science teacher's leg."

"No, I'm not. I wish I were. It would be a great joke, but it's real. We spot-checked other areas of the Moon, maria and highlands alike. We got exactly what we expected. We did the work correctly and the instruments are functioning fine. Trust me on this, Marcus. This is what I do for a living. I'm an observational astronomer. I may not know as much about lunar studies as you, but I do know instrumentation."

"But if what you say is true, then the blotch isn't really there."

"No, not exactly. Our eyes are instruments too, sometimes more sensitive and accurate than anything we can build. We see the thing; therefore it must be there. But all our instruments say it isn't."

"How can that be?"

"I have no idea, Marcus, not a single thought. I am as befuddled as you."

Marcus doubted that was possible.

)) ● ● ● ((

DR. PETER BERNARD was not a man given to emotion. He was a physician, a doctor who worked daily in a difficult and taxing field. He routinely heard the schizophrenic ramblings of patients, the heartrending pleas for help, the outcries of terror from those who thought he was the devil in a white coat. Each day, he calmly made judgments that would affect the lives of scores of mentally ill patients. He decided who went home, and who stayed locked in a cell-like room. He dealt with families and government institutions with unflappable aplomb. He often pictured himself as a giant, state-of-the-art ocean liner cruising through troubled seas, too large to be perturbed by wind, too powerful to be deterred by waves.

That was on most days. Today? Well, today was different. The ice water that normally flowed through his veins had congealed into a slow-moving mass of anxiety. His stomach was tied in a Gordian knot of dread. All of the tension, the anxiety, was due to Julie Waal.

He had tried to call Daniel Waal at his office and at his Sacramento residence, but learned that the senator was out of state on a business trip. Bernard left messages, but knew that was not enough. The police would certainly make calls, too. One way or another, the very powerful man would learn that his wife had gone missing and that a hospital employee had failed to prevent it. Senator Daniel Waal would not be happy.

This hospital was Bernard's life. To the world it was the Pacific Institute for Family Care, but to him it was the core of his being. Medicine had been all he had ever cared about. From the fourth grade on Bernard had seen himself as a practitioner of the healing arts. At first he thought he would be a surgeon, but he became attracted to psychiatry during his last year of medical school. Like all med students, he was required to rotate through the various disciplines of the hospital. He spent time in the OR, logged hours in pediatrics, and took his turn observing surgery. During one rotation he found himself standing in the halls of the psych ward. Other students had complained about the rotation, but Bernard was strangely attracted to it. While others found their comfort level pushed well into the red zone, Bernard looked forward to the time he spent observing, being instructed, and working with the hospitalized.

There in those pale green rooms with their antiseptic floors and walls and their wired glass windows were some of the world's strangest people. Except Bernard didn't see them as strange. Alien, yes, but not strange. They were people who lived and traveled in lands he could not see. They were explorers traipsing through unusual worlds like astronauts who have landed on a distant planet. Some of those places were frightening, reducing the patient to a fearful mass huddled on a bed or sitting on the floor, knees drawn to their chest. There were those who talked to people who were not there, preached paranoia about spacemen and government agents.

He walked those aisles, peered into their rooms, aghast at first, then awash in curiosity. In one organ, a gray mass the size of a softball and possessing the texture of Jell-O, was locked away a twist in the strand of logic, a kink in the hose of reason. Now there was a challenge. Cardiologists and surgeons could install pacemakers, replace valves, give medication to the body's most important organ, but it was basically a technical treatment. Doctors were more highly skilled technicians than scientists. Some did original research, but most applied their knowledge in a way that was not very different from a carpenter or a mason. Certainly medicine took much more training and skill, as well as the mental muscles of discipline and composure, but real science required peeking into the unknown. And nothing was more unknown than the human mind. Not the brain—that was the organ where the mind resided—but the enigmatic mind itself.

Despite himself, Bernard fell in love with psychiatry. He finished med school and pursued the advanced education necessary to specialize. The years passed quickly and he discovered, as did his peers, that he had a gift for the job. It was as if he had been handcrafted to fit the part. But treating the mentally ill was not satisfying enough. He wanted to know what happened in the brain, in that seemingly random yet profoundly orderly firing of synapses. Why did alcohol change behavior?

Why did cocaine lead to paranoia? Why were some people prone to addiction while others seemed immune? When a patient saw green or gray aliens from the planet Remelix or whatever the patient called it, did he really see beings? Did he really hear voices? Why were the voices the schizophrenic heard so real, and where did the words come from that told them to hide, to steal, or even to kill?

He had excelled at the work, both clinical and research. His reputation grew with each paper he published in the *American Journal of Psychiatry* and the *Journal of Clinical Psychiatry*. He had learned his skills, but he had learned a few other things as well. There was money to be made. Mental illness was no respecter of wealth. The rich were just as likely to be struck as the poor. The rich, however, could pay for the best treatment, or at the very least, pay to have their family member housed someplace out of sight. It was a niche that Bernard could fill. He raised money, much of it from his brother, and started the hospital. Things had started slow but soon picked up. He would be a wealthy man if it were not for something else he learned. Rich people could pay for the finest care; they could also hire the best lawyers to wage a lawsuit.

Law was something Bernard had no interest in. He turned all such matters over to his attorney, an honest man with a modest record of success. The first lawsuit, brought by an ambitious and impatient businessman in Hollywood, educated Bernard in the simple realization that the truth does not always prevail and even when it does, it comes with a hefty legal bill. The second suit was similar. Each felt that Mom or Dad could be dropped off at the hospital like a car sent to a mechanic believing that in a few months he or she would be returned in perfect shape. Bernard had patiently explained that treating mental illness was not the same as setting a broken leg. The explanation fell on deaf ears. The sheen of private practice had been stripped away by the coarse sandpaper of the legal system.

Bernard lost the first case and won the second. Winning nearly broke him. He was back to square one.

It was in the middle of the second trial that he decided wealth would have to come by other means. Looking at the impaneled jury, two of which were dozing, it occurred to Bernard that his future must rest in something more than the hands of twelve semiconscious jurors, most of whom had little more than a high school education. What he needed was a medical discovery, a patent on some treatment or drug that would be used worldwide. At that moment, in that courtroom, an idea popped into his head. It was the best thing that had ever happened to him.

And then Julie Waal decided to leave through a window in the clinic's kitchen.

○ ○ ● ● ◐ ○ ○

SAND HAD BEEN REPLACED by asphalt and concrete, making Julie's already swollen, cut, and bruised feet protest with fiery pain. Still, she plodded along propelled by the thought that she was near her home. Behind her lay the long miles of beach she had walked from Santa Barbara as well as State Highway 101. At first she thought she would have to walk across the wide, heavily traveled freeway with its four northbound lanes and equal number of southbound. The thought of hiding near the side of the vast ribbon of asphalt after darkness had fallen and waiting for the traffic of cars and eighteen-wheelers to break enough for her to scuttle across on bare feet, climb the concrete median, and then scamper across the remaining lanes had terrified her. She doubted she could make it, but was determined to try. She had left the world of caution behind, too weary to think about anything but her next few steps.

She was spared the mad dash. Instead of going over the freeway, she went under. A concrete culvert used to drain runoff water that ran from the hills on the east side of the freeway provided a better, safer path, but it was not easy. Julie had crossed a stream of water in the sand that ran from under the freeway to the ocean. Lost in her thoughts, her thinking numbed by the pain and weariness that circulated through her body, she stepped over the small rivulet and took several more steps along her journey, then stopped abruptly. At first, she was uncertain why. All she knew was that she had an odd sense that she had just overlooked something important. Standing alone on the sand, she cocked her head and listened. Had it been a sound that caught her attention? She heard the small waves tumbling down on the shore sounding more like a cat's meow than a lion's roar. The rumbling of rubber tires on hard macadam wafted from the freeway twenty feet up the embankment to her left. That wasn't it either. It was the water, the tiny runoff stream she had just stepped over. Turning, she walked back, her bare toes kicking sand in the air that fluoresced in the moonlight. She stopped at the small stream and studied the water. It was little more than a trickle, but it ran over sand already saturated by its constant flow. First she followed its run to the ocean, and then turned her head to look at its source.

There was an opening in a steeply angled bank that ran from a long stretch of rocks that paralleled the run of the freeway. It was from this concrete tunnel that the water trickled in a sinuous and smooth flow. To Julie the opening looked like the gaping maw of some prehistoric creature, waiting for some unsuspecting prey to step in and be swallowed. The sun had set hours ago and the night was dark, lit only by the waning Moon. The culvert, however, was an abyss of the unknown. Its black seemed deeper, thicker than was possible. What was inside? Julie didn't want to know.

She turned ready to resume her southward trek, looking for some way to climb from the beach that was twenty feet lower than the freeway and a spot from which to make her dash across the highway. The thought made her ill. She doubted that she had the strength to dash ten feet, let alone a hundred and twenty feet of busy roadway. Again she looked at the yawning concrete mouth that drooled on the sand.

"Yea, though I walk through the valley of death, I will fear no evil," she uttered. That was all she could remember. And Julie Waal feared every evil.

Standing at the outer edge of the tunnel, Julie peered into the blackness and saw nothing. There was no light at the end of this tunnel, at least not that she could see. To her it seemed a horizontal pit, a mine shaft laid on its side with no outlet. The gentle music of the ocean faded behind her; the sounds of the freeway evaporated. Julie stared a moment longer, then placed one ragged foot inside the jaw of the narrow conduit and stepped down on the cold water. It stung her feet, but she ignored the pain. She had so much of it now that a little more agony made no difference. The next foot followed, and Julie walked into the culvert's black gullet.

))) ● ● ● ((

JOHN JACOB DEMPSEY WAS COLORING. Like a child bored with television on a day too rainy to play, he sat cross-legged on the floor of his apartment surrounded by sheets of lined paper. Each page was the same, displaying a crudely etched circle that covered the whole surface. Instead of the crayons a child might use, Dempsey utilized the only thing available to him, a dull No. 2 pencil. The pencil bore the scars of contemplative chewing. The circles had been drawn with pressure, the fiber of the paper tearing beneath the firm pressure of the pencil lead. Every one of the twenty or so pages that were flung around the room had the same circle and in that circle was another but smaller disk inscribed in the upper left. The smaller circle was colored in with pencil marks, slapdash across its surface. It was where the man on the news had said the red spot was. The Stiller Enigma, he called it. Stiller Enigma! How could they apply a man's name to something so important? That's the way the world was, always taking credit for what was not its own doing.

"'The sun shall be turned into darkness, and the moon into blood, before the great and the terrible day of the Lord come.' Joel 2:31." He was muttering. A small head of saliva drooled down his chin through black and gray stubble and dropped onto the paper. Dempsey wiped his mouth with the back of his hand, then threw the paper to the side. Taking the pad that had been nearly stripped of all its paper, he slowly peeled another page free, set it on the bare floor in front of him, and gouged another circle. "Terrible day of the Lord come . . . terrible day of the Lord . . . terrible day."

CHAPTER
SIXTEEN

I DON'T THINK YOU BELIEVE THAT, SON." JAMES STILLER finished reeling in his fishing line, leaving enough hanging off the end of his pole so he could reach the cylindrical lead weight and three-pronged hook. He pulled the rig into the boat. The hook was bare again. He set the pole to the side, resting it against the wood-trimmed edge of the small fiberglass rowboat.

"I do," Marcus said. There was a slight tremble in his voice. It wasn't often the sixteen-year-old disputed his father. "It's the only thing that makes sense."

"Is it?" James dipped a finger into a box of Velveeta and scooped out a wad of yellow processed cheese. Wiping the glob in the center of his palm, he rolled it into a ball by gently rubbing his hands together. "Are you sure?"

Marcus watched as his father gently placed the now round cheese on the hook, being careful to conceal its barbs. "Look, Dad, I'm not trying to start an argument. I just see things differently than you."

"Who's arguing?" James said, tossing the baited hook over the side. He picked up his pole, released the catch on the reel, and let the lead weight pull the hook down. They were sitting in a rented boat on Lake Poway, a man-made reservoir in San Diego's north county. It was one of Marcus's favorite places. He and his father came here at least once a month, weather permitting, and had done so since Marcus was five. In the early years, the trips were often postponed because his father was at sea, but that was the only reason. If he was home, they went fishing. "I'm just trying to understand your point."

Marcus had not intended to bring the subject up, but in the idle talk of fishing the subject unexpectedly popped up. His father wanted to know how school was going and Marcus, a straight-A student, began talking about his classes. As an honors student he was allowed to take advanced classes and was enjoying honors physics, a class normally reserved for seniors. Marcus was a junior, one of the youngest in his class. In the discussion he had mentioned his desire to go to Caltech. His dad had asked why. It was his way. For his father it was never enough to know what you wanted to do, but why you wanted to do it. Marcus could remember being six years old and explaining to his father *why* he wanted an ice cream cone. He tried every angle he could think of: ice cream was made of milk and therefore good for you; he was a kid and kids ate ice cream. What other reason could there be? Finally in frustration he had said, "Dad, it just tastes good!" His father nodded approvingly and said, "That's a great reason."

In explaining why he wanted to go to Caltech to study astronomy, he had said that science was based on facts, not "other things." As soon as he said it, he knew he had opened a can of wriggling worms. There was no closing the lid now.

James Stiller was no longer in the Navy, having retired after twenty-five years. Marcus had been twelve then; now, four years later, his father had completed his college education and had become pastor of his first church. It was a big change for the family. It was a greater change for Marcus. They had always gone to church, attending every time the doors were open. His mother worked with the women's groups, his father with the deacons and Sunday school. That was different. In those days, they were just like everyone else in the church, sitting in the pew, singing hymns, and listening to sermons and Bible studies. Now they were the pastor's family, and life had taken on a fishbowl quality. He was no longer Marcus Stiller, one of the "young people"; he was Reverend Stiller's boy. It didn't take long for Marcus to discover his disdain for the new role.

Marcus looked up at the blue southern California sky and wondered if there was any way to get out of his predicament. It was impossible. They were seated in a rowboat in the middle of a lake. There was no escape, not unless he could learn to walk on water, and that wasn't likely. Still, for a moment, he thought of giving it a try.

"What other things?" his father asked. His voice was as flat as the lake.

"You know, Dad."

"Politics? Business? Military? Cooking shows?"

"No—" Maybe a fish would bite. That would help. If a big trout hit one of their lines, then the conversation would be put on hold. Seconds passed but the fish refused to cooperate. Marcus could imagine them below the surface of the green-gray water looking at the boat thinking, *Well? Speak up, boy.* He took a deep breath. "I'm not saying that there is no God, I'm just saying that science is based on hard facts."

"Hard facts, eh?" James nodded. "So you're saying that faith is based on something other than facts, is that it?"

"I guess so."

"This is an awfully important topic to be guessing about." James shifted his weight and the boat rocked gently. "I didn't think science-minded people made decisions based on guesses."

"They don't," Marcus shot back. "There's the scientific method. It's an orderly process that leads to fact-based conclusions."

"Fact-based conclusions," his father repeated. He rubbed his chin, and Marcus could hear the rustling sound his father's fingers made against the graying stubble. James never shaved on fishing days. He had once told Marcus that the uglier the fisherman, the better his luck.

"Dad, we're just different people, that's all. You have faith and that's fine, but I need evidence, proof."

"Facts."

"Yes, facts," Marcus admitted. "I'm not saying there's anything wrong with faith, or that I'm not a believer, just that science provides facts."

James nodded his head and pushed out his lower lip. It was what he did when he was lost in thought. Marcus waited for the conversation to resume, which it did a minute later.

"Maybe we should go home," his father said.

Marcus's heart sank. He had hurt his father and spoiled the fishing trip. "Dad, I didn't mean to ruin our trip—"

"You didn't. Don't be silly. I mean we should go home because there are no fish in this lake."

"What? How do you know that?"

"Have you caught anything? Have I?"

"No, but that doesn't mean anything," Marcus protested.

"Have you *seen* any fish?" James leaned his head over the boat rail and squinted. "I haven't."

"You can't see the fish from here," Marcus said. "The water is too deep and clouded."

"What evidence do we have that there are fish in this lake?" James asked.

"We've caught some ourselves."

"Not today we haven't."

"No, but we have in the past. And we've seen others catch them. The guy on the boat dock told us that the lake was stocked with trout."

"Maybe they're all gone. We haven't seen anyone else with a stringer full of rainbows, have we? And who cares what others say. Maybe they just made it up or were deceived. Perhaps it's just wishful thinking."

"Okay," Marcus said with a small smile. "This is one of those object lessons, isn't it? You're trying to make a point."

"And I thought I was being clever."

"I understand what you're trying to do, but I think you're stretching."

"Let me ask you something. What do you think faith is?"

Marcus thought for a moment. "You've said that faith is the same thing as trust. It's believing in something you can't see."

His father harrumphed. "I'll need to be clearer in the future. Faith is trust. Actually it's deposited trust—trust in someone or something. Like this boat we're in. We had faith that it would support us and keep us out of the water. But faith is more than that—much more. Faith is not based on wishful thinking, but on evidence." He paused for another moment, fiddled with his reel, then said, "Do you know what Hebrews 11:1 says?"

"I couldn't quote it." Marcus felt a second of embarrassment. Scripture memory was something his father encouraged but never demanded.

"'Now faith is the assurance of things hoped for, the conviction of things not seen.' There are three key words in that verse. Do you know what they are?"

Marcus repeated the verse in his mind a few times, then replied, "Assurance, hope, and conviction." Marcus had been asked questions like this before. It was his dad's favorite way of making a point.

"That's right. Now what do the words mean?"

"You're the Bible scholar," Marcus said.

"First key word," James said like a professor before a full class of students, "is *assurance*. Some translations, like the King James Version, use the word *substance*. It's from the New Testament Greek word *hupostasis*. It's a compound term of two words . . . both used in science, by the way."

"*Hupostasis*," Marcus repeated. "*Hypo* and *stasis?*"

"Exactly. Now what do they mean?"

"*Hypo* means 'below,'" Marcus ventured. "Like hypo-dermic needle." His father nodded. "*Stasis* means 'to remain the same.'"

"Right."

"To stay the same under? That doesn't make sense."

"Sure it does. It refers to something that is real, tangible, and undeniable. It refers to the real nature of something. The word is sometimes used to mean confidence . . . a confidence based on facts."

"Facts?"

"That's right. What's the next key word?"

Marcus ran the verse through his mind again. "Hope."

"*Hope*. That's an important Bible word. It's also one of the most misunderstood terms. What does hope mean to you?"

"A wish for something . . . I think."

"That's what it means in English. I say, 'I hope the San Diego Padres go to the World Series this year—'"

"That's not going to happen," Marcus interjected with a laugh. The local major league baseball team was having a dismal year.

"Exactly. My hope is going to be disappointed. But that's not surprising, because in English, the word *hope* always carries with it the idea of doubt and uncertainty. That's not true for biblical hope."

"And the Greek word is?"

"You're not mocking your old man, are you?" James asked with a broad grin.

"Never," Marcus shot back. The constant chiding and kidding was part of their relationship and Marcus loved it, especially now that he could keep up with his father's wit.

"That's good, because I could baptize you again right here in the lake. I'd hold you down until you blew bubbles."

"Maybe I could see the fish then."

"As I was saying, *hope* is used differently in the Bible than the way we use it in English. The original word *elpizo* means 'a confident expectation.' It doesn't carry the same idea of doubt."

"You did know the Greek word."

"It's one of my favorite verses, smart aleck. What's the next key word?"

Marcus didn't have to think about it. "That would be *conviction*, Professor."

"Professor, eh? Well, listen closely, son, or you may flunk this fishing trip. *Conviction* is a powerful word and it ties all this together. *Elegmos* is the original word, and it means 'proof.' Some translations render it as 'evidence.' It means to be convinced of the truth of something. Do you see what I'm getting at?"

"Not really," Marcus replied.

"Okay, here it is: faith is not wishful thinking. It is not trusting simply because we are told to trust. Faith is fact based, evidence based, just like science. We displayed our faith in the safety of this boat when we got in, but we did it because we have seen and have experienced such things before. You follow what I'm saying, son?"

"I think so."

James quoted the verse again. "'Now faith is the assurance of things hoped for, the conviction of things not seen.'" He looked at his son and his tone became serious. "It's a definition. It's a definition that changes our lives. We believe in God, we place our faith and hope in Christ, not based on feelings or family tradition, but on what we know to be true. Faith is based on our having been convinced of its truth. That conviction is based on facts."

The two fell silent. Marcus looked over the lake, watching its wind-driven ripples move along the otherwise smooth surface. His father was a wise man and no one respected him more than he, but they were different people. Science had captured his heart and mind; faith seemed out of place. But there was something twitching in his heart. In all his years of church, he had never thought of faith in the way his father had just described it. But he had to admit that he had never pursued it the way his father had. What biblical knowledge he had came from the overflow of his father's understanding. Church and faith were family traditions to him, little more.

"Does what I said make sense?" James asked.

"Yes," Marcus said quickly. "I've never looked at it that way before."

"You're not alone, son. Few Christians have."

"Are you saying I shouldn't try to get into Caltech?"

"Not at all," his father responded quickly. "I think you should go and I have no doubt that you'll make it. I just want you to know that science is not the answer to everything and that faith is often misunderstood. You'll need your faith there as much as anywhere, maybe more."

"I promise to pack it, Dad. Besides, that's not going to happen for over a year."

"It's never too early to think about these things, son."

"I know. I'm not an atheist or anything."

"I understand that. You know you can ask me any questions you have. If I don't have the answers, I'll find out who does."

"I'll do that, Dad."

Marcus turned to see his father staring at him, his eyes orbs of concern. "You know you mean everything to me, don't you?"

"Yeah, Dad, I know."

CHAPTER
SEVENTEEN

JULIE PRESSED FORWARD THROUGH THE DARKNESS, PLACING one naked foot in front of the other. Beneath her feet ran the cold runoff water from the hills to the east. The stream carried loose debris and society's waste. Already she had stubbed her toes on rocks and glass bottles. The glass was her biggest fear. A broken soda bottle could sever a tendon in her foot. Walking was already arduous; she would never make it on one foot.

What would she do then? Would she just give up? Take a seat in the muck of the concrete pipe and wait for death? Julie paused and shook her head. Such thoughts were unwelcome and destructive to her flagging hope. Better to focus on the next step. Better to focus on nothing at all than to think what might go wrong.

She moved another foot forward and gently set it down, feeling for sharp rocks, jagged glass, bits of metal, or any other thing that waited piranha-like beneath thin water.

Step followed footstep in an endless and slow march. Julie knew the tunnel couldn't be much longer than the freeway above her ... at least she hoped it couldn't. Again her mind kicked into overdrive. What if there was a grate or iron bars at the other end that would keep her from exiting the drain? What if the opening were too small for her to fit through? What if ... She ordered her mind to stop. *What is, is,* she told herself. *I'll cross that drain when I get to it.* She giggled at her little joke, then felt foolish. She was getting giddy and light-headed. It had been hours since she had last eaten, and she had expended more energy during that time than anytime in the last eighteen months.

She felt odd in other ways. At times her skin would tingle and her vision blur. She saw shadows dancing in the darkness, if that were possible. The back of her eyes ached, and she felt unusually cold. Something else had been missed in the last hours, something that hadn't been missed in a year and a half. At the hospital Julie had been medicated on a regular basis. This was the longest she had gone without drugs since first being institutionalized. Could what she was sensing be related to the meds, or the sudden lack of them? Perhaps, Julie decided, but it made no difference. She wasn't going back.

Julie kept her head down and her arms out to the side. The tube was large enough for her to stand if she bent forward. Her legs and lower back bore the strain of the unnatural position and protested with throbbing pain. It felt as if the muscles in her body would tear under the strain.

Another step. Another. One wet, swollen foot after the other. Perspiration ran down her forehead and over her brows, forcing her to clamp shut her eyes against the stinging sweat. She tried to focus on something else, on her house, the place that had been her comfort, her sanctuary. Would it look different? Would it feel the same?

Pausing, Julie wiped the sweat from her eyes and let the lids part. She saw a sparkle in the water, then another. Raising her head, she could see a dim light at the end of the covered culvert. The light was inviting and called to her to continue. It was ivory and pure, like the light some people said they saw during near-death experiences. It was the proverbial light at the end of the tunnel—the tunnel of light. Is this what she was doing, walking from life into death?

A profound sadness washed over her, encasing her like the black of the pipe. The light didn't bring her joy, didn't cause delight, couldn't encourage her. For a moment, a long moment, she considered quitting. She could lie down in the muck and water and just die. No one would find her for days, maybe weeks, not until a big rainstorm came and the drainage pipe was flushed clean. What was there to live for? How long could she avoid being found and taken back to her room, her cell, at the hospital?

She lowered her head in despair, frozen by hopelessness, paralyzed by the certain knowledge that her escape was an utter waste of time, a fool's mission. "Why bother?" she whispered, and the sound of her voice spiraled down the pipe like water down a drain.

Looking up again, she could see the light better. It was soft, pale in the distance, and round like the culvert in which she stood. Round and ivory like the Moon. The Moon. The Moon. The Moon.

The despair that flooded her heart began to ebb, replaced by an ill-defined, tiny warmth of optimism. It was small but unmistakable, like a birthday candle that burned alone in a dark room. It couldn't give off much heat, but its small, valiant light demanded notice.

Julie took another step, moving further from the darkness behind her and toward the pale light ahead. The aching of her muscles quieted under her determination; the pain of her feet was drowned out by fragile resolve. With grit she pressed on. Death would be easier, but if Death wanted her, it would have to hunt her down.

"Left," she said to herself, and her left foot moved forward. "Right," and the other foot followed. "No looking back. No looking back."

Her heart quickened and she pulled in dank air through gritted teeth. Her labored breathing echoed down the long tube. *It shouldn't be this long,* she told herself. *I should be there by now.*

The light grew stronger and Julie began to wonder why. It was night when she entered; the sky was dark except for the glow of the Moon, and a thin layer of clouds muted that.

An eternity of moments later the tunnel ended and Julie emerged into an open concrete catch basin. The cool night air rushed upon her from above like spray off a waterfall. She raised her face to the black sky and relished the openness of it all. A few faint stars could be seen, but most were awash in the glow of the Moon.

"Thank you," she said to the sky.

Lowering her eyes, she took in her new situation. She was free of the tunnel and on the correct side of the freeway. That was the good news. The bad news was that she was at the bottom of a cement catch basin that was the size of a small bedroom. The walls ran from the base up at a forty-five-degree angle, and Julie wondered if she had the strength to make the climb. The vertical distance was not much, maybe eight feet, but it was eight feet added to a day of many miles. At the top of the basin and circling its perimeter was a four-foot-high chain-link fence to keep people from falling in. It might also keep her from getting out.

She considered resting. Bone weary, she wanted nothing more than to sit down, lean against one of the sloping walls, and sleep for a few hours. *No,* she told herself. *My next night's sleep will be in my own bed.*

She looked around the basin again, this time taking in more of the detail. There was nothing to help her get a foothold, nothing to stand upon. Just loose rocks that had washed down off the hills and not enough of those to pile into anything that would be helpful. There were a few broken bottles and some aluminum cans, again nothing helpful. Turning back to the concrete pipe she made a discovery: The edge of the pipe was not flush with the wall of the basin through which it emerged. It protruded beyond the face about three feet at the top. The sloping wall decreased the protrusion to just a few inches at the base. She might be able to work her way up the wall enough to get onto the top of the round pipe. From there, if she could stand, she could take hold of the chain-link fence and pull herself to the top of the wall. What she would do after that, she had no idea, but that was as far as her mind would take her.

Moving to where the pipe exited the wall, Julie touched its rough surface. Rough was good. It would hurt her already mangled feet, but at least she would have some friction to keep her from sliding back down. She turned and leaned back against the concrete surface, resting her weight on her rear. Then she brought one foot up to the incline, then the next. Leaning back with palms pressed down, Julie began to scoot up the surface backwards. Each scoot moved her up the wall about six inches. Not much, but enough if she were careful and patient. She feared slipping, but the rough surface provided enough purchase to keep her in place. She pushed with her legs again, and slid up the surface another half foot. She rested after each effort, but only for a moment. Her legs were starting to cramp and her back was complaining again. She was going to have to do this as quickly as possible.

Sweat began to pour down her face again, but she continued the backward ascent. *This would be easy in daylight and if I was in good condition,* she thought. But it wasn't daylight, and she wasn't in good condition. She was teetering on the edge of exhaustion. She pushed. She moved.

As she moved up the wall, the edge of the round pipe moved away and Julie had to adjust her position laterally a few times. She discovered that by doing so she could follow the line where pipe intersected wall and that she could simply slide along the top of the culvert until she could place her feet on the curved surface of the pipe. Minutes passed slowly, distance even more slowly, but she made it. Both feet rested on the top of the pipe, serving as a perfect foothold. Her back was to the chain-link fence that circumscribed the basin.

Carefully, her heart pounding as much from anxiety as exertion, Julie turned to one side until she could slip her fingers through the rough galvanized wire that made up the fence. Then she rose on unsteady legs, muscles twitching and threatening collapse. If they did, she would tumble down the sloped wall. She doubted that she would have enough energy or courage to make the climb again, even if she survived the fall.

The concrete pipe felt like sandpaper beneath the traumatized soles of her feet. Shakily, she turned until she was facing the fence and both hands were clinging to the metal netting. What next? At first she thought she would climb the barricade, but deemed the idea impossible. Maybe she could do it at another time and another place, but not today, not as weak and uncertain as she had become, and certainly not barefoot.

The fence posts were anchored into the top of the concrete wall. The bottom of the fence fabric hovered an inch or two above the ledge formed by the thickness of the retaining wall, just enough for her to slip her feet under. Tentatively, Julie slipped her right foot under the chain link and rested her weight on it. Her legs protested and her foot fired bolts of pain. Pulling with her arms she raised herself so that her face and chest were close to the fence, and then brought her left foot alongside the right. There was only room on the ledge for her toes and the balls of her feet. Her heels hung over the edge.

Julie had a plan. She had seen something when she first reached the top of the pipe. A curved concrete ditch ran along the bottom of the hillside that towered above her. She could see its gray-white surface in the ivory light of the Moon. The channel ran along the base of the hills to keep rainwater from cascading down the dirt slopes and flooding the freeway. The culverts would direct the water into the basin where it would then run to the sea through the drainpipe she had just traversed. She was thankful it wasn't raining now. The culvert ran under the fence where it met the catch basin. At that spot, the gap between the bottom of the fence and the bottom of the culvert was wider, maybe as much as one foot. She would try to slip beneath the fence, using the open channel as a passageway. It would be tight, but the chain link could be moved some, pushed back to enlarge the opening a few inches more.

She looked down and her stomach turned. One misstep would lead to injury, maybe death. For a moment she thought about working her way back down to the bottom and spending the night. It made sense. She would be more rested and stronger and there would be more light to see by. It was the light that persuaded her to continue on. While the morning sun would help her see, it would also help the thousands of people that would be using the freeway to see also, and what they would see would be a lone woman walking along the base of the hillside and very near the highway. That would certainly draw the attention of the police, and they were the last people she wanted to see . . . well, next to last. Julie had much less desire to see the hospital or its employees again. At this point, she realized, there wasn't much difference between the two.

One agonizing step followed another and with each slide of a foot, Julie tightened her grip on the fence. The rough metal strands dug at her hands with the same ferocity that the concrete wall ate at her feet. Still, she slid her right foot to the side. Once in place she reached along the fence and took another handful of metal netting. Left hand and foot followed. Step by sliding step she moved, unable to think of anything but the next step. Sweat poured down her hairline, matting the blonde strands even more. Another step on a trembling leg, another fist full of metal wire, another tiny victory.

Half an eternity later, Julie was straddling the juncture of the concrete channel with the concrete basin wall. Of all that she had done over the last hours, of all the distance she had covered, of all the efforts she had made to make her way home, the next was the most difficult. To lower herself by the strength of her hands alone, to slip her legs through the impossibly narrow opening, and to slither like a snake on its back until she was on the other side of the barricade was madness.

"Madness," she said to the empty night. "Maybe I am crazy after all."

To complete the maneuver Julie would have to hold onto the fence, lean back in a jackknife position, and methodically work her feet beneath the metal links. She knew she was limber enough, but worried that she might be too weak. This had to be done right the first time, or she knew that she would be spending her last hours as a broken shell in a desolate concrete grave.

She wondered if Daniel would miss her.

Julie crouched down as far as she could, turning her knees to the side. If she squatted too much she would be unable to slip her feet and legs through the opening. One thing lifted her spirits for a moment: she had misjudged the size of the opening. It was larger by half a foot. For that she was grateful and would have wept tears of joy if she were not preoccupied with her next step.

Gingerly, Julie pushed one foot under the opening as far as it would go—about mid calf. Then came the part she feared most. Tightening her grip until the metal chain link bit into the flesh of her hands, Julie rotated on her left foot, leaning back over the open pit behind her. Her arms screamed in coruscating pain and her hands burned as if holding lit coals. Her left foot slipped forward, sliding under the fence. The metal fiber creased her flesh as the left leg joined the right.

A small scream of pain and fear erupted from her lips and echoed off the hill. Julie waited for the fall and the impact, waited for the concrete base to rise and meet her like a freight train. But there was no fall and no impact. She was sitting in the culvert with her legs under the fence, scratched but whole, and her fingers tightly intertwined in the wire fence. She giggled. The giggle, she knew, was inappropriate. The danger was still there, she was far from safety, but she giggled anyway. Tears joined the sweat that ran down her face.

Taking three deep breaths, Julie wiggled forward until her hips pressed against the fence. Moving her hands down she began the slow process of pressing herself through the small opening. The fence dug at her thighs, hips, breasts, and face, but she continued on. There was no backing out even if she wanted to. No matter how weary, no matter how much pain she felt, she continued the process until she had at last slithered free.

Julie Waal lay on her back in a concrete channel.

Blood covered her legs and arms. She touched one of the scratches on her cheek and it stung as if her finger had been caked in salt. Her limbs, now released from impossible duty, shook involuntarily. Bile boiled in the back of her throat and her stomach churned like a washing machine. She felt sick and on the verge of blacking out. Tears continued to run down her cheeks. Above her hovered the medallion of the Moon, looking down upon her through gossamer clouds.

Julie rolled to her side and began to weep.

)) ● ● ● ● ((

"COMING TO BED?" Lucy asked from the doorway of Marcus's office. "It's getting late."

Marcus looked up from the papers before him and checked the time on his desk clock—1:15 in the morning.

"I don't think so," he mumbled. He was weary but sleep didn't appeal to him. There were too many things to think about. "I want to go over this data again. I thought you went to bed."

"I did." Lucy yawned and walked in. "I don't think you're getting enough rest. You're going through a lot; you need extra sleep."

Marcus gazed up at his wife and was once again impressed with her beauty and intelligence. Her dark skin was smooth and begged to be touched and her eyes, dark as they were, always seemed to sparkle. "I'm okay. I dozed off a little while ago."

"Catnapping doesn't count," she retorted. "Trust me, I'm a doctor."

"I had a dream . . . about my dad."

Lucy ran her hand along Marcus's close-cropped hair. "Was it a good one?"

Marcus smiled and nodded. "We were fishing. I've told you about the times we used to go fishing. We would sit in the boat and talk. I loved those times. That's what we were doing in the dream . . . talking."

"About what?" She walked around the desk and took a seat in a chair near Marcus's desk.

"Life. The future. I was reliving the time I told him I wanted to go to Caltech and study astronomy." Marcus shook his head. "He was a smart man, Lucy. No, not just smart, he was . . . insightful. He not only saw people, he saw *into* them. He certainly saw into me."

"Was that so bad?"

He shook his head. "A little disconcerting at times. It was like he could look at me and know what I was thinking and feeling, like it was printed on my forehead." He paused. "I never really appreciated him until the stroke. Why is that, Lucy? Why don't we appreciate our parents while they're still alive?"

"Human nature, I guess. Too busy being young to notice that older people know a few things, too."

"Yeah, you're probably right."

"What are you reading?"

Marcus returned his attention to the papers. "Dr. Sicarello sent me some findings on the enigma. They're puzzling . . . dumbfounding really."

"What kind of findings?"

"He was able to arrange a spectrograph observation of the spot."

"That should be revealing," Lucy said.

"I wish it were. The spectrometer shows nothing is there."

Lucy cocked her head to the side and narrowed her eyes, something Marcus had come to recognize as her thinking pose. "Nothing? That can't be right."

"It shows nothing different. It's as if the spot isn't there at all."

"But you can see it."

"That's right, we can see it, take pictures of it, measure its growth, but spectroscopically it reads just like any lunar soil."

"They must have made a mistake," Lucy offered. "It doesn't make any sense. How can we see what isn't there?"

"My first thoughts exactly, and I told him so. But the observation was made several times on different instruments. It's there, but it's not."

"A spectrometer measures light, right?" Lucy asked.

"Basically. There are different types of spectrometers but they work in the same fundamental fashion. Electromagnetic energy . . . light . . . can be broken up into its component parts."

"Like light through a prism."

"Right. A rainbow is white light separated into bands of color by airborne water droplets," Marcus explained. "Those colors are spectral lines. Different elements and molecules give off a different set of lines. Those lines are like a fingerprint identifying the element. Astronomers can determine the makeup of stars by studying their spectral image."

"But the Moon isn't a star. It's a cold, dead world."

"Right, but there's more to it than that. Substances can also absorb light. In this case, since we know the makeup of sunlight, we can compare it to reflected moonlight. The difference tells us what portion of light is being absorbed, and since we know what elements absorb what spectrum of light, we can determine the composition of the surface."

"But it didn't work?"

"The observations worked fine. We just didn't get any answers, or at least answers we can believe." Marcus rubbed his eyes.

"Aren't there other tests that can be run?" Lucy asked.

"Observations, dear. Physicians run tests, astronomers observe." Lucy rolled her eyes, forcing a smile to Marcus's face. "Between Dr. Sicarello and Dr. Lansing there have been several approaches taken. Lansing was able to get radar images of the spot from the Goldstone Deep Space Network. That too came back inconclusive."

"Radar?"

"A beam of radar is bounced off the Moon's surface. The echo is converted into measurable data. It's the same thing they did back in 1999 to get three-dimensional images of the lunar poles. They were checking for evidence of water."

"I thought the Moon was dry as toast."

"For the most part it is, but some water is held in lunar soil that is protected from the Sun. The temperature of the Moon in direct sunlight is too high for water to exist. And since the Moon has no atmosphere to speak of, liquid water is impossible."

"But there's ice? Is that what you're saying?"

"That's exactly what I'm saying. Some craters remain forever in shadow. In those areas ice can be found. The radar beam reflects off ice better than off the lunar soil so the image shows white spots."

"And the radar images showed nothing out of the ordinary?"

"Not a thing. This is weird," Marcus admitted. "I don't know what to make of it. Every astronomer in the world is probably looking at this thing. Someone will come up with something."

"Will they come up with it tonight?"

Marcus laughed. "I doubt it."

"Then come to bed. Leave tomorrow's mysteries for tomorrow."

"I really should—," Marcus started.

"Doctor's orders," Lucy said firmly. "I'm going back to bed, and you're coming with me."

Marcus let slip a smile of acquiescence and rose. Lucy left her chair, took him by the hand, and led him across the house to the bedroom.

EIGHTEEN

J ULIE WOKE WITH A START. PANIC DESCENDED ON HER LIKE rain, and she fought back the urge to scream. What had frightened her? Where was she? There was darkness. There was a distant roar. There was a cold wet breeze and the smell of salt. It was the salt that calmed her.

It was returning to her now: the flight from the hospital, the long, painful walk, the concrete drainage tunnel under the freeway, and her climb out of the catch basin. Looking around she saw the ocean in the distance, the light of the Moon dancing on the distant water like sequins. She also saw the hill behind her, the freeway that paralleled the long coast, and the chain-link fence she had just wiggled under. Her body quickly reminded her of the enormous effort she had expended over the last few hours.

But she was still alive and still free.

How long had she been asleep? she wondered. She remembered gazing at the Moon hanging over her like a streetlamp. It had moved. Not far, but some. *An hour,* she thought. *Maybe two, but no more.* She had needed the rest; her body not only demanded it but seized the opportunity to sleep. Now, however, it was time to get moving again. Her house was only a few miles away, three miles at most. She could be there in less than two hours, if she pushed herself. She had become good at pushing herself.

Despite the protest of muscles, Julie rose and began to walk along the culvert. Her joints were stiff and her legs uncertain, but she moved forward.

◖◑●◉◐◗◖

To Dempsey's eye, the spot on the Moon looked like an ocean of blood. He could envision it moving, swelling, and ebbing in a viscous flow. "Terrible day of the Lord," he mumbled to himself. He was standing on the balcony that ran in front of his low-rent apartment. His was one of 150 such units in the complex. Despite the late hour, light from several apartments shone on the common courtyard that was in the middle of the three-story complex. From one apartment came the sound of a baby crying, from another the chipper music of a long-dead sitcom. Dempsey ignored it all. He had other things on his mind. He had the Moon on his mind—in his brain.

Closing one eye, he raised an old pair of binoculars to his face and peered through the right eyepiece. He used only the right side of the binoculars because the lens in the left barrel had been broken many years before, when he was a child.

Holding the scarred viewing device in dirty hands, he directed his gaze to the Moon as he had done scores of times at night.

There it was, an ivory disk with a red splotch in one corner. "It's bigger," he said to himself. "Terrible day of the Lord is coming. Coming, the terrible day of the Lord." He was again filled with terror and odd delight, a mixture of emotions he was coming to enjoy.

The red spot seemed to pulsate as though a gigantic heart beat just beneath its surface. "Bump-bump," Dempsey said softly. "Bump-bump, bump-bump." That's when it struck him. The red spot had a heart that beat in rhythm with his. The thought made his own heart beat faster, and he was sure that he saw the pulse of the red spot increase, too. "The Moon is for me. Terrible day of the Lord."

Dempsey gazed at the Moon through the nearly useless binoculars until his arms ached. Once the Moon dropped out of sight, he lowered the glasses, despondent as if his only friend had left for good. Reluctantly, he stepped over the threshold and back into his apartment. A single lamp bought at a garage sale illuminated the room. Papers with hand-drawn images of the Moon littered the floor. The normally bare walls had similar crudely painted pictures.

Crossing the room, Dempsey plopped down on the ragged sofa, the only piece of furniture in the apartment besides a battered coffee table and a small color television that rested on an orange crate. On the sofa was a copy of the *Los Angeles Register*. He had stolen it from one of his neighbors. He had to steal it. It had a picture of the Moon on the front page—a color picture. He required that picture. He was meant to have it, so he took it without compunction. Picking up the newspaper, he studied the article again. Dempsey had stopped keeping count of the number of times he had read it. There it was, the line he would not forget. He whispered the words as he read, "The Stiller Enigma is named after Marcus Stiller, a science teacher who lives in Pinewood, California." Pinewood. Dempsey

wondered just where that was. He could find out. The library
had maps. It wouldn't be hard to find out. He nodded.
Tomorrow, he would take a trip.

"Marcus Stiller," he said to himself. "The Moon man.
Terrible day of the Lord. The Moon man. Pinewood."

Satisfied with his decision, Dempsey let sleep wash over him.

THE MOON WAS GONE, veiled behind a thick marine layer of
clouds. The overcast sky was well known to all who lived close
to the coast. Each night the blanket of clouds would roll in and
then tenaciously cling to the sky until the late morning sun
could burn its way through. It was a daily battle and to be
expected. Julie was glad the clouds had held off until she had
reached one of the residential streets about a mile from her
house. Without the moonlight, her hike would be even more
difficult, and she had all the difficulty she could handle.
Streetlights washed the sidewalk and macadam road in ocher
radiance. Julie trod through the puddles of illumination, thankful for each one.

The hour was late, but how late she didn't know. She
guessed the previous day had given birth to a new one without
fanfare. Time didn't matter. Walking did. The street was familiar; she had been down it many times in the car barely noticing
the custom homes that lined each side. Before she had simply
driven by; now she viewed each house with fear. Would someone look out and see a lone, tattered, barefoot woman limping
by? Would they call the police? So far no lights shone from the
windows. The neighborhood was fast asleep. Sleep. What a
pleasant desire, what a sweet hope. To lie down, face caressed
by a silk pillowcase, to feel the cool, gentle touch of the sheet
and the firm support of a mattress. She thought of her bed, her
house, and quickened her steps. Bare feet met unyielding concrete. Each footfall hurt, but Julie pushed the pain aside with
happy thoughts of sleeping in her own home.

The headlights of a car washed down the street. Julie immediately thought of the police. They would patrol the area. If they saw her they would certainly stop and ask questions—questions she didn't want to answer. They'd ask for identification, and she had none. Scratched, barefooted, disheveled, she would be taken as a derelict. The green hospital garb she wore wouldn't help. Worse, they might already be on the lookout for her. *Of course they would,* she reasoned. *I'm a runaway from a mental institution.* Julie ducked down next to a parked car and waited, shivering more from fear than the cold.

The vehicle passed and Julie could hear the pulsating beat of a music base line. *Thumpa-thump. Thumpa-thump.* Police didn't listen to music while on duty. That much she knew. The driver must be some kid, a teenager coming home from a party or work at a fast-food joint. Relief rolled through her, but she remained in her hiding place. There was no sense in taking risks. Once the car had passed, Julie rose and started down the concrete path again.

Home was less than a mile away.

○◑●●●◑○

GORDON'S HEAD FELL FORWARD then snapped back. He had dozed off again. He swore at himself, then at Julie. He wondered if he had made yet another tactical error. Maybe she wouldn't return home. Maybe she was headed in the opposite direction. That would be the smart thing, but she wasn't smart, she was crazy. He corrected himself. He wished that were the case, but her insanity had made her clever. She had, after all, outwitted him once already. That memory made him even angrier.

He was due at the hospital in the morning, and if Julie Waal didn't show up, he would be arriving empty-handed and without sleep. It wasn't his usual shift, but Uncle Bernard had demanded another meeting. He was already tired, wearied not just by the lateness of the hour but by the angry emotions he had been harboring. Staying up late was not difficult, not normally. It was his job, after all. But sitting alone in a car in the wee hours was boring and infuriating.

Where was she?

Leaning his head back, Gordon rubbed his eyes hard, until spots began to appear behind his closed lids. "Come on, wake up, wake up," he said to himself. *Maybe,* he thought, *I should make a quick trip to a mini-mart for some coffee.* Coffee sounded good, black and strong and filled with caffeine. That's what he needed, coffee, breakfast of champions. But that would mean leaving his self-assigned post, and that seemed unwise.

Opening his eyes, he gazed down the street and at the house where "that woman" used to live. It looked the same, dark, untouched. *It must be great to be a California senator,* Gordon thought, *a big house here in an expensive coastal community and one in Sacramento.* He wondered how much time the senator spent in this home.

Something caught his attention. A movement. A shadow appeared, then was gone. Gordon fixed his eyes on the house. It had been near the front door. The home had no outside lights on, so Gordon had to rely on the scattered illumination provided by the streetlamps. It was insufficient, but it was all he had.

There it was again. Was it a dog sniffing around for something to chase? A figure, a small figure, was at the front door. Straining his eyes, he could see that it was hunched over and moving slowly, like a dimensionless shadow seeking something lost in the dark. Unexpectedly, the shadow dropped down and then reappeared a moment later.

"Gotcha!"

◖◗◗●●◑◖◗

JULIE WISHED FOR A FLASHLIGHT. She was standing on the raised porch that ran along the front of her house. It had been a place of joy. Memories of summer evenings sitting on an antique bench swing floated on the winds of her mind. Had she been back at the hospital, strapped to her bed, she would have reached for those memories and forced them to stay until they evaporated like morning mist in the sun. At the moment, she was less concerned with the past and consumed with the present. She was searching for the key.

Her brain was as fatigued as her body and her thoughts seemed to lie in a heap, disjointed, unconnected, buried in the debris of too many lost months and too much medication. "I know it's here," she whispered.

There was a key somewhere on the porch. Daniel had placed it there in case they ever locked themselves out. But Daniel was a cautious man, so the key had to be hidden. Placing it under the doormat would not do—much too obvious. It had to be in a place where no one would think to look, but Julie couldn't call it to mind. If it wasn't under the mat, then where was it? She looked under the doormat anyway. Nothing. She glanced around, straining to see in the dim light. Her eyes traced the overhang of the roof and the pot shelf that hung under the front window just to the right of the door. Nothing. Panic began to rise. She had traveled too far, paid too a high price, to be foiled by a missing key.

A sound crawled through the night—a muted thud. Julie ducked down again, her eyes darting up and down the street. She saw nothing, heard nothing. The sound had been familiar. A car door. Someone had closed a car door. Still that didn't seem quite right. The sound hadn't been very loud. Maybe it was a street or two away.

Don't go digging up new problems for yourself, she thought. *You're home. That's all that matters.* Digging! That was it!

Julie scrambled along the front of the house until she came to a long, narrow flowerbed. Perennials covered the rich dirt, flowers she had planted with her own hands when they first moved into the house. At least Daniel had kept up the garden while she was gone. Making her way to the corner of the house she found what she was looking for: a hose bib. Crouching down, she dug beneath the loose soil and pulled up a sealed plastic bag. Inside was a key.

Daniel had insisted that the key be away from the door and out of sight but also in a place easy to remember. Burying it beneath the flowerbed and directly beneath the spigot had been the perfect solution: easy to find and easy to recover. She turned and strode to the front door, her hopes high.

The key fit the lock as it should and the door opened without resistance. A dark part of her feared that Daniel might have changed the locks. It was an irrational thought, she decided. She had so many of those.

Crossing the threshold, she quickly shut the door and locked it. As she did, she heard something, an indistinguishable noise from the front of the house. Her heart spun into high gear and she stepped away from the door. The key she held dropped to the tile floor of the entry, ringing like a tiny bell as it hit the hard surface.

Beep.

Julie jumped and she raised both hands to her face.

Beep.

That sound was familiar. The alarm! She had forgotten the house was wired with a security alarm. *How could I be so stupid?* she scolded herself. The beeping was a reminder, a notification that the alarm was set and a door had been opened. If she didn't enter a prescribed code in sixty seconds, the security company would automatically be notified and the police called. That was the last thing she needed.

Beep.

The security system had a keypad mounted inside the hall that led to the lower bedrooms of the two-story home. Moving through the dark house, one hand on the entryway wall to guide her, Julie took the five steps necessary to make her way to the hall. The keypad was where she remembered it. Without hesitation she punched in 101077—October 10, 1977, her wedding day. The beeping stopped.

Julie leaned forward and rested her head against the wall. She was bone-weary. The hours, the miles, the great expenditure of emotional energy had taxed her beyond what she thought possible. Her legs began to shake and her breath came in ragged inhalations. It felt as if someone had opened a port on her soul and her life was flowing from it like water down a drain. Turning, she leaned back against the wall and slowly slid to the floor.

She was home. The smell of it brought back the warmth of memories, the embrace of recollection from days when her mind was her own, her actions her choice, and her life hers to control. Days that existed eons ago, when sunshine meant happiness and home meant acceptance, centuries ago when family was a treasure and freedom a right.

Julie wanted to sleep. She wanted to lean over until her head rested on the hallway carpet and close her eyes. If she died, that would be fine. She was home, in the house she loved, the place she belonged. To die here would be an honor, a privilege.

"No," she whispered, the single word barely audible to her own ears. "Tonight, I sleep in my own bed."

Rising, she ran her hand along the wall until she felt the smooth plastic switch-plate for the hall light. With a flick, the hall was awash in a gentle light from two overhead fixtures. She hoped that the light could not be seen outside, but she was through hiding in the dark. A little light couldn't hurt.

Letting her sight fall to the floor, she saw dark spots on the beige carpet. Blood. It was her blood; blood that oozed from the soles of her bare feet. Sadness filled her, not for herself, not for her damaged feet, but for the carpet. She and David had handpicked that carpet and now it was soiled.

"A shower," she advised herself. "A shower before your filth and blood ruins the whole house."

Julie trudged upstairs, walked down the short hall that led to the master bath, slipped into the bathroom, flicked on the light, turned on the shower, stripped herself of clothing, and started for the shower. Then, as an afterthought, she returned to the hall and switched off the light. A moment later, she entered the cascade of water. She tried to ignore the stinging of hot water on her cuts. The pain meant she was still alive.

〇〇●●●〇〇

GORDON SLAMMED A FIST into the palm of his hand. He had missed her. Not by much, but she had made it into the house while he was still ten or fifteen yards away. It had been his plan to sneak up behind her, plant his beefy palm over her mouth, and drag her back to the car. If she fought back, well, that would be an added bonus. But he was a big man and big men couldn't sneak quietly *and* quickly. Another few moments and she would have been his.

This might be better, he thought. If something went wrong and she screamed, she stood a better chance of being heard outside the house. All he had to do now was find a way in. He had tried the door, but it was locked. She was cautious. All right then, another means of ingress would be required. He would find it, he decided. He was close now and he felt the excitement of a hunter with his prey in the crosshairs.

CHAPTER
NINETEEN

THE HOUSE WAS A LARGE AFFAIR ON A TINY LOT. THE required side yard setbacks had somehow been diminished, no doubt shrunk by passage of money from builder's hand to key members on the zoning commission. Normally Gordon could have cared less, but the tiny setbacks meant little room to move around the house. He had hoisted his bulk over a wooden fence at the side of the home and lowered himself as quietly as he could. He could see several windows along the wall. He crouched down and lumbered toward the back. If Julie Waal were

to look out one of the windows, he would be seen. For that matter, a neighbor could see him just as easily since their house was
less than eight feet away. There was nothing to do about it
except move to the backyard as quickly as possible.

Nothing. No cry of alarm. No sudden lights from the
neighbors. Not even a dog barking. Gordon decided that this
was his lucky day. The backyard was tiny, consisting of a covered patio and a narrow strip of lawn. The wood fence ran the
perimeter of the yard. Gordon slipped next to the rear wall and
waited, pulling a bushel of air into his lungs. Climbing a fence
and racing in a crouched position had winded him. Maybe it
was the excitement of what he was doing. He didn't know. He
didn't care. His heart pounded as if he were the one being
stalked. Gordon smiled. He was having a good time. Images of
the short battle between Julie and him flashed in his mind. She
had won that one, but only because he had underestimated her.
This time things would be different.

Staying close to the back wall, Gordon surveyed the situation. To his right was a pair of French doors. Slowly he
reached for the handle and gave it a gentle turn. It didn't budge.
The door was locked, as Gordon had assumed it would be. He
could break out one of the glass panes, but the noise would
alert his prey. He had another fear. The house was large and in
an upscale neighborhood; it would certainly be equipped with
an alarm. Forcing his way in would set off the alarm and that
would complicate things. Would he be able to subdue her and
get her to the car before the police could arrive? Possibly, if his
luck held out, but he didn't want to risk it. Sneaking in was still
the best bet.

Leaning forward, Gordon peeked through the French
doors and saw only dark. Moving quickly, he crossed the doors
and came to the next window. Unlike the other windows, this
one protruded a foot or so from the wall. Gordon had seen such
windows before. Called garden windows, the units were
designed to hold plants and were usually installed in kitchens.

On the side was a small sliding pane of glass and a screen. It was open, but it did Gordon no good. The pane of glass was less than a foot square. Only his arm could pass through something so narrow. He frowned, then paused. He heard something . . . a soft roar. It took him a moment, but he realized what he was hearing: water running through pipes. He listened for another moment. The sound was consistent and even. *The shower,* Gordon thought. *She's in the shower.*

His heart rate took another step up. This was ideal. If only he could find a way in, and quickly. He could surprise her in the shower. That would give him an additional advantage . . . he smiled at the other, obvious perk.

Knowing that she was most likely in the shower, Gordon moved with less trepidation, all the time keeping an eye on the neighbors' houses for the sudden appearance of a light that might indicate his presence had been detected. Moving along the wall, he tested each window; none cooperated. Stepping to the middle of the small backyard, he studied the upper floor. A light was shining through a small, frosted window. The bathroom, Gordon decided. He saw two additional windows, both closed and neither within reach. If he could get on the roof of the patio, he might be able to test the windows, but he doubted that they would be unlocked, and he harbored greater doubts he could pull himself up on the flat roof.

His excitement was melting in the heat of his rising frustration. He was so close, yet she lay just out of his reach. In desperation, Gordon rounded the other side of the house. Once again he found himself in the narrow confines of a side yard with the house to his right and the wood fence to his left. There was little to lift his hopes. He could see only one dark window. He approached, still in a half-crouch, and peeked through the glass. The cloud-veiled Moon added just enough light to the streetlamps for Gordon to see a car inside. The window led not into the house, but into the triple-wide garage. There was something else about the window: the slider didn't appear to be latched. Holding his breath, he laid his hand on the glass and gave a firm push. The windowpane slid open with a soft grinding of the aluminum frame over its dirty track.

Gordon stared at the open window, unsure that he was really seeing it. He waited for an alarm to sound, but there was no honking, beeping, or siren, just the silence of a predawn morning. Now all he had to do was haul his considerable bulk through the opening. He judged the window to be three feet wide. It would be a tight fit, but he was certain he could make it. The greatest obstacle was not the size of the opening, but its height above the grade. He estimated the windowsill to be about four feet from the ground upon which he stood. He needed something to act as a step stool.

Looking around the side yard he found a metal bucket near a gate. Inside was a bottle of car wash and a large sponge. Inverting the pail, he emptied it and placed it under the window. He had his step.

Gordon leaned in the window and was relieved to see a workbench just inside. At least he wouldn't have to balance himself on the sill and drop to the floor. The bench was clear of tools and debris. Apparently the good senator was a neat freak. Slowly, Gordon pulled himself through the opening that now seemed smaller than it first appeared. He grunted softly and bit his lip when he barked the skin from one of his hips. He swore under his breath.

The workbench held his weight. It was an effort, but Gordon finally pulled himself through and lowered himself from the bench. The garage was darker than he expected and he fought the urge to turn on a light. With hands in front of him, he took one cautious step after another. He could see the vague shape of a car. He touched it, keeping one hand on its smooth, cool surface as a guide. Slowly his eyes began to adjust to the deeper darkness. Vague shapes began to appear.

Straining his eyes he could see the shape of a second car and a set of shelves. The shelves were less than three feet from the front of the car. Gordon's mind began to race. He felt a new sense of focus. He was close and knew it. All he had to do was be careful and hope for a break. Gordon placed a hand on the shelves and followed them along. The garage was attached to the house. He had seen that when he first drove by. There had to be a door between the house and the garage, and he knew it had to be on the same wall as the shelves. All he had to do was find it.

It was there. The shelves ended and the door was tucked in the corner. Sliding one foot forward, Gordon reached out with his hand until it touched the wall and the molding that ran around the door frame. The doorknob was easy to find. Now came the moment of truth. He twisted the knob.

It turned freely.

THE WATER WAS WARM and velvety, flowing down Julie's body in liquid sheets. She stood in the shower, allowing the hot stream to pound on the back of her neck. Steam wafted around her in white clouds. The hot water stung the scratches on her legs and torso but she ignored the pain. Her feet, swollen from miles of barefooted walking on sand, pavement, and concrete, throbbed. Blood oozed from her abraded soles and mingled with the swirling water at her feet. The water would be good for them, cleaning the wounds of dirt and sand.

Julie could barely believe that she was home—in her home, in her shower, in her master bath. Exhaustion hung on her like ingots of lead. Her shoulders slumped and her knees felt as if they were made of rubber. Her hands began to shake uncontrollably. She was safe and warm and at home and now her body wanted to collapse, no longer pressed to be strong beyond its ability. It took all of Julie's concentration to remain vertical. Leaning her head back, she let the hot flow cascade through her hair. The roar of the water drowned out the real world. Images began to flood her mind. Pictures of the Moon, ivory, but like the water at her feet, tinged with red. She felt herself stiffen, expecting another hideous vision to befall her, but this was different. In the past the nightmares came upon her like a lion upon unsuspecting prey, but this vision was passive, as if she were looking at an abstract postcard. She waited. Waited for it to get worse, waited for the sensation of ants crawling inside her skull, but it never came. Instead, she felt a brief moment of peace, an impression she had not felt for a year and a half.

A smile, small and delicate, came to her face. It felt good. In her mind, the Moon faded.

◗ ◗ ◖ ◖ ◖ ◗ ◖ ◯

THE HOUSE WAS DARK, but Gordon made his way around, fumbling with his hands and shuffling with his feet. The door from the garage led to a kitchen. Blue numbers glowed eerily from what Gordon assumed was a microwave oven. The gentle hum of the refrigerator filled the air. A dim, amber light shone in the distance. Dragging his hand along the cool counter, Gordon worked his way to the light. A few steps later he found himself standing in the open expanse of the living room. He could see the shapes of chairs and a sofa. A dim light coming from the opposite wall lit the room. Making his way to the glow, he saw a round device with a plastic lens. Gordon recognized it as a safety light, the kind with electrical prongs in the back that could be plugged in an electrical outlet. The device served as a night-light but came alive in a power outage. The gentle glow allowed him to see a small switch on the front of the safety lamp. He pushed the switch to one side and a brighter light came on. The designers had made the device so that it could be used as a flashlight. Gordon pulled it from the wall.

Now he could see just fine.

◗ ◗ ◖ ◖ ◖ ◗ ◖ ◯

THE VISION PASSED as gently as it had arrived, like a daydream dissolving in the light of reality. Julie took a deep breath and opened her eyes. Her weariness continued to grow. Despite the seductive call of the shower, a good night's sleep beckoned even louder. Reaching for a bottle of shampoo, Julie squeezed a white glob of it into her palm. Rubbing her hands together, she applied the soap to her hair, then stopped. The shampoo was white. That seemed wrong to her. That wasn't the color of the shampoo she bought. Daniel had been fussy about such things, unwilling to try something new. He preferred the shampoo he had used in college. She shook her head, then chastised herself. She had been gone for a year and half; Daniel may have changed in a number of ways, shampoo being the least of them. She rubbed in the goo and then rinsed the soap from her hair.

The soap frothed in her hands and ran down her bare skin. She could feel the grime rinse away under the steady flow of water. To her it seemed the suds did more than remove dirt and oil from her scalp; they also cleansed her mind, her soul. The feeling was glorious and liberating. Next she quickly scrubbed her body with a washcloth and bar of soap. The soap stung her abrasions, but she washed vigorously, as if she could scrub the last few hours, the last few months of her life away.

Julie did not deceive herself. She was not yet a free woman. They would be looking for her, searching, hunting her as if she were an escaped convict. But she had traveled far, farther than anyone in their right mind would have thought possible. There was comfort in that thought. For now, she felt safe.

○ ◑ ◐ ● ◕ ◑ ◯

THE EMERGENCY LIGHT DID ITS JOB. It wasn't as bright as a good flashlight, but it was more than enough to see by. Gordon was even concerned that it might be too bright, so he draped his fingers over the lens, parting them enough to let some light through. It took only moments for him to learn the lay of the land. The sound of water running through the plumbing guided him and thrilled him. The situation couldn't be better.

Careful not to make any noise, Gordon crept through the house checking each room, being certain that he was alone. Outside, he had seen a light from what he assumed was the upstairs bathroom, most likely the master bath. Once he was certain the lower floor was clear, he found the stairs and began a slow, purposeful ascent. He noticed dark spots on the carpet and touched one with his finger—wet, sticky. Blood. She was injured.

Suddenly, something changed. The house was quiet, the sound of running water had ceased. He had to hurry.

◯ ◗ ● ● ● ◖ ◯

WITH REGRET, JULIE SHUT OFF THE WATER, motivated by the attractive, irresistible thoughts of sleeping in her own bed: cool sheets, warm blanket, feather pillow. Stepping from the shower, Julie toweled herself dry, then wrapped a terry-cloth robe around her body. She looked down at the soiled hospital clothes she had tossed in the corner of the bathroom floor. There was no way she would don them again. She picked up the garments and threw them in the trash. Next, she pulled open one of the drawers under the counter searching for a brush. She didn't expect to find hers, which, along with other toiletries, had been taken to the hospital. Daniel would have a brush she could use.

Inside, she found several brushes, including one with long bristles attached to a large, round head, the kind women used when drying their hair. Julie wondered when she had bought that.

There was a squeak.

Julie froze for a moment, then slowly turned to face the door. The door remained closed, just as she had left it when she first entered the room. Letting her gaze drop to the doorknob she saw it turn, slowly turn. Her breath caught.

Someone was coming in.

Reaching forward, she attempted to turn the tab that would lock the door, but it was too late. The door exploded open, slamming into the side of the tub and shower, cracking the shower door. Julie backpedaled until stopped by a wall.

The fire of her terror blazed hotter when she saw a man standing in the doorway—a large man. Gordon! He leered at her and she watched as his gaze traced her robe-clad figure.

"You have caused me a lot of trouble, woman." His teeth were clenched.

"What ... what do you want?" It was a stupid question, Julie knew, but no other words came to her mind.

"I want you, that's what I want. It's time to take you"— he smiled—"home."

"I'm not going back." Julie tried to press herself into the wall as if she could dissolve through the drywall and studs.

"Oh, yes, you are, and I'm going to be the one to take you back. You embarrassed me, you know. You shouldn't have done that."

"Get out of my house."

He laughed then taunted, "Make me."

"Leave me alone." Tears began to pour down her face.

He shook his head. "Ain't gonna happen, missy. You can come with me quietly or you can make it fun. This time, you won't catch me by surprise."

Julie looked around the room for anything that could be used as a weapon, but saw nothing.

"Let's get you dressed." Gordon said. "I'll help." He started toward her.

Julie felt ill and raised a hand to her churning, fire-filled stomach. The brush in her hand touched the robe.

Gordon reached out with a beefy hand and stroked her wet hair. "You smell clean and fresh. I like—"

Julie lunged forward, driving the business end of the brush into Gordon's belly. He exhaled loudly and folded over. Julie brought a knee up hard and felt it smash into the man's nose.

He screamed an obscenity and took a step back, his hands raised to his face. "You stupid—"

Julie didn't wait to hear the rest. She struck again, this time raising the brush over her head as if it were a knife and bringing in down with both hands. The hard plastic end dug into the soft skin of his forehead just next to the lump left by her last attack. He stumbled back, waving his arms in the air. Instincts took charge. Julie grabbed her attacker's wrists, letting the brush drop to the floor, and pushed, adding her strength to his falling momentum. Gordon stumbled backward through the bathroom door and into the bedroom. His footing slipped and he plummeted to the floor. Behind him was the large double bed that Julie had once shared with her husband. Like most beds, a metal frame supported the box springs. Gordon's head bounced off the frame. There was another scream of pain, then the orderly went limp.

Julie stumbled forward, tripping over Gordon, landing on the bed. Scrambling back to her feet, she glanced down at the man on the floor. He was stunned, but not unconscious. He moaned and raised a hand to the back of his head.

There were only seconds available to her and Julie knew it. She had been lucky so far, but she could not expect to defeat a man of his size and temper. Running was her only option. Racing to the closet, Julie snapped on the light and riffled through the hanging clothes. She was glad that Daniel had kept the garments in place. Without thought she grabbed the first things she saw and exited as quickly as she could. She did not want to be trapped in the walk-in closet.

As she raced from the closet she saw Gordon rising to his feet. With a grunt then a roar, he charged. Julie screamed and turned to run, but her head was snapped back as Gordon grabbed a fistful of hair.

"Not so fast." He spun her around. "I have grown tired of you."

He backhanded her. Julie felt warm blood in her mouth and tasted copper.

"Go . . . away!"

He slapped her again. "I'll beat you into submission if I have to. What's it gonna be?"

Julie said nothing. Gordon held her face close to his, her wet hair still intertwined in his hand. She closed her eyes, not wanting to look at his face.

"What are you going to do now, missy? Hit me with a blouse?" He spun her around again so that she faced the door. He pushed her past the threshold and walked her down the hall, snapping her head back and forth as if she were a doll.

"What do you want?" Julie asked.

"You know exactly what I want. I'm taking you back where you belong."

"What do you care?"

"I don't care. Not really. It's a pride thing. You embarrassed me. Besides, your husband might want to reward my good efforts." He pushed her forward again until they came to the stairs.

"At least let me get dressed."

"In the car, darling. You can change in the car. I like it better that way."

"I don't," Julie retorted.

"Pity, because that's the way it's going to be."

"I'd rather die."

"Don't tempt me. Let's go."

Julie took the first step down the stairs, then the next. Gordon was an arm's length behind, still clutching her hair. Her mind began to spin. She had to do something. She had come too far, paid too high a price, to simply surrender. "I'd rather die," she had said. It was true. Death was preferable to confinement in the mental hospital. Julie became desperate and then acted in desperation.

Without warning, without a word, Julie went limp, drop-ping hard on the treads of the stairs. The carpet tempered some of the impact, but pain still ripped up her hip and thigh. The sud-den move caught Gordon by surprise as he was pulled forward, off balance. He let go of her hair and reached for the handrail. He missed and tumbled headlong over Julie's limp body. There was a crash and she could hear the air leave his lungs.

Julie wasted no time. Scuttling to her feet, she rushed down the stairs, stepping over Gordon's prone body. He was twisting in pain. "My ribs. You broke my ribs." Julie was in pain, too. Everything ached, nerves fired unmercifully, spots swam before her eyes, but she pressed on. Escape was the only thing on her mind.

The lower floor was dark, with just a hint of light from the still open bedroom door. Julie stumbled into the kitchen, landing hard on the tile floor. She ignored the painful impact and rose quickly. She had no time to waste.

Her mind was a jumble of competing thoughts. Part of her wanted to race out the door, but then what. A lone woman clad only in a robe on the streets a few hours before dawn. She needed something more. Walking for miles again was impossible. She could barely stand now, and fighting Gordon was tapping the last reserves of her strength. "Light, I need light."

Turning, she saw the dim shape of a familiar object, the refrigerator. With no time lost to thought, she opened the door and the kitchen filled with its wan light.

"Where is it?" she said to herself. "Where is it?" An idea was forming in her mind, if only she could find what she was looking for. "Think. Think." Still holding the garments, she rifled through the drawers in the kitchen cabinet sensing that she was on the wrong track. "I should know this. Why can't I remember?"

From the base of the stairs came a groan followed by a boiling stream of curses.

The pantry! They hung them in the pantry. Between the back wall and the refrigerator was a floor-to-ceiling pantry. It was large enough for a person to step into, with shelves on every side, and had been Julie's pride and joy. Snapping open the door, she saw what she was searching for—car keys, hanging on a small hook.

She and Daniel had owned two cars, a Chevy pickup and a Lexus sedan, and since Daniel would be in Sacramento for the senate session, both would be in the garage. She grabbed the keys and turned in time to see Gordon lumber into the kitchen. He was holding the left side of his chest. His pain was obvious and so was the dark, threatening anger she could see in his eyes.

He started for her and she backed into the open door of the pantry. Julie didn't wait for him to close the distance. She turned and reached for the door that led to the garage. It was partway open and Julie realized that Gordon had come into the house through the garage.

Julie felt her head snap back hard and she released a cry of pain. Gordon had her by the hair again.

"I'm tired of messing with you. No more tricks."

Julie felt her feet leave the floor as Gordon pulled her up, swinging her around. Then he pushed hard. Julie fell forward, landing on the floor and sliding into the cabinets. The keys she held in one hand and the clothing she held in the other fell. Instinctively she grabbed at the robe that was threatening to come loose.

"I've been too easy on you, woman. I've tried to handle this in a professional manner, but you insist on making it hard. That's fine by me. If you want to do this the difficult way, then I'm happy to comply. I don't think you'll like it, but I will."

He took a step forward, then stopped and coughed, grabbing his side as he did. "I can't believe you broke my ribs."

"Maybe you should see a doctor," Julie said tentatively. She rose from the floor and leaned back against the counter.

"I got business with you first." He coughed again. "At least there's no blood. That's more than you can say. It looks like I messed up your pretty face."

Julie felt something by her hand. It was the edge of a drawer. Gordon took another step forward and Julie pulled the drawer out. It came free of its track and hung in Julie's hand. At first, Gordon recoiled, then laughed when he saw what the drawer contained: pot holders. The soft fabric pads tumbled out of the drawer and onto the kitchen floor. Julie's heart sank.

Gordon closed the distance. The sneer had returned to his face. "Are you planning to beat me to death with a pot holder?" He laughed as he took another step.

The laughter stopped abruptly as Julie swung the drawer as hard as she could, putting everything she had into the last-ditch effort. The act upended her and she crumpled to the floor again. So did Gordon. The drawer had caught him on the side of the head. He dropped like a sack of sand. In the dim light of the refrigerator bulb, Julie watched the big man topple and knew he was unconscious before his head bounced on the floor.

Once again, Julie crawled her way up using the counter to help balance her as she swayed on uncertain legs. She waited only long enough for her equilibrium to return, then picked up the keys and clothes. Tottering out to the garage, Julie pushed the button that activated the garage door opener. She quickly slipped into the clothing she had snatched out of the closet and threw the robe to the bare concrete slab. She wished she had had time to grab a pair of shoes. Slipping into the car, Julie started the Lexus and backed out, tires shrieking. Julie drove off into the predawn darkness.

CHAPTER
TWENTY

THE BEST JULIE COULD TELL AN HOUR HAD PASSED. HER tripping heart had settled; her ragged breathing had returned to its normal rhythm. Her mind, however, continued to spin like a top. Once free from the house, Julie had steered the Lexus down the residential streets, turning at random in an attempt to be sure she had not been followed. With every glance in the rearview mirror, she expected to see the hot lights of Gordon's car. She saw none.

Feeling she was, for the moment, free of danger, Julie made her way to the freeway she had crossed beneath a few hours before and headed south. Despite the early hour, scores of cars flowed through the lanes on their way to destinations known only to the drivers. It was illogical, she knew, but she felt conspicuous, as if those drivers who sped past her could know that she was a woman on the run, a woman fleeing a mental hospital and a madman who worked there. She drove precisely at the speed limit, not wanting to draw attention to herself but also concerned that that caution in itself might be noticeable.

Her thoughts turned to the police. Would Gordon call them? Would he say that she was crazy and attacked him? She was sure he had come into the house through the garage. The fact that the door was ajar was proof of that. Had he seen the type and color of the car she was now driving? Could he give a description of it? Was the Highway Patrol searching for her right now? They were difficult questions for which she had no answer, but she was unwilling to take chances. Julie took the next exit, a small highway that led into the mountains. Perhaps she could find a place to hide the car and a place to rest.

The auto moved easily along the wide ribbon of asphalt. The darkness cloaked the vehicle and Julie found it reassuring. At the moment, darkness was her friend. She pressed down on the accelerator with her tortured foot, increasing her speed. She wished she had thought to grab a pair of shoes or sandals or even slippers. Her feet hurt severely. Still, she was thankful to have seized the clothing she was now wearing. Driving around town dressed only in a robe would be hard to explain. She thought about the garments she had put on: a pair of black slacks and an ivory, collarless top. It would have been a nice outfit to wear for a night on the town. Then it struck her. Something was wrong with the clothing. She had been gone for a long time, but she couldn't recall buying the blouse she was wearing, or the slacks. As she thought about it, the outfit didn't fit right, being just a little too tight in the shoulders and across the breast. The slacks, although they had an elastic waistband, seemed tight.

Like pieces of a jigsaw puzzle, her thoughts began to fall into place and the conclusion was devastating. The shampoo in the shower was a different brand than Daniel used. If it were just that, she would have assumed that her husband had found something else he preferred. Not wanting to, but feeling compelled, Julie tried to think of what else she had seen in the shower. The soap was the same, but there had been other things out of place. A bottle of hair conditioner had been tucked in the corner of the large tub. Daniel didn't use hair conditioner. Another image came to mind. It was something small in size but enormous in meaning. She had barely noticed it before, but upon reflection, Julie could remember seeing a razor next to the shampoo, the kind of razor a woman used to shave her legs.

Tears welled up in her eyes. Although she had spent only a moment in the closet, she saw things that were only now coming to the forefront. There were clothes—women's clothes that were not hers—hanging in her closet.

"No," she said to the empty car. "I was scared, terrified, I just didn't see things right, that's all." The only response was the sound of the engine. She might have believed the lie she was telling herself if not for the garments on her body. She was wearing another woman's outfit, a woman who had been in her house, a woman who felt comfortable enough to move in.

Daniel had replaced her.

The dam that had been holding the vast reservoir of emotion at bay cracked, crumbled, and then completely gave way. The tears that filled her eyes blurred her vision of the road. She wiped them with the back of her hand.

"How could he?" she asked herself. "I was a good wife. I loved him." The sadness gave way to rage. Julie pounded her fist on the steering wheel. "It's not fair. It's not right." The anger was just an emotional ruse, a bit of self-deception to squash the rising gorge of hurt over her betrayal.

Julie veered in the lane but caught herself before she drove off the side of the road. As she pulled the luxury car back into its proper place in the lane, she saw a sign. It was a sign for another road. She took the turn and noticed that it led deeper into the San Bernardino Mountains. Minutes passed at tortoise speed. Images of Daniel holding another woman flashed with strobelike intensity in her mind. No matter how much she struggled to exorcise the mental pictures, they came with greater intensity and detail; her imagination fueled by volatile emotions of rejection made them blazingly clear.

She had been gone a long time and he had replaced her, replaced her with a sane woman, a woman no doubt beautiful in every way. Julie now knew why his visits had become more infrequent. He always pleaded the pressures of service and duty, but it was her ... *that woman!* Apparently Daniel wanted something else, something she had never been able to give him.

It was profoundly unjust. She had not asked for visions, didn't feel the need of professional help, saw no reason to be admitted to a mental care facility. But Daniel had pushed in that direction, making it seem like the best possible solution to a difficult situation. "I just want you well," he would say and then kiss her gently on the forehead. She had heard it a hundred times. "These doctors are the best; they can make everything right again."

Nothing would ever be right again. The fury rose in her like a geyser, bringing despair with it. Her emotions vacillated from extreme to extreme, furious one moment, crushed the next.

Julie drove on, no longer paying attention to the scenery, no longer checking her rearview mirror. Instead, she gazed at the barren road in front of her. There was no more pain in her feet, no more stinging from the scratches and cuts. Those had been overpowered by the hurricane of loss that raged within her. Finally, when the steam of emotions could no longer maintain their damaging energy, apathy set in. Numbness.

A new desire rose in her—a desire that should have been shocking, revolting. Her apathy was metamorphosing into despair. "Why bother?" she asked herself. What difference did anything make? Life was meaningless. Life was just a long sequence of pain and betrayal. If living meant enduring rejection, if it meant running from place to place not even able to go home, if it meant returning to the mental ward, then why bother? Death was better than life and oblivion better than awareness. There was no pain in the grave, no betrayal, just nothingness, forever nothingness. That sounded good to Julie. Death was becoming as attractive as a warm bed.

Her mind staggered back to the moments on the beach where she had been tempted to begin a long, one-way swim into the ocean. "I should have done it," she told herself. "I should have done it and spared myself all of this. At least I would have died thinking that someone still cared about me."

Julie pushed the car along the now-twisting road and wished for a cliff.

No cliff appeared. Instead, there was the road: long, sinuous, dark, hypnotic. Julie drove on. The white dashes that ran down the middle of the narrow highway swept by like seconds on a clock. Slowly, steadily, Julie's mind began to shut down. Thinking hurt too much. Reasoning was too painful. Better was the numbness of the catatonic. Stupor was more desirable than awareness.

The road led higher into the mountains. Pine trees slipped by in the silent night. The clouds that covered her home, clouds sent in from the ocean, had given way to a clear, crisp blanket of black with pinprick stars.

She was alone on the road and thankful for it. Upward the car climbed. The trees thickened, and the road turned left then right, her tires squealing as she made the bends at speeds too fast to be safe. Julie was beyond caring. Reaching the crest of the mountain highway, Julie began a descent down the other side. She slowed. Having no idea how far she had traveled and having never driven the road, Julie felt lost—no bearings, no landmarks, just trees.

"This will do," she said to herself and pulled the car off the road and up a small dirt path. She stopped the Lexus and switched off the engine, then exited the car. Julie left the car behind, the keys still in the ignition. The night was as cold as it was dark and Julie embraced it. Walking down the dirt path, she crossed the road and walked into the woods.

The forest of pines swallowed her.

TWENTY-
ONE

THE METAL CHAIR BENEATH MARCUS WAS UNCOMFORTABLE and wobbly on the uneven grass. He wished he could stand, but his place was in the family row, next to his mother. The minutes dragged on with agonizing slowness. The San Diego morning would soon be afternoon and the chill of the day was giving way to sunshine-baked warmth. Marcus stared down at the dark green grass before him and tried to focus on each blade. The lawn itself was not interesting, but hovering just above it, over a hole that had been covered with a large section of green indoor/outdoor carpet, was a mahogany casket that held all that was left of his father. Better to look at the grass than to look at the coffin.

Cutting his eyes to the side, he saw his mother, head up, eyes straight ahead, her gaze riveted to the awful box. She seemed as stoic as a statue, her emotions betrayed only by the moisture that rimmed her eyes.

How does she do it? Marcus wondered. He felt like a dry autumn leaf bullied along by unseen wind. His mother, however, was like the tree, bending but not breaking. Marcus wished for her strength.

A voice droned on: "I am the Resurrection and I am the Life. Those who believe in me, even though they die, yet shall they live, and whoever lives and believes in me shall never die. I am the Alpha and Omega, the beginning and the end, the first and the last. I died, and behold I am alive forever more." It was Dr. Adam Bridger, pastor and a friend of his father. Marcus knew the man, having met him on several occasions before moving away to college. Dr. Bridger had been his mother's choice, and Marcus could not think of a better man.

"In those three sentences we are reminded that there is a resurrection," the pastor intoned, "that Christ is the life in this existence and in the next, that belief leads to eternal life, and that Christ himself experienced death and resurrection." Several in the crowd said, "Amen." Marcus sat quietly.

Resurrection? Marcus thought. There was a term he had not thought about since leaving home. Resurrection: a new body, a new life. His father believed in that and had preached on the topic more times than Marcus could remember. It was a nice thought, a comforting thought, but he could not bring himself to believe it. It was hard to think of the man in the coffin ever walking and talking again. It was too much to believe. Not without evidence. Not without a shred of proof.

Pastor Bridger continued on. "These are not final goodbyes. The separation is real. We do not attempt to fool ourselves about what has happened, but we do draw comfort from the fact of the eternal life Pastor James experiences now." Marcus raised his head and looked at the man who brought the grave-side message. Bridger was a middle-of-the-road man in appearance, with glasses that seemed too large for his face and a jaw that seemed too big for his head. His father had described him as a scholar, "a man deep in the Book." Bridger's wife, Rachel, a surgeon in a San Diego hospital, was standing nearby. At least they had that much in common, wives who were physicians.

Adam Bridger had conducted the memorial service that was held in the funeral home's large chapel. The place had been full. Everyone from his father's church had come as well as neighbors and distant family. They had all come to say good-bye to a man they loved. Seeing his father lying in the coffin had nearly undone him. "He looks so natural," everyone said. He didn't look natural at all. He looked dead, and no amount of makeup or work by an artistic funeral home employee could make his father look any different.

They came by in an endless procession of mourners shaking hands, wiping tears, and patting shoulders. "He was a great man," they would say first to his mother then to him.

"We loved him so."

"Everyone liked him."

"His sermons meant so much to me."

"He was there when I needed him."

"He's in a better place now."

"The long struggle is over."

"You should be proud of him."

His mother would nod, smile, and then say, "Thank you."

Marcus had found it hard to think. And it wasn't over. After the service, they adjourned and made their way to the graveside for an additional short service. Each moment that passed was another knife in Marcus's gut. While seeing his dad lying in an open coffin was the hardest thing he had ever done, seeing the coffin suspended on straps over a hole in the ground was worse. The cemetery workers had covered the hole with green indoor/outdoor carpeting so that no one could look down into the crypt, but it was for Marcus a useless effort. The carpet sagged over the hole, and the slight depression was enough of a reminder that death was final.

"The apostle Paul reminds us," the minister said, "that to be absent in the body is to be present with the Lord. What we read about this morning, Pastor James Stiller has experienced in fullness. We can thank God for that."

Marcus didn't feel thankful.

A hand touched his knee and Marcus turned to see the wet eyes of his wife. Lucy, who sat to his left, nodded in the direction of his mother. Marcus turned to see streams of tears flowing down her cheeks in a steady trickle. Her lower lip trembled slightly, but the rest of her remained solid as granite. Marcus put an arm around her and felt hot tears run from his own eyes.

Pastor Bridger continued on, but Marcus heard nothing of it until fifteen minutes later when enough words worked through his grief-clogged ears. "In the light of these promises God has given us in his Word and in as much as it has pleased the Lord in his sovereign wisdom and purpose to take from our midst one whom we have loved, we now commit his body to its resting place. This concludes our service."

It was over.

Before Marcus knew it, Pastor Bridger was standing before him, bent over, hand extended. Instinctively, Marcus took the man's hand and shook it.

"He truly was a great man," Bridger said. "My life was enriched by knowing him. If there's anything I can do, don't hesitate to call."

"Um, thank you," Marcus said, not knowing what else to say. Bridger moved on to his mother. Marcus watched as the pastor leaned over and hugged her. There were tears in her eyes and Marcus couldn't help noting that Bridger's face was also streaked with rivulets of sorrow. Then the others came, just as they did at the memorial service, one after another, each clearly filled with sorrow, each with a kind word to say.

The steady stream of mourners touched Marcus in a new way. They were not there out of social duty, but because they too had lost someone they loved. Their hearts had been pierced just as his had. Most spoke of God's love and comfort and did so with a sincerity that shamed him. Why had he not seen how great a man his father was when he was alive? Had he been so lost in his own life, his own scientific pursuits, not to see nobility when it stood before him?

". . . great wisdom . . . proud . . ."

The comments were coming in fragments to him, his mind unable to take in any more.

". . . impossible to replace . . ."

"God blessed us with your father and . . ."

Marcus could hold the pieces together no longer. He bent over, his hands covering his face, and wept bitterly. He felt an arm slip around him from his left, Lucy's arm. A hand patted his knee, his mother's hand. A voice he didn't recognize began to speak, "Oh Lord, grant this young man your peace. Give him your comfort . . ." Marcus didn't know who was praying, nor did he care.

Something in him had just died.

)) ● ● ● ((

DR. BARRY WENHAM SAT on the right side of the sofa opposite the president of the United States. He was uncomfortable but not because of the couch. It was the president's icy stare that made him uneasy.

"That's it?" the president barked. "That's all you've got?"

"I'm afraid so. I wish it were more." Wenham focused on looking cool.

"I wish you had more, too," President Larry Rendel snapped. "I can't do anything with this. This is . . . is . . .

nothing! You're telling me the spot isn't there, when anyone with a decent pair of binoculars can see it?"

"The test results show nothing has changed on the Moon," Wenham said.

"I can see it!" Rendel shouted. "I'm no scientist, but I know when something has changed or not. The Moon has a spot on it. The whole world knows it. Why don't you?"

Wenham cleared his throat. He had expected this. His report was true and accurate. It was also nonsense and there wasn't anything he could do about it. What Wenham didn't expect was to see the weariness on the president's face. A strong man, he always appeared healthy, but this afternoon, he was drawn, and the wrinkles around his eyes seemed miles deeper. "We've done optical observations from several places around the globe, computer enhanced the image, compared it to data from spectrographs and more, but the conclusion is the same: We see it, but it's not there. NASA is in full agreement."

"Do you know how stupid that sounds?"

"Yes, sir, I do and I take no joy in saying it."

"I take less joy in hearing it." Rendel bolted from the chair and began pacing. "I assume you've been watching the news?"

"No, sir, I've been busy gathering information for you."

"The Russians are blaming us. That's not official yet, but they've threatened to bring the matter before the UN. Tell me, Doctor, how does our ambassador to the United Nations respond? Does he say, 'Settle down, boys, it's not really there'?"

"Any country with a telescope and spectrograph can determine the same thing."

"That may cut it in your Ivy League world, Doctor, but in the world of politics and international diplomacy it means nothing—less than nothing." The president walked to his desk and picked up a file folder. "Do you know what this is?"

How would I know that? Wenham thought. "No, sir."

"It's a report from the FBI. I received it from the director who personally briefed me this morning. Survivalist groups are arming themselves in Montana, Utah, Tennessee, and a dozen other states. There have been two cult-related mass suicides, one in Oregon, another in Florida. Both left messages behind talking about the end of world. In Oregon, thirty-three went out in the woods, drank poison, and lay down to die. The one in Florida blew up their meeting hall or church or whatever they called it, immolating twenty-nine people inside and damaging nearby buildings."

"That's horrible."

"I'm getting reports that some people are not showing up at work. Why work when the end is near?"

"I'm afraid, sir, that I don't understand all this talk about the end of the world."

"I don't believe it for a moment either, but that doesn't really matter, does it? A lot of people out there do believe it. The world is going wacky, and this is just the tip of the iceberg, Doctor, just the tip. And to make matters worse, we can't do anything about it." The president paused. "Can we?"

"No, Mr. President, we can't. All we can do is offer rational explanations . . . appeal to the thinking populace—"

"Offer a rational explanation! Is that what you said? A rational explanation? Which one would that be? 'We see it but it's not really there.' Can you see me going on television and saying to the nation, 'Don't sweat it, folks, it's not really there. You're just imagining it.'"

"No, sir. I just meant—"

"No, sir, is right." Rendel tossed the file folder back on his desk. "If I hear you correctly there is no rational answer. Maybe we should make one up. Give the people something to believe in, something they can hang their hats on."

"Misinformation?" Wenham asked, shocked at what he was hearing.

"Do you think that no information is better?" the president demanded.

"It wouldn't work, sir. There are too many scientists, and they would never go along with a ruse like that. The moment you say the enigma is something it isn't, they'll call you on it."

"I'm their president."

"Trust me, sir, they don't care. Most researchers are cynics at heart. They're trained to be that way from their first science class. Every experiment must be observable to others and repeatable. You can't even publish a paper in a decent journal without extensive peer review, and once you do, the letters to the editor section fills up with mail telling the world how stupid you are. We scientists are not a forgiving lot."

"I thought politicians were bad."

"Sharks versus piranhas," Wenham offered. "Either one can eat you alive."

The president returned to his seat. "The Chinese think that we've been testing weapons on the Moon and doing it from right here on earth. They think we've been using the Moon for target practice for our Star Wars defense system and light-based weapons."

"That's ludicrous."

"Not as much as you might think," the president said cryptically. "We've done nothing that could cause this . . . especially if it isn't there."

Wenham nodded. "We're continuing our research. We'll know what it is in time."

"I appreciate your confidence, but we may not have much time. I need answers, Dr. Wenham, and I need them fast."

"There's nothing more that I can tell you."

Rendel leaned back in his chair and pursed his lips. "Who can offer more?"

"No one. I have some of the finest minds—"

"What about this Stiller guy? He saw it first, maybe he knows something."

"I doubt it, sir. He's not a true . . . what I mean to say is that he's not involved in real research."

"It sounds like academic sour grapes to me. He was sharp enough to find the thing in the first place."

"Serendipity, sir. Dr. Stiller is a college instructor, not a professional astronomer."

"I don't care," Rendel snipped. "The world doesn't care. The news media continues to refer to the spot as the Stiller Enigma."

"That's their right. He did discover it and announce it, but I still maintain—"

"Get him."

"Sir?"

"I want you to get Stiller for me. Set up a meeting. He may not know any more than the rest of us, but the world thinks he does. I want to know whatever he knows. I want his thinking on this."

"I'm afraid it would be a waste of time."

The president stood and started for the door. Wenham was on his feet immediately. The president said, "I'll be waiting to hear from you. I'll make sure you can get through to me."

Wenham knew all discussion had ended. President Rendel was in no mood to argue.

"Yes, sir," Wenham said with a nod. "It will be my first priority."

"See to it that it is."

Wenham left the Oval Office feeling as if he had left his dignity behind.

))) ● ● ● ((

"IT WAS A BEAUTIFUL SERVICE," Lucy said.

"Uh-huh," Marcus grunted, his eyes fixed on the road ahead. They were traveling north on Highway 2, a narrow, two-lane road leading to their home in the mountains. The hour was close to ten in the evening and Marcus, normally a night owl, was exhausted beyond description.

"I thought Reverend Bridger said some good things," Lucy added.

"Uh-huh."

"Of course, the clown outfit was a bit much."

"Uh-huh . . . what?" Marcus snapped a glance at his wife. "What did you say?"

"Just trying to get your attention. I've been talking. You've been grunting. Hardly meaningful communication."

"I'm sorry," Marcus said. "My mind is elsewhere." He returned his attention to the road.

"That's understandable, Marc. I just want you to be all right." Her voice was soft and sad.

"I'm fine. Really. I just wish Mom had come home with us. I don't feel good about her staying in the house alone."

Marcus had insisted that Abigail return home with them for a week or two, but she would have none of it. She had said, "I'm not the first widow this old world has seen. I won't be the last. I have to get on with my life. It's what your father would have wanted." No amount of arguing or cajoling could convince her otherwise.

"She's her own woman, that's for sure. Besides, she's not alone. A couple of ladies from the church are staying with her."

"I know. I just . . ." Marcus failed to finish the sentence.

They drove on in silence, Marcus's mind a fog of emotion. In college, he had learned that the effects of gravity diminished with distance. Grief was not affected so. One mile or a thousand made no difference; the hurt remained the same.

"Are you okay?" Lucy asked.

Marcus nodded. "The hard part is over. I just have a few emotions to work through."

"Like guilt?"

"I don't know if guilt is the right word for it."

"What word would you use?" Lucy asked softly.

Marcus thought for a moment, then said, "Guilt." He smiled in the darkness. "Doctor's intuition?"

"No, wife's love. You have nothing to feel guilty about. You were always a good son."

"I never appreciated how loved my father was. The church people were . . . very supportive. Their words about Dad were remarkable. Why is it children never see the greatness of their own parents?"

"Human nature, I suppose," Lucy replied. "I know I never fully understood or appreciated my parents when they were alive. I think I love them more now than I ever did."

Marcus steered the car through the turns of the mountain road, oblivious to anything else. "I used to want to be just like my father. When he was in seminary, when I was about twelve, I used to want to be a pastor and stand in the pulpit and boom out God's Word in powerful sermons. I would even practice in my room, pretending that hundreds of people were caught up in my dynamic and insightful preaching." He laughed. "I'm sure glad no one knew about that."

"Your mother did."

"No way."

"Yup. She told me that today."

"When?"

"When I was helping her pack up some of your father's things. You were sitting in the living room holding court with the guests. She said that she could hear you through the closed door."

Embarrassment rushed over Marcus. "And I thought I was making such a secret of it all."

"It made her proud—very proud. She's still proud of you."

"She's my mother, she's required to be proud." Marcus shifted uneasily in his seat.

"What changed your direction? Why did you give up on being a minister?"

"It wasn't for me. The older I got, the clearer the picture of a minister's life became. I'm not wired for it, Lucy. Hear all the hurts and needs, put up with the pettiness, and . . ." He trailed off.

"And what?"

"And I started having doubts. I fell in love with science and haven't looked back since. I developed a detached view of life. I guess I needed more facts than faith could provide. In short, I drifted away. In college, I focused on my math and physics and astronomy. It made me happy, gave me purpose. It wasn't a reasoned parting. I didn't sit down one day and write down all the reasons why science is better than faith; I just stopped thinking about it altogether."

"I can relate to that," Lucy said. "I think I've always been a person of faith, but seeing your mother's strength through all of this, I wonder. Her faith is . . . alive, vibrant, and real. It's not academic, it's personal." She paused, then continued. "I had always assumed that your parents were a product of their time, you know . . . they were religious because they were brought up to be that way. Now, I'm not so sure. I think they were spiritual because . . . well, because it is real."

Marcus sighed. Lucy was right in so many ways, and if anyone should have recognized it, it was he. "I was going through Dad's notebooks and I have to admit, I'm impressed. The detail of his study, the depth of information he pulled from the pages of the Bible, the orderly way he laid out his notes. His belief was based in an intellectual pursuit. I had always assumed that it was blind faith, all emotion and little brain. I couldn't have been more wrong about my father."

"Are they opposites?" Lucy asked.

"Are what opposites?"

"Faith and science."

"I don't know. Dad didn't think so. I have colleagues who would argue the point. They would say that faith blinds the scientific mind. That a true scientist must base everything on facts and repeatable experimentation." Marcus slowed as he prepared to turn off the highway and onto the small street that led to their house.

"Maybe it's the other way around," Lucy said. "Maybe science blinds the spiritual mind."

"My dad would say that the two go together, that people have erected an unnecessary wall between the two."

"What's that?" Lucy asked.

"I'm not sure how Dad would have put it, but I think he meant—"

"No," Lucy interrupted. "Up the street . . . at our house."

Marcus peered up the street at his house, which was now just in sight. He saw a movement near the front door. At first he thought an animal had run by, perhaps attracted by the front porch light. The mountain community was often visited by wildlife. He had seen deer, raccoon, and once a bear. But this was different.

"There!" Lucy said. "Is that someone at our door?"

"It looks like it. Who would come calling at this hour? It's nearly midnight."

"A burglar?" There was an unmistakable tinge of fear in her voice. "I don't think any well-wisher would be standing around our front door at this hour."

Marcus maintained his speed and moved up the street. "You got your cell phone?"

"Yes."

"Get it. I'm going to drive past the house, park down the street, and walk back. I'll park so you can see me. Be ready to call the police."

"I don't think you should go up there alone. We should wait for the police."

"It may be nothing. I'll be careful. But keep that phone ready. I'll wave if I want you to call."

"Marc, I don't think this is wise."

Marcus passed the house and stared at his front porch. "I don't see him. He must have left."

"I still think we should wait for the police."

Marcus pulled to the end of the street, turned off his head-lights, and pulled a U-turn. He then parked four houses down from his own home. "I think he's gone, but I want to check before you come up to the house."

"I can't talk you out of this, can I?"

Marcus slipped from the driver's seat and walked slowly down the street, avoiding the sidewalk, keeping the curbside autos between him and the walkway. He slowed as he neared his home, looking in every direction for movement. He saw nothing. Approaching his home, he could see that someone had indeed been at his front door. The front wall was covered in red graffiti. A large round circle whose diameter reached from the wood deck of the front porch to just under the eaves had been inscribed on the wall. The paint line traced over the front window, siding, and door. A large red spot was painted in the upper left corner of the circle. Marcus could tell the vandal had let the spray can hover over the spot until so much paint had been sprayed that it ran down the wall in rivers of red. Across the front of the defaced wall were the words MOON MAN IN THE MOON MAN.

Fury filled Marcus. "Perfect," Marcus grumbled to himself. "Just what this day needed!" He turned to make his way back to the car when he heard something. A man had appeared from the side of the house. Apparently he had been hiding behind one of the pine trees that dotted the side yard. Startled, Marcus jumped back and clinched his fists.

"I am his servant," the man said in a raspy, sandpaper voice. He was as tall as Marcus but looked older, maybe in his late forties. His dark hair was a bird's nest of black and gray, and thick dark stubble covered his cheeks and chin. He wore dungarees and a threadbare flannel shirt. His hands, covered in red paint, hung at his side.

"Who are you?" Marcus demanded. He lifted an arm and waved, hoping that Lucy could see his signal.

The man looked in the direction that Marcus had motioned.

"I said who are you and why did you do this to my house?" Marcus felt stupid asking the question. Lucy had been right; he should have waited for the police.

"I am his servant," the man said coldly. "You're the Moon man, aren't you?"

"I don't know what you're talking about."

"I seen your picture on the TV. You're the Moon man." The stranger's eyes narrowed and his lips drew tight. Marcus was certain that he was in danger.

"Get off my property," Marcus demanded, hoping his bluster would be seen as courage.

"The end is coming. Your end is coming. The Moon says so. You're the Moon man."

The trespasser was making no sense. He was psychotic, Marcus decided. It was best to keep distance between them.

"The end is not coming—"

"The Moon says so!" The man screamed and pointed skyward.

"Okay, okay, settle down." Marcus lifted his hands. "No need to get excited."

"'The sun shall be turned into darkness, and the moon into blood, before the great and the terrible day of the Lord come.' Joel 2:31. Joel 2:31: 'The sun shall be turned into darkness, and the moon into blood, before the great and the terrible day of the Lord come.'"

He's psychotic, all right, Marcus thought. "What do you want?"

"Repent. Blood Moon. Terrible day of the Lord. I am his servant." When he spoke, saliva ran down his chin.

This guy thinks he's God's avenging angel. Marcus was aware that there were those who were frightened by the lunar anomaly. He had seen the news reports of the lunacy that had been unleashed, but this was too close to home. *Where were the police?*

"What do you want from me? I didn't do anything to the Moon." Marcus forced himself to remain calm. What he really wanted to do was flee, but that would put the stranger at an advantage. Better to stand face-to-face for the moment.

"Terrible day of the Lord."

The man took a step forward and Marcus took a step back. In the distance was the scream of a siren. He hoped that they would get here in time. The man took another step; Marcus retreated two.

The piercing cry of the siren grew louder. This time the trespasser heard it. His face grew hard, and his lips parted in a sneer. Then he moved faster than Marcus had thought possible. In one fluid motion, the stranger threw the spray can at Marcus's head. Marcus ducked just in time; the can sailed past his right ear and bounced off the hard asphalt street with a clatter.

The sirens were loud now and close. Red and blue lights flashed down the street, but Marcus didn't dare take his eyes from the attacker. The man glanced down the street and then bolted around the house, disappearing into the tangle of trees and bushes.

A police car pulled up behind Marcus and an officer exited.

"He went around the side of the house," Marcus shouted. "Just now. Hurry." Another patrol car sped up the lane and stopped behind the other. The first officer followed on foot, the second stopped next to Marcus.

"What happened?" The policeman asked and Marcus quickly filled him in. "What did he look like?"

"My height, white, unshaven, mid-forties, wearing overalls and a plaid shirt." The officer relayed the information over his radio and then followed his partner into the dark woods.

"Marc! Marc!" Marcus turned to see Lucy running down the sidewalk. He turned and enveloped her in his arms. "Are you all right?"

"I'm fine. He threw a can of spray paint at me, but missed."

She pulled away from him and looked into his eyes. He could tell she was terrified. "I was afraid. Maybe he wasn't alone. Maybe he had a gun—"

"He was and he didn't." He offered a reassuring smile. "He did, however, leave his mark." He nodded to the house and Lucy followed his gaze. She gasped and raised her hands to her mouth. "My house," she muttered. "My beautiful house."

"The police will get him," he said with assurance.

"Well, they had better, because I have got something to say to him. I—"

"Easy now," Marcus said, taking his wife back in his arms. "You don't want the world to know what kind of temper you have." Marcus had only seen Lucy lose her temper twice, and it was two too many times for him. Normally, she was mild and even-tempered as a monk, but provoked enough the kid gloves came off and there was a price to pay. "Let's go inside."

Marcus had feared that the trespasser had somehow made his way into the home. He half expected to see furniture askew and drawers emptied, but everything was in its place, undisturbed since they had left it early that morning. Once inside, he did a quick check of all the rooms. Everything was secure. That was a relief.

A knock came at the door followed by a voice. "Police." Marcus invited the officers in and heard their bad news. The culprit had gotten away.

"Don't you guys have dogs you use to track people?" Lucy asked.

"Yes, ma'am, we do, but the nearest K–9 units are on another call . . . a homicide. By the time they got here, it would be too late. I'm sorry."

Lucy turned and walked into the kitchen. Marcus knew she was struggling to keep tame the volcano within her.

"Have you ever seen the man before?" the second officer asked.

Marcus shook his head. "This is the first time, and I hope it is the last."

"Any idea as to why he would write what he did on your wall?"

"Not really. The circle is the Moon and the red blotch is the enigma."

"Wait a minute," the first officer said. "You're that astronomy guy who discovered the thing on the Moon."

"That's right—" Marcus froze. "Oh, no. My telescope!" He started toward the door, but the officer blocked his way.

"Hang tight, sir."

"You don't understand. I spent a fortune on that rig."

"Small building in the back?" the officer asked. "Round top on it?"

"Yes."

"It's fine. Tight as a drum. We thought he might have tried to hide in it, but it was clear. No graffiti either. It looks like you interrupted him before he could get to it."

Marcus sighed in relief. "You're sure it's safe?"

The policeman nodded. "You can check it in the morning. I suggest you lock up tight for the night and call us if you hear or see anything unusual."

"Okay," Marcus conceded.

The officers turned to leave, then one stopped and stepped back to the door. "I hate to ask this, but can I get your autograph? It's for my son, you know. He loves all that space stuff."

Marcus nodded, wishing he had never seen the spot in the first place.

CHAPTER

TWENTY-
TWO

An entire day had passed since Julie abandoned her car at the side of a mountain road, and now it was late Wednesday night. She walked down a gentle slope, pausing every few steps to catch her breath, breath that came with greater effort because of the altitude. She moved slowly, too emotionally numb to care about her condition, too physically weary to go any faster.

The slope led to a narrow canyon through which burbled a small stream. The Moon was setting behind the trees, and the dim light was fading. Julie drank from the stream. The water was cold and refreshing. Her thirst quenched and no longer able to navigate in the dark, she found a small, flat area of ground surrounded by a clutch of trees that broke the biting breeze, fell exhausted to the ground, curled into a ball, and wished for death.

A few hours later the morning sun pushed through pine branches and fell on Julie's bare arms and face. The stirring of birds awakened her from a comalike sleep. Pushing herself into a sitting position, she gazed at the scene around her. It was verdant and alive with life. Birds sang from their perches in trees, a rabbit bounded by, paused to stare at Julie for a moment, and then continued on its journey.

"He's late, he's late," she whispered to herself, recalling the lines from *Alice in Wonderland*. A half-dozen yards away and down the slope, two deer lapped water from the running brook.

The air had warmed and was redolent with the forest's perfume. Sunlight streamed through the early morning mist, filtering through the canopy of trees, falling on the rich brown of the ground and the white granite rocks that lined the little stream. Julie had rubbed the grit from her eyes and pulled dead pine needles from her hair. Then she noticed her feet. They were red and swollen. She had no doubt that infection was setting in. But what did it matter? She had no life. She was sitting in Paradise, surrounded by a scene no writer could adequately describe, but her heart was as dark as outer space and just as cold. Beauty could not replace love, could not offer hope, and could not encourage a wounded and betrayed soul.

Despondent, Julie wanted to lie down again and patiently wait for the black of death to come for her, but she couldn't. Not right away. Her throat was parched beyond anything she had ever experienced, her lips chapped and cracked. Her tongue felt as if it were made of cotton. She forced herself to her feet, and felt the piercing agony of a body pushed far beyond its capabilities. Nonetheless, she hobbled down to the stream. Her movement startled the deer, which leapt away in graceful arches and disappeared into a blind of trees. Julie felt sad that they had left. It was just one more wound.

Cupping her hands, she drank water, and it tasted sweeter than anything that ever passed her lips. Another handful, then another until her parched throat eased its complaining. Another thought occurred to her. Pulling the legs of her pants up, Julie gingerly waded into the icy water. The stinging brought tears to her eyes, but at the same time there was a sense of relief. She forced herself to stay in the water. As the minutes passed, the pain yielded to the numbing cold. Careful of her balance, she rubbed one foot against the other in hopes of cleaning the wounds. The effectiveness would be minimal, but it might ease some of the agony.

When the water became too cold to bear, Julie stepped from the stream and stood on a bank of small, water-worn pebbles until the air had dried her feet. Then she returned to her makeshift bed of dirt and pine needles, lay back, and fell into exhausted sleep again. Maybe this time death would pay its overdue visit.

)) • ● ● ((

MARCUS AWOKE TO THE RINGING OF THE PHONE BY HIS BED. The sound it of startled him, and he swung his legs over the side of the bed in one swift motion, his mind fuzzy from a fitful night of sleep. The police had taken an hour asking questions and taking photos. Marcus, who had been exhausted by the trip to San Diego and his father's funeral, was then too full of adrenaline to sleep. He spent the next hour pacing the living room but finally went to bed at the request of his wife. At first he had wanted to sleep on the sofa in the living room, feeling he could better protect his home, but Lucy was in no mood to sleep alone.

Every hour, Marcus had awakened, certain that he had heard something at the door or window. Every breath of wind was a voice, every blowing leaf a footstep. When he did doze, he dreamt of hideous demons spray-painting his house chanting, "Moon man, Moon man."

The phone rang again.

"You going to get that?" Lucy asked sleepily.

"Yeah." He forced his weary mind to focus and grabbed the phone. The clock on the nightstand read 6:00 A.M.

"Is this Mr. Marcus Stiller?" the male voice on the phone said. "Or should I call you Dr. Stiller?"

"This is Marcus Stiller, who are you?" Marcus made no attempt to hide his irritation.

"I'm sorry to call so early, but I was hoping to ask a favor."

"No favors until I know who you are."

"Of course. My name is Tom Lawrence. I'm one of the producers for the *Day Show*. Are you familiar with it?" Marcus was, having watched it most mornings. The show emphasized news and interviews and ran from 6:00 to 9:00 weekday mornings. "I would like to schedule you for an interview. Robert Billings is very interested in talking to you. Would it be possible for you to fly out to New York today? We'd be happy to put you up in a nice hotel, and we'd pay all expenses."

"You want to interview me? About the Moon?"

"Yes, sir. We think you have information that would be valuable to our viewers."

Marcus was having trouble taking the request in. "Let me get this straight. You want me to fly from southern California to New York City? For an interview?"

"Yes. Most of our guests really enjoy it."

"How long would the interview be?"

"We won't take much of your time. Most of our interviews last about five minutes."

Marcus sighed. "I'm sorry, I can't help you."

"Excuse me, sir, but we are talking about national exposure. The *Day Show* is seen by millions across our nation."

"I've had all the exposure I want, thank you. I'm not flying three thousand miles to sit in a chair for five minutes."

"But your opinion is valuable. People want to hear from you. You are the scientific genius who discovered the Stiller Enigma."

Despite himself, Marcus laughed. "Scientific genius, eh. Sorry, pal, flattery doesn't wash with me. I'm not flying to New York."

"I see," Billings said. "I suppose we'll have to get some other astronomer to take your place."

Marcus recognized the comment for what it was, an effort to prod his pride into taking action. The mention of another astronomer was the barb on the end of the prodding stick. "There are several good ones who love doing this stuff. I'm sure they'll do a good job for you. Thanks for calling—"

"Wait . . . Mr. Stiller . . . please wait."

"Yes."

"Look, can't we work something out. To be honest with you, my neck is on the line here. I'm going to take a professional beating if you don't come."

"I'm not coming. Sorry."

"What about a remote, then. You know, you go to one of our affiliate stations, and we do everything at a distance. Los Angeles. Can you make it to LA?"

"That's still two hours away."

"The station there is better equipped to do this kind of work. How 'bout it? Can I count on you?"

"When."

"Tomorrow morning, early."

Marcus groaned. "Okay, okay. You win. Los Angeles. I'll give you my e-mail address and you can send directions. Does that work for you?"

"Yes, sir. It works fine."

Marcus rattled off his e-mail and rang off.

"That sounded like fun," Lucy said with a stretch. "You love LA."

Marcus hated big cities. "That's why I chose to live in the mountains." He rose from bed and started toward the bathroom. "I don't want to do this, Lucy. We've already had one nutcase on our porch. What happens when my face is broadcast to millions of homes?"

"People will sell their televisions?"

"Cute. Did someone wake up feisty this morning?" Marcus returned to the bed and sat down next to where Lucy lay. "I'm glad one of us is in a good mood."

"I might as well be. I can be depressed about everything but nothing would change. Today I choose happiness . . . and breakfast out."

"I thought you had to go to the hospital," Marcus said.

"I do, but I have time. We could go to the Snow Top Café and have French toast and bacon."

"You're a doctor, you know that stuff is bad for you."

"Come on, you want some bacon and you know it." She tried to make the sound of bacon frying.

Marcus smiled at his wife's antics. He recognized her effort to cheer him up and he appreciated it. "Okay, you win, but I'm having huevos rancheros—a man's breakfast."

"I'll be ready in half an hour. You make coffee, and I'll make myself beautiful."

Marcus leaned over and gently kissed his wife on the lips. "You are already beautiful, and I love you for all that you've done for me."

Lucy wrapped her arms around his neck and pulled him close. "I was scared last night."

"Me too."

◗ ◗ ◖ ● ● ◖ ◗ ◖

LUCY STEPPED INTO THE LIVING ROOM where Marcus waited. "You must be hungry," he said. "You made it in twenty-five minutes."

"Well, you know how punctual doctors are." She was wearing a tan pantsuit with an ivory top and beige pumps.

"Funny, you don't look like a doctor," Marcus said, rising from his chair. "You look like someone who wants to call in sick and spend her whole day with her good-looking husband."

Lucy chortled. "Tempting, but I've missed too much work as it is. I'm afraid I don't get much bereavement time in a case like this. You'll just have to settle for breakfast."

"The universe is unfair."

"That it is," Lucy agreed. "We're going to have to take two cars. I need to leave right from the restaurant."

"Okay, I'll—" The phone rang. "I don't believe it," Marcus snapped. "If it's that producer again, I'll wring his neck."

"He's in New York. I don't think you can stretch that far."

"I was speaking metaphorically." The phone rang again. "Go ahead. I'll meet you there."

"Don't keep me waiting."

"Trust me. I won't."

Marcus let the phone ring two more times before picking up and saying hello.

"Mr. Stiller, this is . . ."

"No more interviews," Marcus interjected.

"Excuse me?" the male caller said.

"I said no more interviews. Now if you don't mind, I was headed out the door."

"Is that what you want me to tell the president?" the voice said.

The caller may have just been being clever, but it got Marcus's attention. "President?"

"As I started to say, my name is Dr. Barry Wenham at George Washington University. I'm the science advisor to President Rendel." He paused. "Are you still there, Mr. Stiller?"

"Yes, yes, I am. I'm sorry. I've been getting a lot of phone calls and . . . other things."

"I imagine," Wenham said. His voice was deep and smooth and carried the force of confidence. "You sound busy, so I'll get right to the point. The president wants to meet with you."

"With me?" Marcus was trying to convince himself that this was a joke, but he recognized the name of Barry Wenham.

"Yes, that is correct. In fact, he wants to meet with you tomorrow."

"You want me to fly to Washington, D.C., tomorrow?" Marcus asked, nonplussed.

"No. The president, as luck would have it, is coming to you. He is making a visit to your state to shore up votes for some of his party's congressmen. He'll be in Los Angeles tomorrow."

"I just agreed to a television interview in LA. I'll be in town early."

"Excellent. The president flies in tonight, has a breakfast meeting at 8:00 which should last about an hour, then is free for an hour before delivering a speech to movie execs in Hollywood. Can I tell him that you're free to meet him around 9:00?"

Marcus hesitated, still uncertain if this was all a joke. "Yes, but why does he want to meet with me?"

"You discovered the Stiller Enigma. Your name keeps popping up in the news media. You appear to be the go-to guy, as they say."

"I'm afraid I have very little to add. I'm as mystified as everyone else," Marcus confessed.

"I told the president that, but he still wants to meet with you." Marcus detected an edge in the man's voice. "He is not a man easily denied."

"Can I bring a friend . . . an astronomer friend, I mean." Marcus had an idea.

"I suppose. I'll need his name to pass on to the Secret Service. Who is he?"

Marcus gave the name of Ben Sicarello. "He's been fol-lowing this closely and providing much of the information. So has Dr. Philip Lansing, but I doubt he could make it from the east in time."

"Let's just keep it down to you and Dr. Sicarello. I suggest you arrive at the hotel early, say 8:30. The Secret Service will want to talk to you for a few minutes and give you a clearance badge." Wenham gave the address of the Berkley-Benton Hotel, a large luxury hotel near the LA Convention Center.

Marcus hung up the phone and stood as rigid as the pine trees in his yard. Life had become surreal. One day he was a college science professor; now the president of the United States wanted to pick his brains. "Lucy is never going to believe this."

Moving to his office, Marcus looked up Ben's phone number and placed the call. "Ben, this is Marc, what are you doing tomorrow?"

） ） ◐ ● ◑ ◖ ） （

WHEN JULIE NEXT AWOKE on Thursday evening, the sun had passed its zenith and was on its journey down the dome of the sky. Her thirst had returned, and she repeated her earlier activities, drinking water and soaking her feet. Hunger was rattling inside her, demanding attention.

The long nap had been troubled by dreams—dreams of Daniel, dreams of the attack, dreams of the hospital, and dreams of the Moon. Julie was thankful that the latter had only been dreams and not the horrifying visions she had had in the past. For the first time since escaping from the hospital, realization dawned. She had not had an episode, a true episode, since she had been out. At first, she asked herself why, but then dismissed the question. It didn't matter. Nothing mattered.

The night fell quickly, and it brought the cold with it. Huddled in a fetal position, Julie shivered, her body's only defense against the bitter evening. She doubted that the temperature had dropped below freezing. She had seen no ice on the ground that morning, but it was cold enough to make

every muscle in her body ache. She shook. Her teeth chat-
tered. Julie cried.

The sun rose slowly, vacating the darkness inch by inch.
Julie was awake to see it, eager for its arrival. She had endured
a night in a near freezing hell. The amber rays of early morning plunged through the trees and lit up patches of ground
damp from dew. Julie crawled to the nearest splash of light and
sat shivering in its glow. The sunlight felt good, and as the minutes passed the air around her warmed. The shivering relented
and Julie sat in a puddle of light that danced in tune to the moving branches overhead.

Her mind cleared, and after two days of rest, agonizing as
it was, her despair had lessened. The desire to die faded like the
cold night, replaced by a shallow hope. Julie was determined
not to spend another night in the cold, if for no other reason
than while death might be welcome, pain was not. But what to
do? Return to the car? No, someone may have found it. Besides,
she would have to walk uphill, and she doubted she had the
strength to do that. Downhill it was then. She rose, drank some
more water, and began to walk, following the stream. How far
she would be able to walk on injured feet that ached with every
step, she couldn't tell, but she had no other options.

Hungry, worn, and battered, Julie began another journey.

TWENTY-THREE

MARCUS COULD NOT HAVE BEEN MORE UNCOMFORTABLE if he were sitting in a dentist's chair waiting for a root canal. He had arrived at the LA television studio half an hour early. He had allowed plenty of time for traffic, but it meant leaving home at 3:30 that Friday morning and making the two-hour drive into the heart of the city. Now he sat on a well-padded stool behind the desk used by evening news anchors. The local director told him to sit up straight because the cameraman wanted to completely cut the desk out of the shot.

They had patted makeup on his face and wired him with a lapel mike.

"You'll be able to see Mr. Billings on that monitor just to the right of the camera," the director said. "You can see yourself on the monitor to the left. Please put this in your ear." He handed a white earpiece to Marcus. "You can hear the whole thing through this. In a moment or two, Tom Lawrence will come on the line, and he'll have a few questions for you. Just speak in a normal voice and talk right at the camera. Pretend it's your wife."

"My wife doesn't have a red light on the top of her head."

The director chuckled. "Lucky for you. That light will come on indicating that the camera is live. We're only using one camera so you don't have to worry about which of the three to look at. Have you got any questions?"

"No, I don't think so."

"Great. Just sit tight, and the next voice you hear should be from New York."

Marcus waited, feeling conspicuous and alone. Others worked around the set as if he weren't there. What was an intimidating situation for him was the mundane, everyday work of others. Behind him was a stage wall, decorated in all the places the camera could see, bare in all the rest.

"Can you hear me, Dr. Stiller?" The voice was less tinny than Marcus had anticipated. It was the same voice he had heard on the phone the previous morning, the voice of the producer Tom Lawrence.

"Um, yeah. I can hear you fine." Marcus felt silly. He was sitting alone talking to the air. The workers in earshot paid no attention.

"Great. Is it Mr. Stiller or Dr. Stiller?"

Marcus looked at the monitors and saw nothing but black screen. The cameras were off.

"Dr. Stiller. Actually, Marc would be fine."

"Robert Billings tends to be a little formal, so Dr. Stiller it is. He would prefer you call him Robert. Not Bob, but Robert."

"Robert. Got it."

"Okay, here's what's going to happen," Lawrence said. "A few moments before we go on the air, you'll see your monitors come on. You should have two of them in front of you."

"I do."

"Great. We'll be at a commercial break at that time, but you'll be able to see Robert and he will be able to see you, assuming nothing goes wrong. We'll do a couple of quick sound and video checks, then we're off to the races."

"It seems odd to be sitting here essentially by myself," Marcus admitted.

"One of the local directors should be there with you, but if not, don't worry. Some stations operate their cameras from a remote control room. When the red light comes on, your face will be broadcast across the nation."

Marcus found no joy in that knowledge. "I'll do my best."

"You'll do great. The interview will last around five minutes, so expect Robert to get right to the point. He doesn't have much time and he doesn't like to waste what he has."

"I understand."

"Do you have any questions for me?"

"No," Marcus said.

"Okay, sit tight, we'll have you on the air in a few moments."

The minutes passed slowly. Marcus tried to imagine what questions were coming his way, but there were too many to formulate. He just wanted it over. Ben was waiting for him at a nearby hotel. He had planned to do the interview, have breakfast with Ben and plan their discussion with the president, then drive over to the Berkley-Benton Hotel.

What a rare day this was: A national interview and a meeting with the president. Marcus had never felt more out of his league.

"Dr. Stiller?" The new voice came at the same time that the monitors came to life. "Can you hear me, Dr. Stiller? This is Robert Billings."

"I hear you fine, Mr. Billings." As promised, the monitor to Marcus's right and situated on the floor near the television camera showed Robert Billings. He was a dapper man, with coal black hair and a youthful look. Dressed in a dark blue suit, Billings was seated in a brown, padded chair that looked suitable for any upscale office. He was glancing at a sheet of paper while a young woman was attaching a microphone to his lapel. Marcus could hear the mike rub against the cloth of Billings' coat.

"Thirty seconds," another voice said. It was muted and Marcus assumed that it was the floor director in NY.

"Fine," Billings said. "That'll do, Marcie," he said to the woman who was now straightening his tie. "Dr. Stiller, I'll begin with a few opening remarks, just to set the stage, you know, then we'll be on to the questions. It's important not to look at the monitor. Look at the camera."

Marcus realized that Billings could see him on a monitor in New York. "I can do that." He looked straight into the round glass lens of the camera.

"That's better. We're on in ten, any last-second questions?"

Marcus said no. He took a deep breath and tried to organize his spinning mind. Suddenly he was as nervous as a child in a school play. Marcus heard music and glanced at the monitor. Billings was staring straight into the camera, relaxed and clearly comfortable.

The music faded and Billings spoke. "The last few days have been unique in the history of our world. A week ago, a red spot was noticed on the face of the Moon. That spot, scientists tell us, is growing at a remarkable rate. For some this has been a mere oddity, to many more it is a sign of the end.

Over the last two days, we have been bringing you reports of mass suicides by cult groups, and the accusations of countries like Russia and China, raising questions of fault against the United States. What is behind all this? What is happening to the Moon? To help us answer those questions we have Dr. Marcus Stiller, the man who first discovered the red spot and the man after whom the Stiller Enigma is named. Welcome, Dr. Stiller."

The pit of Marcus's stomach dropped like an out-of-control elevator. He looked into the camera. The red light came on. "Good morning, Robert." At least he remembered to call the host by his first name.

"The world is on edge, Doctor, and it doesn't seem to be getting any better. What is going on with the Moon?"

Marcus was puzzled. The question was unclear. Was he asking what was the cause of the spot, or was he asking why the Moon was having such an odd effect on the world? He assumed the first. "Well, Robert, we don't know yet. Just south of the Crater Plato a previously unnoticed feature appeared. It is red in color and seems to be growing."

"Seems to be growing or is growing, Doctor?"

"Expanding would be a better word, I suppose. When I first noticed it, it was relatively small but quickly spread. As of last night, the enigma is about"—Marcus paused to mentally convert kilometers into miles—"340 miles wide and nearly one hundred miles north to south."

"I see. Let me cut to the chase: What is it?"

Marcus pursed his lips. Billings didn't waste time. Marcus decided he wouldn't either. "I don't know."

"You must have some idea," Billings prodded. "Don't people in your field have tests for such things?"

"Not as much as some think," Marcus said, trying not to sound defensive. "Astronomy and astrophysics are not hands-on sciences. The Moon is nearly a quarter-million miles away. It's hard to pick up a sample. That leaves us with observations

with telescopes, radar, and spectrometer. From optical observation we can gauge its size and rate of expansion. We can even
rule out such things as volcanic activity. With radar we can
determine that it's not ice, and with the spectrometer we can
usually judge the chemical makeup."

"And what do those observations reveal?"

"Nothing."

Billings seemed stunned. "Nothing?"

"I'm afraid so. Several observatories and highly qualified
scientists have examined the enigma and have been puzzled to
find nothing there."

"But it *is* there. We can see it."

"Precisely. It just doesn't show up except by visual observation."

"What does that mean?"

Marcus sighed, then admitted, "I really don't know."

"Are there other tests under way?"

"Oh, yes," Marcus said. "The event is being monitored
around the world, but since it's a new anomaly, it is too early
to have specific information."

"Parts of the world are in turmoil, Doctor," Billings
intoned somberly. "Some think things are going to get worse.
What is the world to make of all this?"

"I'm afraid people respond in various ways to the unexpected. The Moon has been our neighbor since the dawn of
man. As far as human history is concerned, it has always been
present and always looked the same. In 350 years of observation a change has never been observed on the Moon. In every
way it appears a dead world. Now something is different, and
people are reading things into it that they shouldn't."

"Such as?"

"Fear. As I said, the Moon is nearly a quarter-million miles
away. Nothing that happens on the Moon is going to harm us
on Earth—short of it blowing up, I mean."

"Is that possible?"

Marcus started to laugh but pressed down the urge. "No, it's not possible. I'll admit that the enigma is unusual, it is fascinating, it is puzzling, but it is not dangerous. The only danger we need fear is our own irrational behavior."

"So this hasn't had any impact on your life?"

Instantly, Marcus thought of the graffiti on the front of his house and the confrontation with the crazed man who put it there. "I've been a little busier, I get a lot more e-mail and phone calls than I used to, but beyond that, my life hasn't changed."

"Your father just passed away, didn't he?" Billings asked straight-faced.

That stunned Marcus. How could he know that? "Um, yes, he did."

"I was sorry to hear that. He was a minister, wasn't he?"

"Yes, a Baptist minister for over twenty years."

"What do you suppose he would have to say about this? Would he have seen this as a spiritual event? Maybe a sign of the end times?"

"I . . . I don't know what you mean." Marcus felt confused. This line of thought was the last thing he expected.

"We've been getting a great deal of e-mail and phone calls from various ministers saying that this is a sign from God. They quote a passage from the Bible . . . I have it here." Marcus glanced at the monitor and saw Billings reading from the paper he held. "'The sun shall be turned into darkness, and the moon into blood, before the great and the terrible day of the Lord come.' Joel 2:31." He paused, then asked, "As the son of a minister and as a scientist, does this make sense?"

Those were the words the crazy man used last night. Just hearing them shook Marcus. "I think it is best to let scientists talk about science and theologians talk about spiritual matters." The words didn't seem right. They seemed awkward, ill fitting, but Marcus said them anyway.

"Perhaps you're right. Tell us a little about the Moon. What's it like?"

Marcus called up his concentration, but it was like lifting a heavy anchor by hand. "That's a big topic, Robert."

"We have two minutes." He gave a little laugh.

Marcus spoke of the Moon, rattling off facts about its size, composition, what was learned from the Apollo missions. It was the fastest lecture he had ever given. When he was done, Billings thanked him for his time and then passed the baton to another cohost. As he did, the monitors went dead and the local director stepped forward and removed the lapel microphone. "You did great," the director said.

"Thanks," Marcus replied without conviction. He rose from the seat and stepped around the prop desk.

"That was an interesting question Billings asked . . . about the spiritual stuff, I mean."

"Yeah. Interesting." Marcus felt drained. He wanted to go home, to go back to his office and think things through. But that wasn't going to happen. He still had to pick up Ben at the hotel, drive across town, and meet with the president. He couldn't imagine how that would go, and he feared it would be worse.

○ ◐ ◑ ● ◕ ◔ ○

JULIE FOLLOWED THE STREAM wondering if she were walking into trouble or away from it. Her weariness was profound. Having not eaten in three days, and having expended more energy in that time than she had the previous month, left her barely able to walk. Every step was an exercise of will, a challenge of the impossible. She wanted to quit, but she was driven by something she could not recognize, could not identify.

She walked on.

A sound pulled her from her foggy pain. She had heard something. Her mind chugged slowly like an ancient diesel engine, no longer able to focus on anything for more than a few moments, but the sound was familiar. Cars—cars moving along a road. She left the brook behind and followed the noise.

The terrain continued to slope down and she feared that she would fall and roll unabated until stopped by the trunk of some tree. Careful step followed cautious step. Peering through the trees she saw familiar objects, white, square objects. Big objects. A few staggering steps later she could see what lay beyond a line of trees. Houses. A neighborhood was a short distance away. She paused at the line of trees that bordered the forest. A street ran from her left to her right. Perpendicular to that was another street—a lane lined with small houses. As she watched, a man walked from one of the houses, entered his car, and drove off. It was early on a weekday. People were headed to work.

Julie stood behind the line of trees that was the demarcation line of wilderness and civilization. The air had changed. It was warmer and rich with smells of food that had been cooked that morning. Food. The smell of it made her stomach ache from hunger. Still she waited. No one else left their houses. No one watered lawns. The street had taken on the ghost town qualities that befell residential communities on workday mornings.

A battle began in Julie. Fear faced off with need. She was familiar with fear. It had been her companion for so long ... too long. If she stepped from her hiding place, someone might see her and report that a strange woman with no shoes was staggering down their peaceful community street. That thought terrified her. Her other option was to die in the woods. She could not stand another night without food and warmth. Julie understood her next decision was a choice between life and death.

Death still seemed good to her. No more pain, no more running, no more rejections. It would put an end to the horrible journey. It would make Daniel happy. He could have his

new life, his new love. Maybe he could find the purpose and
meaning in his new love that he could not find in her.

He would win.

Gordon would win.

The visions would win.

"No," Julie said. "I won't let them win. I've come too far."
Julie stepped from the shadows of the forest into the bright
morning light of civilization.

Crossing the first street, she moved down the right side of
the neighborhood lane, trying not to show the pain she felt with
each step. She wanted to look normal, like she was a resident
out for a morning stroll, but knew that she stood little chance
of success. Anyone seeing her would know that she was out of
place, a stranger in the land of the normal. The stagger in her
walk, her rumpled clothing, covered with dirt and pine needles,
her bare feet, all clues that something was wrong with the lone
woman. Still Julie moved on, uncertain what her next move
would be. Perhaps she should just knock on someone's door
and ask for food. She dismissed the idea. They would certainly
call the police, and the police would take her back to the hospital, back to the room, back to the sadistic Gordon.

She gave furtive glances at the windows of each house she
passed. Was someone watching her? Compared to hers, these
houses were small. These were more like large cabins than tract
homes. Each looked different than the one next to it, obviously
each built to some owner's specific design.

One house caught her attention. Its yard was neat and its
paint fresh, but it was scarred by crudely painted words. The
words stopped her in her tracks: Moon man. Moon man? A
large circle with a red blotch painted in the upper left corner
caught her eye. The Moon.

Was it a sign? More important, was it real? Was she really
seeing the graffiti or just imagining it? Julie approached, taking
the wooden steps that led to the front porch slowly, then crossing the porch itself. Standing inches away from the marred wall,

she extended a hand and touched the paint. It was dry, but looked new. What mattered most was that it was real, tangible.

It was a sign. It had to be. But why? What should she do now? A doorbell button was just to the right of the door. Raising a tremulous finger and suppressing a rising tide of terror, she pressed it and heard a muted chiming from inside. Her stomach flipped and a dark corner of her mind screamed that she should run, but Julie stood her ground.

Nothing. She rang the bell again. Still nothing. Pressing her ear to the door, she listened for the sounds of life: a television playing, water running, anything. More nothing. Against her fear's advice, she tried the doorknob. It was locked. Cautiously Julie looked through the wide front window. The curtains were drawn, but a small slit between the drapery panels allowed her to peek inside. She could see the living room and a sliding glass door at the back wall and beyond that was a deck.

Pulling back from the window, Julie looked to the side of the house and noticed that the front porch led around the side of the home. She followed it until she stood on the back deck. The ground below fell away steeply into a canyon. Julie peered over the railing and shuddered. She hated heights. The deck had a plastic-topped table and some outdoor chairs.

The back wall of the house was bathed in morning sunlight. Several windows were spaced evenly down the wall, making the most of the view. Julie looked in each one and saw nothing. Through one window she saw the kitchen. On a tile counter were a loaf of bread and a bowl of fruit. A banquet!

She tried the wide sliding glass door. It was locked. She tried another window; this one led to a small laundry room. Like the other windows in the house, this one had an aluminum frame and could be opened by sliding one pane of glass past another. She pushed against the pane that was designed to slide and was surprised that it budged. She pushed again, looking at the locking device between the windowpanes. It was not fully engaged and the window slid an inch. Encouraged, she pushed harder and the window moved easily along its track. Julie was now looking through an open maw, but it was too high for her to pull herself through. She didn't have strength for gymnastics.

Her mind was operating in overdrive. Entering someone else's house was something she would never have considered, but the thought of bread and fruit elbowed out every other reasonable thought. Her stomach ached with anticipation.

Hurriedly, Julie pulled one of the plastic outdoor chairs over and stood on it. Her waist now came to the sill of the window. She could easily lean in, which she did. Just beneath the window were a washer and dryer. Julie was thankful for them. They meant that she could crawl through the window putting her weight on the appliances and not have to worry about falling to the floor.

Pushing aside guilt and fear, Julie pulled and wiggled her way through the narrow window and soon found herself sitting on the washer, her feet dangling over the edge. She was breathing hard; the simple effort had expended what little energy she had in reserve. Gently, she lowered herself, opened the door of the laundry room, and once more listened for the sounds of occupation. Hearing none, Julie hobbled through the living room and into the kitchen. Seizing an apple from the fruit bowl, she ate hungrily. The juice of the apple ran down her chin and then her neck. It was sweet, so very, very sweet. Nothing she had ever eaten could match the glorious taste of the apple.

Her stomach grumbled in appreciation and she ate more. She then ate a banana and two slices of bread. The room began to spin, but she continued ingesting the glorious feast before her. Opening the refrigerator she found it a vault of treasure: milk, juice, leftovers. She pulled a carton of milk from the refrigerator and drank. Ambrosia! Thick and rich, the milk soothed her dry throat.

It was wonderful, and Julie began to weep for joy. Food. Food.

The room began to spin more. Setting the carton down, Julie steadied herself by holding onto the counter. The room darkened from the edge of her vision in. She knew the feeling. She was losing consciousness.

Staggering into the living room, she tried to make her way to the sofa, but its short distance was too far.

Julie fell to the floor, and the black of unconsciousness flooded her mind.

TWENTY-FOUR

THE PRESIDENT BOWLED INTO THE ROOM WITHOUT INTRO-
duction. Marcus and Ben were on their feet in a moment,
as much from the startling entrance as out of respect for
the man who held the highest elected position in the
country. Marcus and Ben exchanged glances. Both had
been sitting on a sofa in the sitting area of the presiden-
tial suit. Marcus had picked Ben up at his hotel and
driven across town. They arrived fifteen minutes early
for their meeting, were questioned by the humorless

agents of the Secret Service, escorted to the top floor of the Berkley-Benton Hotel, and shown in.

Once inside an agent motioned to the sofa. The room had other furniture: two heavily padded leather chairs that Marcus guessed cost a fortune. An agent stood next to the door. Another stood outside the door, and two more were at the elevators. They were a cautious bunch.

At first they sat in silence, their hands folded in their laps like a pair of children called to the principal's office. They had talked about the TV interview on the way over, and had tried to make more small talk while they waited. They failed.

The only indication that the president was about to enter the room came when the agent by the door touched his ear and then whispered into a microphone pinned to his sleeve. He also stiffened. A second later the door exploded open and the president entered like an avalanche. Behind him were three men, none of whom Marcus recognized.

"Have a seat, gentlemen," President Rendel said. "Thank you for coming."

"Our pleasure," Marcus said. Rendel shook their hands and then stripped off his dark blue suit coat, loosened his tie, and released the button of his collar. "I hate ties," he said. "It's the only thing about this job I hate."

Marcus was wearing a tie, Ben his clerical collar. The president studied the priest, then added, "I suppose there are worse things than ties."

Ben laughed lightly. "I seldom wear this. Not a requirement in my job."

Rendel nodded. "Gentlemen, this is Teddy Thomson, my chief of staff, and Dr. Barry Wenham." He motioned at a young man whose bright red hair and ruddy complexion could make him the poster child for Ireland. "And Steve Baker, my body man."

"Body man?" Marcus said.

"Yes," Rendel replied, seating himself in one of the leather chairs. "Valet, personal assistant, and more. I couldn't get by without him."

"I see," Marcus said.

Thomson took the seat next to the president; Wenham stood just to his right. The body man disappeared into the back of the suite, and the Secret Service agent stepped outside the door.

"I'm afraid my schedule is getting tighter by the moment, gentlemen, so I'm going to have to dispense with pleasantries and get down to work. Brass tacks, men: What's the deal with the Moon?"

Marcus cleared his throat, then said, "Well, while I was doing some observations with two of my students, I took some photos—"

"Excuse me, Dr. Stiller, I'm aware of all that. What I need to hear is what has caused the enigma that bears your name and what we can do about it."

"Do about it?" Marcus said.

"The world is going . . . for lack of a better word . . . wacky, and all because of this spot on the Moon. Dr. Wenham tells me that no one has come up with any answers. That won't do."

"Dr. Wenham is correct," Marcus said. "I've monitored this as closely as anyone and Ben, um, Dr. Sicarello has been leading the forefront of research."

"And you can't tell me what it is or what has caused it?" Rendel asked pointedly.

"No, sir," Ben chimed in.

"This is the twenty-first century, gentlemen. This country has poured countless millions of dollars into research, not to mention money that comes from private sources, and the best you can do is tell me that no one knows anything?"

"That's correct," Marcus said.

"Well, at least you scientists are consistent. I'm getting the same report from NASA and everyone else I ask." He leaned forward. "I need more. Our country is being accused of causing the problem. Some think it's a late effect of the Apollo mission and others think we're testing Star Wars technology on the Moon. It's all nonsense, but just saying so doesn't cut the mustard with these folks. I need more."

Marcus felt like he was being scolded by one of his college professors. "Sir, every test says it's not there, but we can see it. The best we can do is to continue our observations."

"Guess," Terry Thomson said.

Marcus saw Wenham close his eyes. No scientist liked to guess.

"If I were to speculate," Marcus began, "I would try to reconcile the two conflicting facts we have. One, a red spot has appeared and is growing at a surprising rate. We know this because we can see it and monitor its growth. However, no instrument reading indicates any change. If the Moon had an atmosphere we'd guess that we were seeing a dust storm, but the Moon has no atmosphere to speak of, so that's out. What does the Moon have?

"It has geological material," Marcus continued. The president leaned forward as if missing a single word would be catastrophic. "But that material is essentially unchanging. Some suspect that the Moon has a small liquid core that occasionally results in out-gassing, but—"

"Out-gassing?" Rendel asked.

"The release of gasses above ground. Such things have been observed but are impossible to predict. Most likely, the tidal strains on the Moon allow for the occasional release of gas that is expelled into the airless environment of the Moon. Solar wind disperses it and any particulate matter settles back to the surface and mixes with the regolith—the rocky soil of the Moon."

"That sounds reasonable," the president said.

"But it's not," Ben interjected. "We've been observing the Moon closely since the initial discovery and have seen no evidence of such out-gassing. Nor has any such event of this magnitude ever been seen. Add to that, an out-gassing large enough to cover the area the enigma now covers should be easily visible to earth-based telescopes. There should be a significant geyser."

"I've wondered if there hasn't been a shift in the loose debris that covers the mare revealing something previously unseen." Marcus shifted in his seat. "But that doesn't hold up either."

"Mare is . . . are the dark patches on the Moon?" Thomson asked.

"That's right. Sometimes called seas." Marcus continued, "Anything big enough to affect an area as large as we are seeing should also be observable."

"Let me ask this," Rendel said. "Could the Apollo people have left something back there that has caused this?"

Marcus shook his head. "No Apollo craft landed in the Mare Imbrium, nor have any unmanned vehicles. It's unexplored except by flyover probes like Clementine and Lunar Prospector."

"Maybe we should pick a story and stick with it," Thomson said. Marcus saw Wenham cringe. Thomson saw it too. To the science advisor he said, "What? Do you have a better idea?"

"Bat wings," Wenham muttered. He seemed to Marcus to be an unhappy man.

"What are you talking about?" Rendel demanded. Before he could answer, Marcus smiled and the president caught it. "Is this a private joke or can your president be let in on it?"

Marcus spoke up. "In August of 1835 the *New York Sun* published an article that cited the *Edinburgh Journal of Science*. Supposedly Sir John Herschel had been able to observe the Moon with a new type of telescope. He saw four-foot-tall men with wings like bats. He also was said to have seen beaches, goats, and pelicans, as well as a whole town. The publisher later confessed to the prank. He did pick up a lot of new subscribers."

"Your point?" Thompson asked.

"You can't make up a story," Marcus explained. "It might be believed by the people for a short time, but then scientists around the world are going point out the lie. The only thing a scientist enjoys more than making a grand discovery is pointing out someone else's faulty work. It'd be traced back to you, Mr. President, not to mention the ethical factors."

"That's what Dr. Wenham said." Rendel rubbed his forehead. "You are all convinced that there is nothing to worry about?"

The scientist nodded.

"Then why are Russia and China so up in arms?"

"We always fear what we don't know and what we can't explain." Marcus said. For some reason, he suddenly thought of his father. His words sounded like something his dad would have said. "May I make a suggestion?"

Rendel nodded.

"There are many able scientists in Russia and China. Invite some over for a joint research project. Arrange for them to use some of our equipment. Instead of having them on the outside, bring them in. Show the world we have nothing to hide."

"I'll make time available," Ben said. "I'll have to juggle the schedule and offer a dozen apology dinners, but I can make it happen."

Rendel rubbed his chin. "What do you think, Teddy?"

"I like it," the chief of staff said. "The gesture couldn't hurt and might gain us some currency on the world stage."

"What about the other nonsense going on?" the president asked. "The mass suicides, the radio talk shows that preach this is the end?"

Marcus shook his head. He had no idea.

"I don't think anything can be done about that," Wenham said. "Father Sicarello may have a better take on this than I do, but people are going to believe whatever they want. They don't call it lunacy for nothing."

Moon madness, Marcus thought. Lunacy was a good term for what was going on. He had missed the details of most of the news reports, being occupied with his father's death and his sudden place in the media spotlight.

Steve Baker, the body man, came in from the rear of the suite. "It's time, Mr. President."

Rendel stood, buttoned his shirt, and fixed his tie.

"Duty calls, gentlemen. I appreciate your time and especially your suggestion, Dr. Stiller. You will keep me posted, won't you?"

"Yes, sir," Marcus and Ben said in unison. They had stood when the president had.

"Maybe I can do you a favor sometime." He started for the door, stopped, and turned to Wenham. "Dr. Wenham, please make sure they have your contact information."

"Yes, Mr. President."

President Rendel marched from the room.

)) ● ● ● ◄ ((

GORDON WATCHED AS DANIEL WAAL WALKED AROUND his home slowly, like a man combing the wreckage of a house hit by a tornado. His movements were stiff, his jaw set like a vice. His eyes darted around taking in every detail. Gordon, who was seldom intimidated by anyone, felt a twinge of uneasiness. They were standing in the kitchen, hovering over the shattered remains of the drawer Julie had hit Gordon with, knocking him unconscious. Gordon looked up at his uncle. Bernard returned a bitter stare.

"If it's any comfort, she swings a mean drawer," Gordon said, trying to lighten the mood. He touched the swollen red lump on the side of his head. He had been unconscious for half an hour, best he could judge. Julie was gone, he was in pain, and so he relented and called the police. The police had made contact with Daniel's office in Sacramento. Daniel, who had been out of state on business, got home two days after Julie drove off from the house. He was not happy.

"You had her and you let her go," Daniel said. There was ice in his voice. "Why didn't you just call the police? You had her location."

"I was trying to keep it out of the papers," Gordon said. "You know, save the hospital and you some bad publicity. If the police know about this, then it's bound to get to the press."

"You idiot," Daniel snapped. "The police already know. Dr. Bernard called them when you first let her escape. You know that. Don't trifle with me, boy. I am more than your match."

Gordon did know it, but he was grasping at straws. Nothing about the situation looked good. "I was trying to avoid *more* publicity. Besides, she escaped from the hospital on my shift. It was my job to get her back."

"You failed!" Daniel shouted. "Now she's gone again."

"We'll find her," Dr. Bernard said. "If we keep cool heads and let reason prevail—"

"I can see how well that has worked so far," Daniel retorted. Gordon saw him grit his teeth and instinctively took a step back. Daniel reached for the facing of the shattered drawer—the thickest piece of the remains—raised it above his head, and, in a furious motion, brought it down against the counter. It shattered into three large pieces with an ear-punishing crash. He turned to Bernard, who had backpedaled several steps. "You, I'm thinking of a dozen different ways of suing you into oblivion."

"I don't think you want to do that," Bernard said with a tremulous voice. His words seemed brave, but his voice betrayed his fear. "That would ... reveal too much."

To Gordon's surprise, the senator backed off. He wasn't sure what his uncle had on Daniel Waal, but it must be good. Daniel turned on him. "And as for you," he said, raising a finger, stabbing the air in Gordon's direction, "as far as I'm concerned, she didn't hit you hard enough."

Gordon remained silent.

"What was she wearing?" Daniel demanded.

"I've already told the police—," Gordon began.

"Tell me!"

"Okay, okay, just chill. Yelling at me doesn't help." Gordon paused, then said, "I don't know."

"You ... don't ... know," Daniel said, stretching out the phrase.

"It was dark and ..." Gordon could feel the piercing stare of the senator. "She was wearing a robe."

"A robe?" Bernard said.

"Yes, a robe. She was in the shower when I came in. I think she grabbed some clothes from the master bedroom closet."

Daniel shook with anger. His hands were clenched, and Gordon was sure the man was going to burst into flame. "You attacked my wife in the shower?"

Gordon said nothing.

"You perverted little—" Daniel started for him, but Bernard stepped between them.

"Enough!" Bernard said. "He's not the one with a mistress, you are, so get off your pedestal, Senator. We need to focus on the problem."

Mistress? Gordon thought. *That's useful information.*

A ringing sounded from inside the sport coat Daniel was wearing. He removed the cell phone, read the number on the small screen, and answered, "Daniel Waal here."

Gordon watched as the senator's eyes closed and wished he could hear the other side of the conversation.

"Where?" the senator said. "When? ... Uh-huh ...Where is it now? ... Okay, I'll make arrangements for it to be picked up. Any other word?" He waited. "Please keep me posted." He slipped the phone back into his pocket.

"The police?" Bernard asked.

"Yes. They found the car in the San Bernardino Mountains. No sign of Julie. They're calling out search and rescue. She appears to have wandered off into the forest."

"I'm familiar with the area," Bernard said. "There's a ski run up there. I go a couple of times each year. People get lost in those mountains every year."

"I suppose we can hope for that," Gordon said. "That would solve a lot of problems."

The movement was unexpected. Gordon saw his uncle slip to one side. He realized too late that Daniel had pushed the older man out of the way. A moment later he found out why. The senator's right fist came crashing down on the bridge of his nose. Bright lights flashed in his mind, his legs wobbled then gave way, and Gordon dropped to the floor.

Raising a hand to his face, he found blood running from his nose. Gordon was getting tired of being clobbered by the Waal family.

"How does that help?" Bernard shouted.

"It shuts him up and makes me feel better," Daniel snapped. To Gordon he said, "Get out of my house and stay away from me. Next time I won't pull my punch."

◗ ◗ ◗ ● ◖ ◖ ◖

"WELL, THAT WAS INTERESTING," Ben said.

Marcus steered the car north along the I–5 freeway. He was in the right lane, content to creep along with the slower traffic. This day, all the lanes were slow, something Marcus always associated with Los Angeles. Fortunately, he was in no hurry to get home and there was plenty of time before Ben's plane departed. "The president is stuck between a rock and a hard place. People are looking to him for answers and he knows less than we do . . . and we know next to nothing."

"How are you holding up?"

Ben's question caught Marcus off guard. "I was a little tense before the interview and even more so before meeting with the president, but that has passed."

"That's not what I mean," Ben explained. "Your plate has been filled to the edges: the enigma, the press coverage, and the loss of your father. That's a lot of pressure for a man to endure."

"I'm all right," Marcus said quickly. "A little tired. Things are getting weird." He recounted the events with the spray-painting stranger.

"One more log on the proverbial fire." Ben was silent for a moment. "I don't think you're fine, Marc. I know I'm butting in and have no right to do so, but I think you're more troubled than you let on."

Marcus didn't want to go down this path. "I'm okay, really. Tired and confused, but I'm surviving."

"I see. That's good to hear."

Guilt welled up in Marcus. Ben was trying to be a friend, offering an open ear, and Marcus was cutting him off. Still, Marcus was a solitary man, with few friends. He had never felt the need for companionship apart from his wife. She made him feel complete and whole. Friends were just another complexity.

"I lost my father five years ago," Ben admitted. "We were not close as it appears you and your dad were. Time had put a lot of distance between us."

"What did you say your father did?" Marcus asked.

"Civil engineer. He was gifted in that area."

"You must have been proud of him."

"You'd think so, wouldn't you," Ben replied. "I never expressed much pride in him, nor he in me. He was upset when I decided to study with the Jesuits."

"Not a religious man?"

"The antithesis of faith," Ben explained. "My mother was deeply religious, and she dragged me to church as often as she could. My father tolerated it because he adored her. How they ever hooked up, I'll never understand. She was a music teacher, teaching children piano in the evenings. Her heart was gold and her love immeasurable. Dad was the opposite. To him, if it couldn't be explained in quadratic equations, it wasn't worth knowing."

"They say opposites attract," Marcus interjected.

"They're right," Ben agreed. "I've spent my life trying to blend apparent opposites. My father thought I was wasting my time with religious study, but it pleased my mother. He did console himself that I was studying physics and astronomy."

"Did he ever come around?"

"No. We remained cordial, but never close. That's to our shame—to my shame."

Marcus braked quickly. Once again the traffic came to a near stop. A moment later it started to flow again but at a rate slower than a man could walk. "I'm glad we didn't have this kind of traffic on the way in."

"The president would still be waiting on us."

"I don't think he waits on anyone." Marcus studied the road for a moment, wondering if the lane next to him was moving faster. It wasn't. "I'm guessing you have a point to all this."

"I do," he admitted. "I'm guessing you haven't come to grips with your father's death."

"It's still too fresh," Marcus said. "Time will ease things a bit."

From the corner of his eye, Marcus saw Ben nodding. "I'm sure it will, but . . ." His voice faded.

"But what?"

"I don't believe you'll come to grips with your father's death until you come to grips with your father's beliefs. When my dad died I grieved not only over his death but also over my inability to connect with him in the intangibles."

"Intangibles? Like what?"

Ben sighed. Marcus could tell that he was struggling with the words. "I suppose I mean faith, love, those things that can't be quantified. My mother used to encourage me in my love for science but always warned me that there was more than the physical world. I suppose that's why I became a priest. I wanted to please her, but I also wanted to please my father, so I followed my love of science. The Jesuits seemed the answer. It did make my mother happy, but not my father. Our relationship cooled and never warmed again."

"You didn't feel a calling to be a priest?" Marcus asked.

"No," Ben confessed. "I know many priests who have. For me it seemed like a good compromise. The Bible and prophecy fascinate me, but that's more of an avocation than a vocation. The work has been good, the research exciting, so I have no regrets. Although I had some during the training."

"The training was tough?"

"Two years in seclusion as a novice; vows of poverty, chastity, and obedience; two years in classical study; three years of advanced study in philosophy and science. Then I spent several years teaching. After that were three more years of theological study. Then came my ordination. Following that was another year of theological study and a year of retirement for prayer."

"Wow. And you felt no call to do all that?" The idea that a man would give up family and more in a vocation like the priesthood in an effort to please both parents seemed oddly understandable and sad. "My father always said a man had to be called to ministry. He said he felt the call while in the Navy and set his sights on completing his education."

"I have no sense of call, Marc. I am just what I am. But my point isn't to talk about me, but to talk about you. It seems that you are avoiding the faith of your father."

"Avoiding may be too strong a term."

"What term would you use?"

Marcus gazed through the windshield at the sea of cars before him and thought about the question put him. Had he been avoiding faith? It was true that he paid it little heed since college. A new need rose up in him, a need to be honest. He had not known Ben all that long, but he seemed to be a sincere man, intellectually honest and open. Marcus felt he could trust Ben.

"Ignoring. I've been ignoring it," Marcus admitted. "Truth is, I just don't think about it. I am what I am." He laughed. "Great, now I'm quoting Popeye."

"And I am what I am," Ben agreed but then added, "but is that right? Maybe I shouldn't be comfortable being what I am. Maybe I should be asking what I should be. I'm a priest, not because of deep religious conviction. Don't get me wrong— I'm a believer. I believe in God. I believe in Christ. But that's not why I became a priest. I became a priest to please others."

"Isn't that what life is, an effort to simultaneously please ourselves and others?"

"Perhaps, Marc, but is that what it should be?"

Marcus had no answers and could only offer a shrug.

Ben continued. "I didn't mean to talk about myself. What I mean to do is suggest that part of the burden you bear is not the death of your father but the death of an opportunity to please him."

That struck home like a bullet to the forehead. Marcus said nothing.

"I'm not saying this well," bemoaned Ben. "Your father was a minister, a man of the Bible. People like him see farther than we can with our telescopes. Do you think your father was wrong about faith?"

Marcus shook his head. He had never thought that. Truth was, he avoided thoughts of faith. He was a scientist. Science was the structure of his life. "I can't say he was wrong, but still I have spent my life dealing with the tangible."

"No, you haven't," Ben blurted. "And neither have I. Except for those involved in planetary studies, most in our profession gaze at, take pictures of, make instrument readings of distant objects whose light has taken untold years to get here. In some ways, we are students of the past, historians with fancy

instruments. Much of our attention is directed at things we can-
not touch. We have made math our language and science our
guide, but at the end of the day, it all rings hollow."

"So why are you a scientist?"

"Because I believe the two go together. To be anti-God is
to narrow our vision, and that is the opposite of why science
exists. If we search after knowledge, then we must take that
knowledge wherever we find it. To select physical science as the
only reality is chauvinistic and intellectually dishonest."

Marcus was hearing a man unwind a spring that had
been tight much too long. "Can I ask when you started feeling this way?"

"In recent days. It's the Moon, Marc. It's the Moon. You
know the results of our observations. What if it isn't natural?
What if this is a supernatural event?"

"I can't bring myself to say that."

"Marc," Ben shot back. "Our science, your science, leads
directly to that conclusion. The spot is not there, but we see it."

"We need to make more observations," Marc said.

"And if they say the same thing?"

"We make more."

Ben shook his head vigorously. "Until when? Until we find
what we want to see? Until we create a test that gives us the
answer we want to hear? How is that intellectually honest?"

"I don't know what to say," Marcus admitted. "Why
didn't you mention this to the president?"

"And say what? 'Mr. President, the Stiller Enigma is a sign
from God.' Did he strike you as a man that would sit still for
such a statement? He would lump us in with the cult groups
that are preaching the end of the world."

"You really believe this is from God?" Marcus asked.

"I didn't say that, Marc. I'm just saying that we need to be
open to all possibilities, including that one. What would your
father say?"

Marcus chewed on this for a moment. "He would say move with caution, be aware. He believed in miracles but didn't see them everywhere. I remember him teaching that Christians should not be gullible believing everything that came down the pike. He was big on the Bible and kept saying that the Bible and the Bible alone was our source of authority. I guess he would ask, 'What does the Bible say?'"

"'And I gazed when he broke the sixth seal, and there was a great earthquake; and black as sackcloth made of hair became the sun, and the whole Moon became as blood,'" Ben quoted. "Familiar with the passage?"

"Revelation," Marcus said.

"Right. Revelation 6:12."

Marcus said, "'The sun shall be turned into darkness, and the moon into blood, before the great and the terrible day of the Lord come.' Joel 2:31." He turned to Ben. "The crazy man I told you about . . . the guy that spray-painted my front wall quoted that to me."

Silence filled the car. The conversation was running against Marcus's grain. "Observe, note, and observe again" had been his motto for so many years. Now Ben was suggesting that all that be set aside. "The other night I had a dream," Marcus said. He explained about the fishing trips and the conversations he and his father would have. "He reminded me that faith was a reasoned response, not an emotional one. He wanted me to understand that to be a person of faith one didn't have to check his brain at the door. Is it reasonable to think that God would really do something like this?" Marcus already knew the answer.

"Would it be reasonable not to think about it?"

"I don't know."

"Guys like you and me, Marc, are going to need to know."

The traffic gave and Marcus was able to push the speed up. No matter how fast he went, it would never match the careening thoughts in his head.

CHAPTER

TWENTY-
FIVE

AFTER PICKING UP BEN'S THINGS FROM THE HOTEL, Marcus drove him to LAX and waited with him until he boarded a plane back to Arizona. They continued their discussion and reviewed the latest e-mail each had received from others in the scientific community. Marcus's e-mail box was filled with requests for interviews. He checked his phone messages and found it cluttered with the same kind of requests.

They arrived two hours prior to departure and used the time and Ben's laptop computer to reanalyze every bit of information they had. The end result was the same: the spot was bigger, still growing, and nonexistent to every test run so far.

"Two days from now, the entire Mare Imbrium will be covered," Ben said. "What will the world do when six billion people can look up and see the blotch with the naked eye?"

"I was hoping that it would slow down," Marcus said. "At least until the new moon. No one could see it then, at least for a few days."

"I'm not sure that would be any better. Not knowing may be worse than knowing."

The conversation continued, each man frustrated by the lack of supporting evidence. After Ben boarded his plane, Marcus spent more time in traffic made impossible by an accident. It took him ninety minutes longer to reach Lucy's hospital; still he was early and had to wait in one of the waiting rooms until she was free for the day. To pass the time, he decided to pick up a magazine in the gift shop. The magazine rack was full, but *Time*, *Newsweek*, and *U.S. News & World Report* immediately caught his eye. Each one had a large picture of the Moon on its cover, and each photo showed the enigma, red as a sunset.

Marcus bought a copy of each. The cover of *Time* read "Moon Mystery." *Newsweek* displayed a banner in reverse type: "Lunacy?" *U.S. News & World Report* had the heading "Moon Madness." Marcus devoured the articles but founding nothing new. They had pictures of dead bodies being removed from the compounds of various cult groups. There were quotes from scientists, including one from him that had been taken from the news conference that he, Ben, and Lansing had given on Monday.

Apart from the advertisements, nearly every page contained something about the Moon. Politicians expressed their ideas, military leaders were consulted, and there were quotes from NASA and Dr. Wenham, the president's science advisor.

Boiled down, however, there was nothing revealing and nothing helpful.

When Lucy finally appeared they left the hospital and enjoyed an early dinner at a small Italian place. Over bread and olive oil, Marcus filled his wife in on the television interview. Over a spicy sausage and potato soup, he laid out the meeting with the president. During the main course of lasagna, which they split, Marcus related the conversation with Ben. Lucy nodded patiently and asked pertinent questions. Then she made an observation. "You're exhausted."

"I'm fine."

"I'm a doctor, don't argue with me. I say we go straight home after dinner. I prescribe elevated feet, a pillow behind the head, and meaningless television. No news. Sitcoms and movies only. Got it?"

"Will you make popcorn?"

"If you ask nice."

Returning to the hospital, they picked up Lucy's car and drove home in a two-car caravan.

Lucy was right, Marcus decided, he was exhausted. His head felt as if it was filled with cotton, and his eyes burned. It had been a long day, and an even longer week.

As he waited for Lucy to exit her car, Marcus once again took in the sight of his defaced house. Tomorrow morning's first order of business would be to hire a painter.

"It still frightens me," Lucy said, nodding at the graffiti.

"It still angers me," Marcus replied. "It will be gone by sunset tomorrow."

"Assuming you can find a painter who'll work on a Saturday." They walked up the wood stairs to the porch.

"I'll paint it myself, if I have too. It's not staying another day." Marcus slipped the key in the lock and opened the door. Once inside, he was careful to lock the doorknob and the dead bolt. "What say we don't answer the phone tonight."

"Fine with me. If the hospital needs me for anything they can page me."

Marcus flipped a switch and the foyer light came on. "I'm going to go in my office—"

"No, you're not," Lucy interrupted. "You're going to sit on the sofa and put your feet up on the coffee table."

"You never let me put my feet on the table. Besides, I was just going to turn off the computer. I left it on all day."

"I grant you a special dispensation on using the coffee table as a footrest, and I'll turn off the computer. First, however, I'm going to start the popcorn."

Marcus dutifully went to the sofa, picked up the television remote, and pointed it at the television. Before he could push the power button, Lucy let slip a little scream and took two steps back. Marcus was on his feet in a blink and raced to his wife's side, crossing the living room in three long strides. He let his eyes follow her gaze and his heart stopped then thundered back to life. On the floor before him was a woman. She was on all fours, her head down, hidden beneath a cascade of blonde, matted hair. She swayed from side to side, and Marcus was sure she would collapse in a heap.

He stood frozen for several seconds before deciding on a course of action. "I'll call 911," he said.

"No," came a weak plea. The woman's voice was as frail as her appearance. "No, please, don't. Please don't." She collapsed to her side.

"Look, Marc," Lucy said. "She's been eating our bread."

Marcus saw an open loaf of bread on the counter. A half-eaten apple lay on the counter next to it. A banana peel was on the floor an arm's length from the woman.

"Poor thing," Lucy said. "She must be starved."

"Poor thing? She broke into our house. I'm calling the police."

"No, please no. Don't." The woman tried to right herself from her place on the floor. "I'm sorry. I was hungry. I'll go. I'll leave."

Marcus glanced and watched the expression on Lucy's face melt from fear to utter concern. The doctor was coming out.

"You're not going anywhere," Lucy said. "At least not right now." To Marcus she said, "Help me get her to the sofa."

"But, Lucy—"

"The sofa, Marc. Let's not waste any time."

Marcus walked over to the woman and helped her to her feet. She wavered and staggered back a step. Marcus held her firmly, careful not to bruise her. Lucy came alongside. Together they helped the intruder to the couch, where they set her down gently. Her hair was a nest of knots, matted with dirt. She wore an ivory top and black dress slacks. The clothes seemed small on her.

"Look at her feet," Lucy said.

Marcus did, then averted his eyes. Her feet were red, swollen, and covered with cuts and bruises. "What happened to her?"

"I have no idea," Lucy said calmly, now in doctor mode. "Get our first-aid kit."

"Maybe we should take her to the hospital."

"No . . . no, no . . . no hospital. They hurt me." She began to flail her arms.

"Okay, okay," Lucy cooed. "Just relax. I'm not going to hurt you."

"She's afraid the hospital will hurt her?" Marcus asked.

Lucy shook her head. "I doubt it. I think she meant that she *has been* hurt in the hospital. Something has her terrified."

"I don't get it."

"The first-aid kit, Marc. Please."

Marcus ran into the master bathroom and emerged with a large first-aid kit. The kit was in a small backpack. It was a custom collection of bandages and over-the-counter treatments, compiled by Lucy. She had used it several times to patch up neighborhood kids who fell from bikes, slipped from skateboards, or battered themselves with street football. No sooner than he had handed her the kit, she barked out the next order. "She's dehydrated. Get a sports bottle from the kitchen and fill it with water . . . no, wait. Do we still have that Gatorade?"

"I think so." On weekends, Marcus and Lucy liked to take long walks through some of the mountain passes. They usually carried water and Gatorade.

"Put it in the sports bottle. It will replace her electrolytcs faster."

Marcus did as he was told and brought the sports bottle to his wife. "I still think we should call the police or an ambulance."

"Please, please, no. I'll leave. I won't bother you anymore." The woman's voice was pathetic and stirred strong sympathies within Marcus.

"I let you handle the mad painter last night, let me handle this situation," Lucy stated. There was no anger in her voice, just focused determination and professionalism. "I think we need to listen to her."

"Why do you think that?"

Lucy paused before answering. "I don't know how I know. I just know."

"That's not logical."

"What has been logical in the last few weeks, Marc? Nothing. Let me handle this. See if you can find out how she got in the house."

It didn't take long for Marcus to find the laundry room window open. Before shutting it, he peered outside and saw one of the plastic chairs from his patio set. Small dots of blood dotted the chair, illuminated by the light that poured from the window. He went back into the living room and reported what he found. "I thought I had checked every window last night. I didn't think about the laundry."

"She's not running a fever," Lucy said. "Pupils are equal and responsive and I can't find any injury to the head." Marcus wondered how she could see anything through the mat of hair. "She has bruises on her arms and cuts on her legs and feet. There may be more, but I won't know until we get her clothing off."

"Her clothing? You thinking of letting her stay here?"

"Yes."

"Lucy, she's not a lost puppy. She's a grown woman with some physical and maybe mental ills."

"I need a large bowl of water."

"Why?"

"I'm going to clean her feet."

"Lucy—"

"A large mixing bowl will do. And don't make it too hot. Tepid will do. Also bring me several towels and washcloths."

Marcus knew he was beaten. When his wife got this way, there was no reasoning with her. It seldom happened, maybe two or three times in their marriage, but once Mrs. Stiller became Dr. Stiller it was time to get out of the way. Of course, there had never been a situation like this, but he recognized the signs. His role was now that of helper.

Marcus brought the bowl of water and Lucy tested it with her hand. "That's perfect. Bring the disinfecting soap when you bring the towels."

"Yes, Dr. Stiller," Marcus snipped. Lucy ignored him.

For the next half hour, Marcus watched as his wife sat at the woman's feet and carefully washed her wounds using the yellow disinfecting soap and several washcloths. The woman showed no sign of pain. Instead, she sat quietly sipping at the Gatorade. Marcus watched the color return to her face.

"She's tough," Marcus said. "I'd be wiggling like a child if my feet were cut up that bad."

"It's not because she's tough. It's because she has moved beyond pain. The cuts and abrasions are superficial but numerous. I'm surprised she could walk at all. At least no stitches are needed."

"Thank you," the woman said.

Lucy looked up and smiled. "Feeling better?"

"A little."

"Go easy on the Gatorade. If you drink it too fast, you'll get sick. When did you last eat?"

The woman shrugged. "About three days ago."

"You haven't eaten in three days?" Marcus said. The woman shook her head.

"That explains why you passed out," Lucy commented. "How much did you eat here?"

"I'll make it up to you," she said apologetically.

"That's not what I mean," Lucy explained. "How much food did you eat?"

"Not much. A few pieces of bread, an apple . . . and a banana, I think."

Lucy turned to Marcus. "I'm going to apply some antibiotic to her cuts, then I want her to eat. I need you to make some soup. Chicken and rice if we have it."

Marcus returned to the kitchen and set about making the meal. As he waited for the soup to heat, he watched his wife and a wave of pride flowed over him. She was spectacular in so many ways. Lovely, intelligent, and especially attractive when she was driven.

Lucy was finishing when Marcus brought the soup. She moved the bowl aside, bundled up the towel and washcloths, then returned her attention to the uninvited guest. "My name is Lucy, Dr. Lucy Stiller." Marcus saw the woman's eyes widen. The term *doctor* frightened her. "I'm an internist. Do you know what that is?"

She nodded. "I'm a real-estate agent . . . was a real-estate agent."

Lucy nodded, then pointed at Marcus. "This is my husband, Dr. Marcus Stiller. He's a college professor."

"The Moon man."

"Oh, brother, here we go again," Marcus said with exasperation. "I'm becoming too famous for my own good."

"Did you hear about Marcus on television?" Lucy asked.

"No," the woman said softly. She pointed to the front wall.

"Ah," Lucy said with a genuine smile. "A man decided to decorate our front wall last night."

Marcus asked, "What's your name?"

The woman hesitated, then said, "Julie. Julie Waal." She spelled her last name.

"Okay, Julie," Lucy said. "I've cleaned your cuts and abrasions. Now I want you to eat this soup, but do it slowly. Your body has been fasting for several days, so it's a little uncertain what to do with food. Eat only what you want, then I want you to lie down on the sofa. I'm going to put your feet up on some pillows. That will help the swelling. Also I want you to take a couple of ibuprofen. That will help too."

"Okay." Julie took the soup from Lucy.

"Can you hold it okay?"

"Yes," she said.

She seemed stronger already. Marcus had no idea what this woman had been through, but it was grueling. He doubted that she could have endured any more.

"Will you call the police if I fall asleep?" she asked. Fear draped her face like a mask.

"I think it's best," Marcus said.

"Not if you don't want us to," Lucy said. "I promise."

"Okay," she replied, maintaining the severe economy of words.

As the woman ate, Marcus helped Lucy clean up. He didn't agree with his wife's decision, but he did trust her instincts. He just hoped that she was right.

Julie consumed two bowls of soup and drained the sports bottle of Gatorade. Lucy insisted that she sleep and received no argument. Elevating Julie's feet, Lucy helped her lie down on the sofa and covered her with a blanket. She closed her eyes, and the best Marcus could tell, was asleep immediately.

"What now?" Marcus asked in hushed tones. He and Lucy were seated at the table in the small dining room drinking hot tea.

"We let her sleep as long as she wants. I'll stay out here with her tonight. In the morning, I'll do another exam, help her shower, and apply some more antibiotics. I was worried about infection, but so far she seems free of any of that. That's a bit of a miracle."

"What happens tomorrow when you go into the hospital?" Marcus said in hushed tones. "I have to get back to work on this enigma thing."

"I don't know. I can't take any more time off work. I've used up my free days and called in all the favors I can."

"I'm not comfortable being here alone with her," Marcus admitted.

"I can understand that, but I think she's harmless. There's something about her, but I can't put my finger on it—something special."

"I don't see it."

"I can't explain it. There are pieces missing."

"Yeah, in her—"

"Marcus!" Lucy snapped. "I don't think she's crazy. That's a guess, I know. I just checked her injuries; I didn't give her a psych evaluation. I'm not qualified to do so anyway. Still, she seems rational. Frightened, but rational."

"She's only spoken a handful of words, Lucy," Marcus protested. "What kind of judgment can you make on such skimpy evidence? How do you know she not some schizoid, homeless person who fades in and out of fantasy?"

"She's bathed recently," Lucy said. "While you were getting the towels, I examined her abdomen. Everything is fine there, and I could smell the hint of soap on her. Also, the parts of her body covered with clothing were free of dirt. If she were homeless, I'd expect to see some filth ground into the pores of her skin. The dirt on her face and in her hair is fresh. I'm guessing she's been sleeping in the woods for only a few days."

Marcus glanced at the form sleeping on his sofa. "If that's true, she's lucky to be alive. It's been cold at night."

"Temperatures are still above freezing, but you're right. It must have been horrible."

"Tell me this is not some mothering instinct on your part," Marcus said.

"It's not. It's a feeling I have. Call it intuition if you want, but I think we need her. It's irrational, I know, but I can't shake the feeling."

"Let's just hope we're not harboring a criminal," Marcus said.

Lucy smiled and reached out to touch his hand. They exchanged glances, glances that carried a wealth of unspoken communication. Marcus trusted his wife. He had often said that she was one of the smartest people he had ever met. But she was more than smart, she was intuitive, able to determine his feelings and thoughts without him speaking a word. It made her a great doctor and a wonderful wife. Over the years, he had come to trust her instincts. He decided tonight was not a good night to start doubting them.

The world was not the same as it was just a week ago. Sanity was on vacation. The weird and abnormal had replaced it. This was just another bizarre twist in the storm that surrounded Marcus. He felt as if he were on a white-water raft ride down a raging river: all he could do was hold on to the sides.

"I'll stay out here with you," he said. "I don't think you should be alone."

"No," Lucy said. "Julie's on the sofa and there is only the recliner available. I'll sleep there so I can keep tabs on her. You go to bed."

Marcus acquiesced but made a proviso of his own. "I'm sleeping with the door open. If you need anything, just shout. I'll come running."

Lucy rose, leaned over, and kissed Marcus on the lips. "Thanks for trusting me."

"Would things be different if I didn't?"

"No. Now go to bed."

)) ● ● ● ● ((

DEMPSEY'S HEAD WAS SPINNING and his eyes watered. It was the smell. It permeated the closed confines of his old car. A few minutes of discomfort didn't matter. He was on a mission, a mission he couldn't articulate. He was sent for the Moon man. It was his fault. The terrible day of the Lord was coming and it was Moon man's fault. He shouldn't have called the police on him. After all, he was God's man for the job. He was supposed to set things right. Why couldn't Moon man see it? It was all about the Moon. He had even written it on the wall of Moon man's house like the finger of God wrote "Mene, mene, tekel, uparsin" on the wall of King Belshazzar's palace, a phrase only the prophet Daniel could interpret. Dempsey chortled. "That got the ol' king's attention. Got his knees to a knocking."

Maybe that was the problem. Moon man couldn't understand the message just like King Belshazzar couldn't understand God's message on the wall. "You have been weighed in the scales and found wanting," Dempsey muttered. "Found wanting. Wanting." The time had come. Retribution. Glorious judgment. Moon man must pay. All men like him must pay. They deserved to die. Their science deserved death.

Dempsey rubbed his burning eyes and cursed the fumes, but refused to roll down the window. Someone might notice him, might smell the fumes wafting off the two old five-gallon gas cans seat-belted into the front passenger's seat.

"It's about time," he said. He had been sitting in his car since sundown waiting for Moon man to return. And return he did, with his pretty little wife. Parked near the end of the street he could barely see the house, but the view was sufficient for him to see the lights glowing in the windows.

The lights went out. The last lights on the street to do so.

Dempsey exited his vehicle and closed the door to his car as quietly as he could. Rounding the vehicle, he opened the passenger side door and took the two cans of gasoline from their perch on the front seat. He took a deep breath, happy for the cold, fresh air, and then walked slowly to the house he had been watching.

His head ached. His throat was raw. His eyes bled tears. He didn't care.

"Mene, mene, tekel, uparsin," he mumbled. "Weighed and found wanting. Terrible day of the Lord. Moon shall turn to blood. Found wanting. Terrible day."

With purposeful steps, John Jacob Dempsey walked through the cold night like a man strolling the street in peaceful exercise. Balanced with one gas can in each hand, he crossed the street and proceeded down the concrete walk, marching in time to a beat only he could hear, to do a job only he could understand.

Dempsey paused and looked skyward. The Moon was waning, but the red spot was there—he knew it.

"It will be all right soon," he said to the Moon. "You'll see. I'll make it right. Terrible day of the Lord."

Dempsey resumed his walk.

CHAPTER

TWENTY-SIX

GORDON TURNED DOWN ANOTHER RESIDENTIAL STREET, straining his weary eyes to peer through the dark. He drove slowly as his eyes traced the narrow, tree-lined walkways. The police had called off the search for the night. Uncle Bernard and Daniel Waal had stayed back at the staging camp. Once the police had found Daniel's car there was no way to keep them out of the loop. Since the vehicle had been left on a little used road in the mountains, they assumed Julie Waal had to be nearby.

Daniel played his part well, looking every bit the troubled and concerned husband—except when he looked at Gordon. There was hatred there, thoughts of revenge that bordered on the brutal. Gordon had no doubt that Daniel would find some way to exact revenge for his letting Julie get away in the first place. What happened at his home only stoked the coals of anger even hotter.

Now it was public. There had been some measure of control when they were dealing with the Santa Barbara police. They had been mildly sympathetic to the senator's delicate media situation, but now things had changed. The mountains were in San Bernardino County, and the local sheriff's office was in charge. Too many people had been lost in these mountains, and they were taking no chances. Volunteers with horses rode through the brush and trees looking for the missing woman. Others walked, spaced as evenly as the terrain would allow, looking for any sign of her.

They searched throughout the rest of Friday, but came up short. The news media got wind of it and reporters began to show. Daniel made an impassioned plea for help. "My wife is not well," he had said. "She's been getting treatment. Please call the San Bernardino Sheriff's Department if you've seen her." It was a good act, Gordon decided, but then politicians were actors to begin with, so why should he be surprised?

Gordon had become tired of waiting. He had witnessed how cunning and quick Julie Waal could be. She would either be found dead of exposure, or she would discover some way to escape. Gordon decided that she was a charmed woman and that it was his job to remove the shine from that charm.

Gordon decided to do some searching of his own. His reasoning was methodical and logical. If she died in the woods, then there was nothing he could do about that, except try to stay out of Daniel Waal's way. He might sue the hospital, but what did that matter? Gordon didn't own it. He would be fired, to be sure, but that didn't matter much either.

His uncle and the senator were up to something, hiding something. That would be his salvation. Discover the secret and he would have power over them instead of being their whipping boy. He would discover it, but first he wanted to find Julie.

If she survived the forest, then she would have come to some place of civilization. She was paranoid of people, but her need for food and shelter might drive her to the public streets. But where? Gordon had no idea, so he searched the only way he knew how, driving up and down the streets of the small town closest to where Julie's car had been abandoned. The town was called Pinewood.

Since sundown, he had been driving the narrow streets and lanes, trying not to attract attention. Fortunately the village was small with fewer than fifty streets. Unfortunately, those streets were dark, lacking streetlights. The lanes were also long and some winding. Driving as slowly as he could without attracting attention he worked his way through every street. When he reached the end of town, he returned to his starting point and began again. Weary, angry, frustrated, Gordon pushed on, and as he did, his anger grew.

)) ● ● ● ((

JULIE FELT AN ODD SENSE OF PEACE as she lay on the sofa. She should have been apprehensive, looking for a place to run, a place to hide. She didn't know these people. She had no reason to trust them, but she was so tired, so weary, so filled with pain that she no longer wanted to run.

The woman doctor had been nice to her, even washing her dirty and wounded feet, then feeding her soup. She and her husband could have called the police, but they hadn't. Julie didn't know why.

While she lay on the couch she listened to the hushed voices of the couple whose house she had broken into. The man was nervous, cautious, and Julie couldn't blame him. She was a stranger, and an odd-looking one at that. They should have tossed her back out on the street. They didn't, and Julie wondered why.

Her curiosity faded and the warm embrace of sleep enclosed her. She gave no struggle, but let herself drift then plunge into the beautiful caress of slumber.

Julie was afloat in a warm ocean, her arms outstretched. Above her was a deep turquoise sky, cloudless, unmarred by anything, a perfect blue canvas. She was alone, wonderfully, peacefully alone. No gulls flew overhead, no sound of people playing on some distant shore. Somehow she knew that she was the only inhabitant of this world. There would be no boats to bother her, no sharks to menace her. All that was required of her was to relax and float on the soft pillow of the sea.

A moment's consternation rose as she feared that this was a vision—one of those visions. Would the sea turn to blood? Would the sky darken into a crimson dome and rain down drops of blood upon her? Her heart quickened, but nothing happened. The sky remained its thick azure; the ocean remained its cobalt blue.

Julie let her muscles relax. There was no pain. Her feet felt fine, and her scratches were nonexistent. She was dreaming and loving every moment of it. Tension flowed from her as if the ocean was drawing from the tangled fibers of her being. Each second that passed brought a new sense of peace.

Slowly without threat the ocean began to rise around her, making it seem that she was at the bottom of a bowl. The surface of the water drew together until it closed in upon itself. Julie was now in the center of a bubble, and she floated free of its interior surface until she hung in space at its center. There was no sense of danger, no call for fear. As unusual and unbelievable as it was, it seemed right. Why shouldn't she float free of support at the center of a gigantic bubble? Logic had no place here.

The bubble began to rise from the ocean, floating in the air. It hung a few feet off the surface and Julie could see where it had once been. The bubble rose higher and higher until the ocean beneath began to seem small. Julie watched with the

*courage of detached awareness that none of this was real. A
vivid dream, they called it. Julie didn't care. Compared to all she
had seen in dreams and visions, this was sane and wonderful.*

*Julie was flying—flying in a bubble of warm ocean water.
Bobbing on air currents as the sphere rose higher still. Looking
up through transparent, curved walls, Julie could see the dark of
space above her. Below was the cool of atmosphere and ocean.
Rising. Flying. Sailing. Floating.*

*Her vehicle of salt water increased in speed, but Julie could
only determine this by what she saw, not what she felt. She had
no sense of acceleration. No internal feelings of movement. The
bubble not only shielded her from the cold, airless environs of
space, but it protected her from discomfort.*

*Below her the world drew away at unimaginable speed.
Where once the ocean alone filled her vision, now only the
globe of Earth could be seen, and it shrunk in the great distance.
A sea of glittering stars replaced the ocean of water as her
watery spacecraft accelerated through the black void of space.*

*Something in the vast distance caught her attention: a
circle of light the size of a dime held at arm's length. It glistened
like a gold-yellow medallion hanging from an invisible wire. It
glowed and boiled, and her bubble was headed straight for it.
A moment later, Julie realized that she was looking at the Sun.*

*This should have filled her with alarm; panic should have
roiled in her veins. It didn't. Instead, she felt peace, secure in her
watery bubble of solitude. It made no sense, but she sought no
sense. She knew enough science to know that the indelible laws
of physics forbade what she was experiencing. No watery bubble
could exist the near absolute zero temperatures of outer space.
Without sufficient atmospheric pressure the water could not
remain in liquid form. But it did. The Sun would be no problem.*

*The bubble raced toward the glowing orb called Sol and
did so at speeds that comets would envy. Julie recalled from her
high school science class that the Sun was ninety-three million
miles away. Light took eight minutes to travel from the star's*

surface to Earth. Eight minutes to travel nearly 100 million miles. Julie was moving that fast.

As the seconds ticked by, the Sun grew larger. Instinct said she should cover her eyes, but whatever the bubble was, it protected her not only from the harsh nothingness of space but also from the blinding effects of the Sun.

She could see the corona growing, boiling its gas away in immeasurable volume. Each minute brought her closer to the gaseous inferno. Streaming past her like ribbons of silk were bands of ejected plasma. It swirled in a beautiful ballet of gossamer bands, ethereal dancers on the solar wind.

Julie smiled and raised a hand to her mouth to stifle unbridled laughter. The dream was magnificent. It was participatory art, the kind of thing one chose to recall on their deathbed.

Was that it? Was she dying? She didn't think so. In fact, she had never felt so alive.

The Sun had changed. Its surface was a boiling torrent of gas. A mass too large to comprehend. The face of the Sun was dotted with dark spots from which jetted geysers of particles, charged by nuclear heat, directed by a magnetic field invisible to the eye.

She noticed another spot on the Moon. Not like the gigantic, black sunspots, but much smaller. The sphere careened forward with no indication of slowing. The Sun filled her eyes so that she could see nothing else. The small spot grew in size too. It was situated in the perfect center of the disc before her as she was centered in the perfect middle of the sphere around her. Unlike the sunspots that were irregular in shape, this object had straight edges and perpendicular angles.

It looked man-made.

It looked familiar.

Julie leaned forward, drifting toward the leading edge of the sphere and focused on the odd entity. Slowly it took form. One minute it was a tiny black speck, the next a box; finally she could see it clearly. It was a building, a small building, like a house. She moved closer until her nose was a fraction of an inch away from the watery wall.

It was a house—a familiar house. Her home? No, smaller than that. As she drew closer, the house became clearer. It was the house she was in, the very one in which slept so wonderfully on the sofa. It was the Stiller home. It even had the horrible painted markings on the front wall.

Then it happened. It came with such force that Julie jumped back, reeling in her weightless ball. The house caught fire, bursting into yellow flame. Smoke poured up from it like an ancient billowing furnace. Julie stifled a scream.

The perfect dream had been marred. Assassinated by the gut-wrenching vision of a house consumed by flame. It was unfair. She felt cheated and wanted to scream in anger but stopped. Something at the back of her mind was shouting in muffled tones. A voice, her voice, was screaming a warning. What could it mean?

It came to her.

Julie bolted upright on the sofa, swinging her elevated legs back to the floor. She paused for a moment, shaking off the heaviness of slumber. Something was wrong, very wrong. In the dim light she saw Dr. Stiller sound asleep in a recliner. Her face seemed to change with each flicker of the light.

Flicker?

Julie gasped and turned to look behind her. Light was pouring in the sliding glass door. Bright yellow light. Flickering, dancing light. The light of—

"Fire," she said aloud. "Fire. Fire!" Struggling to her feet she hobbled over to Lucy and grabbed her shoulders. "Lucy, Lucy, wake up. There's a fire."

Julie saw Lucy's eyes open then widen. She raised her hands to defend herself. She didn't understand.

"Look," Julie shouted. "The house is on fire. Get up. Get up!"

Lucy turned her head, saw the light pushing through the glass, and then yelped. She was on her feet. "Marc. Marc, get up!"

Julie took a step back as Lucy plowed past her, headed for the bedroom. "Marc!"

"What?" Marcus barreled out of the bedroom taking Lucy in his arms. He was wearing tan pajamas.

"There's a fire. Look." Lucy pointed to the back.

"Out," Marcus ordered. "Get out! Take Julie with you."

"What about you?" Lucy cried.

"I'll be right behind you."

He raced to the phone. Julie saw him dial three numbers. A hand gripped her arm. It was Lucy. "Let's go. We can't stay here." Julie nodded and let Lucy lead her out the front door.

○ ◦ ● ● ● ◦ ◦

MARCUS TURNED ENOUGH TO SEE LUCY pulling Julie behind her as they scurried from the house. The 911 operator answered on the first ring and Marcus rattled off his address and the words "house fire," then abruptly hung up. His mind was in high gear, fueled by adrenaline. He should grab something, take it to safety outside, but what? The glow from the fire increased. There was no smoke in the house, no sense of unusual heat. Cautiously, he stepped to the back door and peered through the glass. A portion of the redwood deck was on fire, its edges aflame. More flame licked up through gaps in the decking. The fire was below the deck, eating at the supporting wood frame.

"How can that be?" Marcus said aloud. Still the sight gave him some hope. If the fire department arrived soon, then maybe he would lose just the deck and not the house.

"Marcus!" It was Lucy. Her voice was strained but close. She must be right at the front of the house.

"I'm coming," he shouted back and started for the door. He stopped mid step. He turned toward his office. A few strides later he was in the room looking at his books, his computer, his stacks of papers, all of them precious to him. Then his eyes fell on the bound volumes on his desk: his father's notebooks. Marcus snatched them.

"Marcus!" Lucy again, but her voice was different, strained not by fear but by something else. "Marcus, help!"

Bounding from the office, Marcus crossed the living room in four steps, plunged through the open front door, then froze as the light behind him cascaded out of the house and fell on three people: Lucy, Julie, and the man Marcus had confronted the day before. They were standing on the front walkway. The light was dim but adequate enough for him to see something that made his mind seize: The man had an arm around Lucy's neck and a long, shiny knife pressed to her temple. Lucy's eyes were wide with fright. The man's hands were red. At first Marcus thought that Lucy had been cut but there was no sign that she was bleeding. *Red paint*, Marcus decided. *His hands are still covered with the paint he used last night.*

"There you are, Moon man," the assailant said. "I thought you were afraid to come out."

"Let my wife go," Marcus demanded. His voice was weaker and shakier than he had hoped.

"Terrible day of the Lord, Moon man. It's the terrible day of the Lord." The man took a step closer. Julie stood to the side, her hands covering her mouth. To Marcus she looked as frail as a reed. He could expect no help from her.

As the man approached the steps Marcus caught a whiff of a pungent and familiar odor. Gasoline. Marcus put two and two together. He could hear the fire crackling at the back of his house and smelled the gasoline fumes surrounding the man. The trespasser was more than a vandal; he was an arsonist and now an armed attacker.

"In the house," the man ordered.

"You set the house on fire," Marcus shot back.

"In the house," the man screamed. Spittle shot from his lips. "Terrible day of the Lord. IN . . . THE . . . HOUSE!"

Marcus backed up, never taking his eyes off his wife. Slowly he backed through the door. The madman pushed Lucy forward, releasing his stranglehold, then quickly grabbed her by the hair. Her head snapped back, the fearsome blade pressed against her neck. Several steps later he was in the house. Julie followed behind.

What are you doing? Marcus thought. *Run for help. Run to the neighbors.* Julie followed, her eyes fixed on the attacker, her hands now by her side. She staggered as she walked.

Crackling came from the deck. Marcus knew the fire was spreading.

"Terrible day of the Lord, Moon man."

"Am I supposed to understand that?" Marcus said.

"Not so smart are you, Mr. Scientist?" the man retorted. He sneered when he spoke; his eyes were dark and blank, like there was no brain behind them. Marcus saw him as more animal than man.

" 'The sun shall be turned into darkness, and the moon into blood, before the great and the terrible day of the Lord come.' Joel 2:31. You've seen it. You've seen it with your own eyes: the blood Moon. The Moon isn't made of green cheese, it's made of blood."

"You're crazy," Marcus said with a bravado he didn't feel.

"DON'T SAY THAT. Don't ever say that!" He pushed the blade harder against Lucy's skin and she grimaced in pain. Any harder and the knife would pierce her flesh.

"Okay, okay," Marcus said, setting his father's books down and throwing his hands up. "I'm sorry. I'm just scared, that's all."

"Good. You should be scared. The end has come. Life will be gone. Terrible day of the Lord."

Marcus was dying inside. It took no professional training to see that the man was a paranoid schizophrenic. There was no way to reason with him. No logic would be able to work its way through the hate that stewed in his mind.

"Why don't you let my wife go and then you can tell me what you want."

"You're the Moon man. I saw you on the news. You made the Moon red and made the terrible day of the Lord come."

Marcus shook his head. "I didn't make the Moon red, I just reported it. Like lots of astronomers, that's all. I just reported it." Marcus wanted to keep him talking. The fire department would arrive soon and maybe the sheriff's department too. He would be glad to see anyone that might help.

"Liar! Don't lie to me. I know too much. I read the Bible. I know the prophecies. I am the terrible day of the Lord. The end begins here."

"Look," Marcus pleaded. "It's me you want. I'm the Moon man. You don't need these women. A man doesn't hide behind women. You want me. I'm here. Come get me."

"I want you all. You have contaminated them with your science, with your Moon."

Nothing was working. The man was making no sense and Marcus knew that wouldn't change.

"I see the Moon, too," Julie said softly. "Just like you."

No, no, Marcus thought. *You're going to make it worse.* Marcus prayed she would shut up.

"What?" the man screamed.

Crackling, flashing, the fire grew behind Marcus, and he didn't need to see it to know.

"I see the Moon," Julie repeated. "In my visions. In my dreams, I see the Moon."

"You're just trying to mess with ol' John Jacob Dempsey's mind. It ain't gonna work, woman."

At least Marcus had a name to work with. "Listen, John— may I call you John?"

"SHUT UP!"

His words were so strong that Marcus involuntarily took a step back. Lucy struggled in the man's grip. Tears streamed down her cheeks. A hot fury burned in Marcus, hotter than the fire that was eating away at his deck. If John Jacob Dempsey hurt his wife, he decided, he would choke the life from the man with his own hands.

"I had a vision," Julie said softly. "I saw the Moon and I see blood."

Dempsey turned to face Julie. He seemed interested. "When?"

"A day or two ago, I saw the Moon in my mind. I see blood, too, and it scares me. They told me that it was all just a dream. That's what they said in the hospital, that it was all in my mind."

Dempsey's expression changed, softening just a little. "Hospital?"

Julie nodded. "In Santa Barbara—a mental hospital."

"Julie," Marcus said. "Maybe we shouldn't talk about . . . hospitals right now."

"Let her talk, Moon man, or I cut your wife's pretty little throat. Terrible day of the Lord."

"I saw things. Other things. Frightening things." Julie's voice faded to a whisper.

"Like what?" Dempsey demanded.

"I can't say. If I tell you, then they will know." She nodded at Marcus and Lucy.

What is she doing? Marcus wondered. She's feeding his paranoia. *She's going to get Lucy killed.*

"I want to . . . terrible day of the Lord . . . want to know. Tell me."

"I'm afraid. I'm so afraid of the Moon." She paused. "Can I whisper it so they don't hear? They won't understand. Not like you can understand. They don't see it. They don't know it."

Dempsey thought for a moment, and then said, "Okay, okay, you can whisper it."

Julie approached and Marcus watched in horror, impotent to do anything, fearful that his next word could cause the death of the only woman he had ever loved. "Whisper, whisper, whisper," Julie murmured as she approached Dempsey. The reek of gasoline and unwashed flesh filled the room.

Marcus began to pray.

In the distance a siren wailed.

Dempsey leaned over so that Julie, who was shorter by six inches, could reach his ear. Marcus could not hear what she was saying but he could see her lips move. There was another sound that iced Marcus's blood. It was Julie. She had clamped her hands on Dempsey's head and was screaming at the top of her lungs.

Dempsey shouted and instinctively brought his hands to his head. Lucy spun free and stumbled away. Marcus didn't wait for an explanation. He launched himself forward, plowing into Dempsey with all his weight. Julie fell to the side. Marcus seized the front of Dempsey's shirt. The two careened backward, slamming into the opposite wall. A framed picture of a cottage plummeted to the floor.

"Lucy, get out!" Marcus shouted. Then he screamed as he felt the cold steel blade in Dempsey's hand cut into his shoulder.

"Terrible day! Terrible day!" Dempsey bellowed. "Time to die, Moon man."

Dempsey was stronger than Marcus and pushed him off with one hand, the knife blade slashing the air. Marcus twisted and turned, avoiding each sweeping motion that threatened to cut him to the bone. He backed up, bumped into the sofa, and then worked his way around. Dempsey came forward, his eyes fired by pure hatred, fueled by insanity. "Terrible . . ." *Slash*. "Day . . ." *Slash*. "Of the Lord . . ." *Slash*. *Slash*.

"Lucy, get out of the house—now."

But Lucy didn't leave. Instead she raced to the fireplace, removed the long iron poker, and charged, coming at Dempsey from the back. She swung the poker like a batter at the plate, catching the attacker on the right arm. He screamed and dropped the knife, which fell in front of Marcus.

Marcus bent for it, grabbed it, then started to right himself. There was a thud and Marcus felt the air leave his lungs.

Dempsey had charged, driving his shoulder into Marcus's chest. The men plummeted backward, hitting the sliding glass door that separated the house from the burning deck. The glass gave way and the two tumbled into the cold night. Marcus landed on his back. Dempsey rolled over him and onto the deck.

Marcus expected to land in the middle of the burning pyre, awash in flame and smoke. He didn't. The deck was burning at the edges, working its way inward. Flame shot up through the narrow openings of the deck like ghostly fingers grasping at his feet. Instantly, Marcus realized that he was hovering over an inferno that would soon burn through the redwood decking.

The heat was horrendous. Marcus felt like he was suspended over the grill of an oven. Pushing himself to his feet he turned to face Dempsey, who was also standing, his left hand clutching his right arm where the poker landed. Fire licked at his feet, touching his pants legs, but he seemed oblivious to the heat. He opened his mouth and Marcus was expecting to hear "Terrible day of the Lord," but instead, Dempsey let out a scream that chilled the cold night.

Dempsey started forward.

Marcus, who wanted more than anything to run, held his ground to allow Lucy and Julie time to flee. Marcus had never been in a fight, not even as child. He had always been small, quiet, and a loner. Confrontation was something he hated. Marcus threw the first punch of his life. It was a good one, a right cross that caught Dempsey on the jaw. He took one step back, then started forward again. Marcus let loose a roundhouse swing that missed. This time Dempsey had been expecting it.

Dempsey let go of his arm long enough to land a rock-hard shot to Marcus's ribs. What little air was left in his lungs was forced into the night. He could no longer breathe and he dropped to one knee, the fragments of broken tempered glass digging into his flesh, and fire reaching up like flaming serpents. Marcus steeled himself for the next blow. It never came.

"Not my husband!"

There was a swishing sound over Marcus head and he saw Dempsey's feet backpedal. Lucy was still wielding the fireplace poker.

"Not my house!" Another swishing sound and Dempsey took another step back.

Before he could rise, Marcus saw Lucy's bare feet walking on glass and hot wood. "Lucy, run." Marcus gasped but his words had no breath to carry them and they went unheard. Forcing himself to rise, ignoring the screaming pain in his ribs and hot pain of the knife wound in his shoulder, Marcus saw Dempsey easily avoiding Lucy's attempts to strike him. Smoke forced tears from Marcus's eyes but he could see well enough to watch Dempsey adroitly catch the swinging poker and wrench it from Lucy's hand. Now he was the one with the weapon.

"Terrible day—"

Marcus launched himself forward before Dempsey could raise the poker. With head down, Marcus put all his weight behind the attack and his head caught Dempsey in the stomach, plowing the man backward. Marcus fell to his knees again. He was now closer to the edge of the deck where the fire was more intense. He scrambled up and backed away.

Dempsey was doubled over, but righted himself. Fire grabbed at his clothing, smoke billowed around him. He raised his one good arm and shouted, "I am the terrible day of the Lord!"

There was a cracking, a noise Marcus recognized immediately. "In the house," he shouted as he struggled to stand. This time he didn't wait to see if his wife would obey. Seizing her arm he pulled her through the broken glass door. As he crossed the threshold, Marcus turned to see Dempsey still surrounded by fire, arm still raised, but now he was looking down. He raised his head and Marcus saw, for the first time, fear on the man's face. He started forward. "TERRIBLE DAY OF THE LORD . . ."

There was another sound—the sound of timber giving way. Dempsey disappeared into rising flame and circling smoke.

Out front came the wail of sirens and the sound of diesel engines. The fire department had arrived.

"Let's go," Marcus said softly, and led Lucy and Julie to the front door.

○ ◐ ● ● ◐ ◑ ○

ONE ADVANTAGE TO LIVING in a small town was that the fire department was always close. The battle that was waged in Marcus's home lasted less than five minutes, but it seemed an eternity to him.

"The deck," he said to the first fireman he saw. "There's a man down back there."

Marcus did not watch the action. He could barely stand, but he managed to walk on wobbly legs to the ambulance that was parked in front of the fire department pumper and was glad for the department's policy of sending an ambulance with every fire call. He stood at the back of the ambulance, his arms wrapped around Lucy. She was sobbing and it tore at his heart. He could not recall a single instance in which she had broken down so completely. He fought back his own desire to weep.

He raised his head to see Julie standing nearby. She was unsteady on her battered feet and she looked as if she had just traveled through a great desert. Her eyes were fixed on them and there was sadness on her face that went beyond all that had happened. She was alone, standing by the concrete curb while firemen rushed about. If it had not been for her, Marcus realized, Lucy would be dead . . . they all might be dead.

He smiled and reached out for her. She approached slowly and allowed herself to be pulled into the embrace. A moment later she was sobbing with Lucy. Marcus held them both.

"Okay," Lucy said, pulling away and pushing back tears with her hands. "I've got to pull myself together. Let me see your shoulder."

"I'm okay," Marcus said. "It's just a scratch."

"I won't practice astronomy if you won't practice medi-cine," she shot back. "Take off your shirt."

"We have company," Marcus said with a wink, then nodded at Julie. He then looked at his shoulder. The upper sleeve of the pajama top was stained with a patch of blood the size of his hand.

"Take off your shirt," ordered Lucy.

Marcus did and let Lucy examine the cut. She grimaced. "That's going to take stitches, but it looks clean and not too deep. Where else do you hurt?"

"Ribs mostly. I think he may have broken one or two. It's a little hard to breathe."

Lucy pressed on the area and Marcus jumped. "I can't be sure without X-rays, but I think you may be right. Did you get burned?"

"My feet sting." He immediately felt guilty considering the condition of Julie's feet.

Lucy directed him to sit on the bumper of the ambulance. She had plenty of light because the fire truck behind her had its headlights on. "There are some burns, but they look like first degree. No blisters." She pulled a small fragment of safety glass from his foot. She then turned to Julie. "How about you?"

"I'm okay."

"Bravado must be contagious." Lucy did a quick exam and made Julie sit next to Marcus. "It looks like we're all going to the hospital." Julie started to complain, but Lucy cut her off with an upraised finger. "All of us."

"Excuse me," came a baritone voice.

Marcus looked up to see a uniformed deputy sheriff walking their way. He could feel Julie tense.

"I'm Deputy Ross. May I ask you a few questions?"

"Of course," Marcus said, taking the lead. He stood, try-ing not to let the pain show in his face. "I'm Dr. Marcus Stiller. My wife and I live here." He chose not to introduce Julie.

"Can you tell me what happened?" The officer pulled a pad of paper from his front shirt pocket.

"I'll do my best." Marcus began the story starting with last night's encounter with Dempsey and continuing through the moment when a portion of the deck gave way.

"You think this Dennis guy started the fire?" the deputy asked.

"Dempsey," Marcus corrected. "He said his name was Something Jacob Dempsey."

"John," Lucy corrected.

"John Jacob Dempsey," Marcus repeated. "He smelled of gasoline. I feel confident that he was the one."

"Why would he do that? Or is he just a really bad neighbor?"

"He's no neighbor, Officer. Last night was the first time I saw him. As to why, he's crazy. Kept shouting about the terrible day of the Lord. In fact, he was shouting that when the deck collapsed."

"He's a paranoid schizophrenic," Lucy said.

"Are you a psychologist, ma'am?" the officer inquired.

"No," Lucy answered. "I'm an internist, but I did a rotation in the psych ward."

"Oh . . . I see. So you think he is crazy?"

"Professionally speaking, he is crazier than a loon."

"Is he still alive after the fall?" Marcus asked.

The officer nodded. "He fell about fifteen feet, but the ground is pretty soft there. Lucky for him, he fell away from the fire. Paramedics are with him now. He's kinda busted up. I've called for another ambulance for you. They should be here in a moment. Can you think of anything . . ." He trailed off. He had noticed Julie.

"Excuse me, ma'am," Ross said. "You saw what happened?"

Julie nodded but said nothing.

"May I ask your name?"

"I don't want to get involved, I just saw the fire and—"

"It's Julie Waal, isn't it? You know, there are a lot of people looking for you. There's even an APB out on you. You're supposed to be lost up in the woods. How did you get all the way down here?"

"I walked." There was a touch of defiance in her voice. Marcus knew very little about this woman, but he knew she was a scrapper.

"You'll need to come with me." He reached for her, but Julie pulled away.

"You can't take her," Lucy said flatly.

"Excuse me? Why not?"

"Because she's going to the hospital."

The officer smiled, but he was clearly not amused. "Doctor, this is police business, and you don't want to interfere with it. Trust me on that. There are scores of search and rescue people trying to find this woman."

"Then they can find her at the hospital."

"Ma'am—"

"There is nothing to discuss, Deputy," Lucy snapped. "I told you I am a doctor. I am *her* doctor. If you want to interfere with my care for a patient, then you had better be prepared for the burden that comes with it. Put an officer in the ambulance if you want, follow behind in your patrol car, I don't care, but my obligation is to my patient, and I will honor that."

The officer stood as still as a stone monument.

"Has she committed a crime?" Marcus asked.

"Not to my knowledge."

"Then it's not like you're letting a felon walk away from the scene of a crime. You know who she is, you know where she's going, and you know where to find her."

"Okay, but I will have a deputy at the hospital to greet you," Deputy Ross conceded. "I'll let the searchers know she's been found." He turned to Marcus. "I'll be taking the guy who did this into custody. Since he's injured, he'll have to go to a hospital, too. Detectives will want to talk to you, as will a county arson investigator. Do you have insurance?"

"Of course."

The officer nodded. "That's good. Just so you know, the house looks to be in good shape. Your deck, however, has seen better days."

A private ambulance pulled up and stopped in the middle of the street. Paramedics exited quickly. The officer waved them over. A few minutes later, Julie was lying on a stretcher, now too exhausted to stand. Lucy took a place in the back of the ambulance, unwilling to leave Julie's side. Marcus joined her in the back.

"What hospital are we going to?" Lucy asked.

"High Desert Community," the attendant said.

"We need to go to Fontana Municipal."

"I'm supposed to go to the closest hospital," the paramedic said. He started the engine.

"Did you see that man they loaded in the other ambulance?" Lucy said. "Well, he just tried to kill us, and if it's all the same to you, I don't want to go to the same hospital."

"I can't help that, ma'am."

"It's not ma'am, it's doctor, and I want to care for my patients in my hospital."

The other paramedic, a stout woman with kind eyes, said, "Take 'em to Fontana. It's not that much farther."

"Okay, you're the boss." The driver pulled the ambulance away.

Marcus, holding a sterile gauze to his wounded shoulder and wincing at each bump the ambulance hit, leaned over to Lucy. "You sure get a lot of mileage out of that doctor thing."

"I paid enough in student loans for the title. I think I deserve a little courtesy." Lucy then took Julie by the hand. "We owe you an awful lot," she said. "I'm not going to leave you. Do you hear me?"

Julie was shaking. Marcus understood the effects of shock and fear.

"Yes," Julie said weakly. "Thank you. Thank you. Thank you."

Tears began to roll.

THE LIGHTS AND SIRENS were more than Gordon could resist. As he finished one more search of a deserted street, he saw the fire truck pass with lights flashing. He followed, if for no other reason than to end the monotony of looking for Julie Waal. Staying a discrete distance behind, he followed the pumper up one of the narrow lanes and parked where he could see the action. He had a good view of the house, firemen, and ambulance. It wasn't much, but it was entertainment.

Gordon watched until the action settled to a pedestrian pace and was preparing to resume his hunt when another ambulance pulled up the street, blocking the road. He would have to wait. Five minutes later, three people walked to the back of the vehicle; one had to be helped with every step. The attendants removed a stretcher and helped the blonde woman lie down.

At first, Gordon couldn't believe his eyes. He removed his cell phone and was glad to see that he had a signal. It was weak, which he expected in the mountains, but it was enough. He dialed a number and waited.

"Got her." He listened. "Yeah, I'm sure. She's in my sight right now being loaded into a meat wagon." More listening. "All right, all right, an ambulance. Tell the good senator I know where his wife is. I'll follow then let you know which hospital."

The voice on the other end was firm and demanding.

"All right, all right, I promise to wait until you get there." He hung up and waited for the ambulance to leave.

CHAPTER

TWENTY-SEVEN

MARCUS RUBBED HIS EYES AND LEANED BACK IN THE FIBER-glass chair that was situated next to Julie's bed in the ER. He winced at the act. Any movement made his side blaze with fiery pain. The emergency room doctor had said that no ribs were broken but there "looked to be some bruising in the intercostals." Marcus had turned to his wife, lifting one eyebrow.

"He said you hurt your ribs," she explained.

"Really?" Marcus failed to hide the sarcasm. The doctor had stitched up his shoulder and dressed it. For the moment, thanks to the local anesthetic, the wound didn't hurt. He suspected that would change in the next few hours. The burns on his feet as well as those on Lucy's were superficial. The dirt and ash were cleaned away and treated with ointment. Lucy had asked for and received hospital slippers for Marcus and her. Julie's feet were too swollen to wear anything.

Since they had arrived in an ambulance, they had avoided the uncomfortable and degrading ER waiting room. Their needs were seen to in relatively short order. On the way down from the mountain, Lucy had warned them that her being on staff carried no currency in the ER. They would be seen like any other patient. No privileges could be expected. Fortunately, the ER was slower than most nights, at least for the time being. Now each had been seen and attended to. Julie was still dehydrated and weak. How she had the courage and strength to do what she had done amazed Marcus beyond description.

Julie lay on an ER bed waiting admittance to the hospital. The ER doctor would admit her, but Lucy would be the physician of record. She and Marcus waited by Julie's bedside. Lucy stood; Marcus sat uncomfortably in a chair. They were silent, attempting to take in all that Julie had told them. When the three were at last together again, Marcus had said to Julie, "I think it's time you filled us in."

Julie did. She spoke of her visions and the mental hospital, she wept while she related her discovery that her husband was being unfaithful, and she recounted the battles with Gordon. Marcus was stunned.

"Let me get this right," Lucy said. "This Gordon who attacked you. He's an orderly in the hospital where you were confined?"

"Yes," Lucy said.

"And he injected you with some kind of sedative? You're sure he did it, not a nurse or doctor?"

"It was just him and some other orderly," Julie explained.

"In your home, he struck you?" Julie nodded, and Lucy's eyes narrowed in a way Marcus had seldom seen. He knew anger when he saw it.

"When was the last time you had an ... episode?" Marcus asked.

Julie stared at the ceiling for a moment. "The last bad one was in the hospital. I've had some dreams since I left, but they were different from the visions."

"Different how?" Lucy asked.

"In the hospital, I could tell when a vision was coming on. My brain felt like ants were crawling all over it, then I'd collapse. They were frightening. I saw blood and crawling things." She shuddered.

"Is that the kind of vision you were having before you were admitted to the hospital?" Lucy pressed.

Julie shook her head. "No. I saw things. Things I didn't understand, but they didn't frighten me. I told Daniel and he insisted that I get help. A week later I was in Dr. Bernard's private mental hospital."

"Was anything else different when you had your first vision at the hospital?" Lucy inquired. Marcus could tell she had something on her mind. "How did you feel physically?"

"First time?" Julie fell into thought again. "I remember being a little shaky and I could see colors at the edge of my vision. It was hard to think, too. I felt confused and frightened."

"Psychotropic," Lucy mumbled. Marcus saw the muscles of her jaw tighten.

"Wait a minute," Marcus said in a forced whisper. "Are you saying that someone drugged Julie?"

Lucy nodded. She pushed back the privacy curtain. "Nurse," she said. One of the ER nurses came over. "I know you're very busy, but I need to ask for something. I'd like you to do a blood draw." She explained what she wanted and also asked that the ER doctor who treated Julie be informed. A few minutes later, the nurse had drawn several vials of blood.

Fifteen minutes later the three were in a two-bed room on the hospital's third floor. Julie had fallen into a fitful sleep. The other bed was empty. Marcus and Lucy kept vigil, sitting a short distance away.

"How long do you think it will take to get the lab reports?" Marcus asked Lucy.

"Hard to tell. It depends on how busy they are. They may find nothing. It's been days since she ran away from the hospital, not to mention we don't know what we're looking for. It was a shot in the dark, but it doesn't hurt to try."

"So you think that they've been drugging her? Why?"

"Sudden onset of the visions. She described frequent injections. Those could have been sedatives, I suppose, but I think there is more to it. The kicker is the absence of visions since leaving the hospital. She seems rational in every other way. If she were psychotic, her fantasies should have gotten worse the longer she was away from controlling medications. Hers have decreased."

"Could you be wrong?" Marcus asked.

"Sure, but I don't think I am."

"There you are," a voice said from the doorway. Marcus turned to see Deputy Ross. "It wasn't nice going to a different hospital."

"I work here," Lucy said. "It seemed the natural thing to do."

"How is our runaway patient?" he asked, lowering his voice as he entered.

"She's had a rough time of it, but she's going to be fine." Lucy turned her attention back to Julie. She seemed at peace, like a child sleeping on her mother's bed. Only the IV line reminded all that she was a patient.

"I've informed the search and rescue people," Ross said. "I need to get some information from you two about the fire and the man that attacked you."

"I understand." Marcus said.

"In here," came a voice from the hall. A large man dressed in white bolted through the door, almost colliding with the deputy. He came up short and backpedaled a step. Two men followed close behind him. There was a traffic jam in the doorway.

"Who are you?" Deputy Ross asked.

"Um . . . ah . . . ," the large man stammered.

One of the other men, a dapper, balding man, stepped forward. "I'm Dr. Peter Bernard of the Mental Health Institute in Santa Barbara. My articulate associate is one of our orderlies, Gordon Bernard." He didn't introduce the other man.

"You're both named Bernard?" the officer asked.

"He's my nephew on my brother's side," Bernard replied.

Marcus tensed and stepped between the crowd at the door and the hospital bed. So this was Gordon. He was big, just as Julie had described him, but he stood slightly hunched over, one arm close to his ribs. Marcus knew the position well; he was standing the same way. Gordon's face was swollen on one side, and there were two knots on his forehead, the result of Julie's well-aimed kitchen drawer. She hadn't been kidding about the hand-to-hand battle.

"If you don't mind, Officer," Bernard was saying, "I've come for my patient." He started forward but was stopped by the outstretched arm of the deputy.

"Not just yet," he said. "Let's step into the hall."

A piercing scream filled the room and Marcus jumped. Turning he saw Julie pushing herself back on the bed. "Stay away. Stay away."

Lucy ran to Julie's side. "It's all right. It's all right. No one is going to hurt you."

"It's him. He's the one I told you about." She was pointing at Gordon.

"Shut up, woman." He started forward, but the deputy slid in front of him, stopping him in his tracks.

"Deputy," Lucy said. "I'm this woman's physician, and these men are disturbing her."

"Nonsense," Bernard said. "I'm her physician. How dare you try to usurp my authority?"

"I believe this patient has been abused at the hands of these men," Lucy said.

"She's crazy," Gordon shouted.

"He hit me!" Julie cried, still trying to push herself out of the bed. "He hit me."

"Officer, I need to take charge of her, before she hurts herself," Peter Bernard said.

"You're not doing anything until I figure out what is going on," Deputy Ross said.

Marcus watched Gordon's expression turn stormy. He was stymied. So close yet so far.

Ross stepped over to Julie's bed. "No one is going to hurt you, ma'am. Settle down." A fluorescent light was mounted to the wall behind Julie's bed. Ross turned it on and studied her. "These marks on your face, they didn't come from the attack at the house tonight?"

"No," Julie whimpered.

Ross bent over and took a closer look. "I've seen enough domestic violence cases to recognize a slap mark. Tell me what happened."

"Officer, she has fantasies. She's unable to tell reality from fiction." Peter Bernard's voice sounded an octave higher. Marcus could almost smell the fear.

Julie began to sob, but she told the story again, just as she had told it to Marcus and Lucy in the ER.

"It's the same story she told us," Marcus said.

"You're going to take her word over mine?" Gordon spat.

"I might," Ross said.

"Look at my face. She struck me. I want to press charges against her."

"Self-defense," Marcus said.

"You can't prove that," Gordon shouted.

"Turn around," the officer said. "Put your hands behind your back."

"No," Gordon said. "You can't arrest me. No one saw me hit her. It's her word against mine."

"Her testimony gives me probable cause for arrest," Ross said. "Turn around."

Gordon bolted through the door, with Ross on his heels. Dr. Bernard and the other man barely got out of the way. Marcus followed them as far as the door then stopped. There was a crash and a thud. Marcus stepped back in the room.

"He didn't get very far." Marcus smiled at Julie.

"Perhaps I should arrange for transfer later," Dr. Bernard said. "Things are a little confusing around here." He turned to leave.

"I'm running blood tests," Lucy said.

Bernard froze. Even though he was turned so Marcus could not see his face, he knew the words found their mark.

"A full battery of tests, Doctor," Lucy continued. "Any idea of what I might find?"

Dr. Bernard turned again and stepped further into the room. "No." He wasn't convincing.

"I think you do," Lucy said. "What about you, Senator? Any idea what the tests might reveal?"

Marcus heard Julie gasp, but she said nothing.

The third man, who had been hidden by Bernard during the earlier confrontation, spoke. "I don't know what you're talking about. I was just concerned about my wife."

"Concerned?" Marcus said, indignation rising. "Is your mistress concerned too?"

The senator's face paled. He turned his attention to his wife. "You were never meant to find out. I . . . I couldn't help myself. Then it got complicated."

"You cheated on me," Julie said. "I loved you and you cheated on me."

"She was blackmailing me, Julie. I stood to lose everything, my seat in the senate, my business connections, the chance at the governorship, everything."

"I did lose everything," Julie shouted back. "You took everything from me. You stole my life."

"It wasn't supposed to work out this way," Daniel said. "You understand. I had to look at the greater good."

"You are pathetic," Marcus said. "You turn my stomach."

"What do you know," Daniel shot back. "I know who you are. I read the papers. I watch the news. You take a picture of the Moon and, boom, you're famous. Truth is, you're a science teacher at a small college. I am an important and influential man."

"Perhaps," Marcus said. "But I love what I do, I love my family, and they love me. I also know the difference between right and wrong. As for your importance, well, I don't think that will last much longer."

EPILOGUE

EPILOGUE

The mountain air was cold and crisp and the cloudless night lay bare a host of stars that glistened in the ebony sky. A crowd of heavily coated visitors laughed loudly and ate grilled hamburgers and hot dogs. Participating in a summer ritual at the end of November may have seemed like madness to the neighbors, but it was an act of normalcy for Marcus. Removing the last patty from the grill, he closed the lid and walked over to the new patio table and chairs.

"It looks like your new deck is holding everyone up just fine," Ben said. He was seated at the table with several others.

"It's beautiful, isn't it," Marcus replied. "The insurance paid up quickly and the contractor drove the last nail yesterday." Marcus set another plate of food on the table.

"Ah, more burnt offerings," Whiz said.

"Be nice," Terri Lynn scolded. Marcus's students were the first to arrive. It only seemed right that they be present. After all, they had been the ones to take the pictures of the Moon that started it all.

"I was being nice," Whiz countered. "I'm always the perfect gentleman."

Terri guffawed.

Seated next to Terri was Julie. This was her third day out of the hospital and she looked entirely different. Her matted blonde hair was clean and curly, hanging to her shoulders. Her eyes sparkled and danced in the light of the back porch. She had gained close to ten pounds and was looking forward to adding another ten.

"Have you gotten settled in?" Lucy asked her.

"Yes. I've rearranged the house and cleaned out a few things." Julie had returned to her home. Lucy and Marcus helped her move back in and checked on her frequently.

"Still no word from your . . . from Daniel?" Marcus asked.

"No. The court issued a restraining order. He's not allowed to contact me except through his attorney. He also is forbidden to come to the house or within a hundred yards of me."

"I imagine his career is over," Lucy said.

Julie nodded. "Thanks to you. Police found the psychotropic drug in the house. I guess he was keeping it in case he had to make his mistress look crazy, too. Dr. Bernard will most likely lose his license. He provided the unregistered drug to my husband."

"Any word on Gordon?" Marcus asked.

"My attorney tells me that he is facing charges of assault and battery, stalking, and practicing medicine without a license."

"Because he used to inject you," Lucy said.

"And others," Lucy added. "Apparently several patients had complaints. Dr. Bernard was testing the psychotropic drug.

He hoped to find a commercial use for it."

Marcus saw her face cloud over. "That's all different now. What will you do?"

"Go back to real estate. I start back to work next week. I'm looking forward to it."

"No more visions?" Lucy asked.

"None. I feel better and better each day."

"Fifteen minutes," Whiz said. "Should I set up the telescope? You know, get it ready. It's almost moonrise."

"Sure," Marcus answered, then added a jibe. "Do you know what you're doing, or should I send Terri to help you?"

"I'm helping no matter what," Terri said before Whiz could speak.

"Okay, you know where it is. The laptop is over there, too. Let's get this show under way."

"Still haven't changed your mind about the enigma?" Ben asked. "You know your mentor Dr. Lansing thinks you've slipped a cog."

"I know. It's hard to blame him. I wouldn't have said the same thing a few weeks ago. Still, I stand by what I said in the television interview this morning. The Stiller Enigma is not natural. We exhausted every plausible explanation. Nothing in nature could have done that."

"'The sun will be turned into darkness, and the moon into blood, before the great and awesome day of the Lord come,'" Ben quoted.

A chill ran through Marcus. The words reminded him of the battle that took place with Dempsey a few weeks before. "Yes," Marcus said. "Jesus said something similar: 'But immediately after the tribulation of those days, the sun will be darkened, and the Moon will not give its light, and the stars will fall from the sky, and the powers of the heavens will be shaken, and then the sign of the Son of Man will appear in the sky, and then all the tribes of the earth will mourn, and they will see the Son of Man coming on the clouds of the sky with power but great glory.'"

"So that's what has happened?" Ben prodded.

Marcus shook his head. "No. I've been reading my dad's notebooks, studying them daily and using his Bible. In many ways, it's as if he is with me, guiding me in my Bible study. He was far more detailed than I knew, a real scholar." Marcus paused as he thought of his father. Marcus felt foolish. He had been unable to see the giant that was his father. The regret ate at him, but he had resolved to learn from his father and to embrace the faith he had once let fade from his attention. "He thought those verses dealt with end times, things that happen right before the Second Coming of Christ. Both passages mention the changes in the sun. We've not seen that."

Ben smiled, and Marcus could tell he was enjoying the conversation. "'I looked when he broke the sixth seal, and there was a great earthquake; and the sun became black as sackcloth made of hair, and the whole Moon became like blood.' Another verse about the end times. So, if the Stiller Enigma isn't a sign of the end, then what is it?"

"A precursor," Marcus said. "God is still in control and still paying attention."

"You know that Lansing thinks the enigma is an unprecedented combination of out-gassing and solar wind."

"And his evidence?"

"None," Ben said. "I don't know a single astronomer or physicist that can explain it. Ideas are flying around like mosquitoes, but no one can show any proof."

"At least the world has settled down," Lucy added. "There were a lot of frightened people."

The world had calmed but tension remained high as the world wondered what they would see when the new moon gave way and began unveiling its face again.

"Here it comes, guys," Whiz shouted.

Marcus and the others rose and gathered around the laptop. A small edge of ivory was rising in the east. Everyone knew what to expect. Reports began to circle the globe since the face of the Moon began to show again. The first word came from those in Europe and Asia. As the line of night circled the globe, everyone could see that the Moon was once again the color it had been since the dawn of history. Tonight was special because it was the first opportunity to see the Mare Imbrium and the Crater Pluto clearly. Everyone wanted to see if the stain had fully receded.

Slowly the Moon began to rise in the sky, clearing the tops of the trees in its own time, unhurried by the eager viewers on Earth. As it did, Whiz and Terri kept the orb centered in the telescope's sights.

When the Moon could be clearly seen, Marcus opened his father's Bible and read:

"Psalm 8 ...

"'O LORD, our Lord, how majestic is your name in all the earth, who have displayed your splendor above the heavens!

"'From the mouth of infants and nursing babes you have established strength because of your adversaries, to make the enemy and the revengeful cease.

"'When I consider your heavens, the work of your fingers, the Moon and the stars, which you have ordained;

"'What is man that you take thought of him, and the son of man that you care for him?

"'Yet you have made him a little lower than God, and you crown him with glory and majesty!

"'You make him to rule over the works of your hands; you have put all things under his feet,

"'All sheep and oxen, and also the beasts of the field,

"'The birds of the heavens and the fish of the sea, whatever passes through the paths of the seas.

"'O LORD, our Lord, how majestic is your name in all the earth!'"

DR. DENNIS MORTON HADN'T been this tired since he was an intern. He sat in a luxurious leather chair owned by Dr. Peter Bernard, the founder of the Pacific Institute for Family Care. Morton felt a measure of guilt at sitting in the chair and working at another man's desk, but it was his job. Besides, Bernard would probably never see the insides of the office again, not unless some sharp, high-priced lawyer was able to convince a jury that giving experimental drugs to patients without their consent was a noble thing. Not likely, Morton decided.

For the last two weeks, he had been reviewing patient files and making reports to the court that seized the hospital and put it under Morton's custodial care. The workload was crushing, and there were eighty patients to care for. For a moment, he wished he had specialized in dermatology rather than psychiatry. He rubbed his eyes, massaged his neck, and then opened the next file.

There was a knock on the door. "Enter," Morton commanded.

A middle-aged nurse with weary eyes poked her head in the office. "The new patient has arrived. You asked me to let you know."

"Thank you." Morton rose and crossed the office. He had made it a point of professional courtesy to meet each new patient and their family. There would be no family in this case; the patient was being admitted by the State of California. The state hospital was full, and since the court had taken control of the Santa Barbara facility, it was placing patients that normally would never see a private hospital.

The man was in the lobby, standing slump shouldered between two large orderlies. "I'm Dr. Morton," he said to the men. "May I have the file, please?" The burly man on the right held out a medical envelop that Morton quickly read. He nodded. "We've been expecting you, Mr. Dempsey. Your chart says your wounds are healing nicely."

Morton looked at his new patient. His hair was unkempt and his eyes glazed.

"He's sedated, Doctor," one of the orderlies said. "He tends to get a little excited."

"Terrible day ... terrible day ... terrible day," Dempsey muttered.

"Those are the only two words he seems to know," the other man said.

"Okay," Morton said with a wave. "Follow me. I'll show you his room." He led the way down a wide corridor and passed several locked doors with small windows of wired safety glass in them. "Let's put him in here. He should be comfortable. The nurse will see to his immediate needs."

"I'll need you to sign the release in the folder," an orderly said.

Morton stepped to the side as Dempsey was walked into the room. Pulling a pen from his pocket, the doctor removed the release form from the folder and placed it against the wall next to the door. He signed it. As he brought the file down he saw the plastic nameplate on the wall. A piece of paper with the patient's name was slipped behind the clear cover. It read "Julie Waal."

"Nurse," Morton said as he pulled the name tag from its holder. "Please have the front office put the right name on this."

"Yes, Doctor."